DESIRÉE M. NICCOLI

HAVEN COVE, BOOK 1

CALLED
TO THE DEEP

CALLED TO THE DEEP

DESIRÉE M. NICCOLI

CITY OWL
PRESS

CALLED TO THE DEEP
Haven Cove, Book 1

CITY OWL PRESS
www.cityowlpress.com

Cover Design by MiblArt. All stock photos licensed appropriately.

Edited by Tee Tate.

For information on subsidiary rights, please contact the publisher at info@cityowlpress.com.

Print Edition ISBN: 978-1-64898-232-3

Digital Edition ISBN: 978-1-64898-231-6

Printed in the United States of America

PRAISE FOR THE WORKS OF
DESIRÉE M. NICCOLI

"*Called to the Deep,* by Desirée M. Niccoli, is a fantasy romance with a sizeable inclusion of drama. This book entertained and provoked me, making me eager to read more of the Haven Cove series." — *Reader's Favorite*

"A modern mermaid tale perfect for fans of small-town urban fantasy. Lorelei is a strong, sassy heroine and her coastal—sometimes bloody—adventure is a playful, grown-up fairytale for those of us who love and fear the sea. *Called to the Deep* is an oceanic romance you can sink your teeth into." — *Freydís Moon, author of Exodus 20:3*

"*Called to the Deep* is the smart, refreshing, sexy, gruesome mermaid story I didn't know I needed, and now I want more!" — *Agatha Andrews, She Wore Black Podcast*

"Dark, atmospheric, but also swoon-worthy and heartwarming, *Called to the Deep* digs its claws in from chapter one and doesn't let go!" — *Megan Van Dyke, author of Second Star to the Left*

"*Called to the Deep* is a rare and luscious treat...a seductive, decadent romance spiced with pulse-pounding horror. Niccoli's charmingly carnivorous mermaid will absolutely enchant you while making you cast a wary eye to the waves. Scary, delicious fun!" — *Paulette Kennedy, author of Parting the Veil*

"Darkly exhilarating, sexy, and refreshingly sharp, *Called to the Deep* is as seductive as a siren's song and just as addicting." — *Katherine Quinn, author of The Girl Who Belonged to the Sea*

"Niccoli creates a perfect blend of gothic atmosphere and tender romance. From the indulgent small town autumn vibes to the creeping coastal mystery, this book doesn't hold back on the romance while keeping you on your toes with its man-eating mermaid." — *Kate Prior, author of Love, Laugh, Lich*

"Niccoli might be a siren herself with the way she lures readers into a beautiful tale full of passion and terror." — *Charish Reid, author of I'll Come Back for You*

"Creepy, sexy, and oh so full of atmosphere — I sunk my teeth in and couldn't put it down." —*Nisha J. Tuli, author of Wicked is the Reaper*

"Desirée M. Niccoli has created a lush coastal and underwater world with fierce females, soft sweater-wearing men, and a story delicious enough to take a bite out of." — *Erin Rose, author of Christmas Passion and Hot Cocoa Cookies*

To those who know the beauty and danger of the ocean and still answer its call.

AUTHOR'S NOTE

You should always feel confident and safe when reading a book. As such, I've included a list of content information available on my website at: dmniccoli.com/books/called-to-the-deep/

If you have any concerns about the contents of this book, please be sure to check that page first. Thank you and enjoy!

CHAPTER
ONE

L ITTLE REMAINED OF *T HE O SPREY.*

One of her masts, once a towering white pine, snapped clean off in last night's storm. Its canvas sails floated adrift, rippling upon the waves amongst splintered wood. The ocean had swallowed the ship in its gaping maw and spat back out just enough to taunt Captain Killian Quinn with the stark knowledge of how easily his crew could have shared this fate.

As much as the ocean was a mariner's greatest joy, the ever-looming threat of a watery grave also made it his greatest fear.

Steering his fishing trawler through the other vessel's wreckage, two-hundred nautical miles from shore, was a cruel reminder of this fact. Not even a modern hunk of metal like his *Dawn Chaser* was impervious to the raging sea.

Static crackled over the radio, interrupting that dismal thought. "I don't have a good feeling about this, Captain," Will Branson said. Normally unflappable, the lead deckhand's voice shook. "We found a torn immersion suit in the water. Stained with blood. There's no sign of anyone, living or otherwise."

Peering out into the grey early morning haze, Killian pressed his lips together. He reached to turn off the station that was quietly playing the news, left on for the off chance something useful about the storm or *The Osprey* might be said.

"*The U.S. cod fishery hit an all-time low in 2016…*"

He paused, compelled to hear what followed.

"*…but this year's total for the state of Maine is projected to be even lower. Scientists are attributing the decline to past years of overfishing and warming oceans.*"

Exactly why they avoided fishing for cod. He turned off the news broadcast, more of a distraction than a help.

Fog had rolled in when the storm passed, reducing visibility to less than a mile. It pressed in from all sides, curtaining the vastness of the ocean beyond, a claustrophobic, isolating shroud. As far as the eye could see, the world did not exist outside this fishing boat, his crew, and *The Osprey's* ghostly remnants.

And this bloody immersion suit…

The one thing that could keep its wearer warm, dry, and afloat for extended periods of time.

Even if the person survived whatever tore them from it, the water was cold for mid-September. A frigid forty degrees. It only took one or two hours to die of exposure in that temperature, and four had already passed since *Dawn Chaser* received *The Osprey's* 3:00 a.m. distress call. If by some miracle this person was still alive, bleeding out in the open ocean without the fluorescent orange suit, Killian and his crew might never spot them in the water.

The ocean swallowed all other color.

Killian lifted the pilothouse communications radio. "The Coast Guard should be here soon. Just keep your eyes peeled for any survivors. We can at least do that much until help arrives."

They were all just simple, offshore fishermen, hailing from small town Haven Cove, Maine. Keeping his crew alive, ensuring they caught enough to pay them well, returning them home to their families, that's all he wanted. That was his job, his responsibility as captain. While their jobs were never "safe," and they'd fought storms before, this one had been *bad*. It had taken every ounce of his skill to get them through it.

He wanted to bring the other crew home, too, if he could, but he and his band of fishermen were as far from prepared to conduct a proper search and rescue operation as *The Osprey* had been to weather last night's storm.

Before meeting its end, *The Osprey* had been an exact replica of a tall ship, one of the ones that traversed the seas two hundred years ago, resurrected to train modern maritime students and adventure-seeking hobbyists in historic sailing craft. Even knowing that she was essentially a moving museum exhibit, built sometime in the 1980s, Killian felt out of place, out of time, staring at her broken remains.

As he strained to catch a sign of life in the gloom, he glimpsed a dark shadow darting just beneath the surface near a tangle of line. He tracked its path toward the mast where five deep gouges sliced into the fractured wood. Someone must have clung to it with desperate, adrenaline-fueled strength, just before the sea ripped them away.

Or perhaps a shark had dragged them under.

"What will we do with a drunken sailor?"

A chill breeze skated across his skin through the cracked open windows. Though he appreciated a little fresh air to help clear his head, goosebumps prickled the back of his neck.

There it was again. A whispered voice across grey, choppy water, a little louder now than when he'd first found *The Osprey's* remains, but still just quiet enough that he struggled to make out the words. He'd heard bits and pieces of the sea shanty all morning, the normally upbeat tune made eerie by the voice's hushed tones, as if carried in on the wind.

Killian turned to his helmsman McAdams. The man was bent over a navigational chart, tracing a path across it with his finger. "Do you hear that singing?"

Dawn Chaser's foghorn blasted, a deep, trembling bellow that raised the hair on Killian's arms. Though it was a common enough sound in his line of work, nothing about today was normal.

McAdams shrugged. "My ears ring every time the foghorn goes off. Wouldn't call it singing though."

The lilting voice continued. *"Put him in the bed with the captain's daughter."* McAdams rubbed his ear, and Killian waited for him to comment further, because he had to have heard it this time, but the helmsman said nothing more.

Auditory hallucinations then. *Great*. Must be from the lack of sleep.

Draining the dregs of his coffee, Killian tuned out the song. His crew relied on his ability to focus under pressure and this search and rescue operation required his full attention. He had to push past these symptoms, especially if they were to have any hope of success.

And yet, exhaustion or not, he couldn't shake the uneasy, nauseating feeling that hours of searching would yield little, if any, rescuing. There was no sign of the rest of the ship or its crew; it seemed more likely that they'd all sunk to the bottom of the sea.

Remembering the five gouges clawed into the broken mast and the dark shadow darting through the debris, his uneasiness deepened.

A piercing whistle shattered Killian's thoughts and commotion erupted on the decks below. Both he and McAdams whirled around to look out the stern-facing pilothouse window. A second whistle blared, and the rest of the crew rushed port-side. "We've got eyes on someone in the water!" Crackling static punctuated Branson's message over the radio.

"Okay, I'm coming down," Killian replied. Sharing a brief look with McAdams, he handed over the pilothouse radio. "Take the helm."

Switching to his hand-held radio, Killian dashed down the stairs and grabbed a life ring, joining Branson at the gunwale. The lead deckhand pointed one pale, calloused finger to an orange immersion suit bobbing in the distance. Well, how about that. They'd found someone, despite the odds. A surge of adrenaline raced through his limbs, and he gripped the boat's railing to steady his shaking hands. Thrill of the find. Or maybe it was jitters from too much caffeine.

As they drew near, he noted that the person had smooth, feminine features. They'd found a young woman.

Cupping his hands over his mouth, he shouted, "Hang on! We'll get you out!"

Relief wasn't a strong enough word to describe the expression that flooded her face. It was a moment of knowing—that she'd stared utter devastation in the eye, but came out on the other side, living to tell the harrowing tale.

Killian threw the life ring to her, and she kicked her way over to where it splashed in the water. Looping an arm through its center, she gave a weak wave. He hauled her in, hand over hand along rough line, but his palms suffered no chafing. It had been years since he was a deckie—most of his work as captain involved driving and running day-to-day operations—but time hadn't softened the calluses on his hands.

As Killian pulled her in close, Branson lowered a sling, a thick leather strap hooked up to a winch. The next part would be tricky.

Bumping against the side of the boat, the woman released the life ring and reached for the sling. "Try to get it under you," Killian called down. The lines of exhaustion on her face deepened as she struggled to wriggle herself onto it, her movements stiff and clumsy, encumbered by the puffy immersion suit. A bright orange Michelin Man of the Sea. Leaning over the railing, he considered how he might climb down to help her. Maybe rig up a bit of line and rappel over the side…

Gripping the sling, the woman hoisted herself up with one great floundering heave but managed to seat herself. That short burst of adrenaline would only last so long. They needed to get her on deck quickly, but safely, before its absence sapped all remaining energy from her body. Then he really would have to figure out how to get down there and help her up.

Nodding to Branson, whose thumb hovered over the control panel, he said, "As quick as you can but keep her steady."

"You got it, Cap." With the press of a button, the winch kicked into gear.

Killian monitored the woman's ascent. She stared up at him, holding his gaze, barely even blinking. Her eyes reminded him of green sea glass, like the bottles that wash up on shore with messages secreted away inside. While echoes of despair still haunted their depths, a clearer message roiled to the surface: S.O.S. *Help.*

He didn't dare break eye contact; this must've been the first bit of human connection she had in hours, a damn-near eternity out on the open ocean, all alone with nothing but hundreds of miles of sea all around. And until now, no hope of rescue.

"You're almost there," he said, keeping his voice steady and calm, hoping it would be the emotional lifeline she needed.

Tears streaked her cheeks. "Thank you," she managed through chattering teeth. The blue tinge to her lips was worrying. Either the suit had a leak, or she wasn't dry when she put it on, and that made her more susceptible to hypothermia.

As soon as she rose to deck level, he said, "I'm going to put an arm around your waist and one under your legs and pull you in."

She cast a nervous glance down at the ten-foot drop, the twist of her body too sharp, too sudden.

And slipped.

He shot forward, grabbing her around the waist, and held on tight, anything to keep her from plunging to the waves below. The crew behind him inhaled with a collective gasp and a few muttered curses. Despite Killian's firm hold, the woman clung to the sling with a death grip. What little color she had left in her cheeks completely drained, as white as the inside of an oyster shell.

"No looking down. Look at me." His heart thundered in his chest, only settling itself when she nodded, complying despite the cold fear in her eyes. "I've got you," he soothed, hooking his arms around her more firmly. "Now grab onto me."

Shaking violently, either from cold or nerves or both, it took her a moment to let go and lock her arms around his neck. But once she did, he whisked her onboard. "You appear to be borderline hypothermic, so we need to get you out of this suit and into some dry clothes. I can help with the suit and check you for injuries, but then you can do the rest privately if you are stable enough. Do you understand?"

The woman nodded.

In the distance, Killian heard a plane's *burring* propellors. The Coast Guard probably. Maybe they'd have more luck and find others in the water, but for now, the woman's wellbeing was his primary concern.

Sharing a brief look with his lead deckhand, he said, "Take command of the boat and radio this in. I'm taking her inside where it's warm."

Branson turned and shouted across the deck, "Ian, stop messing with the lines and grab a spare blanket from the crew's quarters for the lady." Nearly jumping out of his skin, their newest and youngest crew member dropped the rope he was coiling and darted inside. "Everyone else, I want your eyes on the water."

The rest of the crew returned to their lookout positions on either side of the boat, rubbing their bleary eyes and squinting out into the fog.

Ushering the woman inside, away from the cold sea wind, Killian closed the deck door. "Are you hurt?" he asked, pulling open the Velcro to her hood and unzipping the suit. Trapped scents of salt and seaweed drifted between them.

"No. Just sore."

"Sore how?" he pressed.

Her lips trembled. "My muscles ache. I'm cold. Exhausted. Maybe a little bruised."

"That's pretty good, all things considered." He drew the suit over her shoulders and peeled it down the length of her body. Crouching to pull her feet out, he instructed her to hold onto his shoulder. She reached for him with a pale hand, icy to the touch, but at least her fingers weren't blue like her lips. When he tugged on the immersion suit, the woman's boot caught on the material, throwing her off her balance. She grabbed onto his shoulders, her grip surprisingly tight. A little painful even as his bones creaked and joints cracked beneath her fingers.

Damn, this woman was strong.

Masseuse or chiropractor training? Or just more of that good ol' adrenaline?

Once she steadied herself, and eased up her hold, he suppressed the urge to roll the soreness from his shoulders. Throwing her off her balance again wouldn't be wise. While he wasn't old, he wasn't a young man either, and another bone-crushing grip from her might do some damage.

"Sorry," she muttered, a shade of rosy color returning to her cheeks. "I don't know where that came from."

"It's all right." He freed one foot and then the other. She didn't appear hurt, as she'd said, but seawater soaked her auburn hair and clothes.

Half a beat later, Ian opened the door with a wool blanket in hand and traded it for the discarded immersion suit. The woman shrank against the rush of cold air.

Sputtering apologies, Ian closed the door. "Captain." His voice lowered. "Should I stow this with the other one?"

Killian nodded curtly, glancing over at their rescuee. The woman's expression hadn't changed, so she'd probably missed Ian's question. Thank God. She didn't need to know they'd found another suit—bloody, torn to shreds, and without a body.

CHAPTER

TWO

KILLIAN LED THE WOMAN DOWN TO HIS CABIN, A HOLE IN the wall barely big enough to hold the sparse furniture and twin-sized bed inside. He lifted the thin mattress to access the storage compartment underneath and withdrew a change of clothes and a spare towel. She settled into the chair by his small wooden desk.

"My name is Killian Quinn, by the way." He closed the compartment and set the bundle on top. "I'm the captain of this boat, the *Dawn Chaser*. We've got about a day and a half before we reach our port in Haven Cove, Maine."

Pulling the wool blanket wrapped around her shoulders tighter, the woman met his gaze. "I'm Lorelei Roth, from Marquette, Michigan. Former sailing student and museum employee."

Killian frowned. He wasn't a particularly superstitious man, but given the situation, plucking a woman named after the Rhine River siren from the ocean seemed more foreboding than fortuitous. Even if she did come from the Midwest.

"I know." She grimaced, answering his dubious look. "I'm a terrible singer, for what it's worth."

Under other circumstances, he might've laughed.

"Have you found anyone else, Captain Quinn?" Hope glittered in her eyes.

He hated to dash it but beating around the subject would be a futile exercise. Pausing at the door to turn up the heat, he shook his head. The heat register hissed and kicked into gear, coughing up notes of dust and kerosene. "I'm sorry. You're the first person we've seen."

Sinking further into the chair, Lorelei bowed her head.

"I'll be back to check on you in a bit." Killian gestured to the clothes he left out on the bed. "Please, help yourself."

"Thank you." She sniffed, wiping her eyes with the edge of the blanket.

He retreated from the room.

While he felt bad for not offering more condolences, he didn't know what else to say. It wasn't so much about saying the right words, or that feelings gave him trouble. There were no "right" words when it came to grief and tragedy, but there were thoughtful and meaningful ones, and he cared a lot about expressing them well. Perhaps too much. Awkward silences weren't great, but platitudes always sounded empty to him, even though they weren't intended to be.

In the galley, he warmed, rather than boiled, water for a cup of instant hot chocolate. Couldn't risk sending the borderline hypothermic woman into shock over a well-meant gesture. Taking his time, he stirred in the powder and broke up all the floating clumps against the side of the mug with a spoon. Normally, he didn't fuss over a cup of hot chocolate so much, but he wanted to give her plenty of time to change and settle in.

The beverage wasn't much of an offering, but sometimes the simplest comforts were the best ones.

He waited ten minutes before returning and knocked on the door. A muffled curse sounded from within, followed by approaching footsteps. The door opened just a crack, and Lorelei peeked out.

Framed by the narrow opening, Killian got a good look at her face—square with soft cheekbones that rested in a quiet, pensive expression. A set of mismatched eyebrows—one that curved like a bow over her left eye, and one that arched above the right—topped her sea green eyes, a little too bright and vibrant to be natural, and yet, he did not see the outlines of contacts.

The way she held the door closed and angled her body away from the opening, as if to shield herself from his eyes, snapped Killian out of his appraisal. He took a step back. "I'm sorry. Did I come back too soon?"

A flush creeped up her neck and cheeks. "No, it's just I'm having a little trouble getting undressed."

He rubbed the back of his neck, unsure of how he could help. "I don't have any female crew members."

Worrying her lower lip, Lorelei fell silent for a moment. "Can you help me, please?" Her voice barely raised above a whisper, accompanied by pleading eyes and a deepening blush. He grew warm beneath the collar. It had been a few years since he'd last undressed a woman, but under entirely different circumstances.

Pinching his arm to get a grip on himself, he nodded, and she let him in.

"This is for you." He set the mug he carried down on his desk and took stock of her progress. Lorelei had managed to remove the army drab fleece half-zip she wore, now laying on the floor in a heap, and covered herself with the wool blanket. She continued to bite her lower lip, not quite meeting his eyes. Everything about this situation must have made her nervous.

Be kind. Be gentle. But professionally aloof. Do not spook this poor, traumatized woman.

"Why don't we start with your shoes?" he offered, motioning to the chair beside him. Starting small might build some comfort and trust between them.

The tension in her shoulders ebbed away. "Okay, yeah. Shoes first."

Before taking a seat, Lorelei snaked a bare arm out from beneath the blanket to grab the hot chocolate he brought her. She sipped the liquid and sighed, expression relaxing, seemingly comforted by its warmth and soothing taste. "Thank you."

"No problem." Killian knelt, wincing as he bumped into the bed behind him, and rolled up his sleeves. It was already becoming quite warm in his tiny cabin, but Lorelei's teeth had stopped chattering, and she shivered significantly less—all good signs.

Holding one booted foot between his knees, he pried apart the waterlogged knots with his fingers.

ALL THAT SEPARATED LORELEI FROM THE OCEAN'S GREEDY grasp was *Dawn Chaser's* steel hull. She heard it above the rumbling engines, lapping against the side, searching, reaching. She hadn't escaped it, not really. And it hadn't forgotten about her.

A tug on her bootlaces pulled Lorelei's drifting thoughts back to the person in front of her. Pinched between her and the bed, Captain Quinn filled most of the free space in the cramped quarters. It couldn't have been comfortable, kneeling in a too small space, but he bent to the task of removing her sodden boots without complaint.

Lorelei studied him.

From what she'd seen of his interactions with his crew and her, Captain Quinn's features were a perfect reflection of his personality. He had a strong jawline but rounded cheeks that a smile would make rounder. His nose slanted downward at a sharp angle but softly widened at the bottom. Scruff framed plush lips, and his large, calloused hands were gentle and deft. His hard and soft features matched his simultaneous ease in expressing both tenderness and command.

He was older than her. By how much, she wasn't sure. While the crow's feet beside his eyes, the scruff, and white wind-chapped cheeks matured his face a bit, she didn't think he'd quite reached his late-thirties yet.

"You seem young for a captain," Lorelei observed, trying for light conversation.

The corner of his mouth edged upward. "Tell that to my gray hairs."

She examined the dark brown strands, damp from sea air and sweat, that poked out from underneath his charcoal-grey beanie. "I don't see any grays."

Glancing up, his lips quirked, and stormy blue eyes twinkled in amusement. "There's a few of them under there." That half smile deepened the crinkles beside his eyes. Charming.

Cataloguing his features was proving to be a welcome distraction. And she needed one.

Panic stalked too close to the edge of her consciousness. Though Captain Quinn's presence held it at bay for now, she felt herself floating toward it, her mental fortitude about as sturdy as a leaky dinghy with an improvised plug. The moment he left the room, Lorelei knew it would all rush in with the memories of the horrible events that befell her crew and the terror and isolation that followed.

Out there in the open ocean, all alone, and hundreds of miles from shore with no guarantee of rescue, Lorelei nearly drowned in panic and despair. Only by taking deep, measured breaths and singing catchy sea shanties had she staved off the worst of it and kept her mind from lingering too long on all those killer shark movies she'd regrettably watched.

Lifting her mug, Lorelei breathed in the steam that wafted up and let out a shaky breath before taking another sip. The digging pressure on the top of her foot lessened as Captain Quinn worked the bootlaces loose.

He eased her foot free with gentle wiggling motions and peeled off the sea-soaked sock. He did not comment on her hideously wrinkled toes, but rather picked up a towel and patted her foot dry, barely touching it. Her cheeks heated. Was he grossed out by her feet? Did they smell?

"The patting is just a precaution in case you're hypothermic," he explained, catching wind of her insecurities right away. Damn. Perceptive this one was...And did he say precaution? Her vain worries vanished, replaced by a more pressing one. Survival dos and don'ts. "How's that?"

"Well, just don't rub your extremities. Warming the blood vessels in your limbs makes cold blood rush to your body's core, and that could make your internal temperature drop and put you at risk for cardiac arrest."

Shit. Had she rubbed her arms at any point during her attempts to undress? Her heart felt normal, maybe beating a little fast. And that was from a sudden spike in anxiety, right? Not a medical emergency...

"Hey," Captain Quinn soothed, patting her foot with a little more intention—more for comfort than drying. His kind eyes sought out hers, but it was the calm set of his shoulders that eased the tightness in her chest. "I didn't mean to scare you. I think you're fine. Your speech isn't slurred. You're alert. Your breathing seems normal. I'm just being abundantly cautious."

She exhaled, feeling more of that tension wane. "Is there anything else I should know?"

Captain Quinn tilted his head. "You also don't want to apply direct heat. So, no hot water, no heating pads, or stuff like that. Warm compresses to the neck and chest are fine though. And I think a warm shower later would be all right, too, if you want to take one."

Resisting the temptation to take a hot shower would be the most challenging, but she could do it. She didn't survive this long to be done in by creature comforts. "You're really knowledgeable about first-aid."

He folded the towel, and set it off to the side, not quite meeting her eyes. It was an unnecessary task—he would just need to use it again on her other foot. But maybe he didn't know how to respond to compliments. "I keep my certification up-to-date," he said finally. "I have to be able to take care of my crew if something happens."

Practical. Responsible. And yet, bashfully modest about it.

While Captain Quinn worked on her other boot, Lorelei wriggled her toes, the joints cold and stiff. "How long have you been a fisherman?"

"Since I was fourteen." He tugged off her other boot. "How about you? How long have you been sailing?"

Sailing, right. Short history there. This conversation was quickly and inevitably steering itself in one painful direction. Lorelei tapped the side of her mug with her fingertip twice, tears already pricking her eyes. "Not long. I studied maritime history and museum exhibit design in college, but I'd never seen the ocean in-person before."

She'd always been drawn to water, had loved to swim and dive and watch people and their boats sail across Lake Superior. It wasn't the ocean, but it was so large and wondrous, it was easy to forget there was something even bigger out there. Even as a child, she knew, whatever career path she chose, it would be one that kept her close to the water.

In college, she took a couple courses in marine biology but found she didn't have much of a head for science beyond absorbing cool factoids. But maritime history, the study of humans' relationship to the sea, just clicked. The past held its own intriguing mysteries, and maybe her innate curiosities about her own past, her own relationship to the water, fed the interest.

But the thing about history, and rooting around in the past, was it held pain, too.

When her mom died, the lake felt too small, too suffocating. Too many memories pressing in from all around. And that's when, for the first time, Lorelei gave in to her curiosity about the ocean. It was supposed to be a fresh start.

"I couldn't think of a better first experience than crewing for a tall ship. So, when I found a three-month sailing program in Portland run by Captain Calhorn—" The words caught in her throat.

The captain of *The Osprey* had been a stern, sometimes grumpy old man, but she'd been fond of him. He shouted whenever they fumbled or hauled the wrong lines, but that was necessary to be heard on deck in the blustering North Atlantic wind. He only had himself and a handful of seasoned crew members to ensure no one got hurt.

With fickle wind conditions and finite supplies, he had to keep the ship on course hundreds of nautical miles from shore—all while providing a learning experience to a bunch of clumsy-handed novices. There was a lot of respect in that.

Although *The Osprey* had been equipped with a modern radio and an emergency diesel engine, in a tall ship that far out at sea, with only each other to get everyone back home, a healthy helping of tough love was needed. The sea didn't care if you were too tired to man the square-rigging. And storms didn't care if it was the middle of the night when they hit.

Nature never considered human convenience.

But if she was being perfectly honest, the welling tears in her eyes went a bit beyond the loss of a respected teacher.

At the end of each night, before they went to bed, he'd sit down on a crate and whittle little wooden marine creatures while recounting his maritime adventures. The lack of exuberance he had in his daily interactions with people was more than made up for in his storytelling. He'd begin soberly, even gruffly, but as he warmed up to the tale, his expression would soften.

This evening ritual had the feeling of something started and continued for the love of someone lost—a dearly departed wife, a shipmate claimed by the sea, or estranged children he had little hope of ever seeing again. That had been uncomfortable to witness at first, as if intruding on a deeply private moment. But she'd never had a father figure in her life, and she loved listening to the stories Captain Calhorn told. Her mind wandered. For the span of those evenings only, while the old captain spun his seafaring tales, Lorelei pretended she was one of his long, lost children, reunited finally after years of separation.

It was silly. Maybe even a little childish, but an innocent, private fantasy.

At the end of one of these nights, as her shipmates shuffled off to bed, Captain Calhorn handed her the wooden toy he'd been whittling—a lovely mermaid with flowing locks. He awarded her a rare half smile before retiring himself, and for a moment longer, her little fantasy felt real.

That mermaid carving was somewhere on the bottom of the ocean now.

Feeling the intensity of Killian's gaze as tears spilled down her cheeks, Lorelei swallowed and looked away. If she met Killian's kind, patient eyes, she would lose it. And she wasn't ready for that yet. "We were just a few weeks in," she forced out, past the lump in her throat.

Captain Quinn sat back on his heels. "What happened?"

The trip had all started as a harmless wish for a change of pace, a new beginning with a little bit of adventure, and memories to last a lifetime. She shuddered. She'd certainly gotten the latter. "Seas got rough, and the storm we were trying to avoid took an unexpected turn. Captain Calhorn ordered us all into immersion suits and radioed for help. Everyone was shouting, but I didn't hear a word over the howling wind. The first wave knocked me overboard and carried me away from the ship. Some of my crew mates jumped overboard when they saw the second wave. Their first instinct was to get away from it, but it engulfed the entire ship. I'd hoped that maybe someone got lucky, but—" The sentence died on her tongue, as did her hope.

"Not that we've found," he said with a slight, rueful shake of his head. "The Coast Guard is looking, too, but I fear you may be the only one."

Another tear slipped down her cheek. She hastily brushed it away with her shoulder. The news wasn't unexpected, but the confirmation hurt to hear all the same. Shifting restlessly in her seat, she soldiered on with the story. "Everything went black when the second wave crashed down." Her leg began to bounce. "It was still nighttime when I came to, but the storm was gone. I don't know if I passed out, but in any case, I have no idea how I didn't drown."

The others drowned. Every single one of them.

Everyone but you.

Why you?

Seized by the need to do something, she set the mug down on the table and stood, letting the blanket fall onto the chair. "I guess we can take care of my pants next." Captain Quinn's cheeks reddened a bit, and she crossed her arms. Her muscles hurt too much to peel off her sports bra herself, so she was still covered, but the material was thin.

The captain glanced at her arm and frowned. "Did someone grab you?"

She'd noted purple bruises earlier when she took off her fleece shirt —four distinct lines curled around her bicep and a fifth around the back. It did look like someone grabbed her arm, but she had no memory of such. "I don't know what that's from."

Captain Quinn shuffled a little closer on his knees. He was close, so close.

Face inches from her middle, his warm breath tickled her bare skin. And what a devastatingly handsome face it was. She didn't normally like facial hair on a man, or care for its scratchy feel, but she might not actually mind if he roughed up her skin a little...The way he wore his short scruff did funny things to her stomach—opposing currents clashing together, forming a maelstrom of attraction and near-nauseous excitement.

Sneaking a glance down at his hands, Lorelei exhaled shakily. No ring. Nor the mark of one. But that didn't necessarily mean he wasn't married. Sailors and fishermen didn't wear them underway because of how frequently they worked with lines; the perpetual risk of a degloving accident kept their fingers bare.

Captain Quinn tentatively lifted his hand to the front of her pants and paused, waiting for her permission. His Adam's apple bobbed as he gulped. "It's okay," she whispered, shyness robbing her of volume.

He deftly unbuttoned and unzipped her black cargo pants and, with his eyes carefully averted, pulled them down. As soon as he'd gotten them off her ankles, he stood up, towering over her. He had a broad chest and well-muscled shoulders that even his thick navy-blue sweater couldn't hide. She'd been too shaken earlier to notice them beyond a quick assessment of his ability to lift her onto the boat. But now she was half-naked and mere inches away from this utterly masculine physique.

This should feel more awkward, she thought dizzily. *But damn.*

A violent shiver that had nothing to do with desire wracked her body.

Fixing his eyes to some spot on the wall behind her, Killian worked his fingers under the band of her bra with some difficulty. His brow furrowed. "Did you glue this thing on?"

She grimaced, replying tightly, "I was wondering that myself."

He paused to meet her eyes. Stormy blues framed by long dark lashes—she could get lost in them if she wasn't careful. "Am I hurting you?"

Lorelei blinked and looked away. She needed to get a grip on herself. "It's gonna hurt a little anyway, the way it's clinging to my skin. Nothing you can really do about it."

"I could cut it off."

Tempting, but Lorelei shook her head. "I'll need it later."

"Ok. Arms up." He tugged the bra up over her head, unavoidably brushing her bruises. She winced. Good lord, she was sore.

In a flash, he cocooned her in the wool blanket, but his cheeks flushed, so stricken with embarrassment that she half-expected he'd run from the room. Despite attempts to respect her privacy, he'd gotten a glimpse of her. She was sure of it.

Don't go.

Bit by bit, this man had pried away the ocean's icy fingers from her flesh, her bones and was no doubt capable of chasing the rest away. They were strangers, yes, but warmth and the comfort of simple human touch beckoned, and she was powerless to refuse that call. Had he treated her any differently throughout this whole awkward process, she might have ordered him out. But it had been incidental, and she was both too enamored by him and too tired to care what he saw.

Shivering—and this time not just from cold—Lorelei took a small step toward Captain Quinn. His gaze darted every which way—around her, through her, but never at her. Too afraid to look, but not enough to move. His jaw flexed. No words followed, the struggle with what to do next warring on his face.

Just hold me. She didn't say it out loud, nor did she dare touch him herself, but she sought his eyes, pleading. *Please understand.*

Another shiver wracked her body, chattering teeth hurrying in its wake.

Meeting her eyes, his expression relaxed. "You need body heat," he said, and pulled her into a firm, all-encompassing hug, anchoring her to the present.

She buried her face in the front of his sweater, nestling in the valley where his pectorals met to bask in the heat radiating off his body. The wool was sturdy, almost scratchy against her cheeks, but in this moment, it was the softest, warmest comfort. Intoxicated by his body heat, she closed her eyes, and savored the captain's solid weight.

His scent grew more pronounced, too. Something sharp and spicy beneath the salt that clung to his skin. Nutmeg, maybe, or clove and musk. Whatever it was, it was a good, grounding scent, separate and distinct from the ocean's touch.

If he let her, she could fall asleep leaning against him like this, her forehead pressed to his chest.

"Here, drink some more," he instructed, taking a small step back from the embrace. But only just enough for him to lift the hot chocolate to her lips.

Looking down at her through dark lashes, expression so gentle and focused, Captain Quinn tugged on her heart strings. If this kept up, she would be practically in love with him by the time they reached shore.

When she nodded that she'd had enough, he lowered the mug, eyes glued to her mouth as she licked chocolate from her lips.

Kissing a stranger. How tempting.

Clearing his throat, Captain Quinn took a large step back, banging into the bedframe behind him. "I'll have someone come down and check on you in a little bit. Feel free to use whatever is in my toiletry bag. It's right in there." He motioned to the compartment under his bed and gave her instructions on how to get to the showers. "Is there anyone you'd like me to contact—so they know you're safe?" He pulled a sheet of paper and a pencil from his desk drawer.

A few close friends but no family. Shifting awkwardly, Lorelei took them from his hands, hoping he wouldn't judge the short, sad list she scribbled down.

When he left, she reached for the spare clothes he left out for her with trembling fingers. Somehow, without Captain Quinn's hulking frame, the tiny cabin felt even smaller, its walls closing in all around her as if the ocean pushed at the hull, seeking to claim what had been stolen from its cold, dark embrace.

She pulled his sweater over her head, not bothering to roll up the sleeves that hung well past her hands. A wave of exhaustion washed over her at the thought of folding them into two uniform cuffs. With the little energy she had left, she wrestled on a pair of too-large sweatpants and crawled onto the bed.

Drawing her knees up to her chest, she buried her face in the sweater sleeve and inhaled the captain's scent. She hoped it would ground her, remind her that she was safe, but the waves sloshing against hull drowned out all other sound and churned up the memory of her crew mates' screams, echoing from the deep.

Lorelei wrapped her arms around herself and began to sob.

CHAPTER

THREE

Sliding the door closed with a list of names in hand, Killian let out a ragged, intoxicated breath. Ever since he'd gotten a glimpse of Lorelei's lovely round breasts and rose-pink nipples, he resolutely thought about the smell of fish guts to avoid an inopportune physical reaction. She should feel safe and comfortable while onboard and a horny ship's captain was not going to accomplish that. Even the way she pressed her face into his chest made him feel things he shouldn't for someone in his care.

Darting up the stairs to the main deck, a fresh, chill breeze cooled his skin and sobered his mind. He took off his beanie and ran a hand through his damp hair. Save for Branson and Walsh, their oldest crew member, the deck was empty. The seasoned fisherman sat on a crate, humming to himself while repairing one of the nets, cutting away the damaged pieces, his dark brown fingers smudged black at the tips by engine grease.

Tossing a coil of rope into a box, Branson crossed the deck to join Killian. "The Coast Guard radioed that they have it from here, so I sent the crew to their racks, and McAdams has us on course back to port. We're too far out for them to send a chopper right now, but as long as the lady remains stable, there'll be an ambulance waiting by the docks to take her to the hospital. How'd she seem?"

Killian tugged on the front of his sweater, letting brisk sea air rush in. "Shaken but I don't expect she'll need a MEDEVAC." He briefed Branson on Lorelei's tale. "I got the shivering to stop, and I think we avoided a slide into hypothermia, but can you send Walsh down in ten to check on her?"

"Yeah, of course."

"Great. Thanks. I'll be in the pilothouse if you need me." He put back on his beanie and turned to leave.

"Killian, wait." Branson crossed his arms. "What do you want done with the ripped-up immersion suit we found? It's been stowed, but..."

Puffing out a breath, a cloud of white mist in the cold autumnal air, Killian slid his hands into his back pockets. "We'll give it to the Coast Guard when we get to shore. They'll know what to do with it."

"It's weird, right? That it's all we found of the crew besides Ms. Roth? No body. Just a bloody, torn suit?"

"I honestly don't know what to think." Killian swiped a hand over his scruff. "But there's no use worrying about it. We did all we could."

What a strange and eerie day.

He no longer heard the sea shanty that buzzed in his ears earlier that morning. Though he tried to recall the words, his mind went blank for all but the general gist of its tune. It had been so clear before.

And they never should have been able to find the wreckage as quickly as they did.

If at all.

While *The Osprey's* captain managed to pass on coordinates before the radio fell suddenly and disturbingly silent, it only gave Killian a rough reference point. The storm carried the sailing vessel far, far off its original course.

Finding a needle in a haystack should've been easier.

CHAPTER

FOUR

KNOCK. KNOCK.

Gentle rapping at the cabin door, a hollow echo, cut through her heart's thunderous beat, the rush of blood pulsating in her ears. Lorelei drifted toward the sound, away from the abyss, the memories, the nightmare she couldn't wake from.

Was Captain Quinn back already?

Stiffly, she rolled over onto her back, staring up. She opened her mouth to call him in, but no sound passed her lips. Just shuddering breath. Everything hurt. Her body. Her heart. Her soul. Even her lungs burned, full to bursting, and salt stung her tongue, scratched her throat.

Through tear-laden lashes, she blinked at the reading light hanging directly above the captain's bed. Low buzzing hummed from dying filaments, its waning yellow light flickering with the boat's every sway.

The light would need replacing soon. Better talk to the quartermaster...

She glanced around the cabin, awash in fluorescent overhead light, and shook her head. No idiot, not the quartermaster. Not on this vessel. *The Osprey* had lights like this—one of its few modern conveniences. But this wasn't *The Osprey*. God, she knew that.

The quartermaster from her ship, like the rest of the crew, was lost at sea.

Lost at sea. Touching her throat, she swallowed past the scratchy, sore feeling. She should have drowned with the rest of them. Why hadn't she?

Sniffing, she clenched her fingers around the dampened hems of too-big shirtsleeves and wiped her eyes.

While she'd kept the fluorescent overheads on, illuminating the tiny cabin in bright white light, chasing away every shadow and dark corner, she continued to stare up at that dimming reading light, drawn to it as surely as a fish to an Angler's lure.

How in a room so bright could she still feel the deep dark reaching for her with its cold fingers?

Knock. Knock. "Ms. Roth?" She jumped. Dammit. She'd already forgotten someone was calling to her on the other side of the door.

With a hiccupping, stuttering breath she sat up in bed, wiping her puffy eyes dry. "Come in." Just two short, simple words and yet her voice quivered, on the verge of cracking.

The door opened a fraction, just wide enough for an older gentleman to poke his head in. "The captain sent me down to check on you. I'm Walter Walsh, by the way—one of the lead deckhands. But you can call me Walt. We thought you might want some company. Maybe show you around a bit, too, if you're up for it. Are you good with me coming in, Ms. Roth? I'm sure you were expecting the captain."

Walt's voice was deep and warm, a balm for the soul. A storytelling voice. She waved him in. "Please, call me Lorelei. And I would very much like some company."

He shuffled in but left the door open to the well-lit hallway, carrying a cup in his hand. "It's just tap water," he said, holding it out to her. "But I thought you could use some. Gotta stay hydrated and all that."

Pushing up her sleeves, Lorelei accepted it with thanks and took a long drink.

He hadn't said all that much, and yet, Walt struck Lorelei as a grandfatherly fellow. It wasn't just the clothes he wore—a red and white checked button-down tucked into corduroy pants held up by—not a belt

—but suspenders. It was also something in the gentle, unassuming way in which he carried himself. A calming presence.

Clothing and posture aside, with his thick beard and mustache, Walt looked like Captain Gorton from the fish sticks boxes, just a few pounds heavier with tight, curly white hair and dark brown skin.

Remembering what he said about showing her around, she set the cup down and rolled up the legs of her borrowed sweatpants, so she wouldn't trip over the ends. Some time out of this cramped room might ease the loneliness squeezing the air from her lungs.

"It would be good to know where the galley is," she joked, stomach rumbling.

"Tour time it is," Walt grinned. "Come on."

Lorelei followed him out of the cabin and down the narrow hallway. Two people coming from opposing directions would have to turn to the side to squeeze by one another, but she was used to compact spaces. That was ship living.

Shuffling along at a leisurely pace, he tucked his thumbs under the suspender straps. When the boat rolled, she collided into the wall, an amateur sailor unused to this vessel's motions. But Walt's stance naturally widened, and he continued onward with steady ease, a seasoned sailor and fisherman in his element.

"Head and showers," he remarked, elbowing a door on the left. "Crew's quarters." He nodded to a door on the right. A little further down, he stopped at a darkened threshold dead ahead. "And the best spot onboard." He reached in and flipped a switch, the florescent lights flickering to life above. "The galley."

Her stomach grumbled as they filed inside.

A white plastic picnic-style table stood off to the right, bolted down to the floor. To the left, there was a narrow counter space with a coffeepot and a wooden compartment box filled with tea bags and packets of hot chocolate and sugar. Along the back wall was a kitchenette and a row of overhead cabinets.

Walt slid a white bakery box off the galley counter. Across its top, 'Ian' was written in third grader-quality handwriting, letters large and ununiform, the marker smeared and smudged. Probably a lefty, whoever this Ian was—possibly the gangly kid who brought her the wool blanket.

Flipping open the lid, Walt revealed several rows of large chocolate chip cookies nestled inside. "Go ahead. Have as many as you like."

Stomach gurgling embarrassingly loud, she reached for one, but hesitated, fingers poised just above the treats. Last time she'd eaten was five o'clock last night at dinner. She needed to eat something, but these weren't Walt's to share, and she didn't want to put him on anyone's bad side.

Bad tempers were quick to flare between crew mates in close quarters.

"It's all right," he assured, nudging her hand with the box. "You need a little sugar in your system. And besides, this is a community kitchen. Any food left in the galley is fair game. That's the rules."

Unable to refuse the sweet old man, or her sweet tooth, Lorelei plucked a couple from the box. Each cookie was larger than the palm of her hand.

As she chewed, Walt refilled her glass of water. "Milk pairs better with cookies, of course, but you really should hydrate." She downed the whole glass in front of him to put his mind at ease.

When she finished, Walt gently nudged her with the cookie box. "Here, have a few more."

She laughed, reaching back inside the box. "Okay, just two more. But I won't have room for any more than that. These things are monstrous."

He placed the cookie box back on the counter. "Well, that's it as far as the tour goes. Home away from home. There's the fish hold and engine room, too, on the deck below us, but I doubt you'd want to see that."

Nothing against the business end of the boat, but he was right. "We can skip those."

With a handful of cookies, Lorelei returned to Captain Quinn's cabin. Walt followed a few minutes later with a pair of reading glasses and an e-reader. Drawing up Captain Quinn's desk chair, he asked, "Would you mind if I read out loud a bit? You see, I volunteer at the library and read stories to the children. I've got a few brand-new books on here that I want to practice reading—to get the pacing and the voices right. The guys sometimes let me practice with them, but there's lots of ribbing that goes on, and that's distracting, if you know what I mean."

Lorelei smiled. "I don't mind at all."

When she curled up under the covers, Walt sat down, the e-reader in his hands and reading glasses perched on the tip of his nose. It had been more than twenty years since someone read her a bedtime story, but two stories and a woodland fairytale later, Walt's deep soothing voice lulled her into a dreamless sleep, her thoughts far from *The Osprey* and her crew's fate.

Not even all the sugary treats she ate could keep her awake.

Finally, some peace.

IN THE DEAD OF NIGHT, LORELEI JOLTED AWAKE TO A falling sensation and the taste of the sea on her tongue. She lashed out to grab onto something—anything—and seized fabric. Peering through dim light for a sturdier handhold, her gaze flicked up.

Metal bulkheads gleamed back. Not wood.

This was not *The Osprey's* hold. Nor the ocean's cruel, grasping waves. But that didn't mean she wasn't in danger. Grabbing the bedframe, she steeled herself for the next swell. *Oh God. Have we been caught in another storm?*

She waited for the vessel to lurch, frozen in terror, but the boat remained steady, cruising along on calm seas. Letting out a ragged breath, she buried her face into the pillow, shutting everything out so she could center herself. As she breathed in spicy notes of nutmeg, clove, and musk—a scent she was quickly beginning to associate with the captain—the tension in her limbs seeped away and rational thought returned. She had mistaken a hypnic jerk for rough waves.

I am safe. The ocean could not have her. But dark thoughts about sinking ships and drowning sailors crept in. That was a lie.

The ocean took whatever it wanted.

Hugging the pillow close, Lorelei continued to breathe in Captain

Quinn's scent, tethering herself to the present. No more thoughts about what could have been. After several more breaths, a tenuous peace settled over her, and she fell back to sleep.

WITHOUT A WAY TO TELL THE TIME, IT WAS HARD TO KNOW how long she slept, but she felt well-rested when she woke. After her little scare, it had been a deep, good sleep—just what her body needed after the ordeal it had endured.

Rolling onto her side, Lorelei blinked sleep from her eyes.

The room was dark, save for the flickering reading light above her head. Someone had turned the florescent overheads off. They'd been off earlier, but she'd been too terrified to properly register that fact.

And she hadn't noticed anyone else in the room then.

That wasn't the case now. She had company.

Sitting in a chair across from her, Captain Quinn slept soundly, but silently, with his arms crossed and head slumped forward. The edges of his carved masculine physique were softened by the dimly lit room. He'd taken off his sweater, but he wore a linen button-down shirt underneath, slightly rumpled and unbuttoned at the top. A generous amount of skin along the upper half of his chest was exposed, including the robust curve of his pectorals. She gulped, stomach somersaulting. Many hours were spent in the gym sculpting those.

With him so close, she didn't mind the darkness.

And good lord, she itched to touch him, to pull him into bed with her. It would be hard to think dark thoughts with the weight of his arms and his scent cocooned around her. On such a tiny, tiny bed, there would be no escaping each other's touch. Oh, it was tempting. As tempting as that chocolatey near kiss.

But if he rejected her? Her fragile, foolish heart could not survive that. Not here, not now.

At the least, they should switch places. He may have been comfortable enough to fall asleep in the chair, but he would pay for it in the morning. She wasn't yet thirty herself, and she could already feel the sympathy aches and pains. No, that wouldn't do at all.

Just a quick shake of his shoulder, enough to wake him. That would be all right.

She slipped out from underneath the covers. "Captain Quinn," she whispered.

Palm slid over solid trapezius muscle, gently shaking, and the memory of him kneeling before her, his breath tickling her bare skin, swam across her mind. She snatched back her hand, ignoring the heat curling in her belly, and shoved it inside her sweatpants pocket.

What the hell was wrong with her?

Stirring, he murmured something unintelligible and sleepily opened his eyes. He blinked up at her, a soft smile forming.

Do not lean in, you handsy creep. Leave this poor man alone.

"Captain," she repeated. "Go to bed. You can't sleep here."

He pressed a fist to his mouth and yawned. "I'm fine. It's yours."

"Please, I insist. I'm wide awake. I don't need it now."

He looked reluctant but eventually nodded.

The wooden chair beneath him creaked as he stood. Bleary eyed, he stumbled into bed and pulled the covers over his shoulders. Cradling the pillow underneath his head, he said, "If you need something to do, there's a book of crossword puzzles in my desk and a crate filled with books out in the galley. Help yourself."

This man was exhausted and yet he worried about her being bored.

After rummaging around for the crosswords and a pencil, she pulled the reading light chain. The cabin fell into complete darkness. Shit. She'd thought to return a courtesy—he'd left the light on for her, so she'd shut it off for him, but that had been a mistake.

An uneasy, suffocating feeling settled over her.

The deep was back, calling to her.

As she scurried out, she banged her leg painfully against the bedframe in her escape. It would leave a bruise, but out in the well-lit narrow hall, she felt instant relief.

She never used to fear the dark—even as a child. But now, without the light, she was back in the open ocean, all alone, with nothing but the depths and her drowned crew mates below her. Shuddering, she padded down to the galley and turned on its light.

The clock hanging above the doorway read 3AM. She had a few hours to kill until the rest of the crew woke.

Eying the bakery box on the counter longingly, Lorelei forced herself to move on. She'd already pilfered so many, so helped herself to a cup of sweetened black tea instead. Hopefully, it would banish the oddly fishy taste her morning breath had taken. Probably not, but it would have to do until Killian woke up, and she could ask to borrow his toothpaste.

Once she had the steaming beverage in hand, she sat down at the table with Captain Quinn's crossword book. The dark thoughts from earlier still lurked at the edges of her mind but examining them would be better done with her feet planted firmly on solid ground. Until she reached the shore, the ocean could still claim her.

Well-worn, the book was two-thirds completed. Lorelei thumbed through to the first untouched puzzle. She read the clues, counted the boxes, and filled in answers bit by bit, allowing the mental exercise to carry her away.

CHAPTER
FIVE

For three blissful hours, time and place had simply ceased to exist beyond pencil and paper. The sound of approaching footsteps in the hall brought her back to the present.

"Good morning," Walt greeted cheerfully from the doorway. He was followed by a man who introduced himself as Will Branson.

"It's nice to meet you, Will." Lorelei stood to shake his hand. "And thank you so much for your help."

"Of course." Will smiled. He was a stocky fellow with a full beard and dirty-blonde hair that he wore in a short ponytail at the nape. After giving her hand a firm shake, he turned to make coffee.

A third crew member—a sandy-haired kid in his late teens—shuffled into the galley. Lorelei vaguely remembered him from the day before—he'd brought her a wool blanket after she'd been pulled out of the water. The kid headed straight for the bakery box only to frown when opening it. His mouth moved silently as he counted. "Waaaalt, were you eating my cookies again?"

Ah. This must be Ian.

"That would have been me." She blushed. "Sorry about that."

Frown deepening, Ian sat diagonal from Lorelei in a huff and wrapped his arms around the bakery box like a dragon hoarding treasure.

Will tipped a spoon in his direction. "Ian, you should know by now that writing your name on food doesn't mean shit on this boat. If it's in the galley, it's up for grabs."

"Well, where else am I gonna keep 'em?" Ian mumbled and grumpily took a bite from one of his remaining cookies.

"I don't know." Will shrugged. "Your sea bag?" Ian grumbled something under his breath about not wanting to get crumbs on his underwear.

Walt, who had been silently watching the exchange, pinched the bridge of his nose and sighed. "Lorelei, this is Ian. Ian, mind your manners and say hello to the lady."

Ian sat up straight, but his eyes were still half hooded with sleep. "Hi," he replied robotically, cookie crumbs stuck to the corners of his mouth. "Cookie thief."

Her cheeks grew hotter.

"Ease up now. I told her it was okay to eat them. How about I buy you another box when we get back to shore?"

The kid chipmunked two more cookies and grinned. Despite her embarrassment, Lorelei bit her lip to keep herself from laughing.

Halfway through breakfast, the captain joined them. He smiled and greeted them all pleasantly, despite the dark circles around his eyes and pale, haggard expression.

"Boss, I've got this." Will frowned. "Go back to sleep. You look like hell."

"Do I?" Captain Quinn asked wryly, picking up the pot of coffee.

"Oh no you don't." Will took it from his hand. "We aren't fishing today. McAdams has the helm until noon, and you have to look better than this for the uh—" He paused, glancing at her. "For the welcome committee. And no, coffee won't fix it."

Welcome committee? Shit. Was there going to be press? Her rescue was news. Of course, there would be. And they would expect her to talk to them, microphones and cameras pointed in her face.

Nope. Don't think about it now. Panic on that bridge when you get to it.

The captain shrugged. "I'll be passable."

Crossing his arms, Walt chimed in with a firm, disapproving tone. "You'll give yourself heart palpitations with all the caffeine needed to be passable."

"You're no good to us dead on your feet," Will added, pushing Captain Quinn toward the door. "Go back to bed."

"All right fine," he grumbled, but he only made it as far as the hallway before turning back. At the doorway, he paused, bracing against the frame with both hands and casually leaning forward. Her overeager heart leapt when his eyes met hers. Just the slightest bit of attention and she was already a puddle. "A boat closer to shore than us was able to relay a message to your friends. They know you're safe."

All the terrible things they must have heard on the news...

She clutched her empty mug. "Thank you."

Soon after the captain's departure, Branson left with Ian to join the rest of the crew on deck, and Lorelei and Walt dealt with the breakfast dishes. "How long have you been fishing with Captain Quinn?" Lorelei dried off a cereal bowl as he washed another. Nothing against the guy, but she'd always assumed the captain was the oldest, most experienced member onboard. Not on here. Walt had about thirty years on him, and she would be shocked if he didn't have all the fishing experience to go along with it.

Wrists deep in suds, he chuckled. "About twenty-some years now? He was one of my deckies when I captained my own boat, but I've gotten too old for a twelve-hour shift at the helm. But not quite ready to retire either. So, we swapped roles."

She gestured around them. "This used to be your boat?"

"Oh no. *Marry Me, Marci,* she was called." His eyes twinkled. "I proposed to my beautiful wife with it. The boat's scrap metal now, but we kept parts, which Marci turned into art for our home. That's my Marci. She can make anything into a thing of beauty."

Opening a cabinet to the right, she chanced upon the one with stacked bowls inside and returned the one she dried to its rightful place. "She's an artist?"

Walt handed her another wet dish. "As a hobby. Marci ran our town's bank until retiring last year and has since been using our garage as her studio on a more full-time basis. And I mean that loosely. My Marci is enjoying her retirement, so she does what she wants when she wants. Sometimes when I come home in the afternoon, she's still wearing her pajamas." He chuckled.

Lorelei smiled. "Do you two have any children?"

"One daughter—Lila. And wouldn't you know, she's married to Will —the guy with the ponytail." He motioned over toward the coffee pot, where Will Branson had stood earlier. "They live in town near the Haven Cove Marine Research Center where Lila works."

A cozy little crew. And literally family for half. She got the sense that Captain Quinn was part of it, too, in some way, from the ease in which he accepted their good-natured cajoling. "Is Lila a marine biologist then?"

"Yup. Has wanted to be one since she was a little girl," he answered proudly. "How about you? What do you do for a living?"

That was a little up in the air, at the moment. "Museum stuff." She shrugged. "I helped with programming and exhibitions at the Marquette Maritime Museum near Lake Superior. They lost funding though and had to cut positions, including mine. I don't know what my next move will be. I thought I'd have a couple months to think about it on *The Osprey* but... at any rate, I'll figure it out."

"Believe it or not, I might be able to help you. The research center wants to open a museum and my daughter is overseeing the project. She has plenty of artifacts and whatnot, but she needs someone to help her with the design of the exhibits. Would that be something you'd be interested in doing?"

Say what now?

"I would love to do something like that." She tried not to sound too excited. It was perfect, a literal dream come true, but it couldn't be this simple. Her next step in life shouldn't land in her lap right after the ocean had nearly taken it from her. There hadn't even been time to process the shipwreck, much less what came after.

He beamed. "I can arrange an introduction when we get back to shore."

"I am speechless, Walt. Thank you so much." She swayed a little, reeling from the extraordinary offer.

"You could use a blessing or two from Lady Luck. Now, why don't we sit down," he gestured to the table. "You look a little wobbly."

Lorelei nodded and let Walt guide her by the elbow. Once she sat down, he brought her a glass of water. "I know this is none of my business, so you can just tell me to shove off, but I noticed that you've not mentioned parents or siblings since you've come onboard."

She took a long drink of water, sadness creeping into her limbs and weighing them down. Regret passed over Walt's face—her physical reaction must have been obvious. "It's all right," she replied. "Honestly, I don't know anything about my biological family. My mom adopted me in her mid-fifties, and I unfortunately lost her last year to cancer."

The cancer hadn't taken either of them by surprise. It ran in her mom's family like a deadly guarantee, an ill-fated family history Lorelei didn't share. Whatever defective genes she inherited from her ancestors, she'd never know. But despite the inevitability of losing her mom, her illness and passing hurt all the same, leaving a constant ache in her soul.

There wasn't a day that passed that Lorelei didn't think about her. In the first few months without her mom, it seemed like any little thing could set her off in a fit of tears. That wasn't the case anymore, but she hadn't been mentally prepared to talk about her and, coupled with emotional exhaustion, that freshened the wound.

Misty-eyed, Lorelei distracted herself with another drink of water and recited a tongue twister silently in her head. This emotional wave would overwhelm her if she wasn't careful. "I miss her all the time, but I am thankful she didn't have to deal with this mess. Her heart wouldn't have been able to take it."

"A parent's worst nightmare," Walt agreed. "Look, I know we've just met, but you are welcome at our place anytime, especially while you get back on your feet. Marci and Lila would like you. I have no doubt about it."

Once again floored by Walt's exceptional kindness, she wrapped her arms around herself and basked in his parental affection like seagrass bereft of sunlight. Her heart ached for her mother.

Greta Roth always knew what to say—steadying words that chased away Lorelei's uncertainties and hurts. And she was always there to offer a comforting touch—a cool palm on Lorelei's cheek, gentle hands that swept back her hair and wiped away her tears, and strong, sturdy arms that enveloped her when everything felt like too much. Without Mom to anchor her, Lorelei's mind tossed around in a tempest of longing and grief.

Walt reached forward and Lorelei took his hand, choked with tears she could no longer hold back.

CHAPTER
SIX

CHECK THE FISH HOLD.

The nagging thought, coupled with captain's intuition, led Killian to the boat's walk-in cold storage unit where they stacked crates of fish and bait. And he had been right to heed it. The door hadn't been closed all the way, left just slightly ajar. Goddammit. He'd have to talk to the crew about that.

Grumbling about wasting energy and risking the catch, Killian stepped inside. One of the stacks had fallen, strewing fish and ice across the floor. Sighing, he donned thick work gloves and crouched to pick up the tether that should have strapped it in place. He turned the frayed end between his fingers—it must have snapped during the storm—and added checking the others to his growing list of things to discuss with the crew. More might need replacing.

He scanned the mess in front of him.

A few of the fish didn't look quite right, as if they'd been hollowed out and packed with ice. Odd. Lifting them by the tails, he discovered their flesh stripped, too finely cleaned from the bone to have fallen prey to a larger fish. They would've swallowed their prey whole, bones and all. Could they have been cannibalized by the others in the net? He'd never seen or heard of such a thing.

That his crew hadn't found them when they hauled in the catch surprised him further. He didn't normally have to worry about their work ethic. Even the kid Ian was a diligent, thorough worker.

Killian tossed the half-eaten fish in with the bait. They'd have to comb through the rest before taking them to market. As he restacked and packed the crates, rivulets of sweat streamed down his chest despite the cold. He paused once to tug on the front of his sweater, breath puffing out in a cloud.

After tying down the crates, he exited the refrigeration unit and firmly closed the door behind him. Rather than feel relief from leaving the cold for heated air, he pulled uncomfortably at the front of his sweater again. Though the cold dulled his sense of smell, he walked toward the showers, certain he smelled like sweat and fish. An inevitable consequence of spending any amount of time in the fish hold.

Peeling off his shirt, he rounded a corner and collided into someone.

They jumped back with a distinctly feminine yelp. *Lorelei.*

Freeing his head, Killian saw that she had braided her dark auburn hair since breakfast and still wore one of his shirts, a pair of sweats, and wool socks. The sleeves and ankles were rolled up to account for their size difference. Seeing her at ease in his clothes, as if wearing them was something she did all the time, made Killian smile. He rather liked the thought of regularly finding her in them.

He lowered his arms and one by one pulled off each sleeve, feeling much better now that the air kissed his bare skin.

With a bashful, appraising look, she held her borrowed crossword book close to her chest. She gulped. So, she noticed. Draping his shorn sweater over his shoulder, Killian suppressed a stupid grin. "I'm sorry for almost knocking you over. I should have been watching where I was going."

"What?" She blinked. It was followed by a deep blush and slight shake of her head. "Oh. That's all right. I was just on my way to see if my clothes have dried. Walt—he's such a sweet guy—he said he would put them in the engine room for me if they hadn't."

Putting Lorelei in Walsh's care had been a good decision. The old sea captain had a skill for predicting the needs of others and a judicious mind for minor details—often overlooked but consequential details—in matters such as this.

Killian credited much of his own emotional intelligence to him. Not that he liked admitting it out loud. "I—um." He shifted on his feet, a little embarrassed to say he'd already hung up her clothes. "They weren't dry when I first woke up this morning, so I did just that before coming into the galley." Shit. Should he have asked if that was okay? Touching her things without permission... what an idiot.

"That was sweet of you, Captain." Lorelei smiled, pink cheeks flushing red.

Feeling his own heat, he swiped his forearm across his brow. He hadn't felt this awkward around the opposite sex since high school. She sniffed. Right. Shit. Fish. He quickly stepped back before he suffocated her with the odor. "Sorry for the smell. I had a mess to clean up in cold storage. A few crates fell and there was fish all over the floor."

"It's not so bad." Lorelei blushed even more deeply, her whole face aflame. "Anyway, I should let you go. I didn't mean to keep you from your shower."

"I'm not in a hurry."

That sounded a lot more flirtatious than he meant. Mentally kicking himself, he hurriedly added, "When I'm done, I'll see if my phone is getting a strong enough signal for you to call your friends." Not a smooth recovery, but if he kept talking, he'd only make it worse. Pinching his lips tight to keep more idiocy from spilling out, he sidestepped toward the showers.

"Okay, yeah. I'd appreciate that." She flattened herself against the wall. The only way he'd get by was if he squeezed past her.

Wow. He was an awkward idiot.

In the safety of the shower stall under the water's hot spray, Killian tapped his head against the metal wall, venting frustration and embarrassment. His emotional intelligence and professionalism could use some serious improvement.

Clad in her own dry clothes, Lorelei stood next to Captain Quinn in the pilothouse, reassured by the sight of shoreline on the horizon. She wouldn't go as far as kiss the ground when they docked, but to stand on solid land again… that moment couldn't come soon enough.

Taking a deep breath, Lorelei dialed her best friend's mobile number and pressed Captain Quinn's phone to her ear. It was close to noon, so she might catch her on her lunch break.

Ring.

"Hello?" Just one ring, that's all it took. Katrina must have been anxiously waiting by her phone for news. "May I ask who's calling?" Her friend's voice warbled thickly as if she had been crying.

Relief and grief bubbled to the surface, bringing the sharp sting of tears to her own eyes. So much for composure. She'd bottled her emotions the moment she stepped outside the privacy of the captain's cabin, and Walt's comforting parental presence. But just six words unlocked them, surely and swiftly. Her best friend's voice was the skeleton key to her heart. Sometimes she thought she could hold pieces of herself back, but in the end, she never wanted to.

Choking past the lump forming in her throat, she replied, "Hi, Kat."

"Lorelei?"

"Yes, Kat, it's me."

"Oh Lorelei, thank God!" She started to sob. "Are you okay? Are you hurt?"

"I'm all right." Lorelei hastily brushed her tears away, hyper aware of Captain Quinn standing beside her. Impossible to ignore. In close confines his solid presence was a comfort. But up here above deck, out in the open, she was exposed, and she didn't want him to see her lose control.

She crossed the pilothouse to the far wall. It only put an extra ten feet or so of distance between her and him, but it was breathing room and a modicum of privacy.

"I thought I'd lost you. When they said over the news that they'd only found one survivor…"

"Shh. It's okay. I'm still here." Away from Captain Quinn, and his warm, kind, but ever watchful eyes, Lorelei let her tears fall freely. "It's so good to hear your voice."

"Yours, too," Katrina sniffled. "Uh, excuse me. One moment." Muffled sounds of nose blowing followed. "Sorry. Where are you coming in? I'll book a flight and meet you."

"Haven Cove, Maine. They're taking me to the hospital there. Once I'm discharged, the Red Cross will put me up in one of the local hotels."

On the other end of the line, Lorelei heard clacking computer keys and clicking.

"Looks like the next available flight isn't until tomorrow morning, because of bad weather conditions along the northeastern seaboard," Katrina trailed off. "But let me know where you are staying once you find out, so I can meet up with you."

God, it would be good to hug her. The certainty of death, but not knowing when it would come, made four hours adrift a lifetime. Misery cocktail in concentrate. Living almost didn't feel real—the rescue, Captain Quinn might all be a beautiful but immaterial dream. But if anyone could remind her that she wasn't caught in some sort of afterlife limbo, it was Kat.

This phone call was every bit a gift. She'd been so certain she'd never see her again.

After the call, she rejoined Captain Quinn at the table covered in charts, handing back his phone. He wordlessly slipped it into his back pocket, but there was a firm set to his jaw and his brow was pinched. Something was eating away at him. "What is it?"

"I may have another option for where you can stay." He braced against the table, saying the words slowly, uncertainly. Like maybe he shouldn't say them.

She cocked her head, interest piqued. "And what would that be?"

He busied himself with straightening a pile of charts that really didn't need straightening, occasionally looking up to meet her eye. "The Red Cross will put you up in a local hotel, it's true, but you'll be at the mercy of the press and anyone with a mild sense of curiosity. The people in town are friendly, and mean well, but they'll want to know everything about you. I imagine that might be stressful."

True. That didn't sound ideal. "So, what's my other option?"

He shuffled on his feet, cheeks reddening. What made him shy all of a sudden? It was kind of cute, but they were just talking... "If you're comfortable with the idea, I have a spare bedroom you can use." He sighed, rubbing the back of his neck. "I live in a quiet area by the sea. I don't have any neighbors, so I understand if you aren't okay with that, but you'd have peace and privacy."

Oh.

That was unexpected.

And yet, the offer did appeal to her. Sitting in a hotel room alone with her thoughts, closed in by a town full of strangers, sounded lonely and suffocating. That was the last thing she needed. With Katrina still hundreds of miles away, Killian was the most familiar person within reach, and her gut told her that she could trust him.

She tapped a finger to her lips.

When men made her feel uneasy, it wasn't always easy to point out exactly why, but she'd get an undeniably sinking feeling in the pit of her stomach. She felt none of that now. "That would be nice. Staying somewhere quiet, I mean, until Kat arrives."

He gave a short, curt nod, but the tension in his shoulders eased.

Some might say she should have shot him down—Katrina probably would've—but she was certain she'd process what had happened better in the captain's company.

In more ways than one, Captain Quinn had tossed her a lifeline. She wouldn't stop reaching for it now.

CHAPTER
SEVEN

DAWN CHASER ARRIVED AT PORT AROUND MIDDAY.

McAdams steered them into the harbor, horseshoe in shape and ringed with the signature red and white buildings of a New England shore town. All the lobster boats they shared a dock with were already moored up and quiet. The docks themselves, weathered and grey, were littered with gear in various states of repair—stacks of lobster pots, buoys, and live wells—and bigger equipment, including a haul-out crane, fuel pump, and forklift. Ashore, set off to the right, there was a fish processing warehouse and a tiny wooden shack that held Killian's office.

The docks looked the same as always, save for the parked ambulance and small group of reporters waiting with recorders and the cameramen filming b-roll.

As soon as the crew tied off, an EMT boarded the boat to check on Lorelei and make sure she could walk off on her own two feet. The moment Lorelei came into view on deck, the reporters began furiously snapping photos, a chorus of shutter clicks. She shrunk back, but the EMT leaned in and said something; he couldn't hear exact words over the engine of the boat, but whatever it was, the tone was encouraging.

Together, the two hastened down the gangway, inserting themselves as a barrier, arm raised and ready to stiff arm anyone who got too close.

While the press fired off questions and followed them the entire walk over to the ambulance, no one shouted or tried to get in their way. Not at all the feeding frenzy Killian feared it would be.

Once the ambulance drove off, Killian met with the reporters. Maybe, just maybe he could occupy them long enough for Lorelei to get settled at the hospital. And maybe if he offered himself up as a willing interviewee, they wouldn't approach his crew.

Having all those cameras and microphones pointed in his direction was a little unnerving, but he focused on the people asking the questions, looking them in the eye, and pretended it was a regular, unrecorded conversation.

Most of the reporters were regional for various TV, radio, and print outlets, but two were from Michigan and another was from Connecticut. No one talked over each other and instead took turns asking questions —it was a lot more laid back than he'd expected. They all wanted to know the same things.

Their questions centered around the timeline of events, the nature of the storm, and *Dawn Chaser*'s role in rescue efforts. Killian kept his answers as factual as possible but gave enough detail to leave them satisfied.

But when the reporter from Portland asked, "Is there any hope of finding other survivors?" Killian paused.

Portland was the sailing school's home port and primary student pool for *The Osprey*. Looking at the reporter more closely, he noted dark bags circling the man's eyes, a premature five o'clock shadow, and drained expression. The man might've known someone onboard *The Osprey*. Perhaps several.

"I'll let the Coast Guard answer that one," Killian answered gently.

The Portland reporter's face crumpled, losing all that remained of his professional veneer. Too tired to look away, he openly wept. The reporter from Connecticut also looked dispirited, but persevered, "Can you confirm the survivor's name?"

When they were coming inshore, Lorelei asked that he do so. She had a number of acquaintances who would want to know she was safe. "Yes, it's Ms. Lorelei Roth, a sailing student from Marquette, Michigan."

Most of the group thanked him and hurried off—likely in hopes of getting another shot at an interview with Lorelei at the hospital. But the town reporter from *Haven Cove Daily*, Jackie Gaten, stayed behind. A pen was tucked behind her ear, partially covered by the shock of fluffy, prematurely white hair that hung about her face in a curly cloud. Her aquiline nose, high cheekbones, and thin arched eyebrows gave her a permanently hawkish expression, exuding both keen intelligence and hyper vigilance.

"You did great," she said, giving his arm a friendly squeeze. When he was a kid, she babysat and tutored him for a couple years. She had towered over him in those days. Now, she only came up to his shoulder.

"Thanks. I guess you want to talk to a couple of the guys?" While this hadn't been his first time on the record, Killian had only ever been interviewed by Jackie before and for relatively mundane local fishing industry stories.

"I will, but it can wait until tomorrow." She glanced over her shoulder at the journalist from Portland and frowned. He was slowly shuffling to his car. Like it hurt to move. "I'm going to go look after that guy. Ed, I think his name is. His niece and nephew were on that ship."

Killian swiped a hand over his face. "Shit. Yeah, that's a good idea. He probably shouldn't drive."

"My thoughts exactly. I'll catch you later." Jackie jogged after Ed and put her arm around his sloped shoulders, murmuring something into his ear. They left together in her car.

Across the docks, Branson was showing Ian how to process the offloaded catch—pollock and haddock mostly. They had a Northeast Multispecies federal fishing license—the State didn't allow trawling—but anything beyond three miles offshore was federally regulated waters.

Branson glanced up, and seeing the interview was done, patted the boy's back and strode over. "How'd it go?"

"Fine." Killian hooked his thumbs through his belt loops and watched the exaggerated grimace Ian made as he butchered and cleaned his first fish. The kid was a hard worker, but also quite expressive. "Just expect a call from Jackie sometime tomorrow, but don't mention that torn immersion suit. We'll let the Coast Guard figure out what to say about that, if anything."

"No problem. One of their guys is coming by later today to pick it up." Branson rubbed the back of his neck awkwardly. "So, um. My cousin's been asking after you—blew up my phone with text notifications actually. When's the last time you spoke to her?"

A palpable silence fell between them, broken only by a squawking seagull flying overhead. Why the hell did Branson have to bring Carrie up? They hadn't talked about her in years, and he had been content to keep it that way.

Branson shifted uncomfortably on his feet, likely regretting he'd asked.

"Not since she moved to the city," Killian answered finally. "She hasn't tried contacting me, so it's not like I'm ignoring her. If that's what you're asking."

"Ah, right." Branson relaxed. "She's been talking about moving back to the coast. I think she wants to reconnect."

With a little nod, Killian motioned Branson to follow him back to the boat. If they were going to gossip, they were going to work while they did it. "What about her dream job and fiancé?"

Branson followed him up the gangway. "Not what they were cracked up to be, I guess. Or maybe she misses you more than she loves either of them."

Killian shook his head. "If neither are working out for her, I'm sorry, and I hope she finds the next best thing. But that chapter of my life is over and has been for a long time."

The crane the crew used to lift crates of fish out of the freezer hold and onto the docks kicked into gear. Branson had to shout the next bit to be heard above its mechanical rattling. "You're gonna have to tell her that yourself whenever she reaches out. She won't hear it from me."

When she reached out? Good God, he really should have changed his number. From his dinosaur brick phone to the latest smartphone, he'd stubbornly, and apparently rather stupidly, kept it.

At least she didn't know where he lived.

KILLIAN HANDLED BUYER LOGISTICS AND REFUELING WHILE his crew processed catch and cleaned the boat. Midway through the afternoon, he called a break for an announcement. His seven-man crew gathered around him.

Hooking his thumbs through his belt loops, Killian rocked back on his heels. "I wanted to thank you all for how you handled the storm and search and rescue operation. You were professional and brave, and because of you, Ms. Roth is alive here today. Next round of drinks at the pub is on me."

The last bit was met with a chorus of 'aw thanks Cap.'

"Me too?" Ian chirped up. Ha. The kid was barely eighteen.

"Sorry, Ian, you get a milkshake." The crew laughed, and Ian pulled a face. Branson hip-checked him good-naturedly.

Crossing his arms, Killian continued, "There's something else I wanted to talk to you all about."

The crew quieted, noting his serious tone.

"Believe me, I know it's been a rough couple of days, and we could all could use a goodnight's sleep, but I found the refrigeration unit door open this morning." The crew began to murmur amongst themselves. An improperly sealed fish hold meant spoiled catch and thin paychecks. He continued, telling them about the fallen crates and the fish bones he found but was met with genuine looks of confusion. No one seemed to recall making any of those mistakes.

Killian held up his hands in placation. "Look, I'm not looking for names or anything. Just wanted you to be aware so it doesn't happen again."

On his orders, the crew carefully inspected their equipment for weaknesses, and as the afternoon wore on, no more half-eaten fish were found during processing. What Killian found onboard had been an anomaly.

CHAPTER
EIGHT

THE *DAWN CHASER* CREW HAD JUST FINISHED WORK FOR THE day when Killian answered a call from Lorelei on a hospital phone. He drove over straight from the docks.

She was already waiting for him outside, hands tucked away in her olive drab zip-up, when he pulled up to the hospital entrance. Just standing there with nothing but the clothes on her back. No phone. No wallet. Not even a set of keys. Just a piece of paper with his number scribbled on it.

Must have been an unnervingly naked feeling.

Shifting uncomfortably, she glanced at his charcoal-grey pick-up truck, but was too shy to properly look inside. It was an older model, and a little sun faded in spots, but perfectly reliable—something he'd forgotten to tell her. Maybe she was on the lookout for something shiny and new.

Not that he'd blame her. Fishermen did love sporting the latest gas-guzzler.

Lowering the passenger side window, he called her name. She looked up, recognition and relief immediate, and hurried over. Once inside and buckled in, she sighed heavily, raising the window and pressing her temple to the cool glass.

"You okay?"

"It's been a long day." She wrapped her arms about her middle. "Like two full days squeezed into one. I did interviews in between tests, and between the reporters and the doctors there were just so many questions."

He pulled out of the hospital parking lot, taking a left toward town, rather than the right to go home. While driving through town was a bit of a scenic detour, he thought a little subtle sight-seeing might be calming. Sometimes after a stressful day on the docks, he'd park his truck in town and walk the ocean path that hugged the coastline. The sea breeze always managed to gather up his churning thoughts and carry them away.

"It's your time now." He drummed his fingers against the steering wheel to an internal beat. "You can call all the shots for the rest of the evening. No more answering questions if you don't want to."

A small smile tugged at her lips. "Deal."

They drove through Haven Cove proper, where quaint boutiques lined the town's streets and moored sailboats dotted the harbor's dark blue water with white. The leaves of the trees in the waterfront park had begun to turn in the chill September air, mixing green with brilliant shades of red, orange, and yellow. Lorelei stared out the passenger window, her nose as good as pressed to the glass, drinking in the sight.

Understandably so.

The view was literally a postcard shot. All the gift shops in town carried the print, and tourists traveled hundreds, sometimes thousands of miles just to see it in-person.

As they turned out of town, and onto the country road, Lorelei lowered her window and breathed in deep. Peace settled over her. Forest land surrounded them, surrounded the town, and blanketed the whole State of Maine. Roads were far and few in between in coastal, rural regions such as this one—just passages through towering white pines and beech trees from one pocket of civilization to the next.

Lorelei cleared her throat. "Captain Quinn, do you mind if I turn on the radio? I could use a little music."

He chuckled, lowering his own window, too. "You're not on my crew, you know. Don't have to call me captain—Killian's fine. And I don't mind putting on some music. What do you like? We pick up classic rock, hard rock, country…"

"Soft or classic rock. I usually know the words to those songs the best."

"Same." He tuned into one of his favorite stations and turned up the volume. "Mind if I sing?"

"Not at all."

Singing in front of others wasn't something he normally did—except TV karaoke nights with Branson and Lila from the safety of their living room—but the mood struck him, and it might help Lorelei feel at ease. There was something about having a good song on and choosing not to sing along to it that created tension, and that was the last thing he wanted for her.

Trapped in a vehicle with awkward silence for company was never a good time.

After a few lines into the song, Lorelei joined in. She sang quietly at first, but her volume grew as the song progressed. She hadn't been kidding when she joked about being a terrible singer, but he loved how she enjoyed it anyway. He couldn't stop listening if he tried.

By the last chorus, matching grins plastered their faces, and they belted out the final lyrics together, the wind whipping their hair every which way, and with it the stress of the past few days. No crew to worry about, no storm to survive, no reporters to appease.

Three songs later, he turned down a winding dirt road that cut through the forest to the place he called home. Nestled in a small, sandy inlet between mountains and rocky outcroppings sat the seaside stone cottage he built.

Lorelei stared at it all in wide-eyed wonder.

Watching her watch the waves roll into shore, something she said the day before struck him. She had never seen the ocean before joining *The Osprey* crew. What a rotten twist of fate that her first taste of it had ended in such tragedy.

Unbuckling her seatbelt, she leaned forward, pressing her hands to the dash, drawn closer by the view. Perhaps in the short time she stayed here with him, she'd get to witness the ocean's beauty. Not the terrible force of nature that had devoured her ship and crew.

"I can see how neighbors would be off putting," she said breathlessly.

That brought a smile to his face. He'd been afraid she might be alarmed by how isolated his home was. "You couldn't pay me enough to sell off any of it." And plenty of people had tried to convince him to do so.

She twisted in her seat to face him, eyes sparkling. "How did you come by this place?"

He pulled to his truck in the unpainted, shingle-less barn that stood off to the left of the property. "This plot of land has been in my family for generations. My ancestors settled here when they came to America to log timber for ships, but the original cottage burned down when my grandfather was a boy. My father really wanted him to sell the land to a real estate developer and, as you can probably imagine, he would have gotten a lot of money for it. But Granddad couldn't bear the thought of losing it. So, when I made an offer to buy it off him, he accepted and helped me rebuild."

"Wait. You built all this?" She gestured around them.

"Yup." He hopped out of the truck and grabbed his sea bag from the back. "The barn's brand new though, and I still need to weatherproof it before winter."

"Wow." Lorelei followed him to his front door which, despite the isolated location, he always kept locked. Occasionally tourists came onto his property, mistaking his driveway for a trail to an overlook. "I find the fact that you have a door knocker rather amusing," she teased, tracing the iron ring with a finger while he fumbled for the right key.

"Branson's wife Lila said the exact same thing." Killian fit the key into the lock and opened the door. "She makes a show of using it every time they visit."

She smiled. "She sounds fun. Did Walt mention her museum project to you?"

Reaching in, he flicked on a light switch, and led the way inside.

"Yeah, we talked about it this afternoon while locking up the boat. He said he thinks he might have found you a job."

"Oh, I don't know if it's as simple as that. I'd have to apply and hope she likes me better than the other candidates."

Wait. She was seriously considering applying and moving to the area? His stomach did a funny flip. "That's true," he replied, trying to play it cool. "But he has high hopes for you." Truth was there wasn't much competition. No one local qualified for the job, and most applicants who did qualify weren't seriously committed to moving this far north—Lila had bemoaned that reality on numerous occasions. Not that it in anyway diminished Lorelei's merits, whatever they may be. That was just the professional landscape up here.

"At any rate, I look forward to meeting her." She followed him in and closed the door behind her. "Damn. It looks great on the inside, too. Do you mind if I look around more closely?"

"Be my guest." He watched her make her exploratory circuit, weirdly nervous about what she might think. Until this point, he'd only invited a select handful of friends and family into his home. Even his first love had never been inside; the day he bought this slice of paradise from his grandfather was the day she left him for big city dreams.

Directly across the room from the front door stood the open stone fireplace, flanked by two floor-to-ceiling bookshelves made from reclaimed wood. The ground floor had a plan—all that separated the living room from the kitchen was a modest partition. But Lorelei took her time wandering the space. She crouched to admire the driftwood legs of the kitchen table set; gushed over the iron spiral staircase leading to the second floor; ran her hand across countertops and bookshelves made of reclaimed wood; and almost precisely dated an antique sea chest sitting in a corner adjacent to the stone fireplace.

Seeing her admire his craftsmanship made his chest puff with pride.

CHAPTER

NINE

SITTING ON THE COUCH IN FRONT OF A CRACKLING FIRE, they hunched over steaming bowls of store-bought New England clam chowder, his go-to comfort food in a pinch. There was nothing better at the end of a difficult fishing trip than watching the flames dance, licking at the logs, snapping and popping in the fireplace.

Killian sank into the couch cushions with a sigh. This was home.

Blowing steam off a spoonful of soup, Lorelei sat cross-legged beside him in a pair of borrowed sweatpants, the spicy scent of his body wash wafting off her skin. He didn't own a hairdryer, so she'd braided her wet hair and let it hang over her shoulder. It left a watermark down the front of the t-shirt he gave her—a snug fit on him but oversized on her. And yet, the way the fabric settled over her curves, teasing his imagination...

Hot soup scalded his hand as his bowl tipped.

Cursing, he propped the bowl up with his knee and sucked the flesh between his thumb and index finger where he'd been burned. Served him right. He should have paid more attention to his soup and less on ogling Lorelei. He doubted she'd appreciate him staring at her like some sex-crazed teenager.

She looked up from her bowl. "You okay?"

He withdrew his hand with a quiet *pop*. "Yeah, just a little clumsy."

Her gaze lingered on his mouth, several moments longer than polite. Then she shook her head and dipped a slice of folded, buttered bread into her soup, a pretty, pink blush dotting her cheeks. "Your staircase reminds me of the ones I've seen in lighthouses on Lake Superior."

He pulled a couch pillow across his lap and set his bowl on top. For better balance, of course. He was thirty-eight, after all, not thirteen. "I salvaged it from one," he replied, grateful for the innocuous subject of craftsmanship. "When my grandfather and I built this place, we used as much recycled building materials as we could get our hands on. Some of the reclaimed wood even came from the original cottage. If you look closely, you'll notice that some parts of the bookshelves are singed from the fire."

"A preserved piece of your family's history." She smiled wistfully. "I think they would appreciate how much care you've put into giving it new life."

His dad didn't. Called it 'sentimental, hippie shit.' But that was neither here nor there. He loved this little seaside cottage and seeing it rebuilt made his grandfather happy, the only family member's approval he ever really cared to have after his mom passed away.

Rebuilding it was the first checkbox on Killian's bucket list and the last one on his grandfather's.

Carrie hadn't understood his dedication to it either.

She assumed he'd drop the project and follow her to NYC, into all the noise, the hustle, and grimy city air. When she said he was meant for 'bigger things,' that he should become a harbor pilot, a job that would bring in half a million a year, Killian told her he'd never leave Haven Cove, Maine. Would never abandon this project, his home.

He could have done it.

Made the move. Pursued the job. Brought multi-million-dollar cargo ships into NYC's congested port, but that kind of life and that kind of work would have killed his soul. His dream of being a fishing captain wasn't too small, didn't pay too little. How could it be when he was beholden only to himself and the sea?

He had everything he needed. Home life might be a little lonely…

But those weren't things he wanted to talk about.

"Lorelei, yesterday you said you'd never seen the ocean before. Not even once before *The Osprey?*"

"Nope. Not once. It was quite the 'Never Have I Ever' trump card in college."

"But how? Plenty of folks from the Midwest travel to the coast."

She shrugged, taking another bite of food. "My mom was a freshwater fish, and we lived really close to Lake Superior. There wasn't a reason to make a trip to the ocean, because we already had beautiful beaches for swimming and boating. And then she just got too old to make long trips. She was in her mid-fifties when she adopted me." She stirred her soup around, expression falling. "And eighty-one last year when she died of cancer."

The loss of a mother—Killian acutely knew what that felt like. There one day, gone the next. No matter the age, it always felt too soon. "I'm sorry. What was she like?"

Focusing on the good memories sometimes helped, and Lorelei perked a little at the question. "A tough as nails German woman. She immigrated to the U.S. in her early twenties, studied American law, became a lawyer and eventually a judge for Marquette County. My mom never married—couldn't be bothered with men, she told me, or women for that matter. But she'd always wanted a child. Just didn't act on her desire to adopt until I was left on her doorstep as an infant."

Killian did a double take. She was abandoned on a doorstep?

"Sounds like something out of a fairytale, doesn't it?" Lorelei chuckled. She pinched off a piece of bread and popped it into her mouth. "She didn't know how long I was outside, but I began to cry and that got her attention. It was nighttime, so Mom came to the door with a hardwood rolling pin. She'd just heard a rumor about a serial-killer who lured women out of their homes with a recording of a crying baby, so she was understandably a little freaked out. But she also wouldn't have ever forgiven herself if she didn't check and left a baby out in the cold all night. The rest is history."

What a strange tale. It did kinda sound like something out of a children's book—older, childless woman finding the baby she'd always wanted on her doorstep. He didn't know much about the Midwest, but he didn't think that sort of thing really happened, not anymore. Not with shelters and child welfare agencies being commonplace. There had to be more to the story than what Lorelei's mother told her. Something better left unspoken. "Did she ever find out who left you?"

It didn't really matter. He probably shouldn't have asked, but Lorelei's expression didn't change, seemingly unbothered by it. "No. There was nothing unique about the clothes I wore. There was, however, a note pinned to the blanket I was wrapped in. It said 'LORELEI' in bold red ink. Mom thought my parents must have felt very strongly about that being my name."

The story just kept getting weirder and weirder. "That sounds rather ominous to me."

She shrugged. "She suspected they must have been too poor to take care of me, and were ashamed of it, or I was born out of wedlock. Whatever the case, she was sympathetic and liked that it was a German name."

A million more questions circled in his mind, but he let them drop. He'd pried enough already.

The night ended early. They only talked a little while longer before Lorelei excused herself and left for bed, leaving him behind to contemplate everything she'd divulged.

After getting a beer out of the fridge, he added more wood to the fire and plopped back onto the couch to watch the flames. Lorelei seemed aware of how fantastical her mother's story sounded but had accepted it, content with what she'd been given. Life was full of mysteries, but not all of them needed to be solved. Sometimes they brought too much pain, and Lorelei had a fair share of it already. What good would digging deeper really bring?

He couldn't imagine how she must feel right now. On the outside, Lorelei seemed the picture of composure, but he suspected she hadn't fully processed *The Osprey* ordeal. A part of her mind was still in survival mode. It wouldn't be long before the remaining adrenaline wore off, and when that happened, he just hoped she wasn't alone.

It wouldn't stem the grief—nothing ever really did—but the arrival of her friend tomorrow morning would help. He'd make a point to run errands then. His fridge and pantry needed to be restocked with more than just canned soup, but more importantly, they should have a chance to catch up in private. Expression of grief could be a deeply personal and private thing.

If Walt hadn't told him about Lila's museum project, and if Lorelei herself hadn't expressed interest in it, he might have thought that she'd leave tomorrow with her friend, and he'd never see her again. But the way things were headed, once she got her affairs in order, she wouldn't be gone for long. And not only would Lorelei be coming back, she would also be working with Lila, keeping her close to his personal circle.

Funny how life worked out that way.

Eyes beginning to droop, he spread out the coals and went up to bed himself. Sleep came as soon as his head hit the pillow, sweeping him down into blissful oblivion.

AS THE NIGHT WAXED AND WANED, THE TEMPERATURE inside the cottage dropped, and Killian drifted back toward consciousness, roused by the growing chill.

Hugging blankets close to his body, he glanced at the red numbers displayed on his bedside clock—he'd only slept for a few hours. He curled sleepily in bed, debating whether to leave its relative warmth to turn up the thermostat.

The twist of the guest room doorknob interrupted his pondering and was followed by the sound of footsteps as Lorelei crossed the hallway to the bathroom. No, to the stairs. He tucked his arm beneath his pillow. Probably just getting a drink of water. But long moments ticked by, and he never heard the faucet run.

The front door opened. Maybe she needed some fresh air…

Waves crashed and wind whistled louder. The door didn't shut.

He shot up in bed. What the hell?

Throwing on a sweater and socks, Killian hustled out of his room to, one, close the door, and, two, check on Lorelei. A cold gust of wind blew in from the ocean through the wide-open door just as he'd reached the bottom of the stairs, and it banged loudly against the wall.

Seriously, what the hell was she thinking? Was it really that hard to close a damn door?

He flipped the switch to the outside light and as he reached for the door handle, he saw Lorelei was nearly knee-deep in the waves. Odd time to go wading. He shouted her name, but not only didn't she turn, she didn't even pause. Either Lorelei didn't hear him, or she wouldn't acknowledge that she did and continued moving forward in the water.

This was not the time to go swimming. And something about this troubled him. Grief and trauma affected everyone differently, and given what she'd just survived…

Swearing, Killian sprinted after her, not bothering to put on shoes or close the door.

She had wandered in up to her waist by the time he reached the water's edge. Gritting his teeth so hard his jaw hurt, he sloshed through ice-cold water, his legs already becoming stiff and numb—and yet she didn't so much as shiver or wrap her arms around herself for warmth. "Lorelei, stop!" They were close enough to touch now, and yet, she still didn't turn, didn't even flinch.

Her eyes had a glassy, hooded look as if held in a trance. He'd never seen sleepwalking before, but if there was any explanation for Lorelei's odd behavior, it was this. He vaguely remembered reading somewhere that you shouldn't try to talk to or wake up a sleepwalker and stopped calling out her name.

Keeping a close eye on her for signs of distress, Killian gently took her by the elbow. Her nose flared with a deep inhale, and her face tilted in his direction. He thought she might be waking up, but her eyes still had that dazed look, not quite registering him. She leaned in close, her breath hot on his neck, and sniffed. Not a delicate little inhale either, but a deep, lungs-filling one. He flinched, unsure whether to be flattered or freaked out. Some part of his animal brain yelled at him to run from this unknown, but he tuned it out.

Lorelei needed his help. He wasn't going to leave her to drown just because she liked how he smelled, and her subconscious wasn't shy about showing it.

With a firm guiding hand, Killian walked Lorelei back to shore. She followed without resistance.

When Lorelei's feet touched dry sand, she woke in a panic, frantically patting down her body as if looking for keys or a wallet. But all she had misplaced was herself. "Where am I? Why I am I wet?"

"Shh, I got you," he soothed past chattering teeth. He wrapped an arm around her trembling shoulders as much for her comfort and warmth as his own. God, it was freezing. "Just the beach outside my house. You were sleepwalking... into the ocean."

Horror written across her face, she glanced frantically back at the rolling waves they'd left behind. "I've never had a sleepwalking episode before." Her voice shook.

"It's probably stress-related." With a gentle nudge, he urged her up the sandy slope. They were both soaked through and through. "Come on. Let's go back inside."

She nodded, wrapping an arm around his waist.

Whatever spell the ocean cast over her was broken.

CHAPTER
TEN

FOR MOST OF THE NEXT MORNING, LORELEI LAY MOTIONLESS in bed, staring blankly at the ceiling. She'd made the mistake of checking the news on the laptop that sat on Killian's guest room desk. All along she knew in her heart that her shipmates were gone, swallowed by the sea. Afterall, her mind was haunted by the memory of it. Yet, she still hoped beyond reason that she was mistaken and that the rescuers found someone else overnight.

They hadn't. There wasn't even much hope of recovering bodies.

She replayed the events of that night over and over, grimly fixated on the mystery of her survival while everyone else disappeared beneath the waves without a trace. There was no reasonable explanation for it. The same storm, the same series of mammoth waves had swept them all away.

It wasn't that she wasn't grateful to be alive. It just didn't make any sense. Nor did her sudden sleepwalking into the ocean. Was her subconscious mind telling her that she belonged with the rest of the crew?

The scrape of gravel beneath rolling tires drew Lorelei's attention to a vehicle pulling into the driveway. The quiet hum of its engine sounded nothing like the sea captain's pickup truck.

Sliding out of bed to peek out the window, she saw a car stop alongside the cottage, and jumped off to the side, hiding from line of sight. Pure instinct. She wasn't in any condition to receive visitors, and she didn't really belong there. She was supposed to be in some Red Cross provided hotel room.

What if it was a reporter?

Back pressed up against the wall, and contemplating the car down below, Lorelei's stomach tied in knots and her palms grew clammy with sweat. How in the hell would she introduce herself? And explain why she was staying here in the captain's house? She could give all the reasons she gave herself on *Dawn Chaser* but that required a lot of explaining, which begged the question if it was even the real reason at all.

Sinking to the floor and wrapping her arms around her legs, Lorelei's head spun, each thought circling back to Killian. The troubling truth that she didn't want to admit, because it seemed wrong in the wake of recent events, was that she was spinning head over heels for a man she barely knew. She squeezed her eyes shut, but the levee that held back her walled emotions crumpled, and tears flooded her cheeks.

As she sobbed into her knees, she wondered how her future could look so bright and hopeful when her shipmates were robbed of theirs. It didn't matter that she hadn't known any of them particularly well. They were forever bound by *The Osprey* and that terrible storm.

The least a decent person could do was properly mourn them first. But what she felt for Killian would fade. That was how this phenomenon played out, right? Survivors fell a little bit in love with their rescuers, until the circumstances and proximity that brought them together passed, and life returned to normal, equilibrium restored.

Hearing the car door finally open, Lorelei dried her eyes and peered over the windowsill to see who stepped out.

Katrina.

Thank God.

Tucking long, wavy brown strands of hair behind her ears, and scrunching her cute button nose, Katrina surveyed the property as if unsure she'd come to the right spot. She patted down the pockets of her red peacoat and dove back into the car, presumably to grab her phone or maybe a map.

A wave of relief washed over Lorelei.

Launching herself off the floor, she rushed downstairs. When she burst out the front door, ready to smother her best friend in a crushing hug, Katrina was glaring at her phone and cursing the cellular dead zones of rural, coastal Maine.

In her haste, Lorelei closed the door harder than she meant to. *Slam!*

Katrina yelped, nearly jumping out of her skin.

"Sorry! Sorry! It's just me." Not an angry landowner hell bent on giving an earful on the illegality of trespassing.

"Lorelei!" She darted over, enveloping her in a crushing hug.

Fresh tears sprung from Lorelei's eyes, and she held on tight. "I'm so glad you're here!"

"I'm so glad you're safe!"

They rocked from side to side.

"I've been lucky." Lorelei sniffed, pulling back. "They're saying the search isn't looking good for the others."

She frowned. "Have you been reading the news?"

The truth wouldn't make Kat happy, protective mother hen that she was, but Lorelei wasn't going to lie to avoid a scolding. "Yeah…" She hugged herself, already wincing.

"It's too soon! You shouldn't be reading that stuff."

But how could she not? They were fellow crew and friends. "Those were people I knew," she countered quietly. "I have to know what happened to them."

Kat's expression softened. "I'm sorry, Lorelei. That must be terribly hard."

"I just don't understand it. When the storm hit, every last one of us came on deck, put on immersion suits, and hauled on lines. Anyone who went into the water like me, should have—" She paused to take a tissue out of her pocket, addressing a runny nose. "But I was out there for hours, and I saw no one and heard nothing after the storm passed. The only explanation I can come up with is they all got caught in the rigging as the ship sank."

Line coiled around limbs like tentacles, their one-time sea home now the kraken that dragged them into the deep. The descent would've been too quick, the suction too powerful for a diver's knife to cut through submerged, sodden rope in time.

Tears welling in dark-brown eyes, Katrina pressed her lips into a thin sympathetic line and reached out, arms wide. Lorelei fell into the hug. "What a horrible way to die," she said, voice cracking sharply as a sob pushed to the surface.

With the tenderness and firmness only a best friend can give, Katrina held her up when her knees grew weak, smoothing a hand over frizzy, auburn hair. Soothing nothings caressed her ear, not a word of complaint about her ugly crying. Her rock, her solace in grief's storm.

Ever since she'd come on shore, she'd needed to fall apart, and there was no person she trusted more to guard her pieces than Katrina—and then, when she was ready, assemble them back together.

The hurt, the tears eventually subsided. Sniffing, she pulled back, wiping her eyes. "I'm sorry for laying that out in the open. You didn't need to hear that."

"No, don't be." Katrina rubbed Lorelei's arm up and down. "That's what I'm here for. But why don't we go inside and talk?"

"Do you have bags in the trunk? I'll help you carry them in."

Confusion wrinkled Katrina's forehead. "We're staying here? I can get us a hotel room in town, you know. It really wouldn't be any trouble."

A blush warmed her cheeks. She didn't want to stay in town. Not quite yet anyway. There'd already been too much abrupt change in the last seventy-two hours. One more night here, someplace steady. That's all she needed, and she'd be ready to face other people. Being near *him* would be a nice bonus but definitely not the main reason.

"Killian said we could stay here if we wanted, and I hadn't thought to say no, but we can decide later, if that's all right."

Casting a dubious glance at the little seaside cottage, Katrina said, "Yeah, sure. But let's leave my bags in the car for now."

They left their shoes by the front door and made themselves at home. Katrina sat at the kitchen table while Lorelei put on a kettle and searched the cabinets for tea and mugs. She didn't think Killian would mind. "He's got a real nice place," Katrina commented, glancing about the interior, nodding with appreciation.

"He sure does." She pointed at the dining table set with the spoon she held. "Can you believe he made that from driftwood?"

"Handy." Katrina traced a finger over the wood grain. "So, um. Do you want to talk more about what happened?"

She stilled, cradling two mugs plucked from a nearby cabinet. Between the hospital staff and reporters, she'd told the story so many times it had become a habit to just let it roll off her tongue while her mind launched itself a million miles away. And yet, getting into it again, especially with her best friend, was now too much. She couldn't hide herself away with this retelling, cut open and raw, and Katrina didn't deserve to have the darkness that followed put on her shoulders.

After the rough morning she'd had, Lorelei wasn't sure she'd be able to shoulder it again herself. "I'm not sure what else to say."

"What about the good memories? And your crew mates—what were they like?"

"Oh." She exhaled, setting the mugs down on the counter. Happy memories she could do. "They were really kind, hardworking people," she began. "Everyone looked out for each other, you know?"

Kat nodded, attentive, but gave her space to continue on her own time.

Filling the tea kettle, Lorelei recounted the first two weeks onboard *The Osprey*. Just the highlights. Things like climbing the rigging to the crow's nest and the main topsail yard with a deck full of people cheering below, the joy they all felt yelling 'ah-heave!' while hauling lines, Captain Calhorn's stories, and the stupid amount of singing and childish poop deck jokes. Those moments made her the happiest. It was a shame that tragedy always overshadowed the good. Would there ever be a time, somewhere in the distant future, that she could recall these things without being sucker punched by sadness?

Thinking about her mom didn't always make her sad, so maybe there was hope.

Removing a pair of tea bags from their wrappers and dropping them into the mugs, she smiled a little to herself. "The jokes weren't even all that funny. Just dumb things like 'Gotta go swab the poop deck. What a shitty job!' But we would still laugh every single time. Or there would be times when Captain Calhorn singled someone out for a mistake in front of everybody, which wasn't fun, so we'd all chant 'walk-the-plank' to lighten the mood—because then he was yelling at all of us and not just one of us."

Katrina propped her chin in hand. "Sounds like they were a solid group of people."

"They were. We had a lot of laughs, but we had a lot of tears, too, and some short fuse tempers. The first couple weeks of the program were stressful. We were trying to learn how to work together as a team and haul the right ropes at the right time. But for the most part, we all leaned on each other and persevered. The day it all clicked, and we ran a flawless rotation, I've never felt something so exhilarating. We were sailing as our ancestors had done."

Katrina smiled, and Lorelei continued, "It was a proud moment for us all. The third week in, morale was high. We'd found our rhythm, and the shared experience and camaraderie brought the crew closer together…"

The tea kettle whistled, reaching a screeching pitch as steam rushed out of the spout. Lorelei jumped, whisking it off the burner.

That's where the good memories ended. Their smiles wavered.

"You don't have to go on if you don't want to."

She didn't say anything as she shut off the burner and filled their mugs. After setting a timer, she joined her friend at the opposite side of the table. "It's not that I can't talk about it. Or don't want to. It's just—" She looked down at her palms. "Horrible."

"If you are worried about me, don't be." Katrina took her hand and squeezed. "You can say whatever you like."

"I know. But I'm not sure I want to put that image in your head."

"It's too late for that. I've been following the story on the news. And you've already shared with me your theory about what happened to the rest of the crew."

She slumped. "I'm very sorry about that—that was a morbid thing to say."

"Hey now." Katrina came around to her side of the table. She plopped into the chair beside her, and placed an arm around her shoulders, giving them a light shake. "I wasn't trying to upset you. I'm glad you told me. Please don't feel like you have to keep that all to yourself, because you really shouldn't."

"Thanks, Kat." She leaned into the one-armed hug, laying her head on her shoulder. "Talking with you does help a bit."

"I'm all ears."

"All right." She closed her eyes, centering on Katrina's rhythmic touch as it stroked through her hair. "At the end of the third week, Cap saw the storm approaching on radar. He kept a brave face, but we knew it was bad when he kicked the emergency engine onboard into gear. At the beginning of the trip, when he was explaining the schematics of the ship, he'd said he never had to use it in all his years leading the program. For a short while, we thought we'd gotten away from the worst of it. But then the storm shifted. We couldn't move all that quickly even with the emergency engine, so it rammed us. When I was swept overboard, I thought I was a goner. It all happened so fast. One moment I was hauling lines, the next I was rolling backwards through the water. But I broke the surface, and I'd gotten maybe a few deep breaths before the next wave came and wiped out the entire ship.

"When that second wave came, I closed my eyes, said a prayer, and thought about my mom. I guess I thought that if I focused on her my last moments would be peaceful." There must have been something to be said for the strategy because she didn't remember what happened immediately after that.

The stove timer beeped, so she reluctantly rose to retrieve their tea. When she brought over the steaming mugs, Kat was wiping her eyes with her sleeve. "What happened next?"

"I eventually woke up. The storm was gone. And I was all alone."

"Holy shit. That must have been terrifying!"

Lorelei nodded, sipping her tea. "But I'm here now. Thanks to Killian and his crew."

"I look forward to personally thanking him for that."

When Lorelei first saw *Dawn Chaser*'s blue and white hull cutting through the fog, she thought her mind was playing tricks on her. She was numb, bleary-eyed and had been fading in and out of consciousness for an indeterminable amount of time. Any ship within the path of the storm would have tucked tail and fled for land. For one to be out there with her was simply impossible.

Mirages was a thing of the desert. This had to be a hallucination.

And what a cruel one at that.

Laden by the disappointment, she sung another repeating verse of "Drunken Sailor."

> *Put him on a long boat 'til he's sober*
> *Put him on a long boat 'til he's sober*
> *Put him on a long boat 'til he's sober*

The more Lorelei watched, the larger the ship grew. When its foghorn blasted, she shrieked, having heard nothing but the sound of her own voice and the ocean's hungry call for hours. Its bellowing echoed in her ears, in her body, and in her soul. But that's when Lorelei realized the boat wasn't a delirious figment of her imagination and snapped to attention, fumbling for the whistle hooked to her immersion suit. The thick gloves made grasping the whistle between her fingers rather clumsy, so she scooped it up in her palm, shoved it between her trembling lips and blew as hard as she could. The sound rang out over the water.

Was that shouting that answered? It was hard to tell, so she blew again. She couldn't afford to take any chances they might not have heard.

The ship turned in her direction, joy and relief filling her. Killian wasn't the first to shout out to her, but he was the one she heard clearest. The words "Hang on! We'll get you out!" were so beautiful to hear she wept.

Thinking back to that moment, Lorelei decided she had been too hard on herself earlier about how she felt about Killian and the research center job. So what if she liked him? It wasn't undeserving. And how could she pass up the chance to design a museum from the ground up? That would be foolish. Even if neither went anywhere, she needed something positive in her life to break up the bad—to make the mourning process bearable.

As Lorelei drank tea with Katrina, the conversation steered to discussion of her next steps, which included her plan to stay in Haven Cove to pursue the new job opportunity. After hearing the details, Katrina remarked, "I think it's a marvelous idea. But try to take a little time off if you can before starting. You need to process and grieve and get your affairs in order first."

Boy, did she ever. But it was nice to have something solid and tangible to work toward. "I know. I plan to do that. I first need to get a new phone and figure out how to get my car out of storage in Portland. My keys are at the bottom of the ocean." That would be a fun bunch of conversations.

"We can call the car dealer and get you a new phone tomorrow. Also, I don't mind driving you down to Portland so you can get all your stuff."

Fidgeting, Lorelei agreed those things could wait until tomorrow. But she also needed to accomplish something now. A troubled mind and idleness did not make good friends. "Kat, you know me. I need to do *something*."

She sighed, and waved her hand, bestowing her reluctant blessing.

Lorelei dashed upstairs to retrieve Killian's laptop. When she returned with the computer, Katrina showed her how to set up a temporary P.O. Box and order a replacement driver's license from the state of Maine. She clicked around the government website until she found the correct form. It was a surprisingly simple and painless process. "Once you fill this out, you'll get a digital license that you can print and use until the plastic replacement comes in the mail."

As Killian's truck rumbled into the driveway, Lorelei perked at the sound, sitting straighter in her chair. She'd spent the better part of the morning and early afternoon searching online apartment listings, and while she'd wanted the productive distraction, it was a long time to stare at a computer, especially after she'd gone three weeks without harsh LED lights.

The truck door slammed, and she cast cursory glances at the front door. Apartment hunting was no competition for her attention.

Katrina bumped her elbow, pinning her with a hard stare, brow arched.

"What?" She mouthed, lifting her shoulder in a one-armed shrug.

A moment later, Killian burst in through the front door, sweaty, in gym clothes, and carrying an outrageous load of groceries at once.

"Oh." Katrina sat back in her chair with a huff, taken aback by the sight of him, but in a beat smoothed over her features. She likely expected an older, white-haired gentleman with a fair share of wrinkles.

Lorelei pushed away from the table. "Do you need some help?"

"Nope. This is it. I like getting it all in one trip, if I can." He kicked the door shut and hefted the bags into the kitchen. He set them down on the floor with a huff. "Arms are pretty beat though. Was working on them at the gym."

If Katrina hadn't been sitting right next to her, Lorelei wouldn't have heard her murmur appreciatively, "Yeah, you were." An undeniable observation. There was no mistaking that this man routinely picked up and put down heavy things.

He looked good enough to eat.

Do not drool. Do not droll… she wiped the corner of her mouth. *Shit.*

After washing up, Killian held out his hand. "You must be Katrina. I'm glad to see you found this place. GPS doesn't always get it right."

Sneaking a sly, knowing glance Lorelei's way, Katrina shook his hand, hard and firm, no stranger to brushes with business executives. "And you must be Killian. Thank you so much for everything you've done for my friend."

He nodded and returned to his pile of groceries. While he crouched to put food away in the refrigerator, Katrina spun toward her, hands raised in awe. She animatedly mouthed, "Oh. My. God!" Expectations blown out of the water.

She waggled her eyebrows teasingly, a stupid wide grin plastered across her face. An older, whited-haired gentleman with wrinkles, Killian was not. While pointing to white free space on the computer screen, Katrina snickered behind her hand, eyes glinting with mischief. "Look at the hardwood floors of this place. You just have to check it out."

"Stop it!" Lorelei whisper yelled. But God, it felt good to banter with her best friend. "You're going to make me laugh." Now that it was clear she wasn't the only one getting silly over this total smoke show, her infatuation felt justified. Normal even.

Knees audibly cracking as he stood, Killian promised to make them brunch after he showered and disappeared to the second level.

Katrina giggled. "I get it now." She rested a hand on top of Lorelei's. "We're staying."

"Just for tonight," Lorelei reminded her. "Then it's off to Portland. If you want to see Captain Eye Candy again, you'll just have to come visit me."

"Done." Katrina laughed. "You think you'll keep in touch after this?"

"God, I hope so."

"Okay, let's see what apartments are closest to here." Plopping down in the nearest seat, Katrina giddily wrested control of the laptop.

"No, Kat!" She smacked her arm playfully. "I want to look at what's near the research center."

"Okay fine, you're right. Careers before men."

She hugged Katrina around the shoulders, chin resting where one dipped. "I'm so glad you're here."

A MAN WHO COOKED, AND COOKED WELL, WAS A MIGHTY find. And neither of them was particularly good at hiding this opinion. It was a test of Lorelei's mettle to sit through brunch without kicking Katrina under the table. Too often her friend caught her staring at the captain, and the pointed looks Kat cast her way, furtive and impish, brought bright red blushes to her cheeks.

"Did I put too much pepper in?" His brow pinched, gesturing with his fork to the poblano peppers in the scramble's vegetable medley, oblivious to the friendship antics waging around him at the table.

"No, it's great." She pressed a cool hand to her burning cheek. "Just a fair complexion is all." Fat lie.

Killian nodded, and tucked back in, seemingly appeased by her flimsy explanation.

"It's not the food she finds hot," Kat whispered wickedly, the traitor. Though her voice was low, it wasn't low enough for comfort. Lorelei coughed, glaring daggers.

Kat winked, slowly swiping her tongue up the back of her fork. Obscenely ridiculous. It had to be an act of divine intervention that Killian did not look up at that exact moment, still blissfully unaware.

After brunch dishes were cleared, Killian returned to the kitchen, pulling out more ingredients, things like cocoa, sugar, and vanilla extract. More food? She placed a hand on her near-to-bursting stomach, followed by an unflattering gurgling.

"Making dessert for a house party with friends," he chuckled, glancing in her direction, no doubt hearing her riotous stomach.

Behind his back, Katrina pantomimed swooning, and if it didn't take all Lorelei's self-control not to laugh, she'd die of embarrassment instead. Still, it didn't detract from one simple truth:

A man who baked was god-tier.

"You guys can come if you'd like," he continued. "Walsh would like to see you again, and he's pretty excited about introducing you to Lila."

"I think I'd like that. What do you think, Kat?"

Goofiness set aside, her friend studied her face. Although Katrina kept her expression carefully blank, Lorelei recognized a gut check when she saw one. Shenanigans at brunch was one thing, but a social gathering was another. "That's completely up to you. I'm fine with it. And I have some extra clothes you can borrow."

Lorelei thumbed the fabric of the sweats she wore, a sheepish blush dotting her cheeks; they were in a perpetual state of burning this morning. But Kat was right. It wouldn't do to show up to a house party still wearing Killian's clothes. "You're the best, Kat. You think of everything." Then, more quietly to her friend, she said, "I think it will be good for me to get out."

Katrina squeezed her hand. "We should probably go get ready." They retrieved Katrina's suitcase and bag from the car and carried them up the spiral staircase to the guest room, politely declining Killian's offers to help.

Upstairs, Katrina pulled out a pair of light wash jeans and a woven cream sweater. "How about this?" she asked, holding up the outfit. "Cute and put together but cozy."

Lorelei nodded and borrowed a set of underthings, as well. When she took off her shirt, Katrina sucked air through her teeth. "That's a nasty looking bruise you've got there, Lorelei."

Glancing down at the dark red and purple contusion, Lorelei shrugged. "It looks worse than it feels. I hardly notice it." Truthfully, it hurt whenever she moved her arm, but she didn't want to worry Katrina. She quickly pulled the borrowed sweater on to hide it from view. Out of sight, out of mind. "I don't remember getting it," she added, answering Katrina's questioning look. "Maybe someone tried to grab me right before I went overboard."

Katrina nodded, accepting the explanation, but while it worked for her, it didn't sit well with Lorelei. None of the possible explanations did. Immersion suits made anyone wearing them as bulky as the Michelin Man. Who could squeeze hard enough through all that insulative cushion—their own and hers—to bruise her arm like that? And yet, the size of the markings and the spacing between them really did look too much like fingers to be anything else.

Shoulders slumping, Lorelei climbed onto the bed with Katrina and curled up on her side, hands tucked beneath her head. "There's a lot about what happened that doesn't make sense—there being no other survivors, no bodies found, these weird bruises on my arm. I keep turning it over and over in my head, and I don't understand any of it."

"And you may never," Katrina replied gently, lying next to her, arm tucked underneath her head. "Tragedies like this, they never make sense. And sometimes that's what hurts the most about them and makes them harder to let go. They're an open door you can never close."

"You mean a wound that never heals?"

"I'm a firm believer that 'time heals all wounds.' But life's mysteries? Those never go away. They always leave you wondering." Thinking about her mom, Lorelei's heart twinged. Not all wounds could be healed by time. Only time would tell whether *The Osprey* would be one of them.

"Do you still want to go out?"

Lorelei nodded emphatically. "I do."

Hopping off the bed, Katrina said, "Come on then. Sit up and put on some real pants." She tossed her extra pair of jeans at Lorelei. When Lorelei finished changing, Katrina instructed her to sit on the edge of the bed, so that she could do her makeup and hair.

"I can do it," Lorelei protested, sliding forward.

"Nonsense. I've missed this. Plus, do you see a mirror?" Katrina waved around the room, makeup bag in hand.

"Ah, right." There was only one mirror in Killian's home that Lorelei had seen, and it resided in the bathroom. She sat down and let Katrina fishtail-braid her hair and apply a light layer of makeup. Just like old times, Katrina played her latest favorite playlist from her phone, hips swaying to the beat as she worked.

Humming along and rhythmically tapping her knee, Lorelei felt the most relaxed she had in weeks.

CHAPTER

ELEVEN

Visiting the Walshes' was like returning home. For the better part of his teen years, he had grown up there, or as good as; Walt and Marci were there for him in ways his own parents couldn't be.

Lorelei's eyes lit up as she took in the classic colonial, its whitewashed siding, black shutters—just like any other New Englander's house—except for the sheer amount of outdoor sculpture decorating the lawn. It was a loving showcase, a fixed outdoor gallery of Marci's artwork. Some pieces were left as raw, jagged metal. Others had been sanded down and polished, painstakingly decorated with tiny vibrant bits of glass, stone and shells collected from the nearby shore.

Marci found inspiration in various African cultures—legendary creatures such as Mami Wata, Nyami Nyami, and Abada—and, of course, the Orisha. Yemaya—the Goddess of the Oceans, Mother of the Orishas—and Oya, Goddess of the Wind, were her personal favorites and various iterations and portrayals were sprinkled throughout the house.

The sight of Lorelei absorbing each piece as they walked the path to the front door did something to Killian. Maybe it was the art, but something about the Walshes's home, its aura perhaps, or the unabashed pride in heritage, and dedication to personal touch, that exuded the warmth and welcome of its owners. It had always been his safe harbor. Maybe it could become Lorelei's, too, at least for today.

Toting the chocolate torte he made in a cake container, Killian rang the doorbell, with Lorelei and Katrina standing close behind.

"Coming! Coming!" Walsh yelled from within.

A moment later, the front door swung wide open, the old mariner greeting them with a beaming smile. "Come in, come in." He ushered them inside and took the cake container from Killian's hands, placing it on a narrow, wall-side table in the vestibule. Wafts of spiced fish and fresh-baked popovers drifted from the kitchen to the front of the house.

As Lorelei began shrugging off her jacket, he said, "Allow me," and slid the garment from her shoulders, hanging it on a nearby coat hook.

She smiled, a cute blush dusting her cheeks a rosy, red, and murmured "Thanks." Walt offered the same courtesy to Katrina.

Glancing back, he saw the women sharing matching cheesy grins, there and gone so fast he'd almost missed them. Interesting. Maybe asking Lorelei out on a date wasn't so far-fetched an idea, something he was thinking about doing more and more. Overhearing that she was looking for apartments in Haven Cove sold the decision for him to try.

Not now. There was too much change and upheaval in her life. But once she settled, and the moment was right, maybe he'd work up the courage. A ten-year age gap wasn't so terrible, was it?

Maybe to her it would be.

Lorelei turned her head every which way, her eyes sparkling as she drank in the house's interior. It had a rustic New England design, and all the walls and tables bore family photos, plants, and artwork made either by Marci or other local Mainers' hands. That coupled with the soft, warm lighting, and plush blue area rugs on the hardwood floors, gave their home a happy, lived-in feel.

Picking back up the cake container, Killian followed Walsh into the kitchen where the rest of the family congregated, a predictable, familiar sight. Lila stood at the stove in a flattering burnt orange one-piece, one of those ensembles where the pants and blouse were one, the warm color complimenting her rich brown skin, and her corkscrew curls were held back by a twisted gold headband. With one hand, she flipped haddock in a pan, a recipe Killian knew had a generous heaping of black pepper, cayenne, and cumin, from years' worth of witnessing Walsh-family cooking. With her other hand, Lila held a glass of red wine, expertly splashing neither, while Branson busied himself setting the table.

Marci was in the middle of opening another bottle of wine. Short hair twists swished brown cheeks as she yanked out the cork with a pop, her rainbow painted-wooden cube beads necklace clacking, one Killian had bought her for Mother's Day several years back.

Bowls of peas and roasted sweet potatoes sat out on the counter.

But with the arrival of guests, the family paused and greeted them all with the same exuberance as their host. One by one, Walsh introduced Lorelei and Katrina. Setting down her spatula, but notably not her wine glass, Lila came over and gave Lorelei a firm handshake. "Lorelei, my dad's been telling me so much about you and that you might be interested in helping me with the exhibits for the new museum."

Business talk, right now?

Some innate part of him bristled a little, rising to Lorelei's defense, the challenge to his friend's timing and tact just on the tip of his tongue, but he swallowed it when Lorelei smiled, another blush creeping into her cheeks. That wasn't discomfort in her expression.

If anything, this taste of normalcy enhanced her cheer.

He listened as they set a date for an interview in two weeks, and Lila handed her a business card.

"All right, Lila," Marci interjected. "That's enough business for now. Would you ladies like some wine? I've got Cabernet Sauvignon and Chardonnay." Both Lorelei and Katrina answered affirmatively and gratefully accepted the glasses their hostess handed them of their drinks of choice.

Shifting her attention to Killian, and the cake container he held in his hand, Lila asked teasingly, "So, what did you bring me this time?"

"See for yourself." He relinquished the dessert into her possession.

Setting down her wine, for the first and only time since they entered the kitchen, Lila placed the container on the counter and removed the lid with both hands. Dessert was the only thing that got her to do that.

Seeing what was inside, she squealed with delight and whirled to give him a brief, tight hug.

Quick to smile, Lila had prominent laugh lines and a permanent mischievous twinkle in her eye. They were of a similar height, so when she hugged him, her cheek and tight, springy curls squished up against his face.

Pulling away, and motioning to the chocolate torte, Lila said to Lorelei and Katrina, "Whoever made that saying about food being the way to a man's heart would have done better to think about dessert to a woman's."

"I'll drink to that." Lorelei raised her glass, and the ladies clinked theirs together, comradery already forming between them.

Branson raised a brow at Killian and mouthed, "Stop trying to steal my lady!" But he laughed a beat later; it was all just a bit of teasing.

"Man, I'll teach you how to bake, if you want."

His best friend pulled a face and went to check on the stew. "Babe, do you want me to stir this?" Branson hovered over a steaming pot of homemade mac n' cheese with lid and spoon in hand. Lila returned to his side, slipping an arm around his lower back while pressing a cheek to the top of his head.

While the two fussed over dinner, Walsh passed Killian an open bottle of beer and offered Lorelei and Katrina a house tour.

"Ma, go with them," Lila urged. "Will and I can handle dinner. I'm sure they'll have questions about your artwork." Marci nodded and patted Killian's shoulder as she passed him to get to the front of the group. Her husband led the way into the living room.

Above the fireplace hung the piece of hull that bore the name of Walsh's old fishing boat. It brought a wide smile to Lorelei's face, one of recognition. Walsh must have told her about it, but for Katrina's sake, their host told the story again. As he talked, Lorelei sipped her wine, and Killian caught himself gazing at her lips as they pressed to the edge of the glass.

He silently thanked God Branson stayed in the kitchen to help his wife. His best friend would have ribbed him for staring if he'd seen. But looking up, Marci's eyes were already awaiting his. She smirked at his startled expression and glanced knowingly at Lorelei. Shit. He wasn't going to get away with it after all.

He took a long swig of beer.

When Walsh finished speaking, Lorelei turned to Marci. "Which ones are yours?"

"The paintings aren't mine, but the metal wall hangings and statuettes like that mermaid over there are." Marci pointed to the piece sitting in the far corner of the room, a buxom sea goddess who wore a halo of Bantu Knots and a come-hither smile. Lorelei walked over for a closer look and the rest of the group followed.

"She's gorgeous." Lorelei crouched to examine the piece. "And the detailing is amazing. How long did this take you to make?"

"Oh, goodness. I don't remember." Marci turned to Walsh, pressing a finger up against her cheek. "How long was it, sugar?"

Walsh gazed at his wife affectionately and rubbed the small of her back. "You made her when I was offshore for three weeks. You'd just sanded down all the rough edges when I came home."

Marci adjusted the necklace around her neck. "Right, right. And I was still working at the bank, so I only had the evenings and weekends to work on it." She did some quick math in her head. "About eighty hours, I'd reckon. It was a labor of love. Wanted to surprise Walt with it."

Katrina crouched down for a closer look. "Do you sell any of your works, Mrs. Walsh?"

"Oh please, call me Marci. And sometimes. It depends on whether I can get them out of the house without my husband seeing. You see, he has a habit of falling in love with every piece. If he catches me sneaking something out of the house, or sees something I'm working on that he likes, and knows I'm going to finish when he's offshore, he begs me not to sell."

Walt grinned. Utterly unapologetic. "She can't say no to this sweet face."

"Lord knows why. It really hurts my business model." Marci chuckled and kissed his cheek. "And we are eventually going to run out of room. But it's all right. As long as he upholds his promise to dust it all, making more is a fine way to pass the time while he's away."

"Taking care of your beautiful art isn't a chore," Walsh said softly.

That enviable, tender affection between husband and wife. Killian wasn't the only one to notice it—Lorelei stood with her arms wrapped around herself, almost like a hug. As if she craved the touch. Her face was an open book, melting with admiration and longing at the adoring couple.

Stuffing his hands into his back pockets, he curbed the sudden urge to wrap his arm around her and tell her that she, too, would find the right people to call family. That kind of happiness was still in reach, despite the tragedy in her past.

Katrina rose to her feet. "I'd be happy to give you a few pointers on publicizing your work, should you ever decide to sell." She explained to Marci what she did for a living, her publicist mind working through an array of promotional possibilities as she spoke.

A timer beeped in the kitchen, and a second later, Lila called them back in. The rest of the tour would have to wait until after dinner, but Marci and Katrina brought their conversation with them. When Lila overheard, she was particularly enthusiastic about Marci promoting her work. "Dad can't have everything." She side-eyed her father, hands firmly planted on her hips. Walsh smiled sheepishly, to which, Lila added while waggling her finger, "Nuh-uh. None of those puppy dog eyes."

Smiling warmly at the Walsh-Branson family dynamic, Lorelei slid into the seat next to Killian. She leaned over to whisper, "They are really a lovely family." A longing, and a little sadness, laced her voice. She wore it in her expression, too.

He knew that look—it had stared back at him in the mirror many times.

Loss.

"I miss my mom, too," he whispered back. "But it's not so bad when I'm with these guys. They've become my family."

"How did you know what I…" Her eyes softened, and she edged her fingers closer to where his hand rested on the table. He hadn't really paid her hands more than cursory attention before, but now, with the promise of touch, they were all he could focus on. Her nails were cut short and unpainted but also clean and well taken care of. Calluses lined her palms, and there was a real strength in her hands from working with lines. But even so, some softness remained. Not an easy feat for a sailor.

Skin easily chapped and chafed in cold sea air, but she must have dedicated time to her hands' upkeep to counteract the damage, because they were remarkably uncracked. Weren't red either.

"I'm sorry you lost her," she said, breaking his thoughts, and his stare.

He met her gaze briefly, warmed by the tenderness there, and grazed the side of her index finger with his pinkie. The room, the conversation around them, all faded away. One touchpoint, just the barest brush of skin, and liquid heat spread throughout his body, consuming his every thought, every firing, electric synapse and nerve inside him attuning to *her*.

How could so small a gesture light his heart on fire? And render him so completely enthralled?

But then Katrina tapped Lorelei's shoulder, and she twisted away, hand slipping away from his. The touch was broken, but the spell cast over him was not. He leaned back, but still craving proximity, he draped an arm along the back of Lorelei's chair.

Lila had asked a question that neither of them had heard—where Lorelei had grown up.

After apologizing for zoning out, Lorelei launched into an animated description of the similarities and differences between her hometown in Michigan and what she'd seen so far of Maine. Different forests, and a lake instead of the ocean, but in many ways, very much the same.

As Lila listened, she ladled the stew into bowls and passed them around the table, along with slices of fresh-baked bread. The meal passed with lively conversation, largely fueled by conversation between their hosts and Lorelei.

The fate of *The Osprey* didn't come up once, as he'd hoped. Of course, if Lorelei wanted to talk about it, that was perfectly okay, but the evening seemed to be a welcome and healthy distraction for her, if her smiles and relaxed expression were any indication. Walsh family dinners always had been for him.

He'd just started high school and working on his dad's boat when his mother passed away in a freak mountain climbing accident. Naturally, his dad took the loss hard, but the grief changed him, too, and how he treated his only child. Long hours on his dad's boat over the weekends, his lack of time for schoolwork—let alone friends—and the near constant verbal abuse left Killian exhausted and raw. He hated fishing then.

And then he met Will Branson, Lila Walsh, and Carrie Prior.

Although Killian was a latecomer to the group, they'd always made him feel like he was one of them. Going over to Mr. and Mrs. Walsh's house for dinner and to do homework with Will, Lila, and Carrie was his only reprieve.

Eventually, with the Walsh's support, Killian left his dad's boat, and the house he grew up in, to go live with his grandfather.

That summer, Killian turned fifteen, got his worker's permit with Branson, and joined the *Marry Me, Marci* fishing crew. By senior year, he'd reconciled with his dad—to rare, but semi-amicable speaking terms —and started dating Carrie.

Touching his phone through his pants pocket, he thought about the message Carrie sent him early that morning. It confirmed what Branson said about her coming back to Haven Cove. She wanted to know if he'd like to go out for coffee and catch up. He hadn't yet replied. Not because he was ignoring her, but because he didn't know what to say. The polite thing to do would be to meet up with her. But he didn't want to.

He'd ask Lila for advice later. If he was being unfair, she wouldn't hesitate to tell him.

During dessert, as conversation drifted to favorite restaurants and bakeries in town, Lorelei grew quiet. Nudging her knee under the table to get her attention, he murmured, "You still enjoying yourself?"

She smiled, nudging his knee right back. "I am. Just in a listening mood," she explained, her expression content but tired. Maybe her social batteries were low...

"We don't need to stay much longer."

Her smile broadened a little. "I know, but I'd like to stay."

Table cleared, Marci and Walsh resumed the grand house tour, disappearing into the next room with their guests. Killian pulled Lila aside to show her Carrie's text.

Leaning into his shoulder, she frowned, tugging at one of her curls. "I received a similar message."

"What did you say?"

"I said I'd meet up." She shrugged. "We were good friends once, and we are still family, so I feel obligated to—even though I'm still pissed at her for skipping our wedding to go to London with her Wall Street boyfriend." She sighed, folding her arms across her chest. "I don't want to be the kind of person who holds grudges, but I can't seem to shake this one. Maybe seeing her again will help clear the air. And generally, people deserve second chances, right?"

Most people. But Carrie, his ex? He didn't know if he could be that gracious. While he didn't tend to hold grudges, he did write people off when they badly hurt him. Or vacated his life. "That's not an easy thing to forgive. What do you think I should do?"

"What do you want to do?" Lila countered, swiping the bottle of wine off the table to top off her glass.

"I don't have a problem with her coming back to Haven Cove, but that doesn't mean I want to see her."

Lila sipped her wine. "Then don't. And be honest with her about it."

"You don't think I owe it to her, given what we had?" Five years together. Half a lifetime ago but five years, nonetheless. They'd been each other's first loves.

Lila shook her head vigorously. "I might have said something different fifteen years ago when this was all still fresh, but you both moved on a long, long time ago. I don't see how this would be helpful to either of you. Plus, I really have to wonder, why now, after all this time?"

Killian had wondered about that, too. "If she's really planning on coming back, it's inevitable we'd run into each other every now and again. Maybe she wants to get that first awkward meeting past her."

"Yeah, maybe. But the earlier you set boundaries, the better." She gave him a pointed look. Carrie was… persistent and intense when she wanted something.

Or someone.

"I think…" he trailed, tapping a reply out on his phone. Lila looked over his shoulder, murmuring, "I appreciate you reaching out, and hope you are well, but I don't want to see you."

Killian grimaced. It sounded so much worse when said out loud. "That's pretty harsh, isn't it?"

Lila furrowed her brow and took another sip of wine. "Ugh. This is hard. Um. You could say—sorry, wrong number?"

Killian chuckled. "Tempting."

"Maybe just soften the blow by adding 'We're cool' before 'I don't want to see you'?"

"Oh, fuck it. Let's try that and see what happens." Killian edited the message and hit send. Not a moment later, Carrie was already typing out one of her own. They shared an anxious look. His phone pinged with the responding message:

I thought after all this time we could have been adults about this. You hurt me, too, you know.

Lila huffed. "The nerve. She made her choice knowing full well what your dreams were. It's not like you blindsided her."

Like Carrie had blindsided him with her big city dreams.

He scratched his chin and wrote: *It wasn't a good breakup for either of us. And I'm sorry about how harsh that came across, but there isn't a good way to tell someone you want to keep your distance. I'm hoping you will respect my wishes.*

"Very mature," Lila commented. "If she keeps pushing after that, you have my seal of approval to ignore her."

"Thanks, Lila. Hopefully, it won't come to that."

His phone pinged again.

You're right. I'm sorry. I'll stay out of your hair.

He sighed with relief. Maybe Carrie's return to Haven Cove wouldn't be so bad.

CHAPTER
TWELVE

"KAT, DO YOU HAVE ANY LOTION?"

Pressing her fingers to dry, itchy red skin, Lorelei inspected her neck in the Portland coffee shop's bathroom mirror. Whenever she scratched, flaky skin came away underneath her fingernails, reminding her a little of scales, shimmery and a bit translucent.

Fishing out a travel-sized bottle from her purse, Katrina handed it over. "That's an odd spot to have issues with dry skin." She leaned forward to get a closer look, lips pinched. "Oh, weird."

"What?" Lorelei shuffled closer to the mirror, craning her neck, trying to see what Katrina did in the reflection.

"It's just that there's three lines going across your neck where the skin looks extra dry."

Lorelei ran her fingers along her neck where the skin was rougher. Three lines. Just as Kat said. Straightening, she opened the bottle of lotion, squeezed a generous amount onto her fingertips, and rubbed in the cream.

"Both sides?" Katrina arched her brow.

She nodded. "It's never been an issue before. Maybe stress-related?"

"Yeah. Maybe."

They returned to the coffee shop proper and put in an order. They had driven down to Portland three days prior to get Lorelei's car and belongings out of storage and to attend today's memorial service for *The Osprey* crew. Friends, family, and community members—all needing an outlet for their grief—would be in attendance.

After getting their coffees, Lorelei and Katrina sat down at one of the tables by the window, sipping their drinks and killing time before heading over to the church. Normally they could sit together in comfortable silence, but today she felt no peace in this quiet idleness. But what to do? What to say? Everything to be said was covered on the car trip down. And everything that could be done was done.

Picking up her new phone, Lorelei tapped out a message to Killian. It had been a couple days since she'd last spoken to him. This…whatever it was sparking between them was new, and if one of them didn't nurture it, it was doomed to sputter out.

I hoped we could be friends, she wrote. *Since I'm going to be around for the time being.*

Her thumb hovered over 'send' for a moment before erasing the entire message. The last thing she wanted was to hastily put a label on their relationship and inadvertently friend-zone herself. Romantic aspirations aside, it was a lame way to ask to be friends.

Sighing, she set her phone back down and gazed aimlessly out the coffee shop window at the shoppers passing by.

Before she left Haven Cove with Katrina, Killian had put his number into her new phone and asked for hers. He said it was so she could get a hold of him if she needed to, and that made it difficult to discern whether he had actually been flirting with her at the Walshes' house party or was just being helpful.

Killian had eight to ten years on her, which logically meant he must want a woman closer to him in age and stability. Not a jobless twenty-nine-year-old currently living out of a hotel room and her car. But at the Walshes', she hadn't imagined his stolen glances or misinterpreted his small touches, had she? He didn't need to caress her finger to accept her condolences for his mom or nudge her knee with his to ask if she was having a good time, and yet he did.

There was too much touching for it not to mean anything.

The sheer number of times she drafted a message to him in the last seventy-two hours, only to delete it, was ridiculous. She needed to say *something* before he thought she was ghosting him.

But nothing immediately came to mind, and her thoughts turned to her crew and the years of life and love robbed from them. All the goodbyes never said and feelings never shared.

Shifting in her seat to better see the café chalkboard menu, she chased the thought away and read the list in sheer desperation to keep it from coming back.

It was too trivial of an exercise to work.

Lorelei picked up her phone again, but this time, to check her email. In the past hour she'd received a consolatory email from her former museum boss in Michigan and a calendar invite from Lila, solidifying their interview plans. The job with Lila was far from guaranteed, but at least she had a strong lead.

Drumming her fingers against the table, she contemplated buying another coffee. Even though she usually drank tea, she hadn't been sleeping well and needed the extra caffeine kick to power her through the next few hours. But after a glance at the clock on the wall, she decided against it. Not enough time to drink it.

How was it nearly four o'clock already? Everyone attending the memorial service would be trying to find parking right about now, but it would only take her and Katrina a couple minutes to walk over.

No reason to leave now.

What a busy week she had coming up. In the past two days, she'd scheduled several apartment showings in Haven Cove. Tomorrow she was driving back and needed to find a place to live. Hotel living already wore itself out, but she could afford it a little while longer if need be.

By all accounts, even under the grim circumstances that led her to this coffee shop, her life was on the verge of an upswing. But optimism was far from her mind.

Hand shaking, she reached for her coffee cup.

"You okay?" Katrina leaned across the table. "You've been fidgeting since we sat down and now you are shaking."

Lorelei drained the cup and popped a couple mints from a tin in her purse. She exhaled heavily before admitting, "I've been trying not to think about the memorial service. So, I've been thinking about my current state-of-affairs and what to say to Killian instead."

A questionable coping mechanism to be sure. Katrina frowned. "Oh honey, don't fixate on that stuff. You've accomplished a lot in the past several days—way more than anyone could ever expect you to. And why don't you want to think about the memorial service?"

Since her rescue, her name and picture circulated all over the news, which meant that fellow service attendees would probably recognize her. Smoothing out the skirt of her black dress, she answered, "I'm afraid I'm going to lose my nerve. What if the families don't want me there? Or ask why me and not their sons and daughters?"

"No." Katrina shook her head vehemently. "Don't you dare think that way. That's survivor's guilt talking. No one in their right mind blames you for any of this. That would be messed up. And as much as any of them, you have a right to be there, to pay your respects and to grieve. You hear me?"

She felt herself nod, but she didn't quite agree that she deserved to be there, to grieve, just as much as her crew mates' friends and families. These were people who knew them their whole lives, whose pain and loss would never dull with the passage of time. Lorelei had only known them for a few weeks. And she already had plans in place to move on from this tragedy. "I guess we should head over."

"Come on." Katrina stood, holding out her hand. "We can sit in the back, if you'd like."

She accepted her outstretched hand, and with a gentle tug, Katrina kickstarted her momentum out of the chair. "I think that would help," Lorelei said, donning her black dress coat.

They arrived ten minutes before the service was due to start, but it was already packed. Sitting in the back pew was their only option, whether it had been their original plan or not. A few people recognized Lorelei when they walked in, including the presiding minister.

They nodded respectfully to her but did not approach.

After opening prayers and songs, family by family got up to speak about the loved ones they had lost. Lorelei wept, clinging to their words and imagining her crewmates in the memories described. The minutes ticked by slowly, painfully. The entire service, she struggled to push away thoughts of the mammoth wave that consumed them. That terrible memory would forever be burned into her mind, but she couldn't bear to relive it now. Doing so would unravel the fragile weaving of her composure.

Wrapping an arm around her shoulders, Katrina held her close and dutifully pressed tissues in her hands. When the last family sat down, Lorelei expected the minister to begin concluding prayers, but he walked to the back of the church instead.

Would there be some blessing with incense or holy water? No, those were rituals in Catholic mass…

She expected him to pass, but he made direct eye contact with her, and stopped at their pew. "Hello, Miss Roth," he said quietly. He leaned over her in a way that was probably meant to be innocuous, and conducive to privacy, but she shrunk back, feeling cornered. Stale coffee polluted her air on his exhale. Too close. "I know this is a lot to ask," he began, oblivious to her ridged posture. "But would you go up and say a few words? It would mean so much to these families."

Blood drained from her face. Speak in front of all these people? "I haven't prepared anything." Her voice shook.

He patted her shoulder. "That's okay. Just tell it from the heart."

Her heart? How about her brain? Any semblance of coherent thought vanished as quickly as a puff of smoke in the wind. Still, she stood from her seat, jellied limbs trembling so much she had to steady herself on the pew's wooden seat back.

Giving the minister a scathing look, Katrina grabbed her arm. "You don't need to do this," she whispered. "Don't let him pressure you into doing something you don't want to do. He has no right to ask this of you."

"I should do this, Katrina," she said gently, removing Kat's hand from her arm. "I would regret it if I didn't."

Her friend's expression softened. Choice was what mattered. "Do you want me to go up with you?"

She shook her head, mind carefully kept blank. If she allowed herself to think, letting one iota of rational thought sink in, she'd chickened out. One foot in front of the other, she forced herself down the aisle, letting her body carry her where her mind wouldn't go. Rinse. Repeat.

The minister trailed not far behind, heavy footsteps scuffing against the carpeted floor. She stared straight ahead, but the weight of hundreds of pairs of eyes bore holes into her, accompanied by quiet sobs and sniffling. By sheer force of will, she kept her feet moving. When she reached the podium, she dizziness blurred her vision, but she took a deep breath and turned to face all who gathered to mourn *The Osprey* crew.

God, there were so many people. Public speaking didn't terrify her when she had weeks to prepare a speech, tightening language and spending hours practicing in front of her bathroom mirror. But this...

Speak from the heart, the minister said. But neither her heart nor her brain were cooperating right now, each a void where words went to die. She scanned the back row of pews until she settled on Katrina, drawing strength from her kind, familiar face.

Take it one step at a time.

Lorelei lowered the microphone to her level. Her heartbeat drumming so loudly, she wondered if the crowd could hear it. Or maybe that was her heavy breathing. She took a small step back and gripped the podium with sweaty palms.

Just say something nice. Something already said before.

"Hello everyone," she began, letting out a ragged breath. "My name is Lorelei Roth. You may have heard about me... I was a member of the crew." She paused, grip tightening so hard the wooden podium creaked. "I hadn't expected to be asked to speak, so I'm really sorry if what I say is disjointed. I've heard so many beautiful stories today about Captain Calhorn and my crewmates. I don't know how I could ever follow them. You knew them their whole lives. I only knew them for three weeks. But I will tell you what I told my best friend the other day when she asked me about them. I think if I do that, I won't mess this up."

Lorelei stepped closer to the podium. Though her heart and mind were still empty, the words came, some combination of miracle and muscle memory. Her tongue remembered, even if she didn't. "They were unbelievably kind. And hardworking. And the biggest bunch of history nerds I've ever had the privilege of working alongside. If given the chance, I would have been honored to have each of them as lifelong friends." She fell silent, wracking her brain for a worthy way to wrap up this spur of the moment eulogy. A panicked pause of mental scrambling followed. Minutes had to have passed, not seconds. God, this was mortifying.

And in the silence, and sea of stares, her heart and mind caught up.

Her voice cracked as she forced out her spontaneous closing remarks. "If there is anything you should take away from what I say here today, it's that we faced an impossible storm, and your loved ones fought bravely to the very end."

Trembling, she stepped down from the podium.

As the organ cued for another hymn, she made a B-line for the front pew. She sat down just as black dots blurred her vision. Trying not to collapse, she braced herself. This would get worse before it got better. Her hearing dimmed next.

All fell to darkness. Sense of time and place, too.

Bit by bit, song trickled back, the same one as before. Must not have blacked out long then. Soon after, the rest of her senses returned. Fainting spells, fortunately, always passed quickly for her.

"Miss, are you okay?" A hand clasped her shoulder from behind, firm and steadying. She dizzily turned in the pew to see who checked on her. "Better now," she smiled weakly. The gentleman's eyes were red and puffy from crying, but as she studied his features, surprise quickly followed. She recognized this man. "Were you on the docks the day I was brought back to shore?"

His eyes widened. Probably didn't expect her to recognize him. And she probably shouldn't have, but that day on the docks, she'd zeroed in on every detail of the reporters faces. Scrutinizing, analyzing, remembering. Taking note like they were an enemy to be wary of, which wasn't fair, but some bizarre, offensive instinct had kicked in, shedding the protective, trauma-induced blinders that would have otherwise filtered them out. "Yes, I was attempting to report for the *Portland Press Herald*. Name's Ed Knudsen."

Interesting word choice...

"Attempting?" she prodded gently.

"Mackenzie and Jackson Coldwater were my niece and nephew," he said. "This is my sister and brother-in-law." He gestured to the distraught couple sitting beside him.

"Oh, my goodness, I am so sorry." She addressed her sympathies to all three.

Hunching forward, like it hurt to move, Mrs. Coldwater reached out and squeezed Lorelei's hand. "Bless you, dear, for your words." She shrunk back into her husband's arms as a fresh wave of tears overcame her.

Ed rubbed his sister's shoulder. Then turning back to Lorelei, he asked, "Do you want to get some air?" She nodded. *Fuck yes.*

They snuck out the side door—neither caring to hear the minister's closing remarks. With a shaky hand, Ed pulled a pack of cigarettes from his jacket pocket. "Do you mind if I smoke?"

Under normal circumstances, she would have said she'd rather he didn't, but she wasn't going to begrudge this grieving man what little comfort he had at hand. "No, it's okay. I'll just stand upwind of you."

"Thank you." He lit one and took a long draw. "He shouldn't have put you on the spot like that—the minister, I mean. He was out of line."

"What's done is done." She tucked her hands under her arm pits, ignoring the fact that they were damp with nervous sweat. "But I have to ask, did I make a fool of myself?"

"No. Not at all. The opposite, in fact." He took another drag on his cigarette. "Look, I've read all your interviews, and I'm not morbid enough to press for more details about that night, but could you please tell me how they were before it happened?"

She pulled out a tissue she'd stuffed up her sleeve to dab away the forming tears. "They were happy. Joyful even. You know how some people when they enter a room, they just light it up? They somehow always know what to do and say to get people smiling and having the time of their lives?"

He sniffed then nodded.

"That was them from day one. And it was hard in the beginning.

Really hard. We were a group of strangers trying to learn the ropes and work effectively together. People got frustrated with each other, angry even at times, but before things went too far, one of them would just burst into song. The first time they did it, it shocked the hell out of us, but it felt so right. And once they got a song started, the whole crew would join in. Sometimes it was a sea shanty, something they heard on the radio, or a camp song. One time, Mackenzie actually started shouting 'Mary Had a Little Lamb'. We had just sung '99 Bottles of Beer on the Wall' twice in a row and were ready to mutiny, but that desperate act to improve ship morale worked like a charm. And Jackson was the same way. He never let dignity get in the way of a good laugh."

Tears streamed down Ed's sunken cheeks. He made no move to wipe them away. Must have grown accustomed to having them there. "Thank you for telling me that. That's how I will choose to remember them. Not whatever dark imaginings my mind tends to conjure."

A shift in the wind carried cigarette smoke into her face. "I'm glad I could help." She coughed, waving away the smoke. "What little I could."

Ed resituated himself downwind. "I've needed it. Standing on those docks, waiting for the *Dawn Chaser* to arrive, I never felt more powerless in my life. And I had a mental breakdown on the pier after you were taken to the hospital. I was supposed to go like the others to get a statement from you, but I just couldn't. I was a total wreck. We ended up citing quotes that appeared in your hometown's paper."

"I hope your editor wasn't too hard on you for it."

"She was upset I didn't tell her I had family onboard, but no, overall, she was very understanding given the circumstances."

Service attendees began filing out of the church and Katrina was among those at the front of the pack. She darted over. "Oh my God, Lorelei. Are you okay?"

"I just needed some fresh air, and this gentleman was kind enough to keep me company."

Katrina pulled her into a tight hug. "You did such a great job, but man, I am going to go give Reverend Tactless a piece of my mind. I will be right back." Before Lorelei could protest, Katrina had disappeared into the crowd.

"Good friend," Ed commented, dropping his cigarette and stamping it out.

"I should probably go after her."

"Probably. Well, circumstances aside, it was lovely talking to you." Ed stretched out his hand.

She shook it. "Same to you, Mr. Knudsen."

"Before you go, I wanted to ask if I could make mention of some of what you said at the service—and to me just now—in a column I'm writing about reporting through grief."

"Of course."

Inside, Lorelei found Katrina shouting at the minister in front of the altar. "What's wrong with you? Her face went sheet white! After what she's been through, and you had the nerve..." The minister glanced furtively around. Katrina's yelling was drawing attention. Several small groups of people, who lingered after the service to talk, abandoned their conversations to watch.

"Kat," she said firmly. "Let it go. I'll feel better after I've laid down for a bit."

"See?" Katrina hissed at the minister. His face was turning a dark shade of red either from embarrassment or anger. Lorelei wasn't sure which, but she definitely didn't want to stick around to find out.

Tugging her friend's coat sleeve, she commanded, "Now, Kat." Katrina complied, but not without a parting glare. Lorelei waited until they were out of earshot before saying, "Thank you for standing up for me. I think that was the first time I've ever seen you wield your PR sword."

Katrina linked their arms together. "Honey, that wasn't PR. If I had done that in front of a client, I probably would have been fired. But you're not a client, you're my friend, and I couldn't let that slide." Lorelei pulled her into a side-hug.

Back at the hotel, they kicked off their heels and traded their dresses and pantyhose for pajamas. Jumping under the covers, they passed a bottle of wine and bar of chocolate between them while streaming a movie on Lorelei's laptop. They didn't bother with wine glasses, largely because they'd already gotten comfy by the time they realized they didn't have any. And both had just slightly too much dignity to walk down to the bar in their pajamas to borrow some.

Whether it was the rom com they watched, the memorial service, the wine, or all of the above, Lorelei decided as the credits rolled that life was too short for bottling feelings and reached for her phone.

Can I buy you a drink?

Before she could second guess herself, Lorelei sent the message to Killian. Before regret had a chance to sink in, her phone pinged with his reply. That was fast.

Sure. What time?

She smiled from ear to ear. The sudden giddiness snagged Katrina's attention. To answer her friend's questioning look, Lorelei showed her phone screen. Reading the texts, Katrina's eyes lit up, and she squealed happily.

She tapped out, *does tomorrow night work for you?*

Yup. 7:00?

Perfect.

He continued typing. *Hey. Do you have a place to stay?*

It's hotel living for me until I find an apartment.

She didn't get another message from Killian until nearly forty minutes into a second movie. *Sorry, we were offloading. Came in late from a make-up run.*

That extra trip was because of me, wasn't it?

Not at all, he wrote. *We weren't catching much at the beginning of the month.*

Liar, she thought, sipping her wine, but appreciated the effort to spare her feelings and played along. *I hope you had better luck this time around.*

Much better.

Her phone still indicated that he was typing, so she waited to see what else he had to say. After several halting starts and stops, he finally wrote, *the spare room is still yours if you want it.*

Feeling bold, and cheeky, she shot back, *that's a clever way to get me to come home with you.*

Is it working?

Pausing the movie, Katrina huffed, but with a teasing lilt. "Lorelei, are you even going to watch this?"

"No, but for good reason." She showed her the latest messages.

"Holy fuck! You are getting laid."

Lorelei shrugged, a smirk twisting her lips. "I don't know. That's a bit soon for me."

"All right, fair. Carry on."

I want to say yes.

What are you unsure about?

She rubbed her chin. *Being roommates—even the temporary kind.*

A drink is just a drink, unless you tell me otherwise. I respect boundaries.

It's more the principle of the thing, she wrote. *But since that's my only reservation, I'm willing to give it a shot.*

Whatever you want to do.

And later that evening, he sent, *I can't wait to see you.*

CHAPTER

THIRTEEN

Killian found Lorelei waiting for him in a booth at the pub, sipping a red ale. She wore her dark auburn hair in a loose, over-the-shoulder fishtail braid. Couldn't put his finger on why, but it suited her well. "Hey," he grinned, sliding into the seat across from her. "You look really nice."

"I tried." Cheeks turning a rosy pink, she pushed back the sleeves of her olive-green sweater. The lean muscles in her forearms coiled at the motion, well defined from hauling lines. With slightly trembling fingers, she lifted her drink to her lips. Maybe compliments embarrassed her, like they did him. Or maybe she was just experiencing first-date jitters. "Most of my date-night-worthy clothes are still packed away," she continued, setting her glass down without quite meeting his eyes. "This was the best I could throw together without looking like a wrinkled mess."

"Hey," he said softly, reaching out to touch her hand. "Are you okay? You look ready to jump out of your skin."

Staring at where their skin met, Lorelei gulped. "I'm just afraid I'm going to say or do something stupid. I've never been on a date with an older man before…" She hung her head, a fierce blush overtaking her cheeks. "Gosh, I'm such an idiot. I should stop talking now."

He leaned back, folding his arms on top of the table. "You're not an idiot," he assured. "And I'm nervous, too. But mostly I'm happy to be here. I didn't think this would happen."

She finally met his eyes, surprise chasing away embarrassment. "What? Me asking you out on a date?"

He nodded.

"But why? You're—" she blushed. "You've been nothing but kind to me. And I'm pretty sure we were both flirting at the Walshes'."

Frank. He liked that.

And hearing that it had not been one-sided was a relief. "I couldn't help it," Killian admitted with a small smile. "I didn't come on too strong, did I? I wasn't trying to—I don't know—impose."

Lorelei returned his smile. "Not at all. Honestly, it was a welcome distraction, what with everything that's happened. Not that I think you're just a distraction," she added hurriedly. "But this is a nice reminder that things will eventually get back to normal."

"I know what you mean. But trust me when I say that I'm flattered even to be considered distraction material."

"You should give yourself more credit than that." With a steadier hand, Lorelei took another drink. "I want to get to know you. I'm just sorry it took me three days to figure out what to say. It wasn't until I drank half a bottle of wine that I finally came up with this idea."

Killian chuckled. "Hell, you beat me to it."

"You were thinking of asking me out, too?" Tenderness softened her features, relaxed her a bit. Her nails, painted a muted pink, tapped the edge in time to the music playing overhead.

"Ah, yeah." He rubbed the back of his neck bashfully. "Since the boat, but that wasn't really appropriate. And I didn't while you were in Portland, because I knew you had a lot going on. And then I went underway again. My plan was to ask you out to dinner when you were settled here. I wanted to give you some space. Plus, I felt like a creepy old man."

Lorelei ran a well-manicured finger around the rim of her glass while holding his gaze. "You are neither creepy nor old. Believe me."

If the rapidly rising heat in his cheeks was any indication, he'd turned unflattering shade of red. "Well, thanks. I like how this worked out better."

"Me too." She slid her hand down the length of her glass to rest on the table. When her eyes flicked to his hands, Killian considered lacing his fingers with hers, but she blurted first, "Can I get you something to drink?"

"You don't need to do that. I can go up."

"No, please," Lorelei insisted. "I asked you out after all. And you saved my life. The least I can do is buy you a drink. What do you like?"

Rubbing his chin, he glanced at the chalkboard over the bar. It listed everything the pub had on tap, most of it locally brewed. "They don't serve a single bad beer here. Will you pick one for me?"

Her smile grew. "Sure." She crossed the room and leaned across the bar to order. With her back turned, he couldn't help but sneak admiring glances. *Doesn't skip leg day, that's for sure,* he thought as Lorelei struck up conversation with the bartender about the different beers. When she turned around with a dark brew in hand, Killian quickly averted his eyes. Only as Lorelei set the glass down in front of him did he look up again. The moment their eyes met, she winked. Caught. His cheeks flushed so hot it was a wonder he didn't self-combust.

"The bartender said this one was new, so I hope you like it." She motioned to the beer she brought. While she didn't comment on his obvious ogling, she wore a pleased smirk when she slid back into the booth.

If he was ever really smooth, he'd completely lost his touch. Clearing his throat, he lifted his glass to her. "I'm sure I will. Cheers." She didn't hesitate to raise her own glass to clink against his. After they'd both taken a drink, he asked, "How was Portland?"

A dark look flashed across her face. "Trying," she answered after a time, spinning her glass around in a circle. "But Kat helped me through it." She explained what happened at the memorial service. "The whole thing—being amongst my crewmates' family and friends—was unpleasantly surreal. And it was difficult to not replay that night in my head. When I went up to speak, I was afraid I was going to accidentally say something upsetting. I didn't, but I very well could have. My mind completely blanked partway through."

Damn. As if she hadn't already gone through enough. And yet she still pushed on. Make no mistake, her pretty blushes and date jitters were cute and did funny things to his stomach, but there was something deeper calling to him here. Her strength. Her courage. "You were brave to get up there."

"I don't think it was bravery that got me up there but thank you."

Guilt? Peer-pressure? He hoped it wasn't either of those things. "It's odd what the minister did—you said there was press at the church?"

"Sort of. The reporter I talked to was there for his niece and nephew. You would have met him on the docks."

From the docks…Ah, the devastated man Jackie took under her wing after the interview. "I remember him. Guy was in bad shape."

"If there were others," she continued, "and I'm sure there must have been, I didn't notice. I've been following the story more closely than Kat would like me to, but I just couldn't today."

From what he'd seen and read about Lorelei, she handled the aftermath of the tragedy well. But it had taken its toll, too. When he examined her closely, he noticed that even under the make-up she wore, there was still a hint of shadows beneath her eyes. "I've been following the story," he began. "All I'll say is you being at the service was very well received. And the reporter you talked to—Ed-something—spoke very highly of you in the piece he wrote. As for the minister, my guess is he's a tactless idiot. I'm glad Katrina called him out on it."

"I wonder if he genuinely thought my words would help," Lorelei considered thoughtfully. "From what you've said, it doesn't seem like he was entirely wrong to. I'm not excusing what he did—regardless of his intentions he certainly could have handled that better—but I just can't be mad at him. Maybe I'd feel differently if I botched the whole thing." She paused to sip her beer. "How has all this media attention been for you and your crew?"

Significant for a fisherman in a rural, coastal town, but nothing he couldn't handle. "It's been fine. I took a few calls. A couple crew members did interviews, mostly for the local paper, but it's winding down. The Coast Guard wants to give us some kind of public service commendation. There'll be a small ceremony sometime next year, which might stir things back up for a day or two."

"You guys deserve the recognition." Lorelei smiled. "I don't think I'll ever be able to thank you enough for saving my life."

Uncertainty churned in his gut. She wouldn't have asked him out on a date just because she felt obligated, would she? Like a debt that needed paid with some big gesture. "Please don't feel like you have to keep saying that. Especially not with me. You don't owe me anything."

Thumbing condensation from her glass, she nodded slowly. For a time, she didn't say anything else, and he wondered if he'd said the wrong thing. It had been such a long time since he'd last been on a proper date. He thought about asking if she'd like to play a game of darts, just for something to do, when her voice took a softer tone. "Killian, can I ask you something?"

He folded his arms on top of the table and leaned forward. The picture of relaxed, but internally he braced himself for a hard topic. "Yeah, of course. What's up?"

Head cocked to the right, Lorelei watched him intently. "You said you wanted to ask me out since the boat. What was the moment for you?"

Tension eased from his shoulders.

That was easy. He had been thinking about that moment every day since they met. "In the hall, seeing how comfy you were in my sweats." He smiled bashfully. "I realized I wanted to see more of that."

Eyes twinkling, Lorelei rested her cheek in her palm and gazed at him adoringly. "Sweats, huh? So that's what does it for you."

"Well. They gotta be mine, and you gotta be wearing them."

"Mm. Got it." She beamed, brushing his foot under the table with her own.

Killian stretched his legs so that their ankles comfortably entangled. "What about you? What was your moment?" His overeager heart leapt with anticipation to hear what her answer would be.

Absent-mindedly, Lorelei tore off a soggy corner from the napkin beneath her beer. "It was when you were taking off my boots and telling me about the gray in your hair."

He quirked his brow, bemused. "Really?" he teased. "That's what did it?"

"Okay, okay," she relented. "It didn't happen in isolation. It was how kind and gentle you were being. And the vantage point…"

A wicked thought sprung to mind. That maybe she liked him on his knees…With a lopsided grin, he nudged her foot playfully. "Do continue."

"Oh, leave me alone." Lorelei pinched the bridge of her nose. "I'm botching this completely. You had a cute reason. I guess there wasn't a 'moment' per se for me. I liked everything about you right from the start."

Smiling, Killian gently pulled Lorelei's hand from her face and enfolded it in his. "You're not botching this." Anything but.

Lorelei worried her lip. "It sounded like a better compliment in my head."

"I understood what you were getting at just fine." He stroked the top of her knuckles with his thumb, his heart thudding fast against his chest. He desperately wanted to kiss her, but he wouldn't now. Not in front of people. But if not now, then when? Outside the pub before they reached their cars? His front door? Would she even want to be kissed? What if she expected to be kissed… how would he know when was the right moment? God, he was helpless.

"Now, it's my turn to ask you something." The words flew out of his mouth before he had a chance to think about them, but they sounded confident, so he decided to roll with it.

"Uh-oh."

"Don't worry. It's an easy one. How do you feel about 'the goodnight kiss' at the end of a first date?"

A blush crept up Lorelei's cheeks. "You make it sound so ominous," she replied, withdrawing her hand. She rubbed her neck while thinking about how to respond. Bereft of her touch, Killian regretted asking. It *did* sound rather ominous. "But now that I'm thinking about it," she continued. "It creates a weird, awkward tension I don't like. You are talking about the 'walk her to the front door' kind of goodnight kiss?"

"Yeah, that one. It does feel awfully forced, doesn't it?"

"It does! I think it's because it's expected. I'd prefer my first kiss with someone to happen naturally—in the moment. Oh, and not in front of other people." She visibly shuddered at the thought.

"Agreed. It's a private moment."

Her posture relaxed. "Why? You thinking about kissing me?" she teased.

"It's been on my mind. But don't worry, you aren't in any immediate danger. Besides, we drove here separately and are currently roommates, so our circumstances would make the notorious goodnight kiss a bit ridiculous."

Lorelei nodded in agreement. "I'm actually glad we talked about this. It wasn't on my mind yet, but it would have been on the drive back to your house. Maybe I won't be a nervous, awkward mess now."

Talking candidly about where their heads were at was... Nice. Refreshing. Why guess and make assumptions when they could just hash it out together? "I was starting to feel like a nervous, awkward mess wondering whether or not you expected it. I didn't want to guess wrong."

"If you're ever not sure about something, just tell me. We can talk it through together."

"I'd like that." His smile broadened, stupid wide and utterly incapable of hiding how happy those words made him.

Lorelei looked pleased, as well. "How's your beer, by the way?"

"It's good. Want to try?" He held his glass out to her.

Their fingers brushed as she took it from him, and he itched to take her hand again—to feel the press of her palm against his. As she sipped, Killian stared at the slender curve of her throat, wondering what it would be like to trail kisses there. He pushed up his sleeves at the sudden temperature spike in the room, wishing he'd worn a t-shirt underneath. Should have known she'd have this effect on him.

Humming appreciatively, she returned his drink, but as if reading his mind, captured his hand in hers with a warm smile. "I picked well, if I do say so myself."

BACK AT THE COTTAGE, LORELEI JOINED HIM AT THE FRIDGE for another beer. In what Killian could only describe as adorable, Lorelei tapped a finger to her lips and hummed quietly as she perused the bottles. Once making their choices, they sat down on the couch together, and he wasted no time putting his arm around her.

Grinning, she propped up her knees and snuggled into him.

This close, he caught the scent of her hair—sweet, yet a little vinegary. Apples, maybe? Cider? Whatever it was, pleased him. If this date turned into many, Killian hoped he would soon become intimately familiar with the type of shampoo she used. "How long do you prefer to wait between first and second dates?"

She took a swig from her beer. "It depends on how much I like the guy," she answered cheekily.

"In this case?"

She nudged his side, wearing a teasing smile. "Worried you aren't going to see me for a while?"

He flashed a lopsided grin. "I wouldn't want to assume."

"When do you go offshore again?" she asked more seriously.

"In two days, I think. However long it takes us to fish the bait we need. But we won't be out as far or long. We're getting close to the limit of how much catch can be brought in this month—and that's across the whole fishery. So, we want to get out and back as quickly as possible, before others bring their hauls in. Weather and catch permitting, I'm thinking we'll be gone two to three days total."

"Ah, so the question is do we have our second date before or after you get back?"

"There's going to be a second date?" he joked.

Lorelei playfully slapped his knee, and God, he loved how much she was casually touching him now. "Definitely one when you come back. I'm going to be pretty busy with apartment hunting for the next few days at least, but that doesn't mean we can't spend some time together. Whether it constitutes as a date or roommate time, I don't know, but we can wait and see."

That she actually wanted to spend time with him was a little bewildering, but he'd take it, whatever company she was willing to give.

"Do you have any other questions regarding my preferences?" she asked coyly and politely sipped her beer, lips pressed to the rim. The suggestion wasn't lost on him.

The space at the front of his jeans evaporated as he imagined those lips wrapped around the bottle neck. Or better yet him. But the most tantalizing thought of all, the one that utterly wrecked and ruined all hope of this erection going down, was of him returning the favor, dancing his tongue across her softest parts, thighs wrapped around his head.

"Mm." He traced a finger along her shoulder, sliding her collar back bit by bit. "I'd like to find out as we go." He felt the shiver that ran up her spine and how her skin warmed under his touch.

Her face turned to his—mouth just a breath away. "I'll tell you when you do something I like," she murmured.

He brushed his thumb along the slope of her neck, lips grazing the shell of her ear. "You don't have to use your words. I'll know."

"Dammit, Killian," she inhaled deeply, averting her eyes. The sweater he wore was suddenly quite stifling. Growing hot from hearing his name said feverishly on her tongue, he had to take a deep breath, too, to keep the blood from completely rushing from his brain. Last thing they needed was him launching himself across the couch and mauling her.

Lorelei took their beers and set them aside.

"Too much?" His voice rasped. Man, he was a goner for this woman.

"It would be so easy to get carried away with you." She placed her hand on his chest, almost in awe to be touching him so. Her in awe of him? That blew his mind, but it made his heart soar. "I wouldn't even regret it if we did, but I want to take this a little slower. To savor what we're feeling a bit more. If that makes sense."

He brought her hand to his lips and pressed a lingering kiss to her skin. "I'll follow your lead, Lorelei. But if I test the waters, and you're not ready, I'll stop." And he would—on both accounts.

Smiling, she swept her fingers through his hair. "You know. I couldn't see them at the bar but being this close to you I can see a few of them."

"My grays?" he chuckled.

She bit her lip and nodded. "They're cute."

A weird, but pleasant fluttering twisted his stomach in knots. "Not the first thought to come to my mind, but I'll take it."

"Mm. And these," she continued, running a finger delicately over his crow's feet. "I like how they make your eyes look like they are always smiling."

The fluttering spread to his chest. Lorelei was fond of the things that made him worry he was too old for her every time he looked in the mirror. Knowing she wanted even these things about him, set his heart racing. He tentatively played with her braid, watching her as one might the shore after weeks at sea.

"Killian," she breathed, gaze darting to his lips. The need for her touch called him closer, and his silent wish was answered with the slow, deliberate caress of her fingers, charting a path across his cheek and the scruff of his jawline. Drawn to her like a sailor to a siren's song, he leaned in, and she captured his slightly parted lips in hers. He kissed her with reverence owed the goddess of the sea, but as she wrapped her arms around his neck and deepened the kiss, he sucked in a breath, stunned by how forcefully her touch pulled him into her thrall. Killian sunk rapidly into her embrace, drinking her in like a drowning man starved of breath. Such a death would be utter bliss.

Before he could drown, a smile erupted from her, a breath of life that yanked him to the surface with a need of a different sort. Like him, Lorelei was breathless; she had been drowning right along with him. He grinned against her lips, and just like that, his heart was moored to hers.

CHAPTER

FOURTEEN

LORELEI STRUGGLED TO FIND ACCURATE WORDS TO DESCRIBE the kiss she had shared with Killian. Touching her lips and relishing the memory, she smiled broadly to herself as she made herself a thermos of tea. If she had known their first kiss was going to be that good, she might not have asked him to take things slowly. Rushing into things was probably a bad idea, would her resolve be strong enough to withstand their next kiss?

As perilous and turbulent as a riptide, Killian could easily sweep her away if she wasn't vigilant, and then she would be cast adrift at sea, blind to a maelstrom of potential consequences.

Perhaps it was a good thing they both would be busy in the days leading up to his next offshore run. If they couldn't pace themselves, their obligations and responsibilities certainly would. When she heard Killian leave to go to his office by the docks, the sun had yet to come up, and so she sprawled under the covers in the next room, daydreaming the delicious possibilities between them.

Tempting as it was to lay in bed all day, imagining kisses and clinch positions, she eventually rolled out of bed and readied for the day, the cottage all to herself. It amazed her how quickly it felt familiar to her. Even knowing it would not be the last time she saw its handcrafted splendor, she would miss it when she moved into a place of her own. But still, she was excited to find that home for her next chapter.

With tea-to-go, a folder full of printed research, and a heart full of hope, Lorelei left for the apartment showings she scheduled throughout the day.

She hadn't expected to return later feeling tired and stressed but seeing how pleased Killian was when she walked in the door lightened her mood. That he already had that effect on her seemed auspicious. He took her purse and the other things she carried so she could remove her shoes and jacket. "How'd it go?"

Shrugging, she put her outerwear in the entryway closet and plopped down on the couch. "They're livable and within budget. That's all I can ask for."

"Did you take pictures?" Killian sat beside her.

She showed him the ones she took on her phone. He frowned deeply as he scrolled past pictures of bizarre layouts, stained carpets, moldy bathroom corners, and off-colored well water. Along the way, he pointed out a few things she missed that were symptoms of larger problems. "You see the moisture accumulation on this window right here? It means heat is escaping the building. You'll have a wicked steep heating bill if you pick that place."

That most certainly wouldn't do. She scratched her head. "I have one more apartment to look at, but if it doesn't work out, I'll take one of the others and make the most of it."

Handing back her phone, he said, "You're already here. Why don't you just stay?"

Did he just ask her to live with him? She must have heard him wrong. The kiss had been amazing, no doubt about it, but... "I couldn't impose on you like that," she managed, staring at him in utter shock.

Expression soft, Killian replied, "That's not how I'm thinking about this."

Lorelei swallowed the lump in her throat. "Won't that complicate things between us?"

"If we let it. But I think if we are upfront with each other about our romantic intentions and boundaries as roommates, it will be okay. And with how often I am offshore, you'll have plenty of space."

"I am again in a position where I want to say yes, but I have reservations on principle."

He nodded, understanding. "Don't stay if it makes you uncomfortable. That'll definitely complicate things between us but know my door is always open to you."

"You are a very sweet man, Killian." She rested a hand on his forearm. "Let me think about this and take a look at that last listing. I'll have an answer for you when you return."

He threaded his fingers through hers. "You can take more time than that, if you need it. It's an open invitation."

MOST OF THE NEXT DAY KILLIAN SPENT HIS TIME AT THE docks with his crew loading bait and prepping the boat to go underway. Their second date would have to wait until he returned.

Lorelei spent her afternoon reading a book she'd checked out from the local library. Reclining on the rocks down by the water, she savored the fresh sea breeze and lulling sound of waves rolling into shore, all while losing herself to good storytelling.

When the weather was mild, and her mother's caseload allowed, this was how they spent many of their Saturdays together along the shores of Lake Superior. Remembering freshened the pang of loss, but she could almost pretend her mother sat right next to her, and that brought her comfort. Mom loved to read detective mysteries, but if she had more than her fill of law after a difficult week at the courthouse, she turned to historical romances bought for 99 cents apiece at the independent bookstore in town. Lorelei usually lost herself to fairytale retellings and fantasy, but despite their different reading tastes, they would sometimes swap their favorites, just so they could gush over them together.

The waning light and sound of Killian's truck pulling in drew Lorelei from the fictional world in which she'd immersed herself. After a quiet, but pleasant dinner, they curled up together on the couch. "What are you reading?" he asked. Book in hand, Lorelei nestled between his knees and laid back against his chest. He wrapped his arms around her, careful to avoid her bruises.

"Something light and fun."

Killian peeked at the cover. "It's a romance."

Lorelei reddened, not with embarrassment, but indignation. "I'll have you know it's very well-written and…"

He rubbed soothing circles into her arms. "I have a bunch on my shelves, if you'd like to read them." Lorelei's head snapped to the bookshelves in question. She scanned the planks of wood holding the complete works of Stephen King, Patrick O'Brien, Matthew Woodring Stover, and others until her eyes fell on a shelf entirely lined with well-worn romance titles, many had been her mom's favorites. Her eyes bugged out of her head. How had she missed those?

Killian smiled into her hair. "I have my mom to thank for them. She used to read them to me when I was little—skipped the naughtier bits, of course."

"Mine read me Nancy Drew. I wasn't allowed near an adult romance until I graduated from high school."

"Did you sneak read them anyway?"

She laughed. "Of course, I did. Over summer break, as soon as Mom went to bed, I'd creep downstairs, steal one of hers off the bookshelf, and stay up all night reading."

"Mm. I did that with some of my dad's books." Killian barely stifled a yawn and laid his head against the side of the couch. "Well, don't let me keep you."

While Lorelei read late into the evening, Killian drifted in and out of sleep, occasionally nuzzling her neck or playing with her hair. Close to midnight, when he untangled his limbs from hers, he told her sleepily that going their separate ways at the end of each night was becoming less and less appealing. Lorelei silently agreed, but she needed just a little more time.

Lorelei leaned against the cottage front door, an autumnal ocean breeze ruffling strands of hair from her braid. It was still dark at 4AM, sunrise still hours away. She watched Killian shoulder his sea bag in uneasy silence.

"I'll let you know the moment we're shore-side again," he promised, as if sensing her worry, and reached out for her.

Slowly and tenderly they came together, sharing a kiss that rendered them buoyant and breathless. But when they parted, that weightless feeling was replaced by a sinking in her stomach.

The fishing trip was supposed to be short, but that didn't make watching Killian's leave-taking any easier. The last time Lorelei was at sea, her whole crew had died. *She* had almost died.

One storm. That's all it took.

"I'll be fine," Killian said, caressing her cheek with his thumb. "I've done this my whole life."

She pulled him in and hugged him tight, memorizing the feel of him, and biting back the grim words teetering on the tip of her tongue.

Captain Calhorn had, too.

And the sea devoured him and all but one of his crew.

CHAPTER

FIFTEEN

NIGHTMARES ABOUT THE STORM TERRORIZED LORELEI'S dreams.

Living through it once had been horrid enough. But each night, she relived that tragedy, over and over, thrown overboard and somersaulting through the water in her immersion suit, sea salt burning her throat. She'd surface briefly, only to be pushed back to the underwater world of green-black.

In this torturous conjuring of memory and imagination, she had an impossible amount of visibility beneath the waves, her traitorous brain filling in unwanted details.

With the storm raging overhead, the moon had been hidden that night. There was no doubt in her mind. Its light would not have penetrated the clouds let alone the churning waves. But it did in her nightmares.

Something dark sped past her in the water, circling with predatory intent, but it moved too fast for her to see it clearly. Too lithe to be a shark.

Something grabbed her arm.

Lorelei awoke shaking, and drenched in sweat, before she could see what it was. Turning on the bedside lamp and inspecting her once purple bruise, which had now faded to a jaundiced yellow color, she was reminded of the gaping black hole of her memory from that night. What the hell could have done this, crushed her arm like that? She'd been too far away from the ship to have been caught on a line.

Somehow, someone had given her those marks. She shuddered to think that another crew mate had gone into the water with her and reached out for help—only never to receive it. That there could have been another survivor besides her, if only she had reached back, was an unbearable thought.

Over the next two days, Lorelei distracted herself by researching the Haven Cove Marine Research Center and Dr. Lila Branson's work. Her potential future boss was a rising star in the field of marine biology and practically swam in funding. The Center itself was the largest employer in Haven Cove, Maine and was looking to expand their revenue stream with a museum add-on to take advantage of tourism. She began jotting down questions for the interview and talking points.

The more she read, the more she wanted the job.

If she threw herself into this, maybe she'd think less about the things that plagued her dreams.

ALL HER LIFE, LORELEI MANAGED TO AVOID SMALL TOWN drama—middle school, high school, college. It just never touched her, as if she had an invisible force field protecting her from it. But whatever shield the universe had given her then was gone now.

Returning from an open house event at the Haven Cove Marine Research Center, and her last apartment showing, Lorelei found a black BMW parked outside Killian's house and a strange woman snooping around. Probably one of those want-to-be neighbors or buyers Killian told her about.

Patience worn thin from three nights of terrible sleep and a gurgling stomach, Lorelei lowered her window and called out a little snappishly, "Excuse me, can I help you?"

The dirty-blonde-haired woman looked up from her snoop-fest, surprised. Not because Lorelei had snuck up on her—her aging car rattled too much for that—but because she wasn't expected. She wasn't Killian. The woman's initial surprise passed quickly, and she introduced herself. "I'm Carrie Prior, an old friend of Killian's."

Lorelei wasn't stupid. 'Old friend' really meant 'old girlfriend.' The fact that this one was sneaking around Killian's property got her damn near bristling. She got out of the car, bracing herself for a confrontation. "Is he expecting you? He didn't mention having anyone over to the house today."

Around noon, Killian had called her to say they'd moored but would be down at the docks until 4PM offloading catch—and it was about that time now. With how attentive to detail he'd been up until this point, she doubted he'd forgotten to mention visitors. She moved closer to the woman, so that she could hear her better, and talk civilly, but maintained some distance.

Carrie sighed and shook her head, turning to face the ocean. With an air of ease and belonging and rudeness that irked Lorelei, Carrie leaned against the stone of the house and inhaled deeply as she stared out over the water. "It is beautiful here. The home he's built." A shadow of regret flitted across her face. "I don't know what you've heard about me, if you've even heard anything at all, but we dated, Killian and I. We were high school sweethearts. Everyone thought we'd get married, do the family thing."

Jealousy wasn't something that usually got the best of Lorelei, but it surged through her now. Where'd this sudden territorial behavior come from? Balling her hands into fists, Lorelei pinched her lips shut, not trusting herself to speak.

When she didn't respond, Carrie sighed, pushing off from the wall. "I've tried to reconnect with him since I've been back, but he won't talk to me. That's fine. I broke his heart. But, in our case, heartbreak is a two-way street. I had to come see for myself why he wouldn't come to New York City with me."

Distrusting Carrie's intentions, and her own self-control, Lorelei crossed her arms. But she tried to be diplomatic. "Do you feel like seeing this has given you closure?"

"No," Carrie replied flatly. "The opposite, actually. I'm realizing why he wanted and needed this so badly. It's the inverse of why I wanted, and needed, a big city in my twenties. But I don't feel that way anymore, and it really fucking sucks realizing that I can't be with the person I love, because I didn't want the same things at the same time he did."

Nodding blandly, Lorelei glanced down the dirt road. Killian would be back any minute, and she really didn't want his ex-girlfriend still around when he returned. "Look," she said as gently as she could, despite the awkwardness of the situation. Though she didn't really feel it, she wanted to show Carrie some sympathy. "I'm sorry you didn't get the closure you wanted, but I really need to get inside and start dinner."

Taking the hint, Carrie reddened and shifted uncomfortably toward her car, finally showing signs of embarrassment for her intrusion. "I'm sorry I bothered you. I'll get out of your hair."

Neither wanting to be rude or permissive, Lorelei replied neutrally, "Drive safely. I've been seeing a lot of deer near the road lately."

Thankfully, it worked.

Carrie hurried to her car and drove off. And just like that, she was gone.

Locking her own car and walking back to the cottage, Lorelei didn't know what to make of Carrie's oversharing. She'd never met another person younger than sixty who could just spew their life story to a stranger like that, let alone an ex's new girlfriend. She had a sneaking suspicion that, with a personality like that, this wasn't going to be the last she'd see of Carrie.

And who the hell says, 'I'll get out of your hair?!'

Lorelei had just taken her purse up to her room when she heard Killian's truck pull in. Just their luck. He'd probably passed Carrie on the dirt road. She hoped it wouldn't sour his homecoming cheer.

Hearing the front door open, she dashed down the stairs and crossed the room to meet him. He was shrugging off a windbreaker when she said, "What a sight for sore eyes."

Grinning at her greeting, Killian tossed his jacket aside and tugged her in by the belt loops for a kiss. She hummed with pleasure under the touch of his lips. Mood not soured—excellent. "I missed you," he murmured, hands creeping toward her backside.

"I missed you, too," she returned, slipping her hand into his own back pocket and giving him a squeeze.

"I couldn't stop thinking about you."

"Same. So, how'd it go?"

"Great. We had a large haul but not so big that we broke the fishery's limits. How are you? What have you been up to?"

"I'll tell you in a bit. But first, your ex, Carrie Prior, just stopped by…" Lorelei trailed cautiously.

Killian played with the end of her braid. "Yeah, I know," he said apologetically. "I drove past her on my way in. I didn't stop for an explanation though, because I've asked her to leave me be, and I have no time for people who don't respect boundaries. What happened? Did she knock on the door?"

Lorelei recounted the meeting.

"That was very," Killian began, searching for the right word, "dramatic of her. I'm sorry you had to deal with that. If she does it again, I'll give her a talking to."

As they made dinner, Lorelei told him about her past three days. She initially left off the part about having nightmares, but he specifically asked her how she'd been sleeping. As she described the night terrors, she had to assure him several times that she hadn't been sleepwalking again. While she hadn't managed to convince him, he let the matter drop.

"Is this the first time you are having these nightmares?" He flipped two steaks in a cast iron skillet.

Draining the boiling water from a pot of mixed vegetables, Lorelei answered in the affirmative, nose wrinkling from the smell. It made her oddly nauseated. Wanting to change the subject, she announced, "I've given your offer some thought."

"Oh?" He pulled out two sets of plates and silverware.

"I don't want to live alone right now, and there's no roommate who can better understand what's been happening than you—except Katrina, of course, but she's in Boston."

Killian perked up. "So, you're staying?"

"If you allow me to pay rent or share utilities, I will stay. I would not feel right accepting otherwise."

"Deal," he grinned, removing the steaks from the skillet. "You can pitch in for utilities and groceries. Would you like some help unpacking your car after dinner?"

"I'm certainly not going to say no to that."

When they sat down to eat, Lorelei's stomach roiled in protest at the heady smell of seared meat and boiled vegetables. Thinking it would be better once she ate a little, Lorelei tried to take a bite but nearly gagged. The longer she sat at the table, the more her nausea increased. "I'm so sorry," she said suddenly, holding her stomach. "I need some fresh air."

There was no time to soothe the startled expression from Killian's face. Lorelei rushed outside and vomited along the tree line. Her nausea lessened a fraction but returned when the thick smell of pine filled her nose. Drawn to the water's edge, far from the house and trees, she sucked in lungsful of salty sea air. With each breath, her nausea dissipated, but it was a long time before Killian could coax her back inside.

CHAPTER

SIXTEEN

SITTING AT HIS OFFICE DESKTOP, KILLIAN BALANCED *DAWN Chaser's* digital ledgers and updated the logbooks. Across from him, Branson diligently worked on payroll while the rest of the crew worked on the boat. Such administrative and maintenance tasks typically occupied their time when not at sea.

Removing his reading glasses, Branson leaned back in his chair and stretched. "Want a top-off?" he yawned, reaching for the office coffee pot.

Killian rubbed his eyes and then lifted his mug. As Branson poured, he asked, "Not sleeping well?"

He shook his head. "What's your excuse?"

Branson waggled his eyes suggestively.

"Oh."

"What's yours?" Branson fired back.

He told him about Lorelei's nightmares. His friend arched his brow at the information that they lived together, so he quickly explained that she stayed in his guest bedroom. Branson filled his own mug. "Is there something going on between you? And that's a rhetorical question. I know there is, I just want you to tell me about it."

Killian blew away the steam rising from his mug. "She asked me out on a date, and we've kissed."

"Marci picked up that you've got a thing for her. I guess Lorelei did, too. Must have gone pretty well though for you to ask her to live with you."

Saying it out loud made it sound reckless, but everything just made sense with Lorelei. And maybe it was his age talking, but he saw no point wasting their time on formalities. "I really like having her around," he replied. "My place feels empty when she isn't there. I know it hasn't been long, but I've been in other relationships for far longer and have never felt that way. I think she's it for me."

A cheesy grin broke out across Branson's face. "You too, now?" He explained he'd felt the same about Lila and knew the same was true for Walsh and Marci. Sometimes you click with a person right away, and you just know. All the traditional relationship milestones to follow are only observed for posterity's sake, not because of a lack of readiness. "You're adults. Stop worrying about principle and do whatever's good for you. Lila and I only took things slow because we were barely teenagers when we started dating."

Scribbling absentmindedly across the top of a piece of scratch paper, Killian ventured to another topic, one that had been troubling him and made him grateful that Lorelei wasn't living alone. "I'm worried about Lorelei. Aside from not sleeping well, she barely eats. She tries, but she just throws it back up."

"You a shitty cook, Captain?" Branson joked, but his expression was grim.

Killian crumpled up the piece of paper and threw it at him. "It's probably PTSD-related. She has an appointment with a doctor in two weeks—it's the soonest someone could see her. I've read though that yoga and meditation before bed helps, so she's trying that."

Taking the paper ball that hit his chest, Branson tossed it into the recycling bin. "I hope it gets better for her soon. She's lucky to have you looking out for her."

Compliments for being a decent human being never sat well with him. Taking a drink of his coffee, he switched subjects yet again. "Have you seen or heard from Carrie? She was snooping around my place." He told Branson about what happened between his ex and Lorelei.

Unamused by the news, Branson grumbled, "Lila and I got drinks with her last night. She's—" He paused, searching for the right words. "She's nothing like the Carrie we grew up with. New York City did a real number on her, man."

"What happened?"

Cracking his knuckles, Branson replied, "We're going to need a fresh pot of coffee for this. In summary? Her job was brutal, and her boyfriend of nine years got his secretary pregnant and dumped her."

Killian didn't need any more details, but over another pot of coffee, Branson shared them anyway.

The takeaway was loud and clear.

New York's the city that never sleeps, and Carrie got tired.

CHAPTER

SEVENTEEN

STANDING AT THE FRONT OF THE COFFEE SHOP, LORELEI surveyed the room, looking for her potential future boss. Spotting Lila, she adjusted her purse strap, took a deep breath, and walked over to where she sat.

Wanting to look her best for this job interview, and memorable, she wore her favorite professional outfit: an olive-green pantsuit with a cream silken tie-neck blouse and pointed, caramel-colored leather heels.

When discussing what to wear the night before with Katrina, her friend teased that 'news sensation Lorelei Roth was already memorable.' Recent events—including dinner at the Walshes'—meant it was unlikely Lila had forgotten who she was, but she liked the confidence the ensemble afforded her. The last time she wore it, she'd given a great interview at a press event for her previous job and memories stuck to clothes.

Also dressed to the nines, Lila stood when she saw her, hand outstretched. "Hello, Ms. Roth." With how stunning she looked in her dusty rose skirt suit set and heels, Lorelei was grateful she made the fashion choices she did.

"Hello, Dr. Branson." Lorelei firmly shook the marine biologist's hand. "Thank you again for your flexibility in scheduling this meeting. Having those two weeks was really helpful."

Lila waved it off. "It wasn't even a question. Please, have a seat."

Hanging her purse across the chair back, Lorelei complied.

"How are you doing?" Lila asked, expression soft.

"I've been better," she replied honestly. "But I'm looking forward to working again. Having something to busy my hands and mind will help, I think. You?"

"I'm very excited to get this project started. I'm not on sabbatical per se—that's a university thing—but the research center has given me this year to collect specimens and kick start the museum. I'll miss conducting new research, but it will be amazing to see how all the work we've done comes together in this."

Lila recapped what the position entailed and then inquired into Lorelei's college coursework, past museum experience, and relevant skills. Lorelei described the programming she developed for the Marquette Maritime Museum and showed a portfolio of the work she did for their exhibit designer in her free time. She admitted that it had been an unofficial, unpaid apprenticeship.

"That's okay," Lila assured her. "You still did the work." After discussing her qualifications, Lila invited Lorelei to ask questions about the project.

"I hoped you could clarify some of the details," Lorelei began, retrieving a legal pad and pen from her purse. "Is this going to be a natural history museum, or a museum dedicated to local maritime history and fishing economy?"

"It can be whatever I make it. I have almost total scientific and artistic freedom in the project, which opens a lot of possibilities. All of what you just said is important to this region, so I think it should receive a fair share of attention in the exhibits."

Jotting down a note, Lorelei nodded in agreement. "It does all go together hand and hand. But would you say that the primary intent of the museum is to showcase the center's scientific research and natural collections?"

"Yes, absolutely. And preservation and conservation should be the major themes. When visitors come, we want them to learn how marine life is fundamentally important to the very nature of our planet and to us. We also want visitors to take away how humans impact marine life populations and habitats, and what we can do on a local level to better the health of our oceans. I, myself, and an oceanographer we have on staff, have done a lot of research on these issues. I have his papers right here, and mine, if you want to take a look."

Lorelei skimmed through the pages. While she read, Lila lifted a file folder filled five inches thick with colored prints from beneath the table. Its considerable bulk was held together by three heavy-duty rubber bands. When Lila placed it in front of Lorelei, it hit the table with an unavoidable thud. "When you are ready," Lila explained, "these are images of every item we have in our collection."

After skimming the research, Lorelei flipped through a fraction of the images, nodding in approval at the detailed pages of notes accompanying each photograph. Lorelei laid out her initial thoughts for the project and concluded by saying, "You've done a lot of groundwork here. There's plenty here for me to get started on preliminary proofs, if you'd like."

"Please, and I'll compensate you for the time. The exhibits you showed me in your portfolio were fabulous." Lila placed her hand on top of the stack of photos. "I can't wait to see what you do with this."

Lorelei smiled, relieved to be getting a shot. "Do you have a layout of the space?"

"It's in my email. One moment, I'll forward it to you." Lila picked up her phone and took a few minutes to do just that. "Okay sent. What do you say we reconvene in a week's time to discuss what you've come up with?"

"Same time, same place?"

"Same time, but let's meet at my office at the lab. And if you have any questions between now and then, please feel free to email or call me."

Lorelei grinned, feeling lighter now that the interview was over and had gone well. They both rose from their seats and shook hands.

THRILLED BY THE CHANCE TO PROVE HERSELF, LORELEI spent the remainder of the day pouring over Lila's research findings and notes. Immersed in the task, and drowning in piles of paper, she barely registered Killian coming home from work. It took him knocking on her door with an offering of tea to bring her back to the surface.

"Thank you," she beamed, waving him in and clearing a spot on the desk.

The tight shirt he wore drew her eyes to delectable, sculpted shoulders and pectorals. Feeling warm, she tugged at her collar and wondered when he had turned the heat up.

"How'd it go?" He placed the cup and saucer in front of her. As he bent forward, she caught a whiff of his natural scent and inadvertently licked her lips.

"She wants proofs of the exhibits," she replied. "So, I think pretty well. I don't think she would have asked for them, given me all these materials, and offered to pay me, if I wasn't a serious candidate, right?"

As she motioned to the clutter of photos, notes, and papers, Killian leaned against the doorframe, thumbs hooked through his belt loops. Watching her watch him. She drank in every cord, every curvature of muscle, begging touch and taste. Good god, he wasn't even flexing.

"I think it's a very good sign," he assured, oblivious to her sizing him up. "Listen, if you want to work at the table downstairs, I don't mind. You'll have a lot more room there."

Refocusing her one remaining brain cell, she gestured once more to the heap in front of her. "You sure? I'm going to be working on this all week."

He fondly stroked her cheek with his thumb, frustratingly affectionate and chaste when the mere touch whet her appetite for more. "This really is important. I can spare the table."

Clueless man, just kiss me.

Ever since he'd gone offshore and her nightmares began, distance and mutual exhaustion had starved them of intimacy, and she ached to share it again.

"I'll leave you to your work." He began to turn to leave.

Fuck that. Work could wait. Lorelei jumped up from her chair and caught his hand. Before he could comment, she pulled him into a searing kiss. His surprise wore off quickly, enthusiastically.

Eager to join the frenzy, Killian lifted her onto the table and buried his fingers in her hair, mussing her braid. Her palms slipped under the hem of his shirt to drink in the contours of his body and savor the heat rising off his skin. She needed to feel his blood boiling at the urging of her fingertips. To feel his passion and consume it.

He pressed against her core, and she relished how hard he'd gotten. There'd been a previous conversation about taking things slower—one she initiated—but she couldn't think of one good reason why they should stop now. Pulling her shirt off, and tossing it behind him, Killian clearly saw no reason to either.

He blazed a trail of fire with his mouth, tasting the slopes and curves of her flesh. Circling back to her mouth, he whispered against her lips, "You've soaked through your jeans."

A pleasurable shiver tumbled down her spine. She entangled her fingers in his hair. "Never done that before."

He kissed her hard before pulling her off the desk and kneeling before her. "I'm going to give you the kind of goodnight kiss I wanted to after our first date," he voiced thickly, inching down her jeans and panties.

As if sucked into a riptide by his words, Lorelei opened her legs for him to devour her. She trembled violently under the ministrations of his voracious mouth, keened at the scratch of his scruff along her sensitive inner thighs, and held the edge of the desk in a white-knuckled grip. The veins in his forearms bulged from strain when he added his fingers to the mix, pumping her hard and fast.

Her belly coiled tight, pleasure building at a surprising pace, a rising wave just moments from breaking. Added pressure from Killian's tongue wrecked her sweetly and suddenly.

Unraveling, she screamed his name, and he caught her as her knees buckled.

Lorelei sunk into his arms and pressed her forehead to his. Breathing heavily together, they shared a small, sated laugh. Once she caught her breath, Lorelei wrapped an arm around Killian's neck, kissing him tenderly and reaching for his fly.

She would feast upon the parts of him that desired her touch.

CHAPTER

EIGHTEEN

WHILE HELPING LORELEI UNPACK HER CAR, KILLIAN learned that she didn't own very much. Aside from clothes, books, and electronics, she only had a few personal, sentimental items—her mother's recipes, a set of German China, a box of photographs, and apparently a pair of ice skates. It gave him the idea to suggest skating for date two.

The pond wouldn't freeze over for another few months yet, so they opted for indoor ice skating instead.

At the rink, Killian paid for their admission and guided Lorelei over to the benches so they could lace up. They'd come to a weekday evening session, so while the rink wasn't crowded, it was busy enough. She tossed her skate covers into her bag and, for a moment, he watched her tackle the laces with expert assuredness.

The skates themselves were worn, a slight off-white color. She'd used them often, and had them for a long time, but took good care of them. Pulling on his own skates, he asked, "Did you skate competitively?"

She shook her head. "My mom did though, before she came over from Germany. These were hers actually—her latest pair. I took lessons when I was little, but I mostly just skated with her for fun. Then it was the thing to do in middle school and high school." She glanced over at the skates he'd put on. "Did you play hockey?"

"Pond hockey with friends. It was the thing to do," he grinned. "We still play pick-up from time to time during the winter."

Wistful, Lorelei tied and tucked her laces in reverence for the woman who wore them before her. "That sounds really nice."

Out on the ice, Lorelei weaved in front of him between the groups of skaters with graceful ease. He enjoyed watching her hips and backside sway as she pushed off with each leg. In a less congested spot, he came up beside her and switched over so that he could admire her from the front.

Cheeks and nose rosy from the chill, Lorelei smiled. This woman was gorgeous and fucking adorable.

He held out his hands to her, which she wordlessly accepted, and he towed her along skating backwards, regularly glancing over his shoulder to skirt other skaters. Eyes twinkling, she laughed joyfully at the speed in which he took them around a bend, crossing over into the turn.

"Wow, I know you said you played pond hockey, but you're really good. Too good for just messing around on the ice for fun. You've had training."

Killian grinned, releasing one of her hands, so he could skate forward-facing with her. "Not formally. Branson used to play for club teams, and he taught me everything I know." He pulled her close when a teenager suddenly took a spill beside them, narrowly missing a tripping mishap. "You should see how good he is. He would have made it to the minor leagues if he had the inclination. Maybe even the professionals."

"Why didn't he?"

"He would have had to move, and he wanted to stay near Lila."

She smiled, nodding with approval. "Hey, can you teach me how to skate backwards? I never got any good at it, but I'd like to."

"Your mom didn't teach you?"

"Oh, she tried, but I didn't get a lot of one-on-one time with her at the rink. She worked long hours and long weeks at the courthouse."

"All right, let's see where you're at."

Lorelei skated to a spot where there currently weren't very many people and spun around. Without prompting or direction, she began to move, not at all shy about her inexperience. Her form was mostly good, he observed, but her movements were wobbly and unpracticed. When she jerked backward unexpectedly, he shot forward to catch her, but she'd already righted herself by spreading her arms and leaning forward.

There were plenty more close calls like that, but it didn't deter her from trying.

He was pleased to note that she already had a good habit of checking behind her and wasn't too thrown off by the swiveling motion of her head. But as soon as he said that out loud, she swung sharply into another teenager's path.

To avoid a collision, he grabbed her by the shoulders and redirected her. "Whoops." She laughed at herself and thanked him for the rescue. He offered pointers, which she accepted with good grace and determination.

Several laps around, her motions smoothed, and she'd even picked up a little speed.

They took a break from lessons when Killian felt his phone buzz in his back pocket. Checking to make sure it wasn't about the boat he unlocked the screen.

What the hell...?

He frowned down at the photo awaiting him—one of him towing Lorelei around a bend, not long after they got on the ice. It had been sent by Carrie.

With it, she wrote: *You two looked so sweet together, I had to take this picture. I'm sorry for being creepy about it, but candids really are the best shots.* He stopped abruptly, spraying a wave of shaved ice along the boards, and looked around, trying to spot his ex. He didn't see her first or second pass.

Brows furrowed, Lorelei stopped ahead of him and backtracked. "What's wrong?" He showed her the message and photo. Her eyes widened in surprise. "Wow. She's here?"

"Yeah. She was part of the pond hockey group, but I honestly didn't expect her to be here." Or spy on them and take photos like a stalker.

The more he thought about it, the madder he got. He ran a shaky hand through his hair, trying to keep his composure. "I'm really sorry."

"It's okay. If you want to go say hi to her, I'll be fine skating on my own for a bit." She rubbed his arm in encouragement.

He frowned. "I don't think so."

"Not even just a quick hello to be polite? It is a very nice photo."

His frown deepened. "I'm upset with her," he began, keeping his voice light and calm. "Not in a-I-haven't-moved-on-after-fifteen-years kind of way, but because I asked her not to reach out to me, and she hasn't been respecting that."

"Oh." Lorelei glanced down at the ice and kicked at a chipped piece with her blade. "Was it a bad breakup?"

He shook his head. "It was a hard breakup, because we still loved each other—our life goals and dreams just didn't match. But it wasn't a bad breakup."

Confusion spread across her face. "So, if it wasn't bad, isn't cutting her out and completely avoiding her a little harsh?"

"I don't know," he rubbed his face, suddenly feeling tired. He wasn't sure why she was pushing the matter. Maybe she was the type of person who stayed friends with exes? It never worked out that way for him. But he could be patient for her, even in this. "I never felt like we could be friends after that, and now I just don't want to be. I think she wants to pick things up where they were before we started dating, but it's just not that simple. Not for me, at least."

Lorelei nodded, finally understanding. "That's fair. But would it be okay if I keep the photo? It really is a good one of us."

"Only if you take one with me now, so I can have one of us to keep." Killian sent the candid to Lorelei and then opened the camera app on his phone. He put his arm around her, and she scooched in close so they could take a selfie. He held out his phone and, when they were ready, she tapped the button to take the picture. "Like it?" He showed her the result.

"Love it," she beamed and kissed him on the cheek. "I guess this means we're going steady, huh?"

He sent that photo to her, as well. "It's what I've been hoping. Do you want to get out of here?" Knowing his ex-girlfriend watched them from somewhere within the rink, or had at some point, soured his mood to skating.

"Okay. But just one more lap?" she pleaded sweetly, weaving her fingers through his.

How could he say no? He squeezed her hand. "One more and then dinner? Would you be up for that?"

"Do you like sushi?"

He nodded.

"That's a favorite of mine. Maybe it will sit well with me."

"An odd choice for a sensitive stomach but sure, why not. If the smell makes you sick though, we can leave." She agreed, tugging him onward for one more rotation around the carousel of skaters.

SEATED AT THE RESTAURANT, A WAITER WITH A PLATTER OF sashimi whisked by, and Lorelei commented that they didn't smell half bad. He didn't know how she could distinguish their scent from all the other restaurant smells, but she ordered a platter just like it for herself based on that fact alone.

When her own platter arrived, she peeled off her gloves, revealing nails repainted a sultry cherry red. Plucking the chopsticks from the table, she ate every single piece on the bed of rice with a genuine enjoyment for food he'd hadn't seen since he returned from his last offshore trip. An odd thing her appetite had become. Of all things, she stomached pure raw fish the best. Killian mentally filed this tidbit of information away for later.

Relieved to see her finally eat something without struggling, he offered his last piece to her. It was a thickly cut piece of yellowtail, so when Lorelei struggled to pick it up with chopsticks, she pinched the fish between two red fingernails and tore off half of it between her teeth. She chewed slowly, savoring the taste and texture. Then she popped the second half into her mouth and did the same. With fascination, he watched her swallow and suck the tips of those two fingers each in turn, leaving her nails glistening red.

Feeling suddenly very hot, Killian chugged the rest of his glass of ice-cold water.

"Are you okay?" The lopsided grin she wore made him certain she knew exactly the answer to that question. When he didn't answer right away, her grin deepened. She leaned forward and whispered huskily, "Do you want to get out of here?"

He took his wallet from his back pocket and threw down enough cash to cover their meals and a generous tip. They didn't wait for a check.

At home, they shed each other's clothes with a frenzied urgency. Laughing and kissing, they stumbled their way up to his room and tore into the box of condoms he kept in his nightstand. He'd recently bought them, hoping their relationship would take this turn. When he reached between her thighs to ready her, his fingers met slick folds. "God, Lorelei. You're so wet," he murmured. He swirled his fingers around her sensitive bud, and she quaked.

With a mischievous grin, she replied breathlessly, "Yes, Captain. I've been thinking about riding your dick all evening."

What little blood remained in his head rushed out. Swearing, Killian pulled her onto the bed with him and onto his lap. Her long, flowing hair spilled over her shoulders and glinted red in the moonlight. Taking him in hand, Lorelei positioned him at her entrance and sank onto him with a sigh. Killian groaned, the back of his head thudding against the headboard. Silently cursing celibacy, he kept his mind carefully blank.

If he didn't, this would all be over embarrassingly soon.

Lorelei rode him while he sat against the headboard, her head tipped back, lips parted in sweet carnal bliss. A sheet of moonlight overlaid her in a pearly, white glow, as she rose and fell upon him like a wave. He loved how he no longer had to avert his eyes from her lovely round breasts and rosy nipples and watched as they bounced before his face in delicious offering. She moaned loudly when he pressed open mouth kisses to them.

He pulled her hips in time with his, rocking with her like a boat in a sea swell. Building, building until her chest heaved and her body crashed down. Cherry red nails raked lines across his chest as she came, his name on her lips.

Anchored, his hips responded of their own accord, bucking upwards, and he groaned through his own release. Lightheaded from elation, he fell back, happily wrecked and reduced to flotsam. Lorelei laid in the crook of his arm.

CHAPTER
NINETEEN

FAR BELOW THE CHURNING OCEAN SURFACE, EERIE, GREEN-tinted water surrounded her. Lorelei's crewmates frantically swam away from *The Osprey* as it sank to its eternal, watery grave. Other crew members, lifeless and still, floated to the surface—the sea having already filled their lungs. Lorelei kicked out with her legs to hasten her ascent, afraid to share their fate.

A dark shape shot past her in the water. She flinched with fear, but before she could react any further, talons enclosed her arm in a fearsome grip. She thrashed wildly, the bubbles erupting from her mouth just silent screams to an unforgiving ocean.

But the creature was not deaf to them. It turned and a beautiful woman stared back at her—a beautiful, monstrous woman with gleaming blue-eyes, a wide mouth filled with wicked sharp teeth, and a terrible, ravenous hunger. It hissed, letting her go, and swam away at a speed that could easily rival a shark. It joined a school of other creatures like it—humanoid beings glowing with bioluminescence and with fish tails from the waist down.

Sirens. Mermaids. Sea folk. Whatever the name, they swarmed the crew, launching at them with vicious fervor, dragging them screaming down into the deep. She heard the horrific feeding frenzy that followed

—the tearing of flesh and sound of teeth scraping against and cracking bones. But even more terrible, she acutely smelled her crewmates' blood and felt their fear down to the very last twitch of life. As they were eaten alive.

And then the merfolk returned to claim and consume the already dead.

But not her.

Lorelei jerked awake from her nightmare only to realize she was already in one.

Disoriented and completely submerged in ocean brine, Lorelei twisted and turned, not knowing which way to go to reach the surface, panic seizing her in its iron grip. Sleepwalking yet again. But the absence of held breath and burning lungs gave her a moment of pause and allowed her to think more clearly.

Gathering in her surroundings, she realized she could see exactly where she was in the dark, murky water—the rocky bottom, and the shoreline fifty feet away. No blown bubbles needed to distinguish up from down. In fact, she didn't feel the physical need to hurry to the surface at all.

She kicked out frog-style to swim toward the coast, but her legs did not part to allow the motion. They felt like they'd been encased in plastic wrap. She looked down.

And screamed.

A fish tail had replaced them, glowing with bright green bioluminescence, like rows of emerald fireflies had gotten stuck to her flesh. And these nodes weren't just along the tail, they lined her arms and hands, too.

With one panicked but deliberate snap of her tail, she propelled through the water from zero to sixty and, before she registered what had happened, her front scraped the sea bottom in a painful slide into shore.

Dragging herself out of the water, body spasming with gut-wrenching sobs, Lorelei heard Killian shout her name from a short distance away—his feet pounding in the sand as he ran. For a moment, in her desire to rise up to meet him, she'd forgotten that her legs were no more. She made a conscious effort to take a step, and in doing so, the scales that bound her legs retreated beneath her skin. Cringing at the tingling, invasive sensation, she stumbled during her first attempt to stand but gained purchase on the second.

Killian skidded to a halt, eyes going wide.

And yet, the words he exclaimed were "Lorelei, you're bleeding!"

Taking her by the elbows, he helped her to her feet and plucked shards of broken shells from her torso. He murmured that they would have to rinse the sand from the abrasions with fresh water. The speedily way in which he took charge, directing her to do this, directing her to do that—he'd gone into emergency-Captain mode, because doing something was easier than doing nothing, but it was just as much of a response to shock has her own flailing hands.

She didn't care about the shells embedding her body. It was the scales she wanted out. Had they been here all this time? All these years, lurking beneath the surface? The thought sickened her stomach. Wherever they disappeared to inside her body, she wanted them gone. They did not belong there or anywhere on her person.

Gritting her teeth, Lorelei bent to dig into the sides of her legs but stopped when she finally noticed her clawed, webbed hands. Holding them out in front of her, she cried, "What the actual fuck?"

Taking her transformed hands into his, Killian flipped them over, a half-hearted joke on his lips, "Yeah, I wasn't going to say anything, but your nail polish is ruined."

Looking at the chipped remains of cherry red, Lorelei choked out a sound halfway between a laugh and a sob. "I don't understand," she gasped. "How?"

Killian's normally calm eyes betrayed a storm of emotions—shock, confusion, fear, and something else she couldn't identify amongst the others. "How the shit should I know? I never would've imagined something like this were possible."

A chill breeze blew off the ocean, and Lorelei felt a strange crawling sensation across her neck when the cold air brushed the skin. Reaching up to touch, she screeched. It didn't hurt, but her fingers grazed over three deep slashes on either side of her neck.

Pulling her hands away, he gently brushed back her hair and

inspected the source of her alarm. "Shh." Even though his hands trembled and his voice shook, he was trying to soothe her. "They look like gills. And now they're disappearing."

Both observations were stated as facts. Reporting exactly what he was seeing because processing wasn't in the cards right now. All that was happening right now was just too much to be born with critical thought. And fuck it all to hell, Lorelei *felt* that.

Like with the scales, her neck tingled as the skin stitched itself back together. She groaned, burying her face in her hands, as her body spasmed with every new and unfamiliar sensation. Killian pulled her into a tight hug, and she wished it was the comfort she needed at this moment.

Stomach growling, his scent elicited a deep, unexpected pang of hunger, and as she peered with disturbing interest at the pulsating vein in his neck through her fingers, she was overcome by an all-consuming urge to bite him.

Just a taste. A small, unnoticeable nibble…

Blood, pulse, flesh.

She lunged.

Her teeth came down hard on her own forearm, instantaneously clearing her mind of predatory thoughts.

Killian jumped back, quick as a cat, and cursed. "What the hell you do that for?"

Overwhelmed by emotion and throbbing pain, tears streamed down Lorelei's face. *What the hell is wrong with me?* Clutching her bleeding arm, she sobbed. "I don't know what came over me. I just—" But she couldn't finish. How could she tell him that for a moment she was going to take a bite out of his neck?

Not only had she thought about it and wanted to—some animalistic instinct overrode all her human sensibilities. If she hadn't enough presence of mind to throw up an arm, she would have torn out a chunk of Killian's neck. And once she did that, she wasn't sure she could have stopped herself from ripping him apart. The merfolk who devoured *The Osprey* crew certainly showed no restraint.

God, I am one of them. The screams of her crew echoed in her memory, and blood tainted water both fouled and disturbingly delighted her tongue. She felt nauseated. *I'm not human.*

"Lorelei, you're shaking. Let's go inside, clean up, gather our thoughts, and talk about this. Okay?" She nodded numbly.

Killian walked alongside her but did not reach out to touch her again.

Inside, the call of the sea and her animal hunger still beckoned but considerably less than at the water's edge. Killian led the way upstairs and instructed her to climb into the bathtub. While she ran the water, adjusting it to get the temperature right, he gathered the medical supplies he kept in the cabinet under the bathroom sink.

As they rinsed the sand from her body and cleaned her wounds, the remaining markers of her transformation mercifully retracted, though her nail beds and gums ached from the unexpected use. Thank God these changes weren't permanent. How else would she hide claws and webbed fingers? Move to the northern wilds of Canada, wear mittens year-round, and avoid people at all costs?

Fuck. Humor wasn't helping.

"For most of my life, I've been a fisherman, and I've never seen anything to hint that mermaids existed," Killian began, breaking the silence. His hands trembled as recapped a bottle of antiseptic, looking so lost and confused, simultaneously in denial while also self-doubting, like he just happened to miss something factual about the natural world. Something as commonplace as knowing deep sea creatures like angler fish exist but not big fin squid. "The stories had to have come from somewhere," he continued. "And I hadn't known to look. Right?"

He stared and stared and stared like he was looking to her as if *she* had the answers. But this was several layers of bonkers. One, mermaids weren't real. And two, she was a Midwesterner for crying out loud. What business did she have being a secret, mythical sea creature?

"There's no denying what you are," he continued, swiping a hand over his mouth. *Oh, she could deny it plenty for the both of them.* "Seeing's believing, yeah? And you can't be the only one. In all that ocean, in those vast, fathomless depths, there's got to be more of your kind out there."

As he gave voice to that truth, a glimmer of wonder and excitement shone through. Then he was smiling and that made her queasy.

"Aren't you afraid?" She leaned forward, dripping water down the side of the porcelain tub as she folded her arms across the edge. Because he really, really should be.

His growing smile wavered. He glanced down at her mouth, her hands, and gulped. "I'm a little nervous about the claws and fangs, if I'm being honest, but you being a mermaid doesn't change the way I feel about you." Despite his lingering anxiety being plain to see in his shaking hands, the more he spoke, the surer, steadier his voice became. It was like his head and heart were ignoring what his body knew—that he was in the midst of a dangerous predator. "It's strange and bizarre, but for someone who's spent most of his life at sea, since meeting you, I've never been happier to see the shore. And what sailor hasn't fantasized about the love of a beautiful woman with fins and a come-hither smile?"

By the time he finished, he was wearing a small lopsided grin.

Brave man. Trying to be optimistic for the both of them.

She didn't deserve that.

Tears streamed down her cheeks, but when Killian instinctively reached out to embrace her, she held up her hand in warning. "I don't trust myself right now."

He froze, waiting for her explanation.

As she recounted her blocked memory from the night of the storm, they both sat cross-legged—her within the tub and him without. He listened quietly, patiently, until she said her crewmates had been eaten. That's when he finally paled, staring down at the bandage they'd wrapped around her arm.

"So, that's why you bit yourself? So, you wouldn't bite me?" Killian rubbed his arms with a vulnerability she'd never seen before.

Nodding, hot tears of shame burned her eyes. "I've been feeling this hunger recently. I couldn't explain it before, why I suddenly despised normal food, but this is the explanation. I'm a fucking people-eating mermaid who gets by on a little raw fish." She ran a shaky hand through her tangled, salt-encrusted hair.

And just like that, his tender, supportive switch flipped back on. "Hey," he coaxed, cupping her face, and brushing away the tears with his thumbs. "You aren't the same. The creatures you saw are feral, wild. You are not."

She hugged her knees. "How can this be happening? And why now?"

"I don't know, Lorelei," he replied, but as he said it, realization dawned. His hands slid from her face to rub her shoulders. He began slowly, "Maybe…You'd never been in the ocean before *The Osprey*, right?" She nodded. "Maybe exposure to salt water triggered it. Maybe… when you were thrown overboard in the storm, it was a survival instinct. A response to the trauma."

Lorelei stared blankly at his chest as a chill ran down her spine, mind reeling. *It's been in me all along. Left on a doorstep with an ominous note.* Killian brushed back her hair and murmured her name. She finally met his eyes.

"A sea monster raised by humans," she said out loud and remembered the mother of her heart—a tiny German woman with a fierce love of law and justice. "I wish I could talk to her right now," she muttered quietly.

Understanding whom she meant, Killian replied, "I know."

"Do you think she would still love me if she knew the truth?"

Without missing a beat, he answered, "Definitely. She raised you. Hell, we haven't known each other long, and I'm still hanging around."

"But why? Other than this obviously being your house."

He folded his arms across the edge of the tub. "I'm really into you. Even with these new surprises, you are still you. And I genuinely think that having an honest conversation about it means we can also work through it. I don't know about you, but I would definitely prefer to deal with this insanity together than alone."

Lorelei gazed at him in wonder. "I don't deserve you."

Killian shook his head. "I'm calling bullshit on that one."

"Aren't you afraid I might lose control and hurt you?"

"I'm not going to lie, I don't think I'm going to let you go down on me for a while," he teased.

She snorted, a flash of cheer cutting through her gloomy mood. "I don't blame you."

"But I see no reason to condemn a relationship for something that has never happened."

"Killian, you really amaze me. Despite the circumstances, I am very glad we met." And even though he'd witnessed first-hand the row of sharp teeth that hid within her gums, he kissed her. Thankfully, it did not elicit any untoward hunger. She would never forgive herself if she hurt him.

When they parted, Killian suggested, "Maybe we should call Lila about this."

No way. "I can't tell my potential future boss!"

"Your potential future boss is a marine biologist. She's a good person to have in your corner."

Lorelei shook her head. "I don't want to tell her."

Caught between night and the coming sunrise, the next morning's gray dimness peered in through the window and roused Lorelei from a fitful sleep. But given how the night had gone, she had little hope of falling back to sleep. Even with Killian's comforting arms wrapped snugly around her, quieting her mind proved impossible after what she discovered about the night of the storm and herself. So not to wake Killian, she quietly slipped out of bed and dressed.

The ocean's call still tugged upon her soul, but more in gentle reminder than demand. She sensed no harm in going outside for fresh air and contemplation, the monstrous behavior that had possessed her had passed.

Sitting down on the sand and hugging her knees, Lorelei watched the waves as they rolled in, gouging the shoreline with greedy claws. Her mind raced with so many questions.

How did a daughter of the sea end up on a judge's front doorstep in Marquette, Michigan? Did the person who placed her there know what she was? Had she been siren-named on purpose? And why did they choose to give her to whom they did? Was it intentional? Coincidental?

If Mom were still here, what would she make of all this?

Out there somewhere in that great expansive ocean, Lorelei had merfolk parents—the predatory, people-eating kind—a far cry from anything warm, familial, or functional. This wasn't Disney, and she was no Little Mermaid. Still, she wondered where they were—if they were even alive—and how a monster of the deep came to be part of this world above the waves.

And her crewmates—how horribly they had died at the hands of her kind. She shuddered at the memory. Why were they there? Did the merfolk tail *The Osprey* through the storm, a ship of old, waiting for the opportune moment to strike? Did they do the same with modern boats?

Even in retrospect, she'd never heard or seen anything that could have been a mermaid attack but was explained away as something else. The bite on her arm looked nothing like a shark bite. It didn't look human either. And she reasoned that plenty of people survived the open ocean, and concluded that, on many fronts, *The Osprey* was likely in the wrong place at the wrong time.

Lorelei doubted she would ever get solid answers to these questions, but her mind still puzzled over them. Absentmindedly, she picked up a rock and chucked it out into the water, making a satisfying *kurplunk!* when it hit.

How was she going to tell Kat? Was she a danger to her, to Killian, and everyone else? That, she supposed, would be answered in time. There was plenty of evidence to suggest she was capable of great harm— the deep, jagged bite wound she'd given herself, for starters. But she clung to Killian's belief that she was different. That being raised human gave her human inhibitions and control.

And then there were the questions that excited her the more she gazed out over the water—a literal ocean full of possibilities. *How fast can I swim? How deep can I dive? Can I breathe underwater indefinitely? What mysteries will I discover, and what wonders will I see?*

Moving far away from the ocean and pretending everything was normal was an option, but she didn't want to do that. Not unless she became a real threat to others. Her mother had always said 'when you're dealt a tough hand make the most out of it.' In this case, she took it to mean that she should try to figure this out and embrace it, at least the bits that didn't include eating people.

Maybe something good would come from the ordeal.

The sun had fully risen by the time Killian joined her on the beach. He sat beside her with a huff. "Been out here thinking?"

She nodded. "There's a lot to think about."

He rubbed her back, large soothing circles along her spine. "I have to take the boat back out, much sooner than expected," he told her ruefully.

"Today?"

He nodded. "There's an ocean storm due to hit our fishing area later this week. We need to get out there and back before it hits." Lorelei fell silent. Maybe this was too much for him to handle after all. She really couldn't blame him, but it made her feel awful.

Reading her thoughts, Killian explained, "I'm really sorry, Lorelei. I'm not creating a work trip to get away from you, I promise. I really hate the idea of leaving you right now, but we need to bring in catch so I can pay my crew."

Detecting no lie, she smiled weakly, relieved at least to hear that. "It's okay, I understand. And I'll be all right."

"You sure? I could call Lila or Kat for you."

She shook her head. "I'm tougher than I look."

"You are, but I'm still going to worry."

"Don't," Lorelei reassured him, watching herself burrow her toes into the sand. "I'm going to use this time to figure myself out. And I know you need to figure some things out, too."

"Lorelei, I've already figured out that I'm standing by you." He leaned in, searching out her eyes.

Meeting his gaze, she touched his cheek. "Please, while you're gone, use the time apart to let that choice, and all that comes with it, sink in. This has been a whirlwind romance from the start—I won't be mad if you change your mind."

His eyes flared, first with anger, then fierce determination as the corners of his mouth twitched upward into sly grin. Placing his hand on her knee, he promised in a low, rasping voice, "I'll think it all over very seriously. And when I return, I will tell you the exact same thing, tear off your clothes, and make you scream with pleasure." He kissed her forehead with a gentleness that belayed the ferocity of his words. And stood. "I have to go get ready," he stated bluntly, and walked back to the cottage, leaving her speechless.

Killian hated being the reason for the crestfallen look on Lorelei's face when he told her he was leaving. But he was responsible for both his crew's safety and their pay. When he checked the NOAA app on his phone, as he did every morning, it displayed the oncoming storm as plain as day. He had to move up *Dawn Chaser's* timetable so they didn't miss that week's offshore run entirely.

As they pulled away from the pier, Killian texted Lorelei: *I can't wait to see you again. Third date?* If Lorelei responded, it wasn't in time to reach him before he lost cell service, but finalizing plans wasn't his aim. He just wanted her to know that he was thinking about her and eager to come back.

Killian had panicked when he woke to find Lorelei missing again, terrified that the ocean had beckoned, and she answered its call never to return.

While witnessing Lorelei's transformation had been shocking, and he didn't yet know how this change might impact his life, it didn't make him want to come home to her any less. Whatever lay ahead, he wanted to try figuring it out together. And if he was being perfectly honest with himself, he found this new layer of intrigue alluring. The glowing eyes, the almost too-wide wicked smile. Even the teeth, claws, and scales did not bother him. He might even be seduced by them.

If she'd responded any differently to her hankering for human flesh, he would have ended their relationship for his own safety, but Lorelei still possessed all her human faculties and sanity. He could deal with an accidental nip here or incidental scratch there. What worried him more was that Lorelei might try to distance herself in fear of accidentally hurting him or decide that this fledgling romance was more trouble than it was worth.

During his downtime in the days to come, Killian would think about ravishing his lovely Lorelei, and what he could do to erase any remaining doubts she had about his feelings. She was right about the progression of their relationship being a whirlwind, but it wasn't fleeting.

Later that night, Branson temporarily relieved him from the helm so he could stretch his legs and get some fresh air. He made a few rounds about the deck, nodding to Walsh who was coiling line, and then leaned over the side to enjoy the ocean breeze and a moment of peace.

Lost in thought, he intently watched the water stream past the boat as they moved. They hit a patch of bioluminescent plankton that left a glowing blue trail behind them—a biological marvel Lila sometimes called "enchanting."

That's when he noticed a dark, streamlined shape moving alongside the boat. He stared at its barely visible silhouette beneath the surface and searched for more distinguishing features. But all he caught was a glimpse of its tail fin as it dove. It couldn't be one of them, could it? If merfolk were following them and a storm is due... His heart raced over the implications. But it wasn't supposed to hit until later this week.

The memory of a torn, bloody immersion suit flashed across his mind, and Killian's blood ran cold. He envisioned his own men in the water and gripped the railing in front of him to steady his trembling hands. *We need to get back to shore.*

The creature breached, blowing a geyser of water at him. Killian leapt back swearing.

It had only been a porpoise playing in the boat's wake.

"A little jumpy, eh Captain?" Walsh chuckled.

Killian swiped a hand over his mouth, suddenly understanding how a little grog could make a sailor see mermaids in the place of porpoises and manatees. "Yeah, that one got me."

"Porpoise?"

"Yup."

Shaking his head amusedly, Walsh stowed a length of coiled line in a deck box. "You've been daydreaming a lot today. Anything on your mind that you want to talk about?"

Killian stuffed his hands in his pockets. "Lorelei and I have gone on a couple dates."

Walsh smiled. "I knew she liked you."

"It's starting to get pretty serious," Killian added.

The old fisherman came over, and leaned next him, arms folding across his chest. "Just be careful and use your head. The lady's been through some traumatic things recently. So, take your time. You'll both be thankful later that you didn't rush it."

Killian nodded but didn't know what could be done at this point. That ship had already sailed.

CHAPTER
TWENTY

Resisting the call of the ocean, Lorelei did not go near the water for several days. To escape its constant pull, she lugged all her museum exhibition materials to and from the public library each day, working from open until close. When she had to return to the cottage for the evening, she shut herself in her room with her work and blasted music to drown out the sound of the waves and sea breeze. Not hearing them helped some, but the call was in her blood, in her bones. She could not ignore it forever.

The more time passed with Killian still away, the stronger the ocean's call grew, seizing its opportunity to lure her into its grasp. Succumbing to it and her curiosity, Lorelei abandoned her work on her desk one morning and walked down to the beach. She stripped down to her skin and obediently entered the waves. Her entire body tingled and itched from the change, but she resisted the urge to scratch. At first, having scales only appear on the sides of her legs confused her, but the moment she pressed her legs together, the expected scales wrapped around her like a cocoon.

Sitting down on wet, hard-packed sand, Lorelei watched her feet stretch out into fins, gasping at the bright colors that emerged. Brilliant yellows, blues, and greens fanned out from where her feet used to be.

Flexing up and down at the ankle joint, Lorelei's tail fin waved before her, fluid, silky, and horizontally oriented like flukes.

When the tide rolled in, and cold water rushed over her lap, she did not shiver.

The waves rolled out, and Lorelei slid her hands down her tail in wonder, the dark blue and silver scales cool and smooth to the touch. They shimmered in the light at the slightest movement. Bending forward, Lorelei touched her fins, piscine in texture, and a smile cracked across her face.

Pliable translucent bumps formed rows and columns along scale and skin. They must have been the bioluminescent nodes she'd seen glowing green in the dark murk.

And her torso… she ran her hands along her length, pausing to rap against her ribcage. It was harder. Sturdier, like subdermal plate armor.

With the next set of waves, Lorelei swam out into the cove.

Sheer force of habit, she held her breath, staying near the surface. But as water rushed past her gills and filtered oxygen out of the water, she remembered she didn't have to. The lack of breathing in and out was disorienting, but no discomfort followed. If she didn't actively think about it, it wasn't too unsettling.

Would she still get the bends? A question for another time. Making herself sick on the first swim wouldn't pave any roads to self-acceptance. She carefully swam deeper, taking the dive in increments, down until she touched the ocean floor. Just because she could.

The bottom was rocky, littered with the same large boulders found along most of Maine's coastline, interrupted only by patches of muck and seaweed.

Lorelei experimented with her fins to see how far a flick, a slap, and a full-body undulation would send her. She did somersaults, backflips, and twirls. It was amazing how little power and effort it took to whiz through the water, and how much dexterity she'd gained. Many summers she'd spent swimming in Lake Superior, and even that one year she swam on the high school swim team, she had been a painfully slow by comparison. Her legs were practically useless in the water, save for keeping her afloat and eventually getting her from point A to B.

Distances it used to take minutes to cross, she zipped through in seconds.

Once familiar with her shifted form, Lorelei explored the cove more thoroughly, examining the underwater rocks and seeking out critters to observe in their natural habitats. It wasn't until the sun began to set that she realized she'd spent an entire day out in the ocean. The water took on the eerie green tint from her restored memories, sacrificing color for night visibility.

A cold shiver ran down her spine, suddenly feeling exposed and vulnerable out in the open. She glanced over her shoulder, half expecting to see gleaming blue-eyes staring back. But there was nothing. She was considering swimming back to shore when a school of fish swam by. Her stomach grumbled.

Lashing out, she set upon them, snatching one from its path and tearing into it with her teeth—a series of instinctive reactions all made in a matter of seconds. She took pleasure feeling the fish struggle, then twitch in its last throes of life between her teeth. Its flesh and blood were sweet on her tongue, and she groaned with delight, half-drunk on its taste and with predatory satisfaction. The school scattered as she heartily consumed the hapless creature.

Once its bones were picked clean, she continued to hunt, gorging herself on fish after fish until her hunger was sated.

What she had done didn't sink in until after she licked her last victim off her fingers.

Nausea set in.

While she hadn't done the unthinkable and eaten a person, she took disturbing pleasure in the experience of eating something alive. If she had caught the fish, smashed its head on a rock and then eaten it raw, she wouldn't have given it that much thought afterwards. But the vicious delight in devouring it while it died flew in the face of all her human sensibilities.

The sun had gone down completely when she returned to shore, stomach full and mind heavy. After thoroughly washing out her mouth and showering, she sat down at her desk with a mug of hot tea, needing a distraction. Pulling Lila's files in front of her, Lorelei worked on drafting exhibits for several hours.

It was well past midnight when she stopped, and yet, she wasn't tired enough to override the gears spinning in her head. Her brain hurt too much to continue. She needed something mundane to do. Her nails were still terribly chipped...

Rooting around her nail polish box, she blindly selected a new color.

Blood red.

CHAPTER

TWENTY-ONE

EVERY TIME LORELEI SHIFTED AND EXPLORED THE VAST world beneath the waves, it became harder and harder to locate the part of herself that had been human. Each time she swam out, she ventured further and further away from shore, seduced by her birthright and the wonders of the unknown.

She'd been wrong to think of Killian as a riptide pulling her away from shore, hopelessly lost to the depths of desire. That was this hidden thing inside her—a mermaid, a siren, a creature of the sea—and its unwillingness to resist the call of the deep and the taste of human flesh. This terrifying hunger and desire to rend burned within her.

To stave off the worst of it, she hunted live fish.

But, as best she could put it, it was like eating a salad when what she really craved was a thick, juicy burger with all the fixings. If only her dilemma were as mundane as sticking to a 'diet.' Lorelei mourned her loss of taste for human food and was disgusted by what had replaced it.

While hunting a school of live fish, trying to ease her hunger pains, the warbled sounds of a woman talking drew her attention. Lorelei shrunk down behind an underwater rock, clutching her growling stomach. She waited but the woman on the surface did not go away, and instead sat down on the rock above to continue talking to herself, unsuspecting of the danger she was in.

As minutes ticked by, her hunger grew malignant, carnivorous greed thrumming through her veins.

Closing her eyes, she tried desperately to quash it, forget the woman was there, or swim away. But frozen in place, she was unable to do any of those things. So, as she usually did to overcome mental hurdles, she began to sing her favorite sea shanty, opening with the chorus:

Way hay and up she rises,
Way hay and up she rises,
Way hay and up she rises,
Early in the morning.

Hearing small splashes nearby, she opened her eyes and saw the woman kicking her feet through the water.

As a shark smells blood, Lorelei smelled human flesh, and her predatory instincts kicked into overdrive. Before human inhibition could retake control, she struck out at whiplash speed and grabbed the ankles of her prey.

Yanking the poor woman under with inhuman strength, frantic screams rang through Lorelei's ears, bubbling the water around them with precious, expelled air. She marveled with murderous glee at how she could not only smell the woman's flesh but her fear—a thick and heady scent that tickled her tongue. The ocean all around pulsed in time with the woman's rapid heartbeat, pounding in Lorelei's ears, begging her to sate her hunger at last. Her mouth, filled with razor-sharp teeth, watered at the savory meal before her, waiting to be devoured.

Giving thanks to the ocean for this gift of human flesh, Lorelei wrenched the woman's leg to her mouth, sunk her teeth into the calf muscle and tore.

Sweet, sweet flesh filled Lorelei's mouth as the woman thrashed, a surge in fear and pain saturating the frigid water as much as crimson blood. She dug her claws in to hold the woman in place as she savored the taste and swallowed, thrown into a profound euphoria, a high she never wanted to come down from.

Why had she ever held herself back from this joy?

Licking away the blood from her lips, a delicacy she'd craved for far too long, ecstasy and relief overwhelmed her. It was so much like climaxing.

And just like that, with the memory of Killian gazing up at her, eyes hooded in bliss, Lorelei came to her senses.

As if zapped, she released the woman and, for the first time, got a good look at her face, registered her sluggish pulse. *Carrie.* In full panic mode, Lorelei grabbed her arm and shot to the surface. It took maybe a matter of seconds, but the fight had already left the other woman—limp-limbed either from shock or having drowned.

Shit, shit, shit. I think I've killed her.

Lorelei dragged Carrie's unconscious body out of the water and onto the sand. Darting behind the rocks where she hid her clothes, she dressed in record time. Then running back to the woman's side, she checked for a pulse—faint, but still there. Throwing herself into CPR, Lorelei was twelve chest compressions in when Carrie sputtered up water. She turned the woman onto her side and held her while she coughed. Her lower leg wound bled profusely.

Having nothing better to use, Lorelei pulled a sock from the pocket she'd stuffed it in and pressed it to Carrie's calf. In a no-nonsense tone that masked her guilt and panic, Lorelei instructed Carrie to hold it in place and apply pressure. Carrie nodded, all color leaching from her face with a fresh wave of pain.

Lorelei ran to the cottage for gauze and medical tape.

When she returned, Carrie lay curled up on the sand, groaning in agony.

Stomach still roiling with hunger pangs barely tempered by human revulsion, Lorelei had to turn her head away. "Okay, you can let go now." She placed her hand over Carrie's. When the woman's fingers slipped out from beneath hers, Lorelei threw the bloody sock away and quickly replaced it with a wad of gauze.

A sea breeze kicked up and she silently thanked it for carrying away the tangy, metallic scent. She tightly bound the packing in place with the remaining gauze and medical tape. Carrie croaked hoarsely, "What happened?"

Lorelei helped her to her feet, lying with such smooth ease it made her want to vomit. "I saw you hanging out by the rocks. I'd just come out to talk to you when you went in the water. I went in after you."

"Oh." Carrie's face scrunched up in confusion.

"Come on. Put your arm around my neck," Lorelei ordered. "We need to get you to a hospital. You've got a pretty nasty bite on your leg and water in your lungs." Carrie nodded listlessly and hopped to the car. After buckling her in, Lorelei jumped in the driver's seat and sped to the hospital. "Did you see what bit you?" She glanced over at Carrie.

The woman shook her head and winced. "No. Just a bunch of red. But I could have sworn I felt hands—clawed hands—grab my ankles and pull me in. What could do that?"

"I don't know," Lorelei lied, glancing at her badly chipped red nail polish. Fuck. Was that a chunk of skin under them? She gripped the steering wheel tighter to hide the evidence of what she'd done. "Whatever it was, it was gone by the time I got to you. Maybe I scared it away?"

"Yeah, maybe. We'd both be in trouble if it had attacked you, too."

Silence fell in the car. A long, awkward pause later, Lorelei ventured, "What were you doing there? Did you come by hoping to talk to Killian?"

Carrie ground her teeth in pain. "No. Not exactly. I knew *Dawn Chaser* was out at sea because my cousin is on the crew. So, I didn't expect to run into him, but I do want to talk to him—eventually. I hoped that by going out there, I might figure out what to say." When Lorelei didn't say anything, Carrie continued, "I don't know what possessed me to put my feet in the water—it's fucking cold—and yet, I just really wanted to do it all of a sudden. Never fucking going back there again."

If Lorelei hadn't nearly killed this woman, she would have leapt for joy. "Carrie," she reasoned, "creature in the water or not, you shouldn't be coming onto Killian's property. It's trespassing."

"I nearly fucking died, Lori," Carrie snapped. "So, cut me some slack on the stalker ex-girlfriend bullshit."

Lorelei cringed at the name shortening. "It's Lorelei, and are you stalking him?"

"No!" Carrie slapped the passenger side window in anger. "I just—ugh. Who am I kidding? You wouldn't understand."

"Try me."

Carrie eyed her skeptically. "Fine. That place is an extension of Killian. All I want is to be close to him without actually being close to him. Do you get it? It's more of an emotional fix."

"Yeah, I get it. But you really need to move on and going there isn't helping. You're just torturing yourself."

"I keep telling myself that." Carrie slumped her shoulders in defeat. "And yet, here I am, bleeding from my leg in his girlfriend's car."

Lorelei had nothing to say to that. At a red light, Carrie lifted her leg and tried to pull back the bandage to peek at the wound. "Oh my God!" she yelped.

"Don't touch it!"

Carrie's head fell back against the headrest, looking a little grey around the edges. "What could do this?"

"I don't know. Maybe an eel or a small shark?"

"An eel. Or a shark," Carrie murmured numbly when they pulled up to the emergency room doors. And not for the first or last time that day, Lorelei felt horrible.

If it hadn't been for the thought of Killian, a lighthouse beacon in an almost impenetrable fog, she would have surrendered to her animal hunger completely and killed Carrie.

That's when she knew Killian was not a riptide but a guiding light showing her the way home. As lovely a thought as that was, she didn't think it would work very much longer. She needed help. And Lila was the only person she knew who could potentially provide it. If she took a life, Carrie's or someone else's, her humanity would wither away and nothing, not even Killian, could save her from that self-destruction.

CHAPTER
TWENTY-TWO

THE CLOSE CALL WITH CARRIE, THE HUNGER, HAUNTED HER.

Throwing herself into work probably wasn't the healthiest coping mechanism, but it was the one Lorelei knew best. She'd done it after her mom's death, and she was doing it now. When everything went to shit, work was at least something she still had control over.

While she felt confident about her museum exhibit proofs, and her second interview prep, doubt crept in. Something as good as a job couldn't come out of this week, especially not since her post-interview plan was to out herself as a people-eating mermaid.

Monsters like her didn't deserve good things.

There was no way of predicting how badly the marine biologist might react to her secret. Fear. Disbelief. All likely scenarios. But maybe instead of agreeing to help, Lila would have her locked up. Kept for research.

It was a terrifying prospect, and yet, no matter how bad the possible outcome, she had to come clean. Living in fear of herself and for others was not an option.

Looking in her car's visor mirror, Lorelei frowned at her reflection.

Cold compresses and makeup barely hid the visible bags under her eyes, but nothing could hide the monstrous creature that lurked beneath. Staring at her mouth—a mouth that had now consumed human flesh—her stomach turned.

She smacked the visor back into place.

Grabbing her coffee and briefcase, she entered the research center, a red brick building with a modern interior, and signed in at the security desk. An office assistant led Lorelei to Lila's office, making cheery comments along the way about their state-of-the-art facilities, but Lorelei barely registered any of it beyond the glass doors and clinical white walls and tiling.

All she could do was put one foot in front of the other.

Lila's office was warmer than the rest of the building—that much she noticed. The walls were lined with marine animal photography, framed degrees, and awards. Potted native Maine plants clustered together on the windowsill behind her desk. Joe-pye weed, maybe. Some New England asters.

Outside, through a piney tree line, glimpses of the ocean beyond peeked through the gaps between branches.

Lorelei looked away sharply, making eye contact with the marine biologist instead. Her dark, rich browns shone with warmth and excitement. That should have been encouraging, but shame and guilt made Lorelei's stomach churn with nausea. Pretty soon the scientist would learn how unsuitable an employee she'd be.

Portfolio great. Background check? Doomed to fail as soon as she disclosed that she might want to eat her coworkers.

After greetings, Lila sat down to review the proofs, her smile growing wider and wider as she flipped through the layout diagrams and concept art. "How long did you spend on these?"

"About twelve to fourteen hours a day." Nothing like ignoring personal problems to improve work ethic.

The scientist blinked a couple times, surprised. "Well, you're hired," she said, closing Lorelei's portfolio with a firm pat. "And as I promised, I'll pay you for the time you've already spent working on the project. Email me a log of your hours, and on Monday, we can talk about budget and logistics."

That cut through her daze. She expected more discussion. "Wait, really?"

Chuckling, Lila nodded. "I think we are going to make a great team."

Not long ago, Lorelei would have gushed over the good news, but now she plastered a smile on her face and pretended she felt anything but numb.

"I think so, too, Dr. Branson." Though she shook Lila's hand firmly, her words felt hollow. *I don't deserve this.*

"And please, when it's just us, or we are around family, call me Lila."

First name-basis with her scientific superstar new boss? Yet another victory she couldn't truly enjoy. Nausea intensifying with dread, she withdrew her hand from the handshake to wipe her clammy palms on the back of her slacks. It was now or never.

"Can I talk to you about something else?" Her voice trembled, sounding every bit guilty and about to confess wrongdoing.

Worry pinched Lila's brow, but her eyes remained warm, open. Sympathetic, too. Maybe she thought she was about to bring up *The Osprey*. "What's up?"

The words Lorelei rehearsed clogged in her throat, her mind whirring with self-doubt. But moments of awkward silence ticked by, and Lila's patience waned. She forced out, "Actually, it will be easier if I show you. It's at Killian's by the water." Then cringed. That sounded a little shady.

Arching her brow, Lila folded her arms across her chest. "Okay, that's a little cryptic. Can you be a little more descriptive?"

"I'm really not sure how to explain it," she trailed. Oh this was not going well. "You'll just have to see in person."

Conflict warred on her new boss's face. "All right. Let's go," she resigned, grabbing her car keys. Her ultimate decision to humor Lorelei was openly precipitated by a 'fuck it' expression. If it weren't for their mutual connection to Killian, Lorelei doubted Lila would have entertained this bizarre request.

They drove separately.

In her own car, Lorelei tried several breathing exercises to quell her nerves, but her arms prickled with goosebumps, and she frequently wiped sweat from the palms of her hands. It only got worse when they arrived, her resolve faltering.

Staring blankly at the rolling waves over the steering wheel, she thought, *this is a mistake.* It took remembering the taste of flesh and blood in her mouth, and how delicious it was, to propel herself out of the car.

Chickening out came at a steep price she refused to pay.

She beckoned Lila to follow her.

Kicking off their heels, they walked down to the water's edge. There, Lorelei shrugged out of her blazer and draped it across a boulder with trembling hands. Ignoring Lila's intense stare, she inhaled deeply and patched her fractured fortitude by again reminding herself that literal lives were at stake. She waded out to her waist to trigger the transformation.

"Lorelei, what are you doing?" Lila glanced nervously back at her car, undoubtedly already thinking about booking it out of here. Not that she blamed her.

"Give it a second."

As the water caressed her skin, the changes to her body began. Webbing formed between her fingers and her nails extended into razor sharp claws.

Lila's jaw dropped.

"Am I seeing things?" she asked, rubbing her eyes.

If only. Lorelei spread her fingers so Lila could see them better.

Shock shifted to scientific wonder. "Oh my God, would you look at that!"

That was…promising.

Now having secured the marine biologist's attention, Lorelei explained the need to remove her clothes for the full metamorphosis to occur.

"Okay, go ahead." The scientist stared in wild fascination, stepping closer to the water.

"Stay on the beach," Lorelei warned, holding up a clawed hand.

Though a little confused, Lila nodded and did not take another step forward. But she did pin Lorelei with an intense gaze, every bit the marine biologist trained to catch even the most miniscule details.

Dissecting her for study.

Steeling herself, Lorelei tossed her dress and then her underwear onto the sand before sinking beneath the waves. Her bralette stayed on since nothing changed about her torso. Clinging to any iota of modesty was a bit pointless when she'd already flashed her boss, but cling to it she did.

Pressing her legs together, the skin fused, and a layer of scales protracted from her subcutaneous tissue. Her feet expanded and stretched into fins. Unlike the characters in werewolf movies, TV shows, and books, her shifting bones didn't cause her excruciating pain. It was more like a deep, tingling yogic stretch.

With a snap of her tail, Lorelei shot fifty feet away from shore and back, water rushing past unsealed gills. All traces of humanity shed.

She surfaced at waist level and pushed back her hair so Lila could see the three identical slits along her neck.

"Those are...You can...?" Lila spoke in halting sentences, watching the visible flaps of skin gradually disappear.

"This is how I survived the storm." While she didn't remember the gills, they had to be what saved her. It was the only thing about her survival that made sense. "They seal shut when I'm above water."

"Whoa. Okay, do it again," Lila replied, as giddy as a kid in a candy store. "I want to look more closely this time."

Curiosity and wonderment over fear? That was closer to acceptance than Lorelei could've possibly hoped. If the scientist wanted to see how the gills worked again, she'd show her again.

Ducking back under, she waited for the ocean's touch to reopen her gills. As her eyes adjusted to the salty murk, everything beneath the water slid into focus, its silty opacity more of an annoyance than a hinderance.

Then she heard sloshing.

With a predator's acute awareness, she snapped her head in the direction of the sound, spying Lila's legs as she waded through the water.

Shit.

Curiosity getting the best of a scientist? She should have anticipated this. The call to see and to touch was just too much to ignore for the naturally and professionally curious.

Panic seized her, but it was a human enough faculty to keep her from lunging. She swished her tail, prepared to swim away at breakneck speed, but nausea and self-revulsion quelled her urge to bite and kept her humanity at the forefront of her mind.

But that might not last if they weren't careful.

She took a moment to collect herself before popping back up. "Lila, I need you to take a step back." Despite the bile rising at the back of her throat, saliva pooled in her mouth and her hunger flared.

Lila heeded the stern tone, but her forehead wrinkled in confusion. "I'm sorry. Curiosity got the best of me. But, um, why do I need to stay away?"

How to put this without making her run away screaming? "I have… animal instincts I don't have control over. And your scent intensifies it."

Thank God, Lila didn't question that and took a few more steps back. "How's this?"

The wind kicked up, blowing Lila's scent away, and Lorelei relaxed a bit. "That's better."

Craning her head for a better view, Lila asked, "So how does it feel when your gills open and close?"

"Kinda itchy."

"Fascinating," Lila drawled, her eyes burning with scientific awe. Although her feet stayed planted, the marine biologist leaned forward and raised her hand. To touch.

Lorelei flinched away.

"Oh, gosh." Lila straightened. "How did I forget myself already? I'm sorry…"

Sighing, Lorelei tucked her hands underneath her arms. This was going to be a reoccurring problem. "Maybe—maybe, if I hold my breath? But you *have* to promise to get back as soon as I tell you to."

"I promise."

Pinching her nose, Lorelei waved her forward. Lila approached slowly as if to soothe a frightened animal, not with the caution paid to a predator. Dammit. She probably should have disclosed the exact nature of her animal instincts.

As Lila gently pressed and prodded along her gills, Lorelei squeezed her eyes shut, trying to concentrate on holding her breath and keeping the monster within in check. *Don't eat your boss. Don't eat your boss.*

Lila withdrew, far sooner than expected. "Does that hurt?" she asked, worried.

"I don't really feel much." But it was weird.

"Limited nerve endings then. Was this an erogenous zone for you, pre-transmutation?"

A blush crept onto her cheeks. "It was. But I don't know about now."

"Weird," Lila drawled. "But fascinating."

Lungs stinging, Lorelei waved Lila back so she could breathe. She sucked in a breath as soon as Lila was a comfortable distance away. Although Lila's scent still hung in the air, and laced her nose and tongue, the talking, coupled with her own curiosity, helped. The urgency in her hunger pains lessened, too. "Any thoughts why?"

"No idea," Lila marveled, leaning forward once more, unable to stay away and unable to not touch. Lorelei pinched her nose. The love of science and discovery was ironically making the marine biologist a terrible listener. "What are you?"

To answer, Lorelei flicked her tail above the surface, and Lila jumped back.

"Holy fuck! That's a tail. Those are fins. Mermaids are real. And one works for me." Her words tumbled out in an excited, rapid rush. Bending over to examine her tail, Lila whispered, "Oh, thank you, Jesus, for the new species discovery. This is the best day of my life."

Frowning, Lorelei lowered her tail beneath the surface.

If only she could share Lila's excitement. But a part of her prickled at the marine biologist's words. New species. A discovery. Talking at her, not to her. *I'm a person, not an animal.* Remembrance followed, and with it, the intoxicating phantom sensation of Carrie's flesh sliding down her throat. So sweet and savory all at once.

Her irritation vanished. She had no moral high ground to stand on.

Weary, Lorelei suggested, "Why don't we go back up to the house and talk? I'm sure you have a lot of questions."

"Do I ever. Yes, let's go up." Motioning to her state of undress, Lila asked, "Aren't you cold? Goodness, it is freezing out here." The scientist shivered.

"Not when I'm fully shifted." But in human form? Hypothermia was definitely still on the table.

"Wow, just wow. Oh hey, would it be too weird for you if I watched you shift back?"

"No, it's okay." Lorelei flicked her tail, propelling herself toward shore, but kept her distance. Better not to risk getting in biting range. "At first, I thought it happened when I'm exposed to air—like my gills. But I can actually control it with a conscious thought."

In making the mental decision to step forward, fins and scales simultaneously and instantaneously shrunk back. Lorelei sloshed the rest of the way out of the water on her own two feet. "I think I might be able to shift into mermaid form on land, without ever touching the water. I've started to, but it's going to take some practice to get the hang of it. Shifting is much easier when I'm in the water."

Pointing to the scales still poking out from the sides of Lorelei's legs, Lila observed, "These ones haven't retracted."

"I have to press my legs together for the skin to knit into the tail. When I don't, they look like this. I think it's a primed flight response."

"Very interesting. I'd like to test that theory," Lila muttered to herself. Realizing she'd spoken out loud, she apologized hurriedly. "For another time, of course, and with your permission."

Back at the cottage, they both changed into warm, dry clothes and sat at the kitchen table with mugs of hot tea. Inside, away from the ocean, a little more of Lorelei's self-control returned.

Dipping her teabag in and out of the steaming water, Lila resumed their conversation. "Don't get me wrong, I'm beyond thrilled you showed me. But why?"

The moment of grisly truth. There'd be running and screaming now.

Reluctantly, she pulled back the corner of her mouth to reveal partially retracted pointed teeth.

Lila's eyes bugged out of her head. "How did your dentist miss those? Didn't they ever take x-rays of your mouth?"

Lorelei shrugged, silently relieved and a little amused. "Just bite wings. Didn't look far enough into the gums, I guess."

"Okay, sorry. Please continue. What do your extra set of teeth have to do with you bringing me here?"

Swallowing her rising fear, Lorelei told Lila everything. What really happened the night of the storm, her sleepwalking, her near constant hunger for human flesh, and the recent close call with Carrie.

Hearing that final horror, Lila blanched, clasping a hand over her mouth. The fear that rolled off her made Lorelei's stomach rumble audibly and saliva pool in her mouth. The monster inside liked fear, relished in it.

Pinching her nose, Lorelei jumped out of her chair, backed away, and scanned the cupboards for something stinky. Landing on a bottle of vinegar, she unscrewed the cap and inhaled deeply. The sharp scent shot up her nose with such a searing pain, she almost dropped the bottle. She'd never had such a strong reaction to smelling vinegar, but it erased all trace of Lila's scent.

Blinking rapidly as her eyes watered, Lorelei muttered, "That worked better than I thought."

Lila's posture remained ridged. Although she was likely still scared, Lorelei couldn't smell her fear anymore. "Does Killian know?"

"Not about Carrie. He's been underway. But he was there for my first transformation." Lorelei pushed back her sleeve to reveal the scar on her arm. "I almost took a bite out of him when it happened, but I had just enough of my head together, so I bit myself instead. That snapped me out of the instinct to…eat him."

Ashen, Lila held her mug in a death grip. "How'd he respond to that?"

"Freaked out but surprisingly supportive. He suggested I call you, but I just couldn't. I thought I could handle it on my own." She wrung her hands, sensing she only had Lila's ear for a short while longer. If she said the wrong thing, the woman would bolt. "But now I'm scared this hunger is going to get worse, and I'm going to kill someone. I was hoping you could help me prevent that from happening—don't know how—but I'm willing to try anything."

If Lila wouldn't or couldn't help her, she saw no other option than to leave Haven Cove, the ocean...and Killian behind. She'd go back to the Midwest. Or the desert. Somewhere far, far away from the ocean's call.

Rigid in her chair, Lila thought intently for a minute. When a light sprung to her eyes, she relaxed a modicum, some of her earlier excitement returning. "I have an idea. I'll be right back."

Lorelei watched Lila hurry to the door.

Whether or not that was true, Lorelei couldn't say. It could just be an act fueled by survival instinct—to say and do whatever it took to get out. Not that she blamed her. "Lila?" she called.

The marine biologist turned with her hand frozen on the door handle.

Wrapping her arms around herself, Lorelei leaned back against the countertop. She wouldn't leave this spot until Lila was gone. Poor woman was already spooked enough. "I'm really sorry for dragging you into this. And for scaring you. But I didn't know who else to turn to."

Exhaling, Lila replied with a half-smile, "I know, Lorelei. You made the right choice. I think I know how to help you."

OF ALL THE THINGS KILLIAN EXPECTED TO SEE WHEN HE came home, Lila and Lorelei standing together over a table covered in packaged raw meats wasn't one of them. It was quite the assortment, too, like they'd raided the grocery meat department for one of each of everything they had.

"Um, what's going on?" he asked as he hung his keys and jacket.

Tearing the plastic off a tray of beef stew meat, Lila offered it to Lorelei as if serving hors d'oeuvres at a cocktail party. Lorelei plucked a piece and popped it into her mouth, chewing thoughtfully. "It's okay. Almost as appealing as eating live fish."

You ate a live fish?

"She knows?" he asked instead, holding back his first question.

Wiping the corner of her mouth, Lorelei nodded. "She's trying to help me solve my hunger problem. I…" She drew a deep breath. "I may have taken a bite out of your ex-girlfriend."

May have taken a…His stomach dropped. "Wait, what?" She bit Carrie? When? Where? Why?

They both brought him up to speed.

Maybe he should have been more alarmed, but for more reasons than he could count, he was thankful the situation hadn't been worse. Carrie's life should have been at the very top of the list of things to be thankful for, but God help him, he worried more about what accidentally eating someone would do to Lorelei's emotional and mental health.

He reassured himself that Carrie's life came in at a very close second.

Sitting back to observe, he watched Lorelei taste test her way through all the different meats, package by package, and with disappointingly similar results. Nothing was curbing her hunger.

When Lila waved raw chicken under her nose, the only other meat left to try, Lorelei grimaced. "I will never."

"Well, that's it." Killian scratched the top of his head.

"It's hopeless." All color rushed from Lorelei's face. She sat down in the nearest chair with her legs propped up. She hugged her knees looking utterly devastated, and it tore his heart apart to see her like that.

Though he felt lost himself, he went over to put an arm around her shoulder and wracked his brain for something that wasn't an empty platitude.

Rummaging through a grocery bag, Lila said, "Not yet. I saved the best for last."

The woman was a certifiable genius, but to dangle hope like that…

"Ah-ha! Here it is." She cracked open a can, and whatever it was, Lorelei shot up out of her chair, and out of his embrace, nostrils flaring.

"What is that? It smells so good."

Lila handed Lorelei a can of potted meat, and his people-eating woman lit up like she had just been given sunken treasure.

"So, steak's a no go, but if it comes in a can, it hits the spot?" Killian asked incredulously as Lorelei cut up the block of canned meat and ravenously devoured it slice after slice. Weird as shit but at least they had a solution.

Lila launched into an animated description of a Papua New Guinean tribe's cannibalistic funerary rites. "And apparently they say it tastes like long pig."

"For real? Canned pork tastes like human flesh?" Bet those brands' marketing departments would love to hear that.

Shrugging, Lila began dumping leftover meat into freezer bags. "Or they just say that to fuck with the missionaries."

Okay, that was kind of funny.

"It's close enough for me," Lorelei chimed in, happily licking her fingers.

Shoving his hands into his pockets, he quickly buried the thought that his new girlfriend could now make this distinction deep within himself. He changed the subject. "Why didn't we start with this?"

"Scientific curiosity," Lila chirped, just a hair too chipper.

Rolling his eyes, he turned to Lorelei. "That's Lila speak for 'I just really wanted to see you eat a bunch of raw meat.'"

"Hmph. Calling me out." Lila laughed, playfully smacking his arm.

Cradling the empty can in her palms, Lorelei hesitantly met his eyes. "Are you grossed out by the amount of this stuff I'm going to be eating?"

"Not nearly as grossed out as I would be to find a half-eaten arm in the fridge."

"So, an uneaten arm is all right?" she joked, but her voice was hesitant. Uncertain.

It sparked a fierce urge in him to comfort and console her. He enveloped Lorelei in a tight hug. "It wouldn't be ideal."

But would he break up with her over it?

God help him, but probably not.

CHAPTER
TWENTY-THREE

EXHAUSTED FROM THE EVENTS OF THE PAST WEEKS, LORELEI shuffled upstairs after Lila left and fell into a deep and dreamless sleep. No nightmares. No horrific memories. Just blissful, black nothingness.

At some point, when the sun was low in the sky, she had a vague recollection of Killian slipping into bed with her. But no sooner had the thought crossed her mind, she slumbered once more. It had been quite some time since she'd slept this well.

The guilt and shame she felt before weren't gone completely, but they didn't monopolize her emotions either. There was some semblance of peace in that.

She woke early the next morning with Killian's arm wrapped around her waist and his head nestled in the crook of her neck.

So trusting. So much faith in her.

Smiling to herself, Lorelei affectionately ran her fingers through his hair, cutely disheveled from sleep. The grays amongst the brown glinted like silver threads in the morning sunlight. Pinching one between her fingertips, she imagined what Killian would look like with a whole head of them.

When she last brought up the grays to him, she detected a hint of self-consciousness.

It wouldn't be for another fifteen to twenty years before they completely took over, but even if that day came within a few short years, she didn't mind the thought one bit. One day, the captain would make a rather dashing silver fox, and she hoped to be there by his side to see it.

While she caressed his cheek, he snuggled closer as if magnetized by her touch.

She couldn't help but marvel at how quickly this man worked his way into her heart, and how he could lie alongside her lost in sleep, wholly vulnerable and exposed. But the horrible cravings that plagued her no longer troubled her.

For the first time since she discovered what she was, Lorelei had real hope that she could maintain control and justify his acceptance and sense of ease around her.

When she kissed the top of his head, he stirred beneath her.

"Good morning," he murmured, blinking sleepily.

She brushed hair away from his eyes. "Good morning."

Yawning, Killian tightened his grip around her hips, the movement bringing his morning arousal into direct contact with her thigh. A small giggle escaped her lips as he pulled her into the solid crook of his body, enveloping her wholly in his male heat and spicy scent. No hunger, just desire pooled in the pit of her stomach, its liquid warmth spreading from the base of her spine to her limbs.

Thrumming and primed for pleasure, she arched into him, backside teasing and pleading for his attention.

He'd been gone for days, away at sea, leaving her heart and mind roiling in turmoil, as tempestuous as the waves that break upon the shore after a storm. Missing him, craving his touch, but also fearing his return, and what she might do to him, lost to the whims and desires of the monster within.

But yesterday's discovery was a spark of hope in the fog, and for the time being, he was safe in her arms. She'd cherish every bit of him, and every moment spent together for however long this newfound control lasted.

Rotating his hips in slow, delicious circles, Killian rubbed her through his boxer shorts, groaning against her skin. The pressure on her thigh built as he kissed his way up the slope of her neck, eager for more, but not yet taking it.

"Horny, are we?" Though she teased, she was just as breathless and intoxicated by this as he was.

"Mm," he mumbled, scruff rasping against her cheek. But what words didn't say, his body did in definitive answer.

Rough, calloused hands smoothed up her sides, and with a quick yank, he pulled her shirt off, throwing it over the side of the bed. The cheeky grin that followed, so playful and hungry, stole her breath away, leaving her a puddle of sea foam on the mattress.

Cheeks heated. Heart raced. She licked her lips, dying for a taste of his.

To think, a simple fishing captain bewitching a siren. He could ask anything of her in that moment, and she'd sing his name and deny him nothing.

He pushed her pants down next, his voice rumbling against her ear. "I have a promise to keep."

A promise? The past week had been a whirlwind...

She arched her eyebrow, waiting for him to elaborate.

Rising to his knees, spread in a widened stance, Killian thumbed his waistband, unhurried and teasing. Torturer. So, she took what she could. Her eyes flicked down, drinking her fill of his body's topography—the column of his throat, the narrow channel dividing the plateaus of his chest, and the archipelago of muscle at his core. Oh, and that Adonis V, the compass rose to this glorious treasure map, that trail of hair below his navel pointing the way. X marks the spot.

"That day we sat on the beach, before I left?" he reminded, interrupting her perusal with a pleased, devilish smirk. Captain Quinn knew exactly what he was doing to her.

Lorelei nodded, biting her lower lip.

Now she remembered.

The heat in her face surged, streaking the length of her body, down her chest, between her thighs, as quick as lightning. It curled her toes and made her heart thump wildly within her ribcage. For how hot and taut her skin felt, she must have been as red as her hair, ripe with anticipation.

"After very serious consideration," he drawled, *finally* inching his boxers down, over the jut of his hipbones, past his raging erection, "I've come to the conclusion that I want you for as long as you'll have me. And I'm going to…"

He paused, brow arched, and grin wicked, waiting for her to finish the sentence.

Fisting the sheets in her hands, and squirming under his fierce, relentless gaze, Lorelei answered breathlessly, "Captain, are you going to make me scream?"

Grinning, he tossed his boxers behind him and, with a wink, parted her legs, all at once ending her agony and continuing the exquisite torture. Under the mercy of his insatiable tongue, the devourer became the devoured. And she loved it.

The way he pleasured her with his mouth and fingers, attentive to every part of her, each sensitive bundle of nerves, made her clay in his hands. With every lick and stroke, he molded and sculpted her, until her desire was two tectonic plates meeting leagues under the sea, coiling her muscles tight, on the collision course toward release.

Killian sucked her clit, long and hard, and curled his fingers inward, demanding cataclysm.

Quaking muscles clenched as her body erupted, lifting her off the mattress in a sinuous arch, each peak of flesh bared, a pelagic mountain range reaching toward the surface, toward the sun. Pulse after pulse ripped through her, and she screamed his name, nails digging crescent moons into his shoulders.

Dizzy, Lorelei closed her eyes, letting out a ragged, sated exhale as she sank back down into the mattress, chest flushed and heaving. Moments ticked by in blissful, easy silence, the bubbling magma beneath her skin already beginning to cool.

Kneeling back, Killian wiped the corners of his mouth on his forearm. "I will never tire of that."

Good, because now she was addicted.

Languid, Lorelei rolled over, reaching inside the nightstand drawer for a condom, but her fingers found a can of meat instead. What the...?

She held it out in front of her. "What's this doing here?"

Stroking lazily over his length, Killian shrugged sheepishly. "Thought it might be good for you to have a snack before going down on me."

She sat up straight, trading the canned meat for a condom. "Very romantic," she quipped sarcastically, just before launching forward to tickle his sides. He squirmed away with a shout and caught her wrists in his hands.

The discovery of Killian's ticklishness amused her.

"Practical," he corrected, holding the instruments of tickle-torture far away from his body.

Though she had the strength to break free, Lorelei just leaned in to kiss him.

THEIR GRUMBLING STOMACHS EVENTUALLY DREW THEM from the bedroom and down to the kitchen. Waving Lorelei over to the cupboard by the refrigerator, Killian grinned, "This one's all yours. Open it."

Wearing nothing but one of his shirts, Lorelei cheerfully opened it to find rows of neatly stacked canned pork and two boxes of assorted chocolates on top. The reaching motion caused the shirt to rise, and she could practically feel Killian's eyes glued to the exposed cheek.

"When did you do this?" She glanced over her shoulder.

He casually leaned against the fridge and crossed his arms, wearing nothing but a pair of sweatpants that sat low on his hips. "Yesterday, while you were asleep."

Her heart swelled too big for her chest. This sweet, thoughtful man was hers?

Smiling, he nodded toward the cabinet, as if to say, *go on.*

Plucking a box of chocolates from the cabinet, Lorelei ripped off the cellophane and sampled one of the confections. After taking the bite, she closed her eyes and moaned, its sweet and salty flavors delighting her tongue.

"Thank God," she breathed. "I was afraid chocolate was ruined forever for me."

Killian laughed. "So, you can eat more than just raw fish and potted meat."

She demolished another chocolate, this one filled with coconut cream. "Not craving either of those things right now," she replied, licking her fingers. Not even a hint.

Opening the fridge and peering inside, he asked, "Want to give traditional human breakfast another try?"

Laying her arms across her grumbling belly, she nodded enthusiastically. Eggs, bacon, breakfast potatoes—she'd eat it all.

This time she wasn't nauseous as they cooked and ate breakfast. Her taste for human food had returned, at least for now.

Not knowing when the next switch might come, or how suddenly, Lorelei tossed canned meat into her purse and gym bag. Stashed a few in her car, as well. She couldn't afford to assume this unexpected return to normalcy would be permanent. Letting unprecedented extremes of hangry catch her unprepared could have disastrous consequences.

Killian locked up the office and walked with Branson over to the pier-side lobster pound for lunch. As they paid for their lobster rolls and were about to sit at one of the tables, he heard a voice he hadn't heard in a long time.

Even after fifteen years, she sounded the same as he remembered.

"Killian!" Carrie cried. Picking up a set of crutches, she excused herself from the table of friends she sat with and hurried over. The dress she wore was medium-length, so he could see the bandages that wound around her calf.

Before he could blink, let alone react, she pulled him into an awkward one-sided, one-armed hug. Then hopping back, she said, "Wow, you look great."

Shifting uncomfortably on his feet, he suddenly wished they'd asked for their lunches to go.

Branson, who stood beside him, muttered gruffly, "Hello to you, too, cousin."

"Oh hey, Will. You guys getting something to eat?" she chirped, either oblivious to the awkward tension between them or completely ignoring it.

Although the answer was obvious, Killian bit back the urge to say something smart. Branson, however, had no such qualms. "We're taking a lunch break, because it's lunch time."

She brushed off the snark. "Do you want to join us?"

"No, that's okay"—Branson started, just as Killian blurted, "Got to get back on the boat!" At least they were on the same page.

She glanced between the two of them, brow creasing. "Well, why don't we sit and catch up while they get your food ready?"

God, she was relentless. Did anything discourage this woman?

"I'm gonna go check on our order." Branson slapped Killian on the back and abandoned him with his ex-girlfriend. He inwardly groaned.

Son of a bitch.

Seeing no other polite option, Killian sat down at the nearest open table, and Carrie plopped into the chair across from him, leaning her crutches against the wall.

"So how have you been?" she asked, nudging his arm in too familiar a manner.

"Good," he replied, leaning away. "You?"

Straightening out her leg, Carrie winced. "Settling in. Or trying to at least. Lori probably told you, but the weirdest thing happened to me last week."

Lori? Killian almost corrected her but that would have required more talking. He crossed his arms. "She did."

Although it made her grimace, Carrie lifted her leg and began to unwind her bandages. "Carrie, don't." Fucking hell, people ate here. "You should keep that on…"

His next words about proper wound care and restaurant hygiene died in the back of his throat when she peeled back the gauze pad. He sucked air in through his teeth, a tremor racing up the length of his spine.

Fuck.

A chunk of her calf muscle was completely gone, and a circular skin graft lined the concave wound, stitched into place. The surrounding skin shone, swollen, red, and badly bruised.

It looked like a small shark bite. Although that wasn't entirely unexpected, he hadn't allowed that reality to sink in before. Now that this tangible evidence of how dangerous Lorelei could be stared him right in the face, his blood ran cold. He couldn't ignore its severity any longer.

Killian nearly jumped out of his skin when Branson clamped a hand down onto his shoulder. His friend apologized and held up a to-go bag of their food, having discreetly changed their order during his disappearance. "Time to head back."

If only he'd rescued him sooner. Not just because Killian didn't want to be in Carrie's company. The darker side of Lorelei's transformation was staring him right in the face, and he would have rather escaped coming to terms with that reality entirely.

As Killian stood up, practically quaking in his boots, Carrie warned, "You and Lori be careful not to get too close to the water. That thing is probably still out there."

He nodded numbly and followed Branson out the door.

With their backs turned to the restaurant, Branson asked, "Killian, you all right? You look a little shaken."

"Just freaked out by that bite."

"I know, man. It's gnarly. She showed it to me the other day and to just about anyone else who'll take a look."

The wound had been deep. Lorelei hadn't just nibbled; she'd burrowed her teeth into his ex's flesh, as close to the bone as she could reach.

CHAPTER

TWENTY-FIVE

First day at her new job, Lorelei got the official employee tour and spent most of the morning discussing museum budget and logistics. But in the afternoon, Lila signed out a boat from the lab and took them out on the water to collect specimens, research samples, and underwater videos.

As Lila steered them to their destination, far from prying eyes, Lorelei inserted a radio earpiece and pulled a mask with an audio transmitter over her mouth. She also shouldered a pack full of containers and baggies and strapped a video recorder to her hand that could transmit live, underwater footage to Lila's field laptop. The marine biologist begged her to be extremely careful with it, as it was a very expensive piece of equipment.

It all was. That Lila entrusted her with it made her stomach somersault.

Once geared up, Lorelei dove in and shifted into mermaid form. She swam to varying depths to conduct sound and video quality checks.

For the first half of the afternoon, Lorelei served as Lila's eyes and hands on the ocean floor, happily catering to the marine biologist's every scientific whim and curiosity. And as she explored, she listened to Lila's steady stream of factoids and educational commentary. It was one thing to observe the ocean's wonders all on her own, but to know and understand what she was actually seeing?

That was magic shone in a brilliant, brand-new light.

Lorelei didn't even hesitate to give her consent when Lila asked to run tests on her, because she, too, wanted to learn everything that could be learned about her mermaid metamorphosis, beyond what her eyes could see.

Clutching her clipboard to her chest, eager and excited, Lila leaned over the side of the boat. "Can I take a blood sample? Skin samples? Scale samples? All the samples?"

Nodding, Lorelei grabbed the edge and hoisted herself over the side. Sitting on a crate on deck, she presented her tail, wincing slightly when Lila took the samples. Taking a sterile swab, the marine biologist swabbed the inside of her mouth, as well, and dropped it into a sample tube.

Glancing down, Lila selected a fresh cotton swab. "I have an awkward question. Do you, uh, have any idea how you reproduce? Like do you have eggs that are fertilized, or do you have a fish…vagina?"

Scrunching up her face, Lorelei replied, "I don't know. I've never tried, but let's save the gynecological examination for another time." Or never.

Lila immediately put the swab away. "Right. Sorry. Let's focus on your diet, capabilities—things like that instead."

She described how she regularly swapped between a human and mermaid diet, which Lila had a slew of questions about, including how much raw fish and canned pork she needed to eat in a day and whether she gravitated toward any particular kinds of fish. Or avoided others. Still figuring all these things out for herself, Lorelei answered as best she could. With a little nudging, she eventually agreed to keep a food journal.

Food wasn't all they discussed.

"What's the deepest you can dive? And do you have to pace yourself?"

She gave an estimation for depth—deeper than humanly possible, she learned—but she'd sensed in her swims that she'd still get the bends if she took a dive too fast.

Taking a piece of equipment out of her field kit, Lila said, "Let's time how fast you can swim—just through the water, not a dive. We'll first measure your normal swimming pace, then a sprint."

"How?"

Holding it up, Lila pointed to different components. "This is a GPS wildlife tracking device. I'll be able to extrapolate your speed from the timestamps and the distance you go. We usually use implants to track the migratory patterns of marine animals, but I figured you'd prefer something you could take on and off."

Lorelei nodded and held out her arm so that Lila could belt it around her wrist.

When the device was secure, Lila pulled up a program on her laptop. "Okay, we're all set. Let's start with your casual swim speed, so just, uh, swim around out there for ten minutes or so."

Sitting on the edge of the boat, Lorelei adjusted the radio earpiece she wore and put back on the mask with the audio transmitter. "Just call me back in when you have enough data." And then because she thought it would make her look cool, she dove backwards like she'd seen divers do on National Geographic.

The rush of water up her nose made her immediately regretted it.

Underwater, she blew out air to clear it and then swam away.

She was a terrible judge of time, but she thought she'd swam for more than ten minutes before Lila called her back in.

When she popped up alongside the boat, Lila called out the numbers to her. "Cruising speed of about sixteen point five kilometers per hour— that's about ten miles per hour. Okay, now I want you to swim as fast as you can for as long as you can."

Lorelei nodded and darted off. She swam as hard as she possibly could and didn't stop until her whole body ached and burned with lactic acid.

Exhausted, she let herself float limply to the surface like a dead fish.

Static crackled through the earpiece before she heard Lila's voice. "You okay? You just stopped, rather abruptly."

"I've died," she whined, flinging an arm across her eyes.

"Well, let's see." Lila paused to calculate the speed. "You went twenty-eight miles per hour for two miles...Damn, Lorelei. No wonder why you're tired. You kept that speed for about four minutes and sixteen seconds. That's way faster than a harbor porpoise and a little faster than a bottlenose dolphin."

"Great. Can you come get me, please?"

"Yeah, I'll be right over."

By the time Lila reached her, Lorelei had mostly recovered, but she was still splayed out on the surface of the water.

"You okay down there?" Lila peered over the side of the boat.

"Yeah. I think if I train, I could go even longer." She roused herself from her resting position and hoisted herself onto the boat. "I wonder how fast the ones who actually live out there are."

"I was thinking the exact same thing." Lila helped her up.

"All right, what's next?"

"Well, I've gathered that you can breathe underwater indefinitely." Lorelei nodded in affirmation. "So, I guess that leaves us with one last thing I wanted to test today. And that's whether your partial metamorphosis allows for you to shift quicker."

For the next half hour, Lorelei dove off the boat several dozen times, both in states of partial transformation and no transformation. They discovered that in the former state, she shifted completely the moment she hit the water. But when she jumped in fully human, it took anywhere from ten to twenty seconds of time in the water before the transformation completed.

In conclusion? Her ability to remain partially shifted on land was likely connected to flight response, just as she'd predicted.

While Lila jotted down notes, Lorelei occupied herself by diving for shells. Grabbing two of the most sizable ones she could find, Lorelei sprung from the water some distance away holding them over her breasts. In a terrible sing-song voice, she spouted lyrics from a popular children's movie about a mermaid.

Glancing up from her notebook, Lila smirked and flung a piece of seaweed stuck to the boat at her. "You are ridiculous."

Lorelei stuck out her tongue. It was the lightest she'd felt since chomping down on Carrie's leg.

"Very mature." Lila stood and started packing up the equipment. "Now, get your mermaid ass back up here, so we can leave."

CHAPTER
TWENTY-SIX

UNABLE TO RETURN HOME WITHOUT FULLY PROCESSING HIS fear, Killian stayed late at the dockside office, staring at the wall.

He knew Lorelei hadn't meant to bite Carrie. He knew she responsibly handled the aftermath. And he knew she sought help and figured out a way to prevent it from ever happening again. Hell, he was the one who stocked the house with a crate-load of canned pork. He also had a pretty good idea how much she cared for him.

But seeing what Lorelei's teeth had done to Carrie's leg, Killian no longer thought he could take an accidental "nip" as he once did.

Afterall, it wasn't just a "nip." Lorelei had actually *eaten* a piece of her. As much as he didn't want to dwell on that fact, it turned over and over in his mind. Even if she hadn't torn out a bite of his ex, and had truly only nipped her, Killian still wasn't sure he'd feel that much better about it. He didn't think he could take her teeth on any part of his anatomy and be okay with her after. The fact that it had been an accident should count for something, but it did little to put his mind at ease.

And yet, despite his valid fears, guilt gripped his gut.

Lorelei didn't ask for any of this.

Life dealt her an unfair hand, and she dealt with it as best she knew how. No matter what happened, he couldn't push her away. She needed support, not shunning. And it wasn't as if they hadn't figured out a good solution to curb her cravings. What happened with Carrie might not ever happen again.

Checking his phone, which had been on silent, he saw that he had several texts and missed calls from Lorelei and his friends. More time had gotten away from him than he'd meant to. Under normal circumstances, he would have been home several hours ago.

Swearing, he called Lorelei back. She answered right away and sounded so relieved to hear his voice. "Killian, are you okay?"

"I'm good, just had some personal things I needed to work through at the office."

The line went quiet, but not dead. She took a deep, shuddering breath, like maybe she was about to cry. "We were afraid you'd gotten in a car accident. Will's on his way back to the office to check on you."

God, he was such a thoughtless ass. He really shouldn't have disappeared like that without a word.

She sniffed. "Do you want to talk about whatever was bothering you?"

He didn't want to hurt her, but he thought the truth was the best explanation for why he'd gone radio silent that evening. "I saw Carrie's leg. It was stupid, but she took the bandage off to show me…"

…*what you did.*

Though left unspoken, the words hung in the air between them.

He pushed on, and Lorelei listened quietly as he told her how badly that bite was screwing with his head.

When he finished, she replied, "Lila mentioned today that Carrie's been posting a lot of pictures on social media. So, I looked. All the posts about the attack are public, for sharing purposes, so I had no problem seeing them. I really don't blame you, Killian. What I did to her was awful. You should take all the time you need, but you may want to call Will and Lila to let them know you are okay."

Without another word, she hung up, just as Branson's truck pulled in. Killian felt pretty shitty.

As Branson neared the door, he could hear him talking on the phone with Lila. "Yeah, he's here," he said. "I'll text you when I'm on my way home. Yup, I love you, too." Once inside, Branson snapped, "Forget how to answer your phone? What the hell's wrong with you?"

The dude was pissed, and if Killian didn't already know he'd fucked up, this would be the wakeup call.

As much as he wanted to explain—not excuse—he couldn't tell his best friend the truth. The mermaid stuff? Not his secret to tell. There was nothing left to do but lie through his teeth. "Seeing Carrie today opened up some old wounds," he forced out, the words like acid on his tongue.

Pulling over his office chair, Branson sat down. "Do you want to talk about it?"

Killian leaned back and blew out a puff of air. "It just threw me off-guard. I was hoping to work through it before going home."

"Is everything all right between you and Lorelei?"

"Yeah, I just didn't want to drag her into my mess. And it's been a while since I've dated, so I forgot to send a check-in text. Or look at my phone." Too long living the bachelor's life. Accountable to no one but himself.

Seemingly satisfied by that answer, Branson stood and clapped a hand on his shoulder. "We've all been there. Wanna go grab a drink?"

Killian nodded, grabbing his phone and keys.

Maybe several.

CHAPTER
TWENTY-SEVEN

IT WAS NEARLY MIDNIGHT WHEN KILLIAN FINALLY CAME home from drinks with Will. The sound of him clomping up the stairs and closing the door to his room roused Lorelei from sleep.

Emotion rose in her chest, remembering his call earlier that night to explain his run-in with Carrie at the lobster pound. It had taken all she had to keep her voice steady on the phone. Then, after a good cry, she got over herself, made a cup of tea, and curled up in the guest bedroom with a book. The thought of sleeping alone pained her, but she knew it was the right choice for the both of them.

Now that he was home, all she wanted to do was hug him, but Lorelei had to keep reminding herself to give him space. He needed it. And she needed it.

Unable to clear her mind, sleep eluded Lorelei for the next couple hours.

When morning came, and her alarm clock blared, Lorelei did not remember falling asleep. She stared at the ceiling in denial and hit snooze in case she accidentally dozed off.

Day two at her new job was going to be a bitch.

A minute later, Killian knocked on her door. "Come in," she croaked, and winced at the sound of her voice.

The door creaked open, and Killian peeked in holding an offering of hot coffee, a divergence from her usual black tea. That he suspected she'd need the extra caffeine made her chest tighten and eyes burn. She couldn't decide whether to be pissed off about that or lean into the sob she felt coming.

But he was here now, ready to talk.

So, she patted the bed beside her, ready to listen.

Though he smiled as he sat down, it didn't quite reach his eyes, which were underlined by dark circles. He hadn't gotten much sleep either.

Going to bed separate and upset was the absolute worst.

"I heard you tossing and turning last night," he said, handing her the mug. "Thought you might need a little extra caffeine."

"Why didn't you come in?" She tried to leave the hurt out of her voice but failed.

"I had a lot to drink, more than I should have." He swiped a hand over his mouth, the lines of his face deepened by shame. "Didn't want you to see me out of sorts like that. It was stupid, I know. I promise I won't ever do that again—the drinking too much bit and not hugging it out with you."

"Can we hug it out now?" Her lower lip trembled, the tears threatening to spill.

He opened his arms. "Come here."

She set her coffee on the nightstand and launched herself into his embrace, nearly bowling him over.

———

Work was manageable, but when she returned home, Killian's dazzling, infectious smile made everything between them feel right as rain. Their evening began by singing along to the radio as they cooked and ended in his bedroom with their shirts on the floor and her legs around his waist.

It got hot and heavy fast, but as she trailed her lips from his jaw to his neck, giving him just a little, teasing nip...

He recoiled, and like a man burned, pushed her away.

Shit, shit, shit. That was stupid.

She jumped back, remembering how freaked out he'd been over Carrie's bite wound. "Oh, God. I am so, so sorry! I wasn't thinking."

He nodded, rubbing his neck, watching her intently but not speaking.

Tears pricked her eyes as she covered her mouth with her hands. Crying after *she* scared him felt selfish, but she didn't have enough emotional control to school her warping features. He had all the reason in the world to be squicked, and yet, his reaction hurt her.

Killian's expression softened, no doubt seeing the emotional battle waging on her face, and he enveloped her in his arms. "It's not that I don't trust you," he rushed. "Or think you're going to *really* bite me. It just makes me think about it, and it gets stuck in my head."

"I'm sorry, Killian," she whispered, not trusting her voice to remain steady at any volume. "I should have known better. That was thoughtless of me."

Hugging her tighter, he kissed her temple. "This isn't personal, I swear to you. I just need a little time."

She pulled back just enough to look him in the eye. "If I do something that freaks you out, please tell me. The last thing I want is for you to be afraid of me. And believe me, I realize that may be impossible, but I don't want to make it worse."

"It's not impossible, by far. You're not a monster, Lorelei. What happened between you and Carrie was an accident. I'm mostly afraid I'm going to react poorly if we have one, a *real* one, and do something I regret."

"If I attacked you, what could you possibly do that would be regrettable? Certainly not self-defense."

"No, but I could take it personally. Lash out maybe."

"I think that's a normal response."

"But you also deserve a little understanding. This is all new to you, too."

"I don't know if this will put your mind at ease, but I haven't had a single one of those urges since canned pork, of all things, has become my new dietary staple."

He tucked a strand of loose hair behind her ear. "It helps," he said softly, nuzzling her nose. "But could you maybe just use your hands when showing affection? Just for a little while?"

Lightly brushing her fingers across his lips and down the slope of his neck, she promised. But it broke her heart to make it.

CHAPTER

TWENTY-EIGHT

HEFTING A BUNDLE OF SHINGLES FROM HIS TRUCK, KILLIAN carried it over his shoulder and up a ladder planted firmly in the ground beside the barn garage. The roofing material rubbed holes through the thin plastic holding it together, but it barely chafed his skin. Fishing and barn construction had toughened his palms with calluses. Taking pride in having hands accustomed to hard labor was the one thing he shared with his father aside from blood and fishing.

Branson, waiting for him on top of the roof, whisked the unwieldy package out of his arms as soon as it was in reach. Setting it down with a thud, they both ripped off the plastic. Between the two of them, they were making good progress, working their way up the roof. Lunchtime was still hours away, but the felt paper was laid down, and they'd already nailed in several rows of shingles.

If they kept up this pace, they'd be done before the day was out.

The sounds of classic 70s rock music, hammers hitting nails, and languorous waves rolling into shore, filled Killian with a sense of contentment. Every so often, he'd pause to take in the view of the ocean, the land's rocky outcroppings, and the dense pine forest framing his cottage. Breathing deep the scents of home—pine sap and sea salt—peace and calm settled over him.

On the adjacent side of the barn, Walt and Marci giggled and laughed about something while dipping their rollers into trays of white paint. Later, during a break, Killian saw that they had splattered each other head-to-toe with it. Over forty years of marriage, and they still got silly with each other.

Frickin' adorable was what it was.

When the Walshes had found out from Branson that he was weatherproofing the barn on his day off, they insisted on coming over to help. He'd learned from experience that refusing was futile; they'd just come over anyway. That's just what family did. Still, he was grateful for the help and had invited them for coffee and breakfast beforehand. It was the very least he could do.

They'd come over early in the morning, early enough so that Lila and Lorelei could join them before work.

While setting the table, Marci accidentally opened the cupboard filled with canned pork and chocolate. She sucked her teeth at the sight. "That ain't right. You're going to give yourselves heart attacks eating this stuff."

Out of the corner of his eye, Killian saw Lorelei sneak a can out of her purse, and hiding it under her blazer, she excused herself and darted upstairs. Must have been having a craving.

"Ma," Lila drawled. "That's Killian's emergency winter protein stash. Way out here plowing is less reliable." That wasn't true—Killian paid a guy to plow for him—but he was thankful for the quick save and didn't correct her.

"Oh, but your blood pressure." Marci quickly closed the cabinet with a frown. "I can't unsee that."

Once they all sat down to eat, Marci pushed the fruit salad bowl directly in front of his plate and fixed him with the look. He didn't eat anything stored in that cupboard, but he sure as hell still scooped two helpings of mixed berries onto his plate.

Lila and Lorelei had to cut out a little early from breakfast so they could get to work on time. On their way out, Lila kissed her husband goodbye, while Lorelei blew Killian a kiss from the door. He winked in return.

Marci smiled at the sweet exchanges, and while Killian put on a good outward show, his heart twinged. He missed the touch of Lorelei's lips, but he feared the teeth behind them even more.

Around mid-morning, a too familiar BMW drove up the dirt road.

"You gotta be kidding me," Killian groaned. He hit the nail pinched between his fingers with extra force.

Pausing in his hammering to look up, Branson's eyes widened as he watched his cousin's car park next to the Walshes'. "This will be the third time?"

"That I know of." Killian drove the rest of the nail in with one solid hit.

Carrie crutched over from her car and planted herself right below where they worked. Leaning against one of her crutches, she shielded her eyes from the morning sun with her hand and squinted up at them. "Killian? Will? Be careful up there, or you're going to fall and break a leg!"

Annoyance flared within him, and Branson grumbled unintelligibly under his breath. Neither had an issue when Marci said those sorts of things to them. To them, she was Mom. But Carrie not only used to be a friend, she was once also the group's daredevil. As a teen, she hiked knife's edge trails and climbed steep cliff faces the rest of them refused to go near. Always the one to push them to try something new, the next adventure, the next thrill, she was fearless, unstoppable. She'd had spitfire in her soul; it was what Killian once loved about her.

And then she outgrew Haven Cove and him and became someone else entirely.

One of the Walshes turned down the radio. "Carrie? Is that you I hear?" Marci called from around the side of the barn.

"Hi, Mrs. Walsh!" She called back, walking over to greet them.

He overheard snippets of their conversation.

Walt said, "Hi, sweetie. It's so good to see you. How you doing?"

"Not bad..." He missed a piece. "...it's good to see you, too."

Marci scolded, "Child, we know you've been in town. Lila mentioned...Just when were you planning on coming to see us?"

"Oh, you know...trying to settle in. I was going to stop by soon." Even from on top of the roof, Killian could hear she was weaseling around the truth with that lame answer.

"Mm hmm," Marci tutted. Carrie never could get away with anything when Marci was around. None of them ever could. But the conversation was over too soon, and Killian heard the crunch of gravel, marking Carrie's return. She called up to him, wanting to talk.

Emboldened by Marci, he looked over the edge. "You really don't respect personal boundaries, do you?"

Carrie frowned. "Don't be a jerk. I'm here because of this." She pointed to her leg.

All right. That was a big deal.

Sighing, Killian set his hammer aside and climbed down.

She led them down the road a bit, presumably so they wouldn't be overheard. Something as serious injury couldn't be brushed off outright, but he trudged after her grumpily. Carrie was right to be upset about the bite, and yet, rather than feel sympathy or concern, Killian just felt annoyed. Maybe that made him heartless.

The wind kicked up and blew Carrie's hair every which way. Unable to let go of her crutches, it kept whipping in her face.

Should he offer to help, in some way? He wasn't sure what he could do, but before he could ask, she stopped. Leaning against a nearby tree, Carrie dug a scrunchy out of her purse and wrangled her disheveled hair into a ponytail.

He folded his arms across his chest. "All right. What did you want to talk about?"

"Animal services," she replied simply.

"Animal services?" he repeated. Was he was supposed to know what the hell she meant by that?

She smoothed lumps out of her hair. "Yeah, have you called them?"

"Excuse me?" Killian bristled. She'd said it like they'd already discussed this, and he'd agreed to do it. Whatever 'it' was.

Carrie fixed him with a hard look. "Killian, something in the water over there tore off a piece of my leg, and I don't know if I'm ever going to walk right again. It's your property. Aren't you going to do something about it?"

"Who's to say I haven't?"

My girlfriend eats potted meat now, so you can chill. It's taken care of.

"Me." She dropped her arms with a huff. "I checked. Nothing's been reported."

For Chrissake. As his temper rose, he struggled to keep his volume low. "For real, Carrie? If you want it done, do it yourself."

She placed her hands on her hips. "Aren't you the least bit concerned someone else might get hurt by that thing?"

"Not especially. Whatever attacked you is gone. We've been keeping an eye out and haven't seen anything."

"Killian, this isn't something you can just brush off. You really need to get professionals here to handle this. Like, how well were you really able to look? The water's deep over there. It wouldn't be hard for it to hide. You're lucky I'm not the suing type, because I could've filed a lawsuit for getting hurt on your property."

"Could you?" he challenged. "This isn't a public park. It's private property, and you were trespassing."

Doubt flickered across her face, and she shuffled uncomfortably. "Okay, maybe not, but it's still out there, and chances are this isn't the only place it swims."

He couldn't quite put his finger on it, but something about her tone and how she said things just pissed him off despite the validity of what she said. It was no excuse for a temper, but he just couldn't let these Carrie-isms roll off his back.

Feeling bad about it, he said more gently, "Look, I've got it handled. I am sorry you got hurt, but you were trespassing. And now, not only are you doing it again you've got the nerve to tell me what to do on my own property." Okay, so much for being gentler…

"Killian, you're not listening to me!" she fumed, balling her fists. "That thing is dangerous. Everything else doesn't matter. If Lori hadn't pulled me out of the water when she did, I would be dead. I'd lose my mind if something like that ever happened to you." Killian raised his brow. "Or anyone else," she hastily added. "I can't say or do nothing."

"Believe me, you've said plenty, and while I do appreciate the concern, I don't appreciate the delivery. And for crying out loud, stop calling her Lori! Her name is Lorelei."

If it weren't for Carrie's stricken, watery-eyed expression, he might not have realized he'd raised his voice. "I'm sorry. I shouldn't have snapped at you like that."

"Just promise me you'll be careful," she pleaded, genuine concern etched on her face.

"I will. Now, please," he gestured to her car. "I have to get back to work."

To his relief, she didn't try to press him further, and instead got into her car.

As she turned her vehicle around, Killian saw her wiping at her eyes, and despite how obnoxious she'd been, he kind of felt like an ass for making her cry. Maybe in hard lining on his boundaries, and protecting Lorelei, he'd sacrificed some of his basic human decency.

But remembering how Carrie did whatever she wanted, whenever she wanted, and demanded that others follow along, he shook off the guilt. He could afford losing a little decency.

CHAPTER
TWENTY-NINE

RACING THROUGH THE WATER, LORELEI UTILIZED CURRENTS to propel herself forward faster, an experience not unlike running down a travelator at an airport. With each sprint, she pushed herself to cover more distance, help or no help from the ocean's currents.

She was building up her speed and endurance, because, as Marci pointed out, adding canned meat to her diet wasn't doing her heart any favors. And this form of exercise was much more fun than anything she would otherwise be doing at the gym.

For her heart's sake, she hoped her cravings would lessen, but, if not, she would pay the price of increased cardiac risk if it meant not eating people. It also gave her a lot of time to think.

And she needed it.

Lorelei had begged her friend to fly up again, and she would arrive soon.

Katrina's visit filled her with dread.

While she stood by the decision to invite her up for the purpose of spilling secrets, not knowing how her best friend would react was terrifying. There wasn't much of a precedent for revealing her oceanic origins. Killian witnessed the first transformation, and honestly, how well he received that was a miracle. And with Lila, the blow was softened by her scientific curiosity.

But how would Kat take it? Could Lorelei maybe lose a decade-long friendship?

Although that risk weighed heavily on her, treating it like a secret and hiding it from Katrina would be much worse. And if nothing else, her best friend had a right to know for safety reasons.

When Lorelei picked Katrina up from the airport that evening, her friend begged her for an explanation for the urgent visit, but Lorelei held firm. They'd have to wait until they got to Killian's house. Showing her in-person was the only way. Katrina reluctantly let the conversation shift to her own life, and a cute girl she met at the gym, but she fidgeted in her seat the entire way.

At home, they passed Killian on his way out the door, clipboard in hand.

"Hey Kat! Welcome." He grinned, giving her friend a brief, reciprocated hug. "I've got to run into the office for a bit. There's some last-minute stuff to take care of before we head offshore, but I'll see you both later when I get back."

Kat waved him on. "No worries. Duty calls."

He made eye contact with Lorelei, smiling warmly, but in that moment when a peck on the lips or a kiss on the cheek would normally follow, he just waved and hopped inside his truck. "Make yourself at home!" he called out the open window, then drove off.

Her heart sunk a little at that. If Kat wasn't standing right next to her, impatiently waiting for her to finally spill her guts, she might've dwelt on it more.

Grabbing a can of canned pork and a bottle of vinegar from her car's backseat, Lorelei ignored Katrina's horrified looks when she ate the first and sniffed the second. Stomach full, and olfactory senses deadened, she took Katrina straight down to the beach for the demonstration, which she awkwardly prefaced with "this is going to get weird, so bear with me."

With a nervous laugh, Katrina followed her to the water's edge and muttered under her breath, "Things are already weird."

IT WAS DARK, GIVEN THAT THE SUN SET BEFORE 4PM THIS time of year, but between a cloudless night, a full moon, and her bioluminescence, Kat would see well enough.

When Lorelei shifted, Katrina shrieked and fell backwards onto the sand, and yelled about being *Punk'd*, head on swivel for hidden camera men amongst the rocks. It took yanking on her teeth and inspecting her gills and bioluminescent nodes for her friend to accept they weren't elaborate costume prosthetics and street magician trickery.

Silently brushing the sand from her backside, Katrina's complexion turned peaked. Even in the moonlight, Lorelei could see the blood rush out of her face. She noticed weird things like that now...murderous mermaid superpowers.

Gently taking her by the arm, and squashing down the hurt of her flinch, Lorelei guided Katrina inside the cottage and sat her down on the couch. Kat stared ahead like she had blinders on, not once sparing a glance at her, even when she gave a little wave in her periphery.

In a motion that was almost comically robotic, Kat lifted her phone to her face.

If that wasn't a sign that some space was needed, she didn't know what was.

While her friend watched funny cat videos on her phone, Lorelei dressed and fetched a box of chocolates from her personal stash.

Joining Katrina on the couch, and rubbing circles across her back, Lorelei held out the box and encouraged her to eat a little sugar. Eyes glued to the screen and all the cute furball silliness, her shaken friend mechanically ate one after the other. As the assortment dwindled from twenty-one pieces down into the single digits, Lorelei jokingly asked whether she was going to leave her any.

Jolting from her robotic preoccupation, Katrina glanced over and gasped when she saw how many remained. "You let me eat all those chocolates!" she exclaimed, pink returning to her cheeks. "Lorelei!"

She shrugged, crossing her legs. "They were good, weren't they?"

Katrina shoved her playfully. "You are the worst."

"Hey now. I shared most of my chocolate with you. I think that makes me the best."

"Eh. With the news bomb you dropped on me," Katrina trailed off. "How long have you known?" Lorelei explained everything from the beginning, and what she'd been up to since finding out. Nodding along, Kat waited for her to finish, and then said, "I do understand why you had to show me in person. You technically could have video chatted me, but this was easier to digest. Pretty sure I would have thought you were just cosplaying, otherwise."

"So, we are good? You're okay?" Lorelei gripped the edge of the couch to keep herself from wringing her hands.

"It's a lot to take in, so I'm sorta internally screaming, right now," she admitted, talking a mile a minute, but then gestured between the two of them. "But of course, you and I okay. Just because this is blowing my mind, doesn't mean it's bad or whatever. Are you okay? I hope you're okay. It's not like you have any control over this, or anything to be ashamed about, but I guess an unexpected change is kinda scary, right? Not really a precedent for this sort of thing either."

Kat scrunched her nose, falling abruptly silent. She did that when she was nervous and thought she was talking too much.

"It's been a bit of a rollercoaster ride, but I think I'm on the upswing."

Throwing one leg over the other, Katrina eased back into the couch cushions. "Embracing your inner mermaid, huh? I'm seriously glad to hear it."

Puffing out a breath, Lorelei laughed, releasing her death grip on the armrest to bear hug her friend. "Do you really mean that?"

A whoosh of air rushed out of Kat, along with the words, "Good frickin' God, you're strong," but once Lorelei loosened her grip, she continued, "I mean I never thought I'd say that literally. It's WILD, bonkers shit that mermaids are real, but yeah, I totally mean that. It's like finding out you're Spider Man, but way, way cooler. And girl, I can't believe you took a bite out of Killian's stalker ex-girlfriend of all people."

Lorelei snorted. "Not my finest moment."

"I know, I know, but also kinda badass. Am I a terrible person for thinking that?"

"I could have killed her, so yes, you're a little bit terrible."

Katrina shrugged. "And yet, I don't feel all that bad."

Picking fuzz from her sweater, Lorelei mumbled, "You would if you saw it in person."

Katrina pushed the box of chocolates to her. There were two left inside. "Is that why there was limited PDA between you and Killian when he left?"

She pressed her finger onto a broken fragment of chocolate laying at the bottom of one of the trays. The heat from the touch melted it enough that it stuck to her finger when she popped it into her mouth. Her tongue tingled with the taste of bittersweet. "You noticed that, huh?"

"Yup."

Lorelei sighed, rubbing her forehead. She hated the halting way they now danced around intimacy. "I don't think our relationship is doomed, but we are at a bit of a stalemate. And Killian's gonna be on this offshore run for the next two weeks, after you leave. So, we can't exactly work on it. I can't even send him a goodnight text. They don't get cell service out there."

"Hmm." Katrina tapped her lips once before excusing herself to get a glass of water. She brought one back for Lorelei, too. Sipping thoughtfully, Katrina said, "Here's a daring thought. Why don't you put those fins of yours to use and swim out for a surprise, late night hook-up? How far out is he?"

"Sixty miles."

Katrina whistled, doubt crossing her face. "How far can you swim?"

Picking a chocolate from the box and biting through the caramel and nougat center, Lorelei mulled the idea over. In mermaid form, her baseline endurance was strong. Even without training, the furthest she swam offshore, incidentally, was about twenty nautical miles. Once out there, she played with harbor porpoises, hunted fish, and lazed about before swimming home. It took her about an hour to swim out and an hour to swim back. Which meant, when swimming with a purpose, she could maintain a speed about twenty nautical miles per hour without thoroughly exhausting herself.

While a one-hundred-and-twenty-mile round trip was not a forty-mile round trip, Lorelei's doubts were of a different sort. "I could do it. But the real question is, should I?" She sucked caramel and chocolate from her fingertips. "Killian is frightened enough of me as it is. He won't think I chased his boat in the middle of the ocean for a friendly visit."

"It won't take much to prove him wrong on that one," Katrina hinted suggestively. "But whether or not you go, he still has to get over his fear and accept all of you if your relationship is going to last."

If her relationship with Killian didn't work out, Lorelei joked that the inescapable fate of spinsterhood lay ahead of her. Katrina suggested they make a pact to live together as eccentric cat ladies if neither of them landed a long-term partner in the next ten years. Laughing, Lorelei thrust out her hand and shook on it but wondered out loud whether there was a chance the MMA fighter Katrina mentioned meeting on the car ride over, might render this pact moot.

Blushing, Katrina shrugged. "Too soon to know. If Killian wants to actually see a scary woman, he should see Rosie in the ring." Grinning goofily, she pulled up several videos she recorded of fight nights on her phone. Lorelei watched in wide-eyed wonder as Katrina's crush pummeled another girl senseless. "You wouldn't guess it from watching this, but she's normally soft-spoken and sweet."

Lorelei bumped Katrina's shoulder. "I can't wait to meet her."

Chuckling, Katrina bumped hers back. "Girl, I gotta ask her out on a date first. Not everyone moves as fast as you and Killian."

She stuck out her tongue. "It made sense at the time."

"You guys will figure this out," Katrina assured confidently. "From what you've said, Killian doesn't strike me as a runner, and it's obvious that he's practically in love with you. He'll come around."

Feeling her cheeks heat, Lorelei looked down at her lap. "You really think so?"

"Totally. And if you swim out there, he might be a little freaked out at first, but once he realizes you're not going to eat him, at least not in the bad way, I bet it knocks his socks off. And everything else he's wearing," she teased. "Mermaids have got to be a fisherman's biggest fantasy."

Emboldened by Katrina's confidence, Lorelei made up her mind to give her suggestion a try. It was all or nothing now. While that thought scared her, she had to know which it would be.

CHAPTER

THIRTY

THE GENTLE ROCKING OF THE BOAT HAD LULLED KILLIAN into a deep sleep.

He dreamt of Lorelei, a sleek, pale form gliding gracefully through the water, dark auburn hair billowing out behind her. As she swam, the muscles in her core rippled with each undulation. Even the barest flicks from her shimmering tail powered her onward. Her dual life as both daughter of Gaia and child of Poseidon had made her unbelievably strong.

A haunting, seductive song roused Killian from sleep.

There were no words, just an evocative crooning that quickened his heartbeat and set his skin tingling with anticipation. He bolted straight up in bed and threw off the covers, compelled by a desire to find the song's source.

That voice. That call, such a pleasant thrumming in his veins, a pull on his very bones, down to the marrow, urging him onward. Maybe he could deny it if he tried, but he didn't want to. And he knew it, didn't he? Heard it, felt it, once before.

But where? When? He scrambled for the memory but came up empty-handed.

Only one way to find out.

Not bothering to put on a shirt, he hastened topside.

As he peered in the dark across the deck, a clawed hand reached over the side, followed by the dripping, wet form of what otherwise appeared to be a woman. Little green spots of color along the bridge of her nose, her temples, her hands, her haunches, illuminated her in the night, bright as dancing fireflies.

She dropped down onto deck, in a crouched position, the sides of her legs covered in blue and silver scales and more of that bioluminescence.

But brightest of all were those gleaming sea green eyes he knew intimately well. They locked on him in a predatory stare, and a wicked smile played on her lips, over a mouthful of wicked sharp teeth. And she was beautiful. The most beautiful and terrifying he'd ever seen her.

Slowly, Lorelei began to rise.

Rooted in place by awe, Killian watched the sultry sway of her hips as she sauntered to him, his alluring sea goddess. His Aphrodite. Seeing her this way made his blood boil and head spin, but he also trembled at the uncertainty of her intentions.

In silent answer, she delicately touched his face, the tips of her claws gently resting upon his cheek and charted a course down. A shiver, born of both desire and fear, rippled down his spine, knowing that the claws that sensually touched his skin could also easily rip it to shreds.

Stopping at his navel, Lorelei withdrew her hand, eyes flicking to the passage below deck with heated intent. Dizzying desire triumphed over fear.

Nodding, he followed her wordlessly to his cabin.

Water ran in rivulets from her sea-drenched hair down the small of her back and dripped onto the floor, leaving small, foot-shaped puddles in her wake.

Distracted by passion, Killian didn't care how soaked she was when they fell into bed together, a tumbling tempest of kisses and entangled limbs. When he first pressed his lips to hers, it was without thought to the pointed teeth that lay behind them. But an incidental, innocent, prick of his tongue on their sharp edge, and the subsequent taste of his own tangy blood, froze his fevered movements with a burst of clarity and panic.

He laid in bed with a predator, sooner to eat him than give and take pleasure.

Lorelei's nostrils flared, but she slowly pulled back and exposed her neck.

Killian was confused at first, but when she didn't move, it gave him a chance to think. He recalled that wolves exposed their bellies, the most vulnerable part of their bodies, when showing submission. This similar gesture, exposing the very parts of her that allowed her to breathe underwater, was meant to demonstrate that she wouldn't attack him. Her posture was loose and relaxed as she patiently waited for him to realize that and make the next move.

Lowering his mouth to her neck, Killian delivered an open-mouthed kiss. His teeth grazed and nipped at her skin, eliciting a rumbling sound from the back of her throat. He was both relieved and pleased that it sounded more like a purr than a growl.

She lay languid beneath him, arms splayed wide. Relaxing himself, he sank into her embrace. When his fears of teeth and claws had long been forgotten, Lorelei pushed him onto his back.

Bestride, Lorelei was the ocean, rising and falling in waves. Lips parted, she watched him with a glowing, hooded gaze, and scales roughed his hands as he caressed her thighs. He churned beneath her, their bodies straining with need. Sea met gale again and again in frenetic passion. When her back crested, she rolled her hips through the peak of her pleasure and coated his thighs.

A love drunk sailor at the mercy of a siren's call, Killian drifted in the bliss of his own release.

After, as they lay together on his bed, he trailed his fingers down her spine, across the grooves of muscle on her back, wanting to learn and worship every inch of her. Whispering into her ear, he asked, "Would you be willing to show me your tail?" He'd never seen it.

Rolling onto her side, Lorelei pressed her legs together and scales rippled from the waist down in a shimmer. Her feet gracefully stretched into brightly colored fins streaked by many shades of yellows, greens, and blues.

Raising his hand to touch, his eyes flicked to hers in a silent request.

Lorelei's glowing sea green eyes met his in the dark—her answer given with the slight inclination of her head. He lowered his hand to her tail, and even this simple touch was a flirtation with beauty and danger. When he stroked downward, her scales were both silky and cool. Upwards, and they rasped against his skin, rough like a shark's. If he wasn't careful, he could cut himself on them.

"Your tail is quite beautiful," he marveled. Every single scale faded from a thin strip of dark blue to silver. "All the different colors, the way they either blend together or accent one another—reminds me of a betta fish."

With a wide toothy grin, Lorelei replied, "As you say, Captain."

Lorelei had called to him that night with her siren's song, swimming miles from shore to the *Dawn Chaser*, and summoning him from a deep sleep to satiate a primal need. And he found he did not care one iota about the immense, terrifying power she possessed—how easily she could bend him to her will and tear into his flesh with teeth and claws.

The truth was she wouldn't. She had grappled with the creature of the deep, harnessed its strengths, and quashed its unsavory impulses. He no longer feared her touch, but rather longed for what it might lead to.

THE OCEAN WAS QUIETER AT NIGHT. LESS NOISE FROM shipping traffic. The water more still.

Off in the distance, Lorelei still heard the rumbling engines of *Dawn Chaser*, but that sharp, scraping sound was finally dimming.

Hearing sensitivity had some perks. It allowed her to hear a wider range of sounds, and with it she could distinguish previously imperceptible nuances like a boat engine's unique vibrations. Even miles and miles away, *Dawn Chaser* had a distinct sound, one she learned after her rescue tucked inside Killian's cabin.

But hearing sensitivity had its challenges, too.

Those same engines up close were like a TV's volume being turned up slightly too high. Other ambient ocean noises were like that, too. Uncomfortable, and annoying, but not unbearable. It helped that much of the hearing sensitivity went away when she shifted back into her human form.

Not all her amplified senses gave her trouble.

At night, the ocean was an impenetrable inky black to the human eye. But Lorelei wasn't human. In the dark, her eyes expanded, picking up even the barest traces of light. Even on a cloudy night such as this one, there was always some surface light filtering down into the depths like strands of tinsel.

And she rather liked the deep. The more she swam and dove, the more she felt suited to its cold, pressing embrace. It was somewhat quieter, too, especially during the day, but she was careful not to go too far down, past the epipelagic zone.

That's where the truly monstrous creatures lived.

As Lorelei swam back toward Haven Cove, a pod of sleeping whales floated in the distance. A family just drifting along.

So sweet. So peaceful.

Something *whooshed* by in the water, tearing Lorelei from her reverie.

She should have paid more attention to her surroundings. Even for a siren such as herself, sticking to the uppermost pelagic zone, being alone in the open ocean was dangerous. Any number of creatures would find her easy prey, possibly even her own kind.

As Lorelei whirled around to see what it was, something slammed into her side, and she was thrown back through the water. If she had been on land, and making use of her lungs, the impact would have knocked the wind out of her.

Claws closed around her waist and razor-sharp teeth buried into her shoulder from behind. Howling, bubbles rushed from Lorelei's mouth and momentarily blinded her, so she didn't see another set of claws slash at her abdomen until they'd already sliced through her flesh. Lorelei doubled over from the attack, nauseated from the fiery, salt-searing pain, the taste of her own blood as it permeated the water, and the reek of her attackers' hunger.

The siren that grappled her from behind yanked her up by the hair, its claws scraping across her scalp. The motion forced her to meet the gleaming blue eyes of the siren who slashed her belly. Hair as black as midnight flowed around her face, and the blue-eyed siren's lips drew up into a snarl, the bioluminescence outlining her body flashing in angry warning.

Recognizing the creature from the night *The Osprey* sank, and remembering the awful fate of her crew, Lorelei twisted out of the other's grip, seething with rage. The claws binding her raked her flesh, but she didn't care. The cuts were only superficial, and she returned the damage done with a fearsome vengeance by ripping out the offending siren's jugular with her teeth. They weren't the only ones who could be lethal.

Bitter and sour filling her throat, she gagged on the unappetizing taste of kindred flesh, but the creature shrieked and fled, clutching her neck. Judging from the amount of blood flowing from the gaping wound, it wouldn't be long before she bled out.

Drawing up, chest puffed out in challenge, the blue-eyed siren's body began to glow from within, the silhouette of her bones dimly illuminated by blue bioluminescence, her whole human-piscine skeleton on display as if under x-ray. When she flexed her tail, the light brightened and an electromagnetic pulse starting at the base of her fins rippled up the length of her body.

Pissed off was putting it lightly.

But Lorelei would not cower.

Glaring at her opponent, she spat out the foul-tasting flesh and hissed.

Anger flared across the siren's face, but instead of retaliating, her glow dimmed, and she followed her mortally injured companion, electric blue fins snapping with haste.

Lorelei wasted no time and booked it out of there.

If more of her kind didn't come for her, sharks attracted by her blood would. Adrenaline and fear of another attack powered her the rest of the way back to shore, despite the severity of her wounds. It was the longest few hours of her life.

Crawling up the beach to Killian's cottage in the wee hours of the morning, Lorelei felt woozy from blood loss and salt-caked wounds. She only just managed to get in the door and text a S.O.S to Lila before passing out.

CHAPTER
THIRTY-ONE

A CAR DOOR SLAMMED OUTSIDE.

Dizzy and too stiff to move, Lorelei drifted toward consciousness. Ocean wind blew in off the water, over torn flesh, salty and searing. She sucked in a hissing breath, as black spots dotted her vision once more.

The pain was like no other. Like someone had doused her in kerosene and lit a match.

A moment later, Lila rushed in through the open door. Seeing the lacerations on her stomach, and bite on her shoulder, her hands flew to her mouth. "Oh my God, Lorelei! What the hell happened?" She fell to her knees beside her.

Lorelei groaned. "Family reunion."

Jumping up, Lila ran to the kitchen and grabbed a handful of towels from a drawer. "We need to get you to a hospital," she called, and when she returned, she pressed the bundle of towels to her abdomen to stanch the bleeding.

White hot fire burst behind Lorelei's eyes as pain raced up her spine, her whole body spasming. It was pure agony, but the surge passed.

Helping Lila hold the clothes in place, Lorelei shook her head furiously. "And how would we explain this?"

"We could say the same thing Carrie did."

"But this didn't happen near shore. If we tell them that it did, it would cause unnecessary panic. Lila, you gotta stitch me up."

Hands pressed to her temples, Lila cried, "Lorelei, I'm a marine biologist not a marine life veterinarian! I don't know how to do stitches. And I'm not sure I want to!"

"Please Lila," Lorelei begged and motioned to her still visible scales with one claw-tipped finger. "I'm too weak to fully shift back. And if I'm outed, they're going to stick me in a lab somewhere, or worse, they'll think I had something to do with what happened to *The Osprey* crew. I couldn't live with people thinking that."

Tilting her head back, Lila let out a long string of curses. "Fine," she sighed. "Someone's probably written a DIY blog post on this. But we're only doing it if we can get that bleeding to stop. This isn't worth you dying over. Where does Killian keep his medical supplies? And sewing kit?"

Lorelei told her, and Lila dashed upstairs. She brought down the first aid supplies, linens, a pillow, and a repurposed Danish cookie tin that must have been filled with sewing materials. Spreading a sheet over the couch, Lila set up a workstation, her hands trembling.

Then crouching down, Lila inspected her wounds. "Bleeding's slowing," she murmured, more to herself. A small, brief flash of relief softened the tension in her brow.

Still, just to be safe, the marine biologist opened a packet of clotting sponges and dressed her wounds with it, praising both Jesus and Killian in the same sentence for keeping such an impressive first aid kit at home. While continuing to add pressure, Lorelei wondered out loud why he had it, and Lila guessed it was from when he built the barn and frequently worked with power tools.

Once the bleeding stopped completely, Lila carefully helped Lorelei to her feet and supported her on the walk over to the couch. They moved slowly, so her injuries didn't start bleeding again.

Tears streamed down her face from the misery of engaging her core. Lorelei laid down and rested her forearm across her forehead.

Frowning, Lila handed her a glass of water and opened a bottle of Non-NSAID pain reliever. "Here. Drink this and take a couple of these."

Lorelei wordlessly obeyed, and Lila briefly disappeared into the kitchen. She heard her rifling through the cupboards and running the kitchen faucet.

A moment later, Lila returned with a mixing bowl filled with warm water and a handful of clean linen towels.

Soaking one of them in the warm water and wringing it out, Lila gently cleaned her wounds, rinsing and repeating often. Lorelei sucked her teeth at the sting, but otherwise didn't make a sound. She was thankful when Lila told her that they wouldn't be using any rubbing alcohol, because it was too harsh and actually damaged tissue and slowed healing.

No doubt she would have blacked out from the pain of that.

While Lila read a reputed survivalist's blog on self-medical care, Lorelei indirectly applied ice to the flesh surrounding her wounds to numb and reduce swelling. "How long did it take for the bite on your arm to heal?" Lila asked, opening a box. "It's just a scar now."

"About a week. I've always been a fast healer but more so now."

"Thankfully for the both of us, butterfly closures should work on most of this." Lila peeled off the wrappings, pulled her skin together, and began to apply the adhesive. "But there are a few spots across your belly and on your shoulder that need actual stitches." Lorelei winced through the procedure. "We will get the worse out of the way first," Lila continued, gesturing to her abdomen. "And we can take breaks as often as we need to."

When Lila pulled over an empty bucket, Lorelei raised her brow. Holding up the smallest needle she could find, Lila explained, "This is probably going to hurt like a bitch and feel weird as hell. You might puke."

Paling, Lorelei gulped nervously and tried to focus on her breathing, so she didn't psyche herself out. In truth, she wanted to go to the hospital and receive professional medical treatment. But the long-term consequences of going in partially shifted terrified her. As her thoughts raced, Lila unscrewed the cap and wetted a cotton ball with rubbing alcohol to sterilize the needle.

"Nylon. Polyester. Silk. He won't have silk," Lila muttered to herself as she searched through the spools of thread in the sewing kit. "A-ha! Nylon." But eyeing the spool closely, Lila huffed, "I don't care what that famous survivalist says. I can't stitch you up with this. We need surgical sutures and one of those curved needle thingies." She looked back down at her phone and read further. Her eyes widened. "Oh my God! I can't do this."

"Why? What does it say?"

"Lorelei, it says that stitching human skin is like sewing leather. I've never tried sewing leather before, but that doesn't sound easy. What the hell are we doing? This is a bat-shit idea."

Resolve shattered by the fallibility of "experts" found on the internet and imagining Lila trying to force the needle in and out of her skin repeatedly, Lorelei relented.

Pulling out padding, antibacterial ointment, and gauze to temporarily dress the wounds for the ride over to the hospital, Lila continued, "We're trying to tackle the wrong problem. We should be trying to hide your metamorphosis. You don't have any injuries on your legs, so we can just cover them up with sweatpants. I can clip your claws. If you keep your fingers together, they might not notice the webbing. But if they do, some people actually have webbed extremities, so it's not too hard to explain away. The teeth—damn, I don't know what to do about the teeth."

"You'll just have to do most of the talking," Lorelei said. "Tell them I was camping, forgot I had a bag of peanut butter crackers in my jacket, a bear got in my tent, and we both freaked out. With Carrie, I mentioned that the bite kind of looked like an eel's or a small shark's. No one would ever believe that in my case, but they might believe a small, frightened bear did this."

"You told them it looked like an eel bite? And they bought that?" Lila asked incredulously. "A Moray maybe, but you won't find those here. We have American eels, but they have tiny teeth and weak jaws—"

Lorelei cut her off. "Lila, focus. I know it was a flimsy lie. And this one is, too, but what other choice do we have?"

"Okay. Okay. Let's give this a shot. I'll go get you some clothes and nail clippers."

THE TRIP TO THE HOSPITAL WENT AS WELL AS COULD BE expected.

The nurses and doctor, of course, had a lot of questions, but Lila managed to answer most convincingly. And throughout the whole visit, Lorelei kept her hands out of sight by either burying them in her pants pockets or sitting on them. When she had to speak, she hid her teeth by carefully tilting her head. The doctors and nurses tried to convince Lorelei to allow them to examine her more thoroughly for additional injuries, but she did not consent, and they eventually let her be.

On the way home in Lila's car, she ate iron-rich foods from a to-go box purchased from the hospital cafeteria. With the worst of the ordeal behind them, Lila asked her to explain what happened, because "family reunion" and "it didn't happen near shore" weren't enough to go on.

Between bites of food, Lorelei told Lila that she swam about sixty miles offshore to visit Killian on the *Dawn Chaser* but didn't run into any trouble until she left him to swim back to shore. When she described the attack, and the siren she recognized, Lila glanced over at her from the driver's seat, a frown creasing her features.

"Lorelei, they could smell Killian on your skin."

CHAPTER
THIRTY-TWO

CURSING KILLIAN'S LACK OF A DOWNSTAIRS BATHROOM, Lorelei awkwardly hobbled up the spiral staircase with Lila's help, all while trying not to jostle and irritate her wounds. It was slow going, but they eventually made it up and across the landing into the master bedroom.

The medication given to her at the hospital was kicking in, making her woozy, and no sooner did her head hit the pillow, did she lose herself to the oblivion of sleep.

For once it was deep and dreamless.

When consciousness found her once more, sunlight was streaming in through the windows, bright and blinding. Squinting at the bedside clock, Lorelei grumbled, then buried her face under the covers in the blissful darkness.

10AM.

Either she hadn't slept for very long, or she'd passed out for a whole day and night.

The need to use the bathroom compelled her out of bed. If it weren't for that, she'd happily stay put another day, as motionless as possible. With every slight movement her abdomen twinged something fierce— and sliding out of bed hurt like a bitch.

She was way overdue for another dose of pain medication.

After washing up, Lorelei found Lila in the guest bedroom with a sketchbook in her lap, a pencil in one hand, and a spare jutting out of her hair, which she'd piled high onto her head in a puffy bun and secured loosely with a large hair tie. A silk scarf lay curled upon the comforter at her side, and donned in familiar cozy socks and jammies, the marine biologist had evidently spent the night and had helped herself to the spare clothes in Lorelei's dresser. As she should.

Holding her bandaged middle, Lorelei leaned against the doorframe. "Doodling?"

Lila looked up from her drawing. "Oh good, you're awake. How're you feeling?"

"Like a truck hit me."

"Wanna sit?" Lila patted a spot beside her on the bed, the covers rumpled and unmade.

She winced. "I think I'm just going to stop moving for a little bit."

"Fair enough." Spinning the sketchpad around, Lila showed her a drawing of a wet suit, a chainmail vest, and a harpoon, the linework and shading impressively rendered. Marci wasn't the only artist in the Walsh family, apparently.

"It's shark armor," Lila explained. "For you. I thought that maybe if you wanted to go back out again, we could make sure you were better prepared."

The truth was, despite being almost gutted, Lorelei *did* want to go back out. Needed to. But damn, why hadn't she thought to take protective measures for herself on her own? She knew better than anyone how dangerous the ocean could be. For Chrissakes, she watched a pod of carnivorous mermaids devour her entire crew.

It was stupid, so, so, stupid. If Lila hadn't gotten her text, hadn't been awake to see it and rushed over, she would have bled out on Killian's floor.

And yet, now that she'd faced the creatures of her nightmares, and of her worst memories, it wasn't fear she felt, but a fierce, territorial instinct to fight back and give as good as she'd gotten. Pay flesh and blood in kind.

Just...not without protection next time.

She pressed the heel of her hand to her forehead, frustrated with herself. "You must think I'm an idiot for going out there like that."

"Mm yeah, a bit," Lila snorted. "But I think I get it. Booty call aside, it's in your nature to be drawn to the deep. That's your species' natural habitat." She thumbed a sketchpad corner. "In a way, I feel it, too, that draw. Every day the ocean beckons to me, challenges me to uncover its secrets. And I am too mesmerized to even consider another path. Marine science is more of a calling than a job."

"So, you don't think I'm an idiot for wanting to go back?"

Setting aside the sketchbook with a sigh, Lila hugged her knees and propped her chin on top. She looked...guilty? "No, it makes sense biologically, but I have selfish reasons for not trying to talk you out of it."

Lorelei froze. "What do you mean?"

"There's just so much I can learn from you," Lila admitted, scrunching her nose. "I know how that sounds. It's the scientist talking, not the friend, but I want to be real with you about what's going through my head right now."

Maybe it was time to sit down.

Shuffling over to the desk, Lorelei slowly lowered herself down into the chair, grimacing. *Speedy mermaid healing, heal faster, dammit.* She'd need to go find the pain medication after this.

Lila puffed out a breath. "I'm just gonna tell it like it is, get it off my chest, all right?"

Lorelei nodded, bracing herself.

"What your biology achieves, morphing from human to mythical fish creature and back—it's a wonder to behold and an incredible discovery on its own. But there's even more I can learn if you continue exploring. With your help, I can learn the unknowable mysteries of the ocean, things other scientists couldn't even dream of if they tried."

An experiment. A fact finder. That's what a marine biologist saw in a mermaid. It didn't come as a surprise, not even a little, but a part of her had hoped that scientific value wasn't the only thing she saw in her.

"But Lorelei, that's the scientist in me. I also see you as a friend, and friend-me wants to shield you from scientist-me's voracious thirst for knowledge and from anyone else who may want to take advantage of you. You're a person, not a data-extracting curiosity quest. Just the thought of my colleagues, or myself, intruding on your life, and shucking your anonymity like frickin' corn..." Her fingers dug into the fabric of her pajama pants. "Well, it makes me mad and ashamed. There's plenty of biologists out there who would do it, too, without a single care for the ethics. My field has its fair share of vultures, and I've dealt with them my whole career, even in undergrad."

Lorelei exhaled, and in a soothing voice, said, "But you haven't done any of that. All our little experiments help me learn more about myself, too. And when I'm making dives, being your eyes and hands on the ocean floor, I'm learning about where I come from. I might be able to see and touch things you can't, but I don't know what I'm looking at, what I'm holding. But you make sense of it all. I'm..." She swallowed, feeling tears sting her eyes. "I'm podless. So, you see, exploring the ocean on my own could feel really lonely, but it doesn't because you're there, talking to me over the radio."

Glassy-eyed, Lila fanned herself. "Girl, you're gonna make me cry."

Lorelei wiped her eyes. "Yeah, well, you've literally saved me twice. First with the flesh-craving problems, and second with getting me to the hospital. So, thank you, Lila. Thank you so much."

"Dammit," Lila slid out of bed, tears streaking her cheeks. "I'm coming to give you a hug."

"Just go easy on me, okay? The quick healing hasn't kicked in yet."

"I'll be careful."

Careful not to irritate her abdominal injury, that is, but her shoulders were fair game, apparently, as Lila squeezed them tight, squishing their faces cheek to cheek. "You're not podless, Lorelei," she said effusively. "You've got Killian, and you've got us."

Ignoring the fiery pain shooting up her stomach, Lorelei bear hugged her friend.

CHAPTER
THIRTY-THREE

K ILLIAN PUSHED THE SPEED LIMIT ON THE WAY HOME, EAGER to rejoin the woman that swam out to *Dawn Chaser* just to ravish him. On empty, country roads, he could afford to be a little reckless.

She was gone from the boat when he woke the next morning and did not return for the remainder of the offshore trip. Had it not been for the smell of sea salt on his pillow, his nakedness, and the evidence of her pleasure on his skin, he would have thought her visit nothing more than a vivid dream.

While he wasn't the type to daydream, he couldn't stop replaying that night in his head—a fantasy he never could have conceived would be fulfilled.

Lorelei met him at the door with a warm smile, likely having heard his truck pull up the gravel driveway, but something was off. When he bent to hug her, she stretched out a hand to keep him from coming any closer.

For a long, agonizing moment, he thought he had done something wrong, but he couldn't figure out what he might have done to upset her.

Then she reached up to caress his face, but he noticed that her movements were stiff and pained. He cupped her upper arms. "Lorelei, are you okay?"

"I've been better." She lifted up her shirt to show him the bandages wrapped around her torso. With a small, lopsided shrug, she added, "My shoulder is wrapped up, too."

Stomach knotting up from fear, he pressed, "How bad is it? What happened?"

"I had to get stitches. Come upstairs, I'll show you. I was just about to change the gauze."

Killian gulped and followed her to the bathroom.

A roll of bandages, antibacterial ointment, and a container of cotton swabs sat on the countertop. Sore from her injuries, she winced as she attempted to remove her shirt. Killian helped her with bitter nostalgia for the circumstances under which they met.

Unraveling the bandages from her waist and removing the pad from her shoulder, Lorelei said, "There will be scars, but I've been healing nicely. No infections."

The butchery wrought upon her nearly brought Killian to his knees. Four slashes crossed the width of her belly, one bisecting her navel, and the bite mark on her shoulder reminded him of the one she gave herself. "It looks worse than it is," she tried to assure him, but he trembled and clenched his fists.

"What happened?" he repeated, his voice firm and low.

She applied ointment and rebandaged her wounds while she talked. Listening to Lorelei explain what her own kind had done to her, and Lila's near attempt at DIY medical care, doused his vision in shades of red. These were near fatal wounds. Just a little bit deeper and... "What were you thinking swimming that far and all alone?" he yelled.

Surprised by his outburst, Lorelei squared her shoulders, folding her arms across her chest. "I wanted to see you."

"Lorelei, you know better than most what dangers wait out there in the open ocean! You should never have taken the risk."

"You didn't have a problem with it that night," she fired back. "In fact, I remember you looking very pleased."

"I wasn't thinking clearly. If I was, I would have said something, but you literally bewitched me."

Her eyes flashed with anger. "Excuse me?"

"You're a siren, and you called to me. Of course, I came. And then you were on deck, and I just couldn't look away or—" Lost for words, he ran a hand over his face.

"Oh my God." Lorelei blanched, covering her mouth with her hand. "Did you want to? I didn't force you—" she trailed in horror.

Realizing the implications, and how his words came across, Killian's anger vanished. *Shit, that's not what he...* "Oh God, no. I didn't mean it like that. I wanted you. I wanted you so bad it was overwhelming, but I definitely, definitely wanted you."

Relief washed over her face, and he continued in a softer, gentler voice. "Lorelei, never in a million years did I expect to see you there. But there you were, emerging from the sea like a goddess out of a goddamn myth, and it was so fucking hot and surreal." His gaze drifted from her eyes to her lips. "I am going to cherish that memory until the day I die."

She took a step toward him and reached with her good arm to brush his lower lip with her fingertips. "Then why did you yell?"

He pressed his forehead to hers. "I yelled because I was scared—and still am. When I came home today, I never considered the possibility of you not being here. I almost lost you, and I had no idea."

Lorelei nodded, accepting his explanation. She leaned into him. "Are you still afraid of me?"

"No." He met her lips in an unhurried, tender kiss. Tugging the hairband from her braid, he combed his fingers through her tresses, savoring their silky texture. When she reached for his belt, he stilled her hands, heart racing. "You need to heal." He tried to sound stern, but the words fell out desperate and needy.

"This will help, if we go slow and easy," she soothed, charming him, seducing him.

He wanted her, to be as close as possible to the one he almost lost, but he didn't want to hurt her. It would be selfish of him to readily agree to this.

"Please Killian," she begged softly, unclasping her bra and letting it fall to the floor. "I need you. And I think you need me, too."

A groan rumbled in the back of throat. *Dammit, he really did.* He took her hand, unable to resist any longer.

They undressed in his bedroom, peeling away layers slowly and carefully. He eased her down onto the bed with her legs hanging over the edge. To help her relax, he lit a candle and played quiet, soothing music. He would take great care in where and how he touched her.

"Promise me you won't swim out to the *Dawn Chaser* again," he pleaded, maintaining eye contact as he smoothed his hands over her thighs, and pressing kisses in their wake.

Fire burned in her gaze—he knew a sharp disagreement was coming —and he'd hear what she had to say, but he desperately wanted a taste of her first. Easing her legs open, so not to jostle her abdomen, he licked her slow, rolling his tongue over her most sensitive bits, savoring her taste, sticky and sweet like saltwater taffy.

"You're trying to distract me," she moaned, her legs trembling against his cheeks. "So, I agree when I can't think straight."

After a long, drawn-out suck of Lorelei's clit, one that made her clench around him, he rose from between her thighs, crawling onto the bed on both hands and knees to straddle her body, carefully keeping his weight off her. "I would never," he said, hovering so close their noses brushed.

She stared up at him in fierce challenge, pinching her lips tight. "I'll be better prepared next time."

"No amount of preparation is going to make it safe enough for you, or anyone, to be out there all alone. Not that far out at sea."

For the briefest moment, he spied a flicker of doubt, one he could've easily missed if he hadn't been watching her so closely. But then her expression hardened, and he knew she'd squashed it and was going to double down.

He captured her lips in his, wanting to kiss away the stubborn, reckless set of her mouth. She threaded her fingers through his hair, giving into him one moment, tearing their mouths apart the next. "I'm a mermaid," she growled, yanking his hair. The brief, sharp sensation pulled a hearty groan from his mouth. *Damn*, he liked it when she was a little rough with him. "I belong in the ocean."

Fear and a sharp spike of anger raced through him. He was making no headway in getting her to take this risk to herself more seriously. What if the merfolk sought revenge for the brethren she probably killed?

Murderous mermaids didn't strike him as the forgive and forget type. Lorelei may be able to fend off two or three of them on her own but an angry swarm? He would never know if she was in trouble or how to find and help her.

An hour of pleasure wasn't worth the constant fear for her safety.

When he voiced these thoughts to Lorelei, her features finally softened. "They took me off guard once, but they won't again," she promised, cupping his cheek. He frowned, but before he could protest, she added, "I'm not fragile out there. They swam away when I drew blood. And I need the ocean as much as I need to see you. I always feel its pull."

Unhappily, Killian relented. It wasn't his choice to make.

When the tailor-ordered shark armor and wetsuit arrived, paid for out of Lila's own pocket, Lorelei watched the marine biologist demonstration how its custom features would work in all stages of transformation.

Unwilling to sacrifice speed, they opted for a black-link chainmail vest that would protect Lorelei's vital organs from attack. It would overlay the wetsuit, the latter of which had a skirt split down the middle. Hook and loop tape along the front and back of the split allowed the material to be strapped around her tail or individual legs.

She would not only need the wetsuit as a layer between her skin and the armor, but also to cover herself during research expeditions, and to hide herself from the eyes of other boaters. Naked ladies out for a swim weren't exactly inconspicuous.

The wetsuit, despite its unusual structure, fit Lorelei like a glove, and strategically placed fabric and fastenings ensured she was fully covered no matter how it was worn. As Lorelei lifted the vest from the box, her eyes widened at the lack of weight.

Noting her surprise, Lila commented, "Light, isn't it? We have recent advances in materials fabrication to thank for that. And the brand boasts increased maneuverability."

She couldn't wait to try it on in the water.

"I also got you a small underwater video camera that hooks to the vest, so you can record hands free," Lila continued, pointing out the play button and a marine spotlight feature. "If you're willing, it'd be wicked if you could get footage of your next run-in with the sirens."

"The light might mess with my night vision, but I know we won't see anything on the video without it."

"We will test it before you go out that far again."

"I'm going to feel like such a badass wearing this stuff."

Lila grinned from ear to ear. "Oh, just wait until you see what else came in."

Every nerve in Lorelei's body vibrated with excitement. "The harpoon?"

"The harpoon."

LORELEI'S WOUNDS HEALED WITH THE SPEED OF HER supernatural heritage. What should have taken weeks, possibly months, only took days. Those closest to her cautioned rest, but she was a livewire of adrenaline, itching to get back into the ocean.

She practiced wielding her new harpoon beneath the waves, twirling, thrusting, and slashing at invisible enemies. In this, and in her swimming, she worked on speed and endurance, pushing herself through the aching and burning of her muscles.

The sirens of the wild were hardened by a life of survival.

To defend herself against them, she needed to be in peak fighting condition. She put in the effort not only for the occasional romantic visit to the *Dawn Chaser*, but to expand Lila's personal research, and to explore her own curiosity about the greater depths of the sea.

Lorelei understood the risks. And while she didn't want Killian to worry about her, she wouldn't let fear—his or her own—get in the way of living her life to the fullest.

LORELEI SWUNG HER LEG OVER *DAWN CHASER'S* RAILING AND grinned mischievously. Killian stood on deck waiting for her, half-aroused and with a grumpy expression on his face.

Breathing hard from the exertion it took to get to the boat, but no less energized, Lorelei crossed the deck, stripping off her diving belt, harpoon, and shark armor. She let each slide from her fingers onto the deck with a soft thud. It occurred to her that they could be caught, but she didn't care. She was riding high on her adrenaline rush.

When Lorelei unzipped the top portion of her wetsuit, Killian's eyes fell to her heaving, flushed chest. A choked sound escaped his lips, but he tore his eyes away, and looked up, ready to scold her for risking her life. Before he could do so, she grabbed the front of his sweater and crashed her lips onto his. He swore against her mouth but returned the kiss voraciously and pulled her into the space behind the pilothouse stairs. Her back hit the wall hard, but not painfully so.

Killian kissed his way down her body, ripped open the fastenings, and peeled off the wetsuit. More swearing followed when he tasted how wet she was. "Captain," she moaned, pulling him to his feet. Despite the cold sea air, he yanked off his sweater. He, too, breathed heavily, and his pupils were blown wide.

"Please," Lorelei pleaded, wrapping her arms around his well-muscled shoulders. She slung a leg around his waist.

"You shouldn't have come," he murmured gruffly, his breath a warm puff of air against her cheek. And yet, he pushed down the front of his sweatpants, and hoisted her other leg, unable to deny her. They joined with a gasp.

"I needed this," she whispered back, rolling her hips. Heated skin to her front, cool hard metal to her back. His forehead fell to her shoulder, reluctantly grumbling defeat. He'd needed this, too. Rocking into her, in time with the ocean's swell, against the wall of his boat—there didn't exist a better cure for cabin fever.

FASTENING THE BELT HOLDING HER DIVER'S KNIFE AROUND her waist, and securing her harpoon behind her back, Lorelei sat on top of *Dawn Chaser*'s deck railing. She gave each weapon a tug, and once satisfied that they would stay in place, she braided her just-washed hair to keep it off her face. She'd showered to remove Killian's scent from her body, hoping the mermaids wouldn't find her if they couldn't smell her human lover in the water.

Killian looked on at her preparations in reserved fascination.

This time he'd had enough presence of mind to be grumpy with her for risking her life. But she regretted nothing about tonight. What happened last time wouldn't be repeated. She'd been caught off-guard, unprepared, but thanks to Lila, she was far from either of those things now.

After she fused together her tail on deck and enclosed herself in the wetsuit, he cupped her face in his hands, pleading, "Be careful. Please."

So much fear and worry shone back at her in those storm-grey eyes. It cut through her steely resolve and a measure of regret twinged in her chest. Not for what they shared, or for wanting to try swimming in open water again, but for not considering Killian's feelings more. There really was no way for him to know whether she made it back to shore safely until he did in several days' time.

Maybe proving she could take care of herself would put him at ease.

"If any of them give me trouble, they will regret it," she vowed. He wasn't relieved by her confidence. "I'll be fine," she winked and dove backwards. This time, she remembered to pinch her nose closed before she hit the water.

Through prior testing, Lorelei learned that the spotlight feature of the video recorder was too bright and blinded her in the water, but Lila replaced it with a night vision lens attachment that produced a clear picture. It was expensive, but Lila didn't want to miss another opportunity to obtain footage of her murderous kinfolk.

The moment Lorelei sensed something near her in the water, she pulled the harpoon from her back and pressed play. Blood pumping with adrenaline, she kept her head on a swivel for attack. Either they could still smell Killian, despite Lorelei's thorough washing, or they recognized her scent.

The first mermaid attacked from the side.

But Lorelei was ready and slashed a gash in her chest. Gravely injured, the mermaid fled without attempting another attack.

Hearing a disturbance behind her, she whirled around to thrust the harpoon into the tail of a second one. The impaled creature swiped at her with razor sharp claws, but they glanced uselessly off the shark armor vest she wore.

A third siren sped up at her from below.

Lorelei yanked out the harpoon and flipped, cracking the newcomer over the top of the head with the shaft. The impact jarred her wrist, but it brought the siren to a sudden halt. Dazed, she floated past Lorelei to the surface with a flaccid expression.

A fourth grabbed her hair but let go when Lorelei drove the butt of the harpoon into her stomach. While this attacker doubled over, Lorelei wound up to deliver a second, more damaging blow.

The blue-eyed mermaid—the nightmare of her memories—darted in and blocked the strike with a trident. Without missing a beat, Lorelei whipped out her diver's knife from the holster on her hip and pressed the blade to her enemy's throat. Their eyes locked in fierce challenge.

About half a dozen other mermaids circled warily, but kept their distance, as if awaiting command or readying to flee.

Pressing the knife harder, Lorelei drew a small amount of blood.

The blue-eyed siren accepted defeat with a slight inclination of her eyes and backed off with reluctant respect. Blue-eyes waved the rest of them away, and they retreated as a pod, heeding her command without question. She must have been their leader.

The rush of Lorelei's victory made the return home fly by.

Her next run-in with the sirens was unlike the others.

They were drawn in by Killian's scent, just as before, but this time they recognized her. And without so much as a hiss, or a backwards glance, they dashed away as they might from another dominate predator.

Did this mean she'd earned a measure of respect? Or fear? Either one suited her just fine.

CHAPTER
THIRTY-FIVE

Peeking his head out into the narrow hallway between his cabin and the crew's quarters, Killian checked if the coast was clear. While the crew should be fast asleep in their bunks, they couldn't be too careful during Lorelei's nighttime visits. Never knew who might be out of bed getting a late-night snack from the galley or making a head run.

It was quiet. Empty.

He waved Lorelei out into the hallway.

As she tiptoed out of his cabin and slinked toward the stairs leading to the main deck, the door to the head swung open with a creak.

Walsh emerged, bleary-eyed from sleep.

Well, shit.

"Lorelei?" The older fisherman blinked, then rubbed his eyes for good measure.

At least she was already decked out in her shark armor, wetsuit, and harpoon combo. Nakedness would make this situation a hell of a lot more awkward. Silver linings.

Observing the get-up, her glowing eyes, Killian watched the gears turning in Walsh's sleep-deprived head, trying to rationalize Lorelei's presence so far from shore. With a straight face, he asked, "Are you a secret Navy Seal and are those night vision contact do-dad's?"

Oh, Walsh. Of all the fantastical theories, only this sweet old man would come up this one. Maybe they could get away with humoring it tonight. But come morning? Not a chance.

Not that he wanted to lie to Walsh, the Patron Saint of Too Good for this World. It made Killian sick to his stomach. Lying to his best friend had been bad enough. He could not repeat that decision with the man who'd welcomed him into his home, had given him his livelihood, and shaped him into the man he'd become.

To Lorelei, he nodded toward the stairs. "Go on. I'll meet you topside in just a minute."

She tugged at the end of her braid, fingers twisting around the loose strands. "Are you going to tell him?" she whispered.

"Not right now...but I can't lie to him, Lorelei. Please don't make me lie to him."

When she frowned, he thought she might protest, but all she said was "we'll talk topside" before darting up the stairs.

"What's going on, son?" The old man was more alert now.

Sighing, Killian threw an arm around Walt's shoulders. "I've got something to tell you about Lorelei, but can we wait until the morning to talk about it? I need to have a conversation with her first."

"We can do that," Walt nodded, patting his hand. "Go talk to your lady. Sort it all out."

Killian watched Walsh shuffle back to bed, then raced topside.

It was cold up on deck, his breath clouding in front of him. He pushed down his sleeves, head on a swivel, looking for Lorelei.

Two green orbs stared out at him from the dark nook underneath the pilothouse stairs. Waiting. A chill ran down his spine, and it was not from the frigid rush of sea air blowing across deck, ruffling his hair and knifing through his clothes.

If it weren't for that lambent gaze, he never would have seen her tucked away in the shadows.

She stepped out from beneath the stairs, and into the moonlight, mouth pinched tight. Irritated. Scared. And rightfully so.

"I know it's not my secret to share," Killian said, trying to find the right words. He shoved his numbing hands under his arms for warmth.

"I don't want to lie to Walt either." But her shoulders were squared off, stiff.

Maybe knowing who the old fisherman was to him would help her understand.

"Walsh was the dad I needed when my own old man turned into a real shit."

The tension in her shoulders gave out. "I didn't know that Killian. I'm sorry."

"It was after my mom died," he continued, sniffing from the bite of the wind against his nose and cheeks. "My granddad took me in, taught me carpentry, masonry, and a number of other skills, but *who* I am wouldn't be the same if it weren't for Walsh. I looked up to him. Still do."

An arm draped across her chest, Lorelei leaned against the wall, pressing her temple to the metal. "I'm torn. I don't like lying, but I've got to keep *what* I am secret. Walt's a good, honorable man. I know he is, but what if he hates the monster in me and tells someone? I've been lucky, so far. You and Kat and Lila have all handled it really, really well. But what if it's too much of a burden and the wrong person finds out... I'm a lab experiment."

He shook his head. That wasn't the old fisherman at all. "Will he be shocked? Yes. But he's not going to out you, and he's definitely not going to fault you for something beyond your control. I promise you can trust him with this. Come on. You know he's a big teddy bear."

That brought out a small smile. "That's true." She came forward, slipping her arms around his middle, and nuzzled her face into his chest. As he enveloped her in the hug, she said, "I never had a dad, but if I did, I would have wanted him to be just like Walt."

The wind died down.

"Tell him, Killian."

FROM ONE FISHING CAPTAIN TO ANOTHER, AND ONE seafaring son to his father, Killian told Walsh the truth—that the sailors' stories about mermaids and sirens weren't drunken fiction. They were real and beautiful and deadly. And Lorelei was one.

With the help of video footage, Killian explained everything as delicately as he could. He didn't want Walsh to fear Lorelei, but he also wanted him to have realistic expectations when it came to her people-eating kin.

While Walsh sat with his hands clasped under his chin, quietly absorbing Lorelei's story, his expression was hard to read. When Killian finished, the older fisherman nodded, lost in thought. "I'm glad Carrie's injury hadn't been worse," he began quietly. "How're you handling all this? Do you feel safe around Lorelei?"

"I'm adjusting, but I'm willing to make whatever accommodations are necessary to keep her by my side. If the ocean becomes too much trouble for her, and she needs to move away, I'd follow her and give *Dawn Chaser* to Branson. I'd keep the cottage for visiting, but I couldn't continue living there if she wasn't in it. It wouldn't be home without her."

A bashful grin tugged at his lips, and the next words just poured out of him. "Do I feel safe? Let's just say, she's a scary lady, but she's my scary lady, and I love her."

Walsh answered with a warm, knowing smile.

Wow. He just said that out loud, hadn't he? That he loved Lorelei. But he knew in the depths of his soul that it was true. His feelings for her had always been intense. Was it really any surprise that love soon followed?

"Do you think it will come to that—her needing to move away?" Walsh tilted his head, watching him carefully.

Killian mulled the question over. "It's hard to know what's going to happen, but for the time being, no. There've been hiccups, but Lorelei's struck a pretty solid balance between these two separate parts of her life. Lila knows, and you know Lila when it comes to marine studies. I think her excitement over this has really helped Lorelei embrace it.

Katrina also knows and is coming around to it. I know. And now you do, too."

"That I do," Walsh replied, taking Killian's phone again and replaying the first of many videos.

In this one, Lila recorded Lorelei's playful spins and leaps out of the water; the marine biologist's commentary and laughter could be heard throughout. At the end, when Lorelei did her infamous Little Mermaid schtick with a pair of seashells, Lila turned the camera to record herself rolling her eyes and grumbling, 'Work wife's thinking she's funny and being cute. AGAIN.'

"They're having such fun, aren't they? And your lady looks happy."

"I'm really glad they get along," Killian replied, wearing a stupid grin. Man, he was besotted. "Lila's approval means a lot to me."

Walsh looked up from the screen. "It means a lot to me, too."

And that's all Killian needed to hear to know exactly how Walsh felt.

CHAPTER
THIRTY-SIX

As Lorelei sped through the water, she came upon two mermaids hunting a school of fish. Their eyes widened at the sight of her. With the flick of their flashy silver and orange tails, they abandoned their hunt and fled with their prey.

That brought a much needed smile to her face.

Now that she wasn't beholden to eating human flesh, she found that she rather *liked* thinking of herself as a dominant predator beneath the waves. It made her feel powerful. In control.

With not another creature in sight, Lorelei took solace in the quiet, peaceful sea, pretending she had it all to herself, mistress of her domain. She needed that illusion to get the rest of the way home, because on the surface, her secret was rapidly slipping out of her hands.

By morning, Walt would know. If she lost one more person she cared about…her stomach tied in knots. *Don't think about that.*

Out of the corner of her eye, a dark shadow swam toward her.

So much for being alone.

It was bigger, more powerfully built than her mermaid kin. *Shark.* Heart racing, she unstrapped her harpoon from her back and turned to face it head on, bracing for attack.

But it wasn't a shark.

Two golden eyes peered back at her in the dark water from a male, humanoid face. He drew up just close enough for Lorelei to see his features but stayed far enough away to keep out of range of her weapon. At the sight of her, his lips turned upward into a malicious, predatory grin.

She tried swimming away but didn't get far before the merman cut her off. Only a jab from her harpoon kept him at length.

For the next mile, he stalked her, persistently testing her defenses, waiting for her to make a mistake. It took all her energy, all her focus to keep track of his movements—to not make that mistake. With about forty miles of ocean between her and the shore, the thought of having to fend him off the entire way distressed her. How much longer could she keep this up? He was all alone, and yet this one merman made Lorelei far more uncomfortable, and in far more danger, than the swarm of angry mermaids.

The smell of her fear permeated the water, pungent even to her own senses. He grinned wider, cockily spinning through the water around her, and her stomach soured knowing he smelled her fear, too. She didn't recognize the scent he exuded in response, but it sent a cold shiver down her spine. Before she could follow her instincts to launch an offensive, the blue-eyed siren sped up from the depths with her trident and a retinue of four others holding broken off spear points.

Lorelei flinched away, expecting attack.

But she wasn't their target.

They stabbed and clawed the merman with brutal ferocity. Their collective anger rolled off in waves, so potent it drowned the taste of his fear and anguish. The surrounding water became so red with blood, Lorelei could only see an occasional glint of flashing steel or the shimmer of a flicked tail.

Frozen in place by the scene, Lorelei could only watch, clutching her harpoon in a two-handed death grip. The merman was nothing more than minced meat when they were done with him. His limp, shredded body ascended to the surface where he'd likely become food for fish and scavenging sea birds.

Neither of them expected that's how his evening was going to go. But thank God, that's how it did.

When the bloodied water dissipated, a row of five mermaids hovered in the water facing her, chins held high, but weapons lowered.

For the first time, Lorelei took a moment to truly appreciate their incredible, terrible beauty. Each had brightly colored fins as varied and vibrantly patterned as betta fish. Two of the mermaids who bore similar facial features, also shared similar colorings—fins fanning out in several orange shades and slashed with the same silvery color as their tails. Perhaps they were family. Sisters or cousins.

Another mermaid's coloring was a magenta gradient from waist to fin. And the fourth a kaleidoscope of greens.

Of the five, only the blue-eyed mermaid met her gaze directly, but it was without any challenge or threat. Unlike the others, her tail was as black as her midnight hair and flecked with white specks like stars. Bioluminescence aside, only her fins bore color—electric blue and silver.

Begrudgingly, she nodded her thanks, and the blue-eyed siren returned the gesture before leading the others back into the deep. While she hated what this mermaid and her kind did to *The Osprey* crew, she couldn't ignore the fact that they had just saved her.

Shaken and emotionally exhausted from this latest confrontation, Lorelei swore off future *Dawn Chaser* visits. It had finally lost enough appeal to keep her close to shore—at least as long as she was alone.

At home, she trudged despondently up the stairs and into the shower where she sobbed. She slept through most of her Saturday and, on Sunday, curled up on the couch in front of a fire with hot chocolate and a book.

In the office Monday morning, after showing Lila the recording, the marine biologist agreed at Lorelei's bequest not to show it to Killian.

CHAPTER
THIRTY-SEVEN

Toes buried deep in the packed wet sand Lorelei gazed out over the water. Sea wind loosened tendrils of hair from her braid, and blew them about her face, sticky, and damp from the salty spray. She breathed in deeply, trading the scent of pine and earth for brine and kelp. As the tide rushed out, Lorelei felt the ocean's pull, rolling over her feet and tugging at her heart.

It called her to the deep.

Even after the violent encounters with her kinfolk, the last happening only a few short days ago, she wanted to answer that call. She missed her explorations and the freedom to speed through the water, fully shifted in mermaid form.

Gripping her harpoon in the palm of her hand, Lorelei inched toward the waves. No matter the peril, she could no more resist the sea than a sailor could a siren's song.

Lorelei left behind a pile of clothes and her human fear on shore.

The sea rushed up to meet her in a welcoming embrace. As hard as she'd tried to stay away and forget it, it would never leave her, never forget her, its daughter. And maybe that hold wasn't something to fear, any more than a home was or family.

With hard snaps of her tail, she raced toward the horizon. Not to seek out *Dawn Chaser* and her human lover onboard. Nor to collect samples and specimens for a marine biologist. She avoided her kin's territories and *The Osprey's* watery grave, too.

The ocean took, but it gave, too, and she needed to stake her own claim.

On her way to pelagic waters, Lorelei swam through a seagrass meadow. Green and sun-kissed, the seagrasses tickled her fingers as she swept her hands through them and across the sleek mussel shellbacks latching on. Further beyond, she overturned a rock that drew her eye to find an angry lobster beneath. Cornered between her and other surrounding rocks, it raised its claws, pinching at empty space, ready to fight.

Bubbles erupted from Lorelei's mouth as she laughed. *Okay Sebastian, you win.* She lowered the rock and swam away, allowing the lobster to dart back underneath. There was no point in frightening it further. A mermaid befriending a lobster was as farfetched as one befriending a crab.

Lorelei rose toward the surface and a small pod of three harbor porpoises joined her.

Although normally shy, elusive creatures, they gently bumped their faces against her in greeting. They actually recognized her...She'd met them weeks back, after freeing one caught in an abandoned fishing net. She stroked that poor creature's blunt, rounded head. Its body bore a latticework of scars.

Another porpoise took the harpoon strapped to her back between its spade-shaped teeth and gently tugged her upwards. Lorelei followed. Releasing her, the porpoise shot out of the water in a tremendous leap, arching its body in the air to show off its acrobatic prowess. Another shot up after it and reached even greater heights than the first.

She knew dolphins leaped, but harbor porpoises...that was rare. Some didn't think they did it at all. Most of what the science community knew about them came from the animals they rescued or that were killed as bycatch in fishing nets.

Little was known about their behavior in the wild, because they avoided humans.

Smiling, Lorelei clapped at each performance. After each pod member had taken a turn, she unstrapped her harpoon, letting it float on the surface, so she could join in on the fun. Undulating her torso and tail in short, quick bursts of motion, she shot out of the water and twisted artfully in the air. Her dive back in made very little splash.

Getting the hang of this mermaid thing.

Beneath the surface, the pod encircled her, all bobbing their heads up and down, their inward-curving mouths open in what looked like smiles.

She bowed with a grin plastered on her face.

Before parting ways, Lorelei hunted with the porpoise family. A silvery school of fish scattered before them, but with the slap of her tail, she sped after a few and snatched one in her clawed hand. She delivered a killing bite before devouring it and chucking the bones.

Although she enjoyed her time with the harbor porpoises, the ocean called her deeper still. Even if they couldn't quite understand her, she waved her goodbyes.

Miles and miles from land, the shoreline long gone from sight, Lorelei dove through the brine to the seabed far below and discovered a sea cave. Brandishing her harpoon in case the space had been claimed by other creatures, she swam through the mouth with caution. But nothing lashed out at her or swam away in fright.

Still, she explored the cavern's six tunnel paths with care, each leading to its own separate chamber the size of Killian's cottage. They were all empty. Swimming from floor to ceiling, Lorelei deemed them cozy, but still roomy enough to swim around in. Sitting on a rock shelf, she leaned back and contemplated the natural treasures she might collect and bring here. What she might do to mark it as her own.

She'd steer clear of sunken ships and their sunken treasures. Not even curiosity stemming from her love of maritime history could chase away the tragedy and death lingering on their once-seafaring remains. Lorelei would no sooner walk through a crypt. *Everything that fills my cave will be alive,* she thought, imagining it filled with sea plants. *Well, maybe not everything. A shark jaw would look pretty cool hanging above the entrance.*

Settling on the rock shelf, arms behind her head, Lorelei lost herself to home planning and eventually fell into a deep sleep. In her dreams she saw more days like this one, and the promising life the ocean offered her beneath the waves. All she had to do was seize it.

So tempting...And yet, why shouldn't she give it a go? Who would stop her?

She woke sometime later to find herself all alone in the empty cave.

With nothing and no one to fill it apart from herself, loneliness crept in, and her thoughts turned to Killian. How long had she been down here? She had no way of telling the time. It could have been hours or days.

Days...

Lorelei fled the cave in a wild panic, racing back to shore. If Killian came home from offshore fishing to find her gone, and her clothes in a pile on the beach...Her stomach tied in knots. He'd fear the worst.

When Lorelei emerged from the sea, returned to the shore once more, Killian was just getting out of his truck. He grinned and waved to her. Forgoing her clothes on the sand, she ran up the beach and jumped in his arms, filling her nose with pine, earth, and her lover's warm, comforting scent—cinnamon, clove, and musk.

"What's this about?" he chuckled, holding her tight even though it drenched his shirt.

Anchored to her heart's greatest desire, relief washed over Lorelei. She nuzzled his shoulder, and in too quiet a voice for him to hear over the roaring waves, she murmured, "You're my home."

CHAPTER
THIRTY-EIGHT

LATER THAT WEEK, LILA TEXTED KILLIAN AND LORELEI: *IF MY dad knows, I gotta tell my husband. And dad's gotta tell mom. It's a family matter though, so we'll keep it in the family.* Killian was ready to tell Lila 'no' on Lorelei's behalf, but when he looked over at her on the couch, tears glistened in her eyes.

"They think of me as family," she sniffed into her sleeve.

"You are family," he murmured, pulling her in close. Fresh tears streaked her cheeks, but she was smiling as she draped her legs across his lap. "I felt it the first week you were here," he added.

She gazed up at him. "You did?"

Nodding, he caressed her jawline with his thumb. "I knew that if you left, it wouldn't feel like home anymore. You're it for me, Lorelei. Wherever you go, I go. If the ocean's call becomes too much and you move inland, I'll follow you inland. If it's too much and you go out to sea, I'll take *Dawn Chaser* and follow you there."

Her eyes widened. "I *have* bewitched you."

He brushed a loose tendril of hair behind her ear. "I don't know that I would call it that."

"What would you call it then?"

"Love."

Lorelei fell back onto the sofa cushions with her hand slung across her forehead. He thought he heard her say 'whoa' under her breath. "You okay?"

"Yup. Just swooning."

"Hopefully not from fright." He grinned, amused.

"Not at all. Just marveling at how good I have it right now."

That was all he needed to hear—that his words were well received. He wouldn't press her for a mutual expression of love. It wasn't something to be rushed, and Lorelei was already experiencing an emotional overload. She would say what she felt when she was ready.

Sitting back up, Lorelei murmured, "It means a lot to me what you've said. And I don't take it lightly."

"I didn't think you would."

"I could never ask you to leave knowing how much this place means to you."

"You wouldn't have to ask. You'd only ever have to ask me to stay if you didn't want me to follow."

She bit her lip. "I don't think I could do that either."

"Then don't."

She cupped his cheek, fingertips coursing over the creases beside his eye. "The idea of letting you give this up feels selfish. Isn't it selfish?"

"I'm not giving anything up yet." He stroked the inside of her wrist with his thumb. "And no. It's my choice to make. It would hurt me more if you made that decision for me."

Nodding, Lorelei said, "Okay, fair. There will be no stealing away in the middle of the night on my end."

A shiver stole down his spine. Had she thought about doing that? "Please don't you ever do that," he pleaded. His heart would shatter.

Crossing her heart, she promised she wouldn't and answered his unspoken question. "I only thought about doing that to protect you after I lost control with Carrie."

"Lorelei, if we ever part ways, please let us reach that decision together. I'll decide what I can or cannot handle. Even if it's really bad—

the worst thing you could ever imagine doing—I still want you to come tell me so I can understand what happened. Just please don't ever disappear on me."

"I won't," she repeated vehemently, brushing back his hair, and he relaxed under her soothing touch. "If I ever lose control—which I don't expect to—but if I do, I will tell you. I'm crazy about you, Killian, and I don't ever want to hurt you. But there's…something I do have to say." Worry creased her brow.

He took her hands in his and squeezed gently. It was his turn to soothe her, whatever the confession. "You can tell me anything."

She nodded, not quite able to meet his eyes. "The ocean called to me while you were gone. And I went. I swam with porpoises and found this really nice sea cave. The next thing I knew, I was imagining what it would be like to live there. And I—I wanted to stay."

When he nudged for her to continue, she met his eyes. "So, I fell asleep there, dreaming of building a new home. But when I woke up, and I realized you weren't with me, I didn't want to be there anymore. No matter how strong this call seems to get, you always bring me back to shore. Home is nowhere you can't follow. And that's as much as I can say right now."

His heart swelled with happiness. "I think that's quite a lot." Better than an 'I love you,' which could mean so many different things to different people at any given time.

"Doesn't it bother you that I thought about staying out there?"

"That nice of a sea cave, huh?" he teased, waggling his eyebrows. *She-cave, sea cave.* She slapped his arm playfully. "You should show it to me some time," he continued. "Take pictures or video with all that fancy equipment Lila gives you."

"Okay," she said a little shyly and with a smile. "It's completely empty though. Nothing much to see. Just a bunch of bare rock walls."

"I can make something you can take with you." He waved around the room at his handiwork. "I'm no Martha Stewart of she-cave interior design, but I think we can figure out something that would fit nicely. No reason why you should be cooped up here all the time when I'm away."

Lorelei's smile widened, and he pulled her onto his lap for a bear hug. She sunk into his embrace, worries forgotten, just as he'd hoped. There was nothing he wouldn't give her.

CHAPTER
THIRTY-NINE

TYPING AWAY AT HER DESK, DRAFTING COPY FOR THE museum exhibits, Lorelei was so immersed in her task that she tuned out everything else, including the pair of scientists arguing down the hallway.

A balled-up piece of paper smacked her hand. *"Hello? Earth to Lorelei."*

"Oh sorry, what's up?" Lorelei saved the document and took a post-it to mark where she left off in her notepad.

"Friend, not boss talking." To accentuate the point, Lila swiveled around in her office chair, more for the 'weeee' factor than anything remotely serious. "So, I told Will."

About mermaid stuff.

Noting Lila's amused expression, she didn't panic. Had the dynamic of the little family Lorelei had been adopted into been any different, she would have guarded her secret more closely and done more to prevent its spread. While the growing numbers of those who knew still made her anxious, it also normalized it and made it easier to embrace.

Pushing off from her desk, she rolled back in her chair to where Lila sat. "Yeah? How'd it go?" She spun to face her.

Smirking, Lila replied, "It was hilarious. I enjoyed it way too much."

"Uh-oh. What did you do?"

"Nothing really. When he walked in the door, I said, 'Hi honey. How was work today?' And he said, 'Blah-blah-blah catching fish.' And I said, 'Boy, do I have a juicy secret to tell you.'"

Lorelei snorted. "You did not say that."

"Yes, I did. Now shush and let me tell the story. So, I asked him, 'Did you know Lorelei's been swimming out to the boat to see Killian?' Of course, Will gave me the what-fumes-are-you-inhaling-at-the-lab look, but I said, 'Here, look at this cool footage of work wifey in action.' I showed him some of the recordings and BOOM!" Lila mimed Will's mind exploding with her hands.

"I sincerely hope that's not how your dad told your mom." Lorelei flicked a paperclip in Lila's general direction. The biologist's hand smacked down to stop it from launching off the desk.

"Oh hell no. He probably poured her a glass of wine and snuggled up or something."

"That sounds more in character."

"Anyway, Will. Poor man didn't say anything more than 'the fuck?' the entire evening. He'd go and get a beer out of the fridge, pause, and say 'the fuck'. Be sitting on the couch and opening a bag of chips. 'The fuck.' Setting the table for dinner. 'The fuck.' Doing his business in the bathroom. 'The fuck.' Pretty much anytime he started anything new, he'd say 'the fuck.' He's okay now though."

"Geez, Lila. You sure?"

"Positive. He's been asking me for pointers on how not to act like a dork the next time he sees you. Told him several times that finger guns were not the way to go."

"I feel like I could use some similar advice. To break the ice, you know?"

"Ah. Well, more good news on that front. It sounded like Mom handled it well. She's been in her studio working on a new mermaid piece and said we should all get together again soon. Will and I offered to host, but she insisted on having the next get-together at their place again. She wants to do a clambake and classic Maine lobster dinner."

Her stomach rumbled audibly. "Well, I guess you know how I feel about that."

Lila chuckled. "The stomach doesn't lie."

"Not to volunteer Killian for making dessert, or anything, but what follows a Maine lobster dinner?"

Without missing a beat, Lila replied, "Blueberry pie!"

Skipping field work that afternoon so she could make more headway on the exhibits, Lorelei lost track of time and stayed later than she meant to. Stiff from sitting in a chair all day, she stretched and texted Killian that she was going for a walk before driving home.

Nearby, there was a winding shore path, lined with beech trees and white pine, that led to a popular tourist site—rocky cliffs overlooking miles and miles of rich blue water. Numerous side paths branched off to overlooks, and private nooks, where visitors could sit in quiet contemplation with breathtaking views of the ocean. Tourists often went off these paths to climb down the large boulders along the shoreline, irritating the local authorities to no end. It was amazing the danger people put themselves in for the sake of a picture.

Lorelei stuck to the main path. While she could breathe underwater, it wouldn't do her any good if she slipped on her way down to the water's edge and cracked her head open on a rock.

Tightening her scarf around her neck, she enjoyed the scent of sea salt mixed with pine, and the unusual peace and quiet. At the height of summer this walk would be teeming with people and horrid, biting black flies, but with the cold creeping in, and the days becoming shorter and shorter, there was no one else but her.

It was dusk now—the sun due to disappear below the horizon at any moment, but Lorelei didn't hurry back. The moon hung bright in the twilight sky, and her eyes adjusted to the waning light. She thought about how she'd persuade the board to install a memorial for *The Osprey* crew at the museum, when she heard a sharp cry followed by a splash.

Had someone fallen in?

When the smell of blood and panic overloaded Lorelei's senses, she had her answer.

Hunger flicked at the edge of her consciousness. She inhaled deeply —the wounded person was just up ahead. If her breakfast that morning had not included a particular canned meat, she might not have been able to stamp down her wild impulse to hunt the wounded person.

Shedding her clothing Clark-Kent-style, Lorelei followed the scent and rushed down to the water. Claws and scales emerged, and she picked her way over the treacherous terrain as quickly and safely as she could. She barely registered rolling an ankle on a loose, wobbly rock.

Fear thrummed through her veins and caught in her throat—a morbid cocktail of her own and the drowning person's below. Her heart pounded in her chest and her limbs buzzed with adrenaline.

She spotted blood on one of the boulders below. The person had not just fallen in, they'd hit their head on the way down.

Once she could clear the rocks, Lorelei dove in.

Cold, churning water rushed up all around her. If it weren't for a powerful snap of her tail, the breaking surf would have smashed her into the rocks. Lorelei peered through the brine, scanning for the person who fell in, but the turbulent water made it difficult to see. She swam onward blind, guided only by her acute sense of smell.

As sharp as the scent of blood and distress was on land, its assault on her olfactory senses spiked tenfold beneath the waves. It led her to the ocean bottom, fifteen, twenty feet down where she saw a teenage boy with a nasty head wound. His eyes were hooded, and his fingers twitched, too stunned by his injury to move.

At the sight of such easy prey, Lorelei summoned all her willpower to ignore the rumbling of her stomach and rescue the poor boy without tearing into him. She swam down and hooked her arms underneath his armpits. There was no time to contemplate the shock in the boy's eyes at the sight of her or the filming GoPro clipped to his shirt.

Snapping her tail, they shot to the surface.

The moment they broke through the boy tried to cough but couldn't. His lungs were filled with seawater; he was still drowning.

"Hang on kid." She dashed for the shoreline with him in tow.

She fought against the waves and the current that carried them dangerously close to the rocks, stealing precious time they didn't have. Her abdominal muscles ached with the effort it took to keep them both from being smashed.

By the time she yanked the teenage boy out of the water, he was unconscious.

Lorelei snatched the GoPro from his shirt and threw it as hard as she could into the ocean—more because it was in her way than because it was recording her. Clasping her hands together, Lorelei began a series of chest compressions to get the water out of the teenager's lungs. "Come on," she pleaded.

The moment he began coughing up water, she turned him over onto his side. His whole body convulsed as he expelled the water trapped inside and sucked in great gulps of air. Patting his back, she coaxed, "That's it. Get it all out."

When he finally caught his breath and turned to look at her, Lorelei saw his disoriented gaze come into focus and zero in on her. *Oh fuck.* Half transformed and completely naked, Lorelei bolted for the ocean path and her pile of clothes just as the sun dipped beneath the horizon.

MINUTES LATER, SIRENS AND FLASHING LIGHTS RACED toward the research center.

Driving on the opposite side of the road, Lorelei continued home with her hands clutched to the steering wheel in a death grip. The red and white lights seared her vision, and its blaring wail left her feeling numb.

She'd saved a boy's life. But she was also seen.

CHAPTER
FORTY

SEEING LORELEI COME IN THROUGH THE DOOR SOAKING WET and visibly shaken, Killian abandoned the chili he was stirring. "Lorelei, what happened?" He turned the burner down and crossed the room to take her purse and help her out of her peacoat.

Without needing more encouragement, she launched into the story of how she rescued a drowning teenage boy but wasn't sure how much he'd seen or comprehended of her transformation. Her words tumbled out hurried and panicked. "I got rid of the GoPro, Killian, but I really think he saw me. What if he says something?"

Though his blood ran cold, he schooled his features, so she didn't see that he was freaking out, too. Rubbing his hand over his face, he said, "You said he conked his head pretty good, right?"

She nodded, wringing her hands.

"I don't think people will believe him if he says he was rescued by a mermaid. It's too fantastical," he reasoned. "They'll attribute it to the head injury. Sure, people will speculate and gossip about the rescuer— it's a quiet, small town. But even if they somehow figure out it's you, they'll never think you're really a mermaid."

Sighing, Lorelei slumped against the wall. "You're right. There's no way they'd think that."

Holding out his hand, he coaxed, "Come on. Let's get you out of those wet clothes." She took his hand and followed him upstairs.

The following day, Branson called him while he was at the gym. He stepped outside to take it and greeted him cheerily.

"I'm gonna take a wild guess and say you haven't been on social media today," Branson said, his halting tone a warning for bad news to come.

Gripping his phone hard, Killian forced out the words, "No, why?" He didn't want to know the answer, but it was probably necessary that he did. While Branson liked to gossip, it never had him rushing for the phone.

"There's a video I think you'll want to see. Carrie's been sharing it with everyone. Here, I'll send it to you." *If Carrie's sharing it, and Branson's calling, this ain't fucking good.* Killian clenched his jaw. He could already feel a headache coming on.

The original post had been shared that morning by the teenage boy Lorelei rescued.

It was an utter nightmare, but he couldn't blame the kid for wanting to confirm what he saw or to share such a discovery with the world.

The original post said:

Guys, I was rescued by a mermaid. MERMAIDS ARE REAL. I repeat. MERMAIDS ARE REAL. This is not a drill, people. P.S. Lost my GoPro, so THANK GOD FOR CLOUD STORAGE.

Killian watched the video, and while there was no mistaking what had rescued the boy, the video quality wasn't good enough to identify Lorelei. That put his mind temporarily at ease. Then he read the comment Carrie wrote when she reshared the post:

PSA: MERMAIDS ARE REAL & DANGEROUS!
I was attacked! It's the thing that GRABBED my ankles and

pulled me into the water! I have a chunk of my leg missing to prove it! Will reshare the pictures. There's no way an "eel" or "shark" GRABBED. ME. BY. THE. ANKLES. No way. Look at those clawed hands. That's what did it! THIS IS NOT A JOKE PEOPLE. New video footage to come. Returning to the scene of the crime today to get it!

"Shit. This is bad," he said to Branson, rushing back inside to get his gym bag. "I gotta call Lorelei and warn her. Carrie might be out there now."

"Lila thinks Lorelei's out for a swim. She and Marci have been taking turns trying to call her, but she's not picking up."

"Fucking hell. I'll call you back later. I need to get home."

"I'll have the ladies keep trying. Good luck, man."

As soon as Killian got his bag, he dashed for his truck, and sped home.

Just as he was about to turn into his driveway, he saw Carrie get into her car and start it. She'd parked near the entrance, away from the cottage, probably so she could sneak onto the main part of his property without calling attention to herself. Pulling alongside her, he prayed she didn't get anything.

When she wound down her window, he did the same, heart thundering in his chest.

"You've got a mermaid problem, Killian," Carrie announced smugly, confirming his worst fears. Her eyes shone with triumph. He opened his mouth to object, but she interrupted him. "If you don't believe me, check out the video I just posted. It proves it. And I'm calling the police, animal services, the fish and game commission, the research center, the paper, and anyone else I can think of to get the word out. Someone's gotta do it so more people don't get hurt."

Without waiting for a response from him, Carrie wound up her window and drove off.

He punched the roof of his truck and let out a long string of curses. As soon as his vision no longer flashed red with rage, he drove up the rest of the driveway and parked his truck. He found Lorelei sitting on a rock and munching on a fish several hundred feet out from shore.

Standing at the tideline, he cupped his hands over his mouth and shouted, "You should have eaten her like a fucking fish stick!"

Startled, Lorelei looked up. Still holding her kill, she slid off the rock and into the water. Moments later, she sprung up fifteen feet from where he stood, scales and claws retracting. "Who?" she asked, joining him on shore.

"Carrie," he fumed.

She quirked her brow in surprise. "Really, why's that?"

"I'll explain, but let's get inside first."

After Lorelei showered, Killian showed her the posts on social media.

Her expression was grave throughout, especially as they watched Carrie's new video together. Distance and swim speed kept her face blurry and partially obscured, but there was no mistaking her tail, fins, and naked torso during her hunt for fish.

"Can you tell that's me? I can tell that's me, but I'm not sure if it's just because I know it is." She clutched his arm so tight it hurt, but he didn't have the heart to tell her to ease up.

"You can't," he asserted. "Carrie would have said something if you could. She just thinks mermaids are dangerous animals. If she suspected this was you or anyone else, she would have written that instead. She's too righteous not to."

Lorelei released him to bury her face in her hands and groan. He rubbed his arm gingerly. That one might leave a bruise.

"I know this could be worse, much, much worse, but this sucks so bad," she grumbled and then dropped her hands with a huff. "Am I only gonna be able to swim at night now? Or only when someone's keeping a look out for me?"

He rubbed his temples. "I don't know. But I'd definitely lay low for a while. People are going to be hanging around the water more, hoping for a mermaid sighting."

Lorelei nodded in agreement, stress lining her brow. "What are we going to do about Carrie? I'm pissed at her, but I don't want to eat her."

"I don't know. I imagine she'll keep coming by, too. Look at all the attention she's getting for this." The likes and shares were quickly climbing into the thousands. "Report her for trespassing, maybe?"

"Gosh. I don't know. What a mess." She hugged a couch pillow to her face and screamed into it. The fabric muffled the sound.

Despite the shitstorm they were in, Killian couldn't help but laugh. "Better?"

"Slightly," she sighed, picking up her phone to text Lila and Katrina.

Katrina advised them to share the boy's video and post their own comments with it, because it would be odd if they didn't acknowledge it. Lila, as any marine biologist would do, already posted something about the mermaid sightings. She tagged her lab saying, "We're looking into this!"

Cringing while sharing the video herself, Lorelei wrote: "Does anyone know if this is real? Or just another internet hoax?"

The skeptics' camp could use another member, Killian thought blandly. He commented on her post: "Been fishing for almost twenty years. Never seen one."

Branson, who must have been lurking, liked Killian's comment and then wrote one of his own: "I don't believe it. Probably a hoax."

In true Carrie fashion, she reacted to her cousin with an angry emoji and replied: "You calling me a liar, cuz?"

"Nope. Just crazy!" he shot back. While his friend was willing to go toe to toe with Carrie, Killian was not and turned off all his social media notifications. Lorelei did the same.

After dinner, Walsh and Marci stopped by for a surprise visit. Their daughter had kept them up-to-date on all the social media buzz, and it worried them. They didn't end up staying long—just long enough to give Lorelei a hug, hear how she was holding up, and invite her and Killian over the next day for much needed family fun.

"Wait. You're not upset? Freaked out?" Lorelei asked.

Walsh and Marci shared a look. "You just saved a boy's life," he countered. "Why would we be upset about that?"

"No, I meant about what I am. It's...a lot."

Marci gave her a warm smile. "We were rattled at first," she admitted. "And it's hard to wrap our heads around, but when you're as old as us, it's better to adapt to change quickly. It just is what it is. There's no use losing sleep over it."

Lorelei nodded, looking relieved.

On their way out the door, Marci said to Lorelei, "Lila's already said she's giving herself and you a half-day tomorrow. Just come on over to the house when you're done."

Walsh patted Killian on the back and murmured discreetly, before following his wife to the car, "Pour your lady a glass of wine."

CHAPTER

FORTY-ONE

WHEN KILLIAN DROVE THEM OVER TO THE WALSH FAMILY home for the get-together, Lorelei wore her hood up and scarf around the lower part of her face the entire way. Even though she wasn't readily recognizable in the videos, she no doubt felt exposed.

Marci practically shoved a glass of wine into her hands the moment she came in the door.

That afternoon, while the clambake slow-cooked, they drank beer and played yard games. Bit by bit, Lorelei's smiles and laughter returned. After the homemade blueberry pie was eaten, Lila's karaoke machine made an appearance. Lila and Killian wasted no time and sang a duet. Walsh and Marci harmonized and tapped out the beat while Branson recorded the whole performance in a fashion that had become tradition.

While Lorelei still couldn't sing unless fully shifted as mermaid, she danced instead, entering from the kitchen with a grand twirl. The way her whole body moved like a reed in the wind—hips swaying, arms waving, and hands twisting in time—Killian didn't know which part of her he wanted to look at the most.

Watching her made him sing louder, bolder, which Lila matched enthusiastically. Their energy fueled hers in turn.

For five glorious minutes, they completely forgot about the viral mermaid videos.

Killian's ringing phone yanked them back to reality.

Pulling it out of his back pocket, his eyes widened in surprise. "It's Jackie Gaten from the paper," he announced to the group. Lila hit pause on the karaoke machine. "Hello?"

"Killian, have you seen this viral mermaid video?" Jackie's tone bordered on accusatory.

His brow wrinkled in confusion. "Uh, yeah, why?"

"Why am I seeing your girlfriend in it? If you try telling me she's wearing a costume, I will scream."

"Jackie, what are you talking about? That's not—"

"Don't you start with me," Jackie scolded. She hadn't been his babysitter for more than twenty-five years but had since perfected that no-nonsense voice. "This is serious. I need you to listen. I went to the hospital to talk to the kid that recorded this—the one that nearly drowned. He has a longer version of the video. He tried posting it on YouTube, but it got taken down for nudity. Killian, it's a close up on Lorelei's face and her goddamn tits."

He swore.

"Yeah. Fuck is right. But lucky for you, I think I've got this under wraps. I bought all his original files. Then I lied and said service in his hospital room was too shitty to use Airdrop. The kid's naïve, so he let me borrow his phone, and I went outside, airdropped the files, and deleted the extended version from the cloud. He'll still be able to share the clip if he wants, but as far as I know, all original copies are gone. Although you never know with technology these days. Look Killian, I did this because I don't want your life to blow up, and I don't want to see Lorelei's face in the public eye again. But if you expect me to continue sticking my neck out for you, you better give me a damn good explanation for all this."

Shit, shit, shit. He pinched the bridge of his nose, trying to think. "Just give me ten minutes."

"Killian, I'm serious. You need to tell me what's going on. Did she attack that other woman? Carrie Prior? Is she a threat? If you give me the run around—"

"Jackie," Killian growled in warning. "Give me ten minutes. I'll call you back."

"You better," Jackie huffed and hung up.

CHAPTER

FORTY-TWO

LORELEI REMEMBERED JACKIE.

The local reporter was the last to interview her in the hospital the day she arrived in Haven Cove, Maine. She'd come late in the afternoon after all the others had left.

Although Lorelei never felt like she was being interrogated by the other reporters, it had always been distinctly clear that they were there to do a job. That had been easy to forget with Jackie. After introducing herself, she talked about the town and laughed and joked about the local populace's eccentricities and the stories one hears and writes as a small-town reporter.

At first, Lorelei did all the listening and asked almost as many questions about the town as she would eventually answer about her ordeal.

As Jackie talked, and left openings in conversation for Lorelei to say as much or as little about herself as she wished, Lorelei felt less self-conscious about the fact that she was being recorded. It had only become distinctly apparent to Lorelei that the interview had "begun" when Jackie asked, "I guess you're pretty shaken up about all this, right?" And even then, she'd felt more at ease than she had all afternoon.

Her chat with Jackie had been as good of an end to a trying day of interviews as she could've hoped to have.

Now, Lorelei could only hope Jackie would continue to extend those courtesies and show sympathy for her unusual situation. Killian seemed to think Jackie was only trying to help them, but she couldn't be so sure. Not with the reporter's pointed questions about Carrie's attack.

If Lorelei hadn't been backed into a corner by Jackie's leverage over her, she would have refused to give a "mermaid demonstration" outright. Her future in Haven Cove hung in the balance. Which way the scales tipped depended on whether Jackie saw her as a threat to public safety.

She never felt the power of the pen more keenly.

"Lorelei," Killian began gently. "I know you probably don't want to, but I think you need to tell Jackie about what happened with Carrie."

She flinched. "If we do that, she'll see me as a threat and out me for sure."

"Jackie can be tough around the edges when she feels she needs to be, but she's far from heartless," Killian replied. "If we explain that it wasn't something you could control until Lila found a solution—"

Lorelei was about to protest, but Lila beat her to it. "Jackie cares about you, Killian. I mean, Jesus, what she did with the boy in the hospital was illegal. And that's exactly why she might out Lorelei. She'll do it if she thinks she's protecting you."

Lorelei nodded emphatically.

Killian swiped his hand over his face. "She'll see through any flimsy lie we try to come up with. Carrie may have bought the 'bitten by a shark' stuff at first, but Jackie won't. If anything, it will piss her off that we'd insult her intelligence like that, and then we'll definitely lose her sympathy."

Lila sighed, pinching the bridge of her nose. "Ugh. I hate it, but you're right. We can't even give her a believable lie like 'another mermaid came close to shore and did it.' If we spread misinformation about mermaids being a direct threat, it would cause a public panic."

Lorelei crossed her arms, her mind whirring.

How naïve she had been to think she'd be able to keep her secret concealed. With each new person to learn the truth of what she was, the more her life seemed to be spiraling out of control. A quickly widening circle of friends knowing had been stressful enough.

She didn't want to tell Jackie, but the reporter had already made the connection between her and Carrie. There was nothing they could say but the truth that would get her to potentially drop it. And as Lorelei once heard Katrina say, 'to control the story, you have to get out in front of it and tell it yourself.'

If they had a chance at truly winning Jackie over to their side, Lorelei would have to take the risk and appeal to Jackie's sense of compassion. "It's the only way," she conceded. "And if the worst happens, and I have to pay for what I did to Carrie, I guess it's only fair."

Both Killian and Lila looked stricken, and began to speak at once, but none of their reassurances comforted her.

Anxiety over the reporter's uncertain intentions fouled Lorelei's mood and flared up her hunger for human flesh. She gorged herself on canned pork before the meeting—almost making herself sick on it—just so she wouldn't be tempted to eat Jackie.

Waiting for the reporter to arrive, Lorelei paced the length of the beach while Lila and Killian helplessly looked on. She was a fish caught in a net and waiting for the fryer.

It made her both irritable and nauseous.

Jackie's arrival only made her grouchier. No polite greetings or niceties—just a hard, expectant stare that burned with impatience and squashed all hope of receiving the same treatment as before.

Refusing to cower, Lorelei folded her arms across her chest and matched Jackie's flinty stare. "What do you want first, the transformation or the story?"

Jackie's expression softened slightly, but her tone remained firm. "The transformation, please."

Lorelei entered the water, shifting, and hated every moment. She swam near the surface so Jackie could see her and waved her colorful tail at group on the beach before forcing herself to leap and twist out of the water. Performing like a goddamn circus sideshow.

In for a penny, in for a pound.

Nausea churned in her stomach as she sloshed back to shore. Hot flashes followed, and she doubled over clutching her middle, vomiting onto the sand. Too much food in her stomach. And too much compounded anxiety and humiliation.

"Oh my God, Lorelei, are you all right? Does that always happen?" Dropping the tough lady act, Jackie took a step forward, apparently now concerned for her well-being.

She glared, eyes flashing a warning, giving Jackie pause.

"Nerves," she replied coolly and spat on the ground.

While her queasy stomach made Jackie unappetizing for the time being, her blood boiled with rage and fear. Poised to attack like a cornered animal, Lorelei couldn't be sure she'd be able to overcome her instinct to claw Jackie's face off if she got too close.

No one attempted to approach her for a good long time. When her animalistic urges finally passed, Lorelei bent down to splash water on her face. The cold cleared her mind and released the tension coiled in her limbs.

Sensing it was safer to approach, Jackie cautiously came forward to put her own jacket around Lorelei's bare shoulders. While still a ballsy move, she recognized and respected the gesture as a show of good faith. Jackie was trying to be cordial and knowing that helped her remain calm.

"Those scars," Jackie murmured. "What happened to you, Lorelei?"

"I'll tell you inside."

ON THE WALK BACK TO THE HOUSE, KILLIAN PUT HIS ARM around her waist and whispered, "The worst part's over, love." She smiled weakly, keeping her doubts to herself.

As the four of them sat around the kitchen table, Lorelei started at the beginning, with what really happened the night of the storm, and ended with her rescue of the teenage boy. To Jackie's credit, she listened intently and did not interrupt once, even as Lorelei described the gruesome demise of *The Osprey* crew and how she got her scars. She left out the bit about Carrie.

For now.

While Jackie didn't say anything, she was visibly disturbed by the story—paling and clenching her jaw so tight they could hear her teeth grinding together.

When Lorelei finished, Jackie got up from her chair. "I need a drink," she announced, rapping the table once with her knuckles. "Killian, where do you keep the strong stuff?"

He pointed to his liquor cabinet, and Jackie helped herself to two fingers of whiskey. She downed it quickly, wincing at the burn but not bothering with a chaser. "Lorelei, I am so sorry for what happened to you. I can't even imagine. But there's something I need to know and understand. And listen, I know you probably don't want to tell me, but keep in mind that I know you saved a boy's life—"

She sighed, stomach twisting in knots. "You want to know if I attacked Carrie Prior."

Jackie nodded. "Obviously, whatever happened hasn't pushed these two away," she said, gesturing to Killian and Lila. "If they can understand what happened, I'm sure I can, too."

That gave Lorelei a glimmer of hope. "I wasn't in a right frame of mind," she began slowly, watching Jackie's face. The reporter nodded for her to continue, and Lorelei told her about the animal hunger she felt before Lila figured out how to curb her unsavory cravings. "But we hadn't figured that out yet, so when Carrie came onto Killian's property—"

"Lorelei was basically starving," Lila interjected. "Right, Killian?"

He nodded. "She couldn't keep down any food."

"I snapped out of it before I could do any worse," Lorelei continued. "And I drove her to the hospital. I feel horribly about it, but how can I apologize to her? Make amends? She would never understand."

Jackie poured herself another drink. "She'd probably try to ruin your life."

Now the question is, are you? Lorelei squeezed Killian's hand beneath the table. Wincing, he leaned over to whisper, "Ease up, love. You're quite strong." She quickly released his hand, an apology on her lips, but he shook his head with a small smile and a wink.

The reporter swirled her glass.

"What happened to Carrie was regrettable, but you didn't ask for any of this, Lorelei. And I'm not so sure I could have handled this any better than you, if I were in your shoes. You needed help, and you asked for it. There's nothing condemnable about that. I can see that plainly now that we've talked.

"I'm going to protect your identity, Lorelei," Jackie continued. "That, I promise you. I swear it on my professional integrity and my mother's grave, may she rest in peace." The reporter raised her glass and looked to the heavens before throwing it back.

Lorelei sighed in relief, releasing her grip on Killian's hand. He nudged her leg with his knee under the table and smiled. Jackie wasn't finished. "But I'm not dropping the story," she said. "The public needs to know about sirens and mermaids. It's a public safety concern. They ate a whole crew for Chrissake."

Killian tensed, and Lila looked to her to see how she would respond. "She's right," Lorelei told them both. "Now that people are ready to believe they exist, they will be looking for them and need to know the dangers involved with that."

Lila spoke up. "While I don't disagree, I also don't think we should start telling people that mermaids ate *The Osprey* crew. Their families have been through enough. And it wouldn't protect Lorelei's anonymity."

"True," Jackie rubbed her chin. "What to do...what to do..."

Lila already had an answer for that. "Let's drive this conversation with science. All the crap circulating online is just anecdotal myth-busting crockery."

Having a sneaking suspicion where this conversation was heading, Lorelei's heart sank. While Lila would never publicly study her, a mermaid from the wild was another matter entirely. Self-preservation was important, but the ethical quandary of subjecting another mermaid to scientific research wouldn't leave her thoughts.

Yes, they ate *The Osprey* crew, but if they were plagued by the same hungers she was, hungers they could not control…

It filled her with doubt.

Pulling out a notepad from her back pocket, Jackie sat back down. "Go on," she said to Lila as she flipped to a blank page. "What are you thinking?"

The scientist practically bounced to her feet, pacing around the table, gesticulating wildly as she spoke. "Educating people about dangerous marine animals—whether it's sharks, squid, or in this case mermaids—it begins with scientific research."

But mermaids aren't animals. I'm not an animal.

Stopping to hover over Jackie's shoulder, Lila tapped her arm and asked, "Hey, can I mooch a piece of paper off you?"

Jackie shot her a look that was very 'calm your tits' but ripped off a sheet. "Want a pen, too?" She was already reaching for a spare from her breast pocket.

"Yes, thanks!" Lila plucked both from her hands and began jotting down what might've been a To-Do list.

"What are you saying, Lila? That we catch one?" Killian asked. He glanced at Lorelei, but she kept her expression carefully blank.

Lila nodded vigorously. "Catch one and study it. If we succeed, Jackie will have more than enough material for an article series."

While Lorelei fidgeted uncomfortably in her seat, Jackie grinned from ear to ear. "I do like the sound of that," the reporter replied.

Knowing they won Jackie over onto their side brought her a modicum of relief, but the looming ethical question hanging over her head did not. She wanted to bring it up, but seeing how excited and energized they were, she kept silent. They were doing this to help her—to protect her anonymity. Why couldn't she just be grateful for that?

Because another mermaid will pay the price to keep my secret safe.

CHAPTER
FORTY-THREE

THE GROUP FOCUSED ON PREPARATIONS FOR THEIR MERMAID live capture expedition.

Killian charted a course based on the location of *The Osprey* when it sank, and Lorelei's whereabouts when she encountered the mermaids. Walsh and Branson made sure their nets and fishing equipment were in good order and that *Dawn Chaser* had plenty of fuel. Lorelei drove to the nearest wholesaler to purchase several crates of canned pork, hoping it would pacify any merfolk they encountered.

And Lila took charge of what came after, the logistics of handling a live "specimen" and bringing her back to shore. Since Killian was bringing his boat into the equation, and would be hauling institution-owned equipment, he went along with her to approach her boss, the director of the Haven Cove Marine Research Center.

He'd driven past the campus plenty of times with its red-brick buildings and perfectly manicured lawns, but this was the first time he'd ever been inside. The buildings were old, around since the late-1920s when the institution was founded, but the interior had been newly renovated. Gutted really.

It was all sterile white floors, clean lines, and glass. The lobby furniture had a futuristic ergonomic design like something out of the

Jetsons. It was cold, clinical. Even the plant pots had no character. Just edgeless, colorless, cylindrical basins.

This was what the multi-million-dollar capital improvement project had bought? New, cutting-edge lab equipment he understood. But this? What the hell was wrong with natural wood and terracotta?

For a bunch of Maine-based, ocean-loving scientists, their workplace reflected none of their life's work or the local ecosystem. And none of the region's character.

But he kept those thoughts to himself. Lila loved the research center and her job, and he wasn't going to be some petty asshole who insulted where she worked.

As he followed Lila down a long hallway, so pristine polished the tile gleamed, he looked behind him, certain he'd see a trail of smudges and scuffs from his boots. *Fuck.* He was. These weren't even his boat pair, which were permanently covered a thin layer of grime and fish-guts.

He picked his feet up higher, like a cat stepping in snow.

Lila glanced back at him, laughter dancing in her eyes. "You all right back there?"

"I'm fucking up your floor. Why didn't you tell me to bring slippers?"

She rolled her eyes and tugged him along by the elbow. "Come on. His office is this way."

As Killian's boots squeaked across the resin, he cast a sincere apology out into the universe to the janitor who'd get stuck cleaning up after him.

Director Phil Simmons was a sophisticated, straw-haired academic who wore pressed slacks, cashmere, and a golden watch that probably rivaled the average fisherman's annual pay. Besides that, and the fact that he ran the research center, all Killian really knew about the man was that he had a private yacht moored up in the harbor.

Oh, and some sort of relation to Branson and Carrie...weird, but Haven Cove was a small town.

As Lila handled introductions, Dr. Simmons seemed friendly enough. Firm handshake. Unwavering eye-contact. A charismatic smile that likely came in handy while schmoozing donors. But more importantly, he seemed to have a healthy amount of respect for Lila, listening without interruption as she delivered her pitch.

That won Phil points in Killian's book.

Having seen the viral mermaid videos himself, Lila's boss authorized her proposal to parse out what was real, if anything, and what was a hoax. He only asked that she keep the pet-project on the down low, used her own funding, and involved as few of her colleagues as possible, which included using *Dawn Chaser* instead of a HCMRC research vessel.

Unless Lila found hard evidence of a new species, the director didn't want the expedition to be public knowledge. It was the kind of wild goose chase the board of directors wouldn't endorse. Better to ask for forgiveness than permission, and all that, but if the mission proved fruitful, the last thing the board would be doing was complaining.

After, Killian followed Lila back to her office and sat at Lorelei's desk, waiting while she filed for a federal research permit to shutdown part of the shoreline.

Typing away at her computer, Lila explained that while it would take weeks for the application to be reviewed and approved, its true purpose was to serve as a red herring. The public needed to think she was taking steps to investigate the areas where the mermaid sightings occurred, even though she never actually intended to.

Crafty, clever woman. Thank God, she was on Lorelei's side.

After the application was submitted, Killian went with Lila to gather various equipment for sample collection, sedation, and restraints—the latter of which was borrowed from a marine veterinarian colleague in her lab. And together with that colleague, they supervised the loading of a saltwater tank designed for animal transfer onto *Dawn Chaser*.

The endeavor raised eyebrows at first, but all Lila had to say to her colleague was that she received permission to discreetly look into the mermaid sightings. "Keeping it on the DL for now," she explained. "Can't have folks think we conduct pseudoscientific research and use our funding to chase cryptids."

It was all very wink, wink, nudge, nudge, and something about it made Killian uneasy. Maybe it was the bit where his girlfriend got lumped into the same category as Sasquatch and the Loch Ness Monster.

"My lips are sealed," the marine vet promised. And then in a teasing tone said, "But in some wild off chance you do find one, loop me in on the action, okay? I'll keep my phone on in case you need anything."

When the veterinarian's back was turned, Killian caught Lila smiling smugly to herself, knowing full well this was no snipe hunt. But this expedition wasn't about her showing up her colleagues.

His stomach lurched. He'd no reason to doubt Lila before, but this new demeanor didn't sit well with him. It lacked the vibe of a friend helping a friend. Or a concern for public safety.

Leaning in, he muttered into her ear, "What are you doing?"

The smile vanished. "Playing a part."

"You sure?" He gave her a pointed look. "You're acting like you've just won a bet."

She sighed, shoulders slumping. "This is going to be the discovery of a lifetime, Killian. I can care about Lorelei and want that, too."

"I know you're excited, but Lorelei's a person first, and your friend." He paused, recalling how quiet Lorelei had gotten at the end of their conversation with Jackie. How effusive Lila had been about researching mermaids, equating them to sharks and squid. And he realized something.

Clasping Lila's shoulder, he said softly, "While she doesn't have any love for her kin, we have to remember that they *are* her kin. You get what I'm saying?"

She nodded her head, but the agreement came a little too quickly.

He wasn't sure she did get it.

Late in the afternoon, Jackie surprised Killian at his office.

He was working on payroll when she rushed through the front door. "You won't believe who I bumped into today," she puffed, offloading her messenger bag onto the floor beside his desk.

Startled, he looked up from his keyboard. "Were you running?"

"You bet. So, any guesses?" She dragged over a chair and plopped down, rubbing the shoulder where the strap had been.

"No. Who?"

"Ed Knudsen from the *Portland Press Herald*," she answered. "The guy who lost a niece and nephew on *The Osprey*."

Killian nodded. He remembered the man.

Swiping a tissue from his desk and dabbing sweat from her face, Jackie continued, "Your ex tipped him off about our Little Mermaid, and he's come to do some investigative reporting. She's really put a bug in his ear with her story. When we talked, he barely mentioned the kid Lorelei saved. I tried to get him to pay more attention to the rescue, but he just brushed me off and said he already knew about it."

"That doesn't sound good," Killian grumbled, folding his arms across his chest.

"I have a hunch he's about to publish a fear-mongering piece. There's not enough time to get ahead of it, but I think I can keep it from building traction. When's the soonest you can get us out on the water to catch a mermaid?"

"Tomorrow morning, all parties willing and able."

"Okay, good. Keep me posted." Jackie bent over to pick up her bag. Killian gave her a salute and watched her hurry back out the door.

It was time to make some phone calls.

CHAPTER
FORTY-FOUR

"CREATURE OF LEGEND, NEW APEX PREDATOR?"

Lorelei let out a heavy sigh, moderately soothed by the circles Killian rubbed across her back. Making the news yet again as her life went to hell in a hand basket was becoming a bit of a pattern, and she didn't like it one bit. But at least this time around she had a lot of loved ones to lean on when it all got to be too much.

Huddled together with the Walsh-Branson family, they gathered around a laptop at Killian's place to video chat Katrina about Ed Knudsen's article. The fact that they had to scroll down the newspaper's list of recent stories to find it seemed to bode well.

"Well, I'll give him this, it's a catchy title," Katrina said. "But yeah, it looks like the editors tried to bury it on the page a bit. The writing screams tabloid and conspiracy theory, so I'm a little surprised they ran it. Let's see. His bio says he's been with the paper for twenty years. That's probably it. Guy's got some weight to throw around."

"Jackie called it," Killian grumbled beside her, looking mighty pissed off. "It's all based on Carrie's shit and only mentions the rescue briefly."

That was rather annoying, and unfair. Leaning in to get a closer look at the featured photo, Lorelei grimaced. "I look rather vicious there, don't I? I wasn't even trying to eat the poor kid."

Katrina nodded. "Yeah, I hate it when reporters pick and choose like that. He quotes Carrie up and down the whole article but uses a still from the boy's video for the featured photo, because you look scarier. In Carrie's video, you're just lounging on a rock, snacking on a fish—very Disney-esque, minus the gross fish eating." Lorelei made a face, which Katrina ignored. "But in this kid's video, the image is dark, and you're this pale form with clawed hands and glowing eyes coming toward the camera."

Rereading the article on her phone, Lila just kept shaking her head. "It's riddled with inaccuracies. It says the mermaid is an 'apex predator that lives close to shore and is a lone hunter.' This is the exact kind of speculative, misinformed garbage we have to shut down. Maybe it won't spread much beyond Haven Cove, but it's gonna start a panic here. And don't get me started on the animals that will die when they're mistaken for 'shore-loving apex predators' and are hunted down."

Lila looked like she could and would keep ranting until Will smothered her in a bear hug. "Honey, we're gonna help you put a stop to all that."

"So, what's your verdict, Kat?" Lorelei asked. "Is there any hope this blows over?"

"I think it'll gain traction with the small, loud group of people that want it to be real. But right now it's just kooky, local news. Let's hope it stays that way. It's getting around but people outside Haven Cove mostly think it's a hoax and that the guy who wrote this is unstable." Katrina promised that once they had irrefutable proof, she would help them get their story out to all the large national news outlets.

"So, what are we going to use as bait?" Walsh folded his arms across his chest. "I'm not okay with putting anyone near the water."

"Definitely not," Killian agreed. "I already talked about this with Lorelei. We can use a mannequin and my blood."

Once the video chat ended, everyone agreed to meet down at the docks the next morning for their maiden voyage as mermaid chasers, and Killian shot a heads-up message to Jackie so she could meet them there for the ride-along.

Neither Lorelei nor Killian could sleep after everyone went home.

Bundling up, they went down to the beach and laid a blanket out on the sand. They snuggled close for warmth and bodily comfort, watching their breath dissipate into the chilly autumn air. While Haven Cove produced very little light pollution to begin with, way out here, isolated from all civilization, the Milky Way shone bright in the sky above.

Lorelei laid her head in the crook of Killian's shoulder and entwined her gloved fingers with his. With his free hand, he tugged her beanie down to fully cover her ears and pulled her scarf up around the lower part of her face.

"No scruff to keep you warm," he grinned.

She smirked. "What a shame."

They watched the night sky in companionable silence, only occasionally breaking it with a comment about a constellation or shooting star.

Stargazing had once been a summer pass time Lorelei shared with her mom. Sprayed head to toe with bug repellent to keep the mosquitoes at bay, they would lay out late into the night. Sometimes they took turns naming the constellations or talking about the books they read. Other times, they talked about serious things—like Lorelei's future. Or difficult things—like her mom's cancer.

Needing a little peace from all their troubles, Lorelei and Killian did not talk about gravely serious or difficult things when they eventually struck up conversation. "I don't know why I couldn't get the words out when you told me you loved me," Lorelei commented softly. "It all seems so silly now."

"It wasn't silly. You've had a lot going on—pretty much nonstop since we met."

"True," she accepted. "But I want you to know that you're it for me, too. I love you, Killian."

His grin spread from ear to ear. "Yeah?"

"Yeah." She nodded. "You're my guy."

"Grays and all?"

"Mm." She withdrew her hand from his to poke a finger under his charcoal gray beanie. "Every last one." He kissed her deeply, leaving her warm and breathless despite the dropping temperatures. "Should we go inside?" she asked when she'd caught her breath.

"If it weren't so cold, I'd have you right here," he whispered in her ear.

"You don't think I can keep you warm, Captain?" Lorelei ran her hand down his side. "And, if you recall, I don't feel the cold so much when I shift—" she trailed, waiting to see how he'd respond to her unspoken suggestion.

Killian propped himself on his elbow, wearing a mischievous, lopsided grin. "I would be a liar if I said I hadn't thought about it."

Sitting up, Lorelei began shrugging off her jacket. "Well, I'll leave it up to you how much of your clothes stay on." Though he helped her out of hers, he remained bundled.

Goosebumps erupted across Lorelei's skin as they knelt face-to-to face, her back to the ocean, his to the trees. Pushing off his beanie, her claws slowly emerged, gliding through his hair. He let out a ragged breath but did not break eye contact, and she saw her own glowing green eyes reflected in his.

As scales sprung forth and encased her legs, Killian ran his hands along her waist, his palms grazing the rough ridges of her scars. Her tail fin twitched into shape, and the cold seeped away. Pulling her flush against him, Killian's lips descended upon hers and his tongue entered her mouth slowly and with great care. He had gotten good at not cutting himself on her teeth.

As she tugged on his zipper, Lorelei tasted nervousness on Killian's trembling lips. With the way his hand splayed across her lower back, and the other entangled in her hair, she didn't think it was fear. But still, she paused, searching his eyes.

"Is everything okay?"

Twin spots of color rose on his cheeks. He smiled bashfully. "I don't know where to…"

"I'll show you," she murmured softly, guiding him to where her scales parted, and she ached with need.

Killian moaned, his forehead falling to her shoulder, insecurities forgotten.

CHAPTER
FORTY-FIVE

EARLY THE NEXT MORNING, IN THE DARK HOURS BEFORE sunrise, Killian and Lorelei met Walt, Will, Lila, and Jackie down at the docks. The older woman carried a monstrous thermos of coffee that she sipped while the rest of them unloaded their vehicles.

"Does that thing fit a whole pot?" Will stared at it incredulously.

"Pretty close to it." Jackie lifted it to her mouth for another sip. Filled, she had to hold it with two hands to manage the weight.

Walt teased, "I can see you have no intention of sharing."

"Didn't sleep well last night," she shrugged. "Too hyped up."

Looking forlornly at his own thermos, Will mumbled, "I need one."

Lila rolled her eyes, hoisting a carrying case filled with equipment out of her trunk. "You don't need that much coffee all to yourself. And that thing's not gonna fit in your cup holder."

Helping her with the case, Will countered, "Au contraire. Where there's a will, there's a way."

'Really?' summed up the look Lila gave him before announcing to the group that he once bought five different thermoses just to see which one fit best in his truck's cup holders. "You're gonna be mad when it doesn't fit," she insisted, closing her trunk.

"It's true," Will admitted, gracefully accepting defeat. "I do hate it when thermoses don't fit in my cup holders."

Onboard, while Lila triple checked her equipment, the three *Dawn Chaser* crew members stowed the crates of canned pork below decks, and Jackie went with Lorelei to stock the galley. They couldn't be sure how long they would be offshore, but they'd planned for three days maximum. Killian couldn't postpone his own fishing trips any longer than that—not without possibly losing his crew.

Not having a break in between trips would be tough on the fishermen, but they'd all managed it before. It didn't happen frequently, but it wasn't unusual for them to spend three consecutive weeks out at sea.

Then again, they'd never before gone underway without the rest of their crew. And they'd never tried catching a mermaid.

As the engine roared to life and Will steered them out of the harbor, the sun just peeking up over the horizon, Lorelei wondered how this discovery would affect their lives.

DRESSING A MANNEQUIN IN AN OLD SET OF HIS CLOTHES, Killian prepped the bait while Lila sterilized a syringe. When he rolled his sleeve past his elbow to expose the veins there, Lila paled, no doubt remembering her failed attempt at playing doctor with Lorelei.

He clenched his jaw and mentally prepared himself for the discomfort of hesitant, untrained hands poking him repeatedly with a needle.

"It's okay, honey," Walsh said, coming to both his and Lila's rescue. "I've got this. Did a stint as a medic back in the day."

A medic? The things you still learn about a person even after decades of knowing them.

Relieved, Lila handed over the syringe without protest, and Walsh's confidence helped Killian relax. While Walsh pulled on a pair of latex gloves, Lila took a blue latex tourniquet from her kit and wrapped it tightly around his upper arm, making his veins pop. After cleaning the blood draw site with an alcohol wipe, Walsh deftly inserted the needle and drew a vial of his blood.

If Killian hadn't known better, he would have thought the old fisherman was still moonlighting as a nurse. As Walsh slapped a Band-Aid on his arm, he asked, "When's the last time you stuck someone with a needle?"

"Oh. About that. I was never a medic. Just said that so you'd relax."

"Dad!" Lila was horrified on his behalf.

Rolling back down his sleeve, Killian muttered, "Glad you didn't go too deep."

Utterly shameless, Walsh nodded with enthusiastic agreement and held out the syringe for him to take. "Want to do the honors?"

Taking the syringe, Killian emptied its contents down the front of the mannequin. It was bizarre seeing his blood seeped into one of his shirts like that. It looked like he'd just committed murder. Or was faking his own.

Pulling a sharpie out of his back pocket, Branson drew facial hair on the dummy's face to make the body double look more "authentic."

"You're such a child," Lila laughed, rolling her eyes.

While Killian watched with a bemused grin plastered on his face, Lila plucked the used syringe from his grasp and disposed of it in a biohazardous waste bag. Walsh set to work on baiting the net purchased specifically for this expedition—a gill net.

Apart from this expedition, *Dawn Chaser* never used them.

One, it wasn't the type of fishing they did. And two, their tendency to entangle bigger bycatch like sharks and whales was a serious environmental problem. However, its invisibility in the water made its use on this trip necessary up against a sentient creature who would otherwise just avoid the net.

As a marine biologist, Lila despised the use of gill nets and cringed when it went into the water. She took some comfort knowing Branson was monitoring it and the surrounding area with the boat's sonar fish finder system. They also rigged several underwater cameras that would send a live stream to Lila's field laptop. That way, mermaid or not, they would know when something caught in their net.

Now all they had to do was wait.

It only took a matter of minutes.

"We got something!" Lila announced suddenly, pointing to something on her laptop screen, and startling everyone to attention.

"What is it? Is it a mermaid?" Jackie shot over and hovered next to Lila, eyes scanning the screen.

"Dunno. Zoomed in fast but couldn't see what it was. Just a dark shape in the water."

"All right. Let's haul it in and see what we've got." Killian radioed an update up to Branson, who piloted the boat up top.

Crowding the stern, the group waited on bated breath for the net to clear the surface and reveal what they had caught. When they saw what was tangled in the net with the bait, there was a collective groan on deck.

"It's just Jaws," Killian said, using the winch to lower the wriggling shark gently down on deck. "Gotta detangle and toss him back in."

"On behalf of Captain Quint, I resent that," Lorelei laughed. "One does not simply toss Jaws back into the ocean."

"It's gonna take all of us to heave it over the edge," Walsh remarked, taking in its size. He passed out pairs of heavy-duty gloves to everyone.

Jackie cracked her knuckles. "Time to embrace our inner Steve Irwin."

Lila looked scandalized. "Ouch. Or not."

"Too soon?" Jackie donned the pair given to her.

"Always," Lila responded, sliding her hands into her own work gloves. "The crocodile hunter was killed by a stingray of all things."

"Right. Don't embrace that. No one gets bit, okay?" Jackie remedied.

"Do pep talks often, Jackie-O?" Walsh teased.

"Shut up."

A few bumps and scrapes later, they dumped the shark back into the ocean with a splash. It was unhappy but swam away just fine. Breathing heavily, they surrounded what was left of their bait. "Killian, your body double knows how to party. Top buttons busted. No pants—" Jackie chuckled.

"Jackie, what parties are you going to? No pants? No legs is more like it," Walsh ribbed, head cocked at its missing extremities.

"He's a little chewed up." Lila crouched, pulling the bloodied shirt over the dummy's chest. "At least we still have the important part."

"All right. Let's try again." Killian was not at all discouraged by the false alarm. Patience was a particularly important virtue in his line of work.

The mannequin looked worse for wear when they returned it to the ocean, but the plastic fellow was securely attached to the netting.

The good humor faded into silence as they waited.

And waited.

Lila squinted at the underwater camera footage.

Jackie paced the deck, frequently looking out into the water, but never nearing the gunwale.

Walsh hummed quietly to himself, busying his hands with fixing a bit of netting.

Lorelei frowned, folding and unfolding her arms, casting questioning looks his way. Killian gave her a reassuring smile. "It just takes time," he said.

Fishing required patience. For all the trips they filled the hold to the brim with fish, there were the others when they barely pulled up enough catch to cover the cost of fuel. And yet, for all that Killian had made a career out of waiting, he felt none of that usual patience now.

Surely the scent of human blood would draw a ravenous mermaid up from the depths? Short of chucking an actual living person in, there was no better bait than what they'd offered.

Dawn Chaser chugged steadily along the leisurely chop of waves, Branson steering them in a grid pattern across what they believed to be merfolk territory. Minutes, then hours ticked by. Lorelei stared out at the horizon, arms folded across the gunwale. Lila slumped over her field computer, cheek squished against her palm, and Jackie sat on the deck with her legs crossed, doodling in her notepad. She'd drawn a tiny boat, a bucket with a flag sticking out of the center, a bunch of "Vs" that might be birds, and a huge, gaping-mouthed mermaid stick-figure with comically large teeth.

Anxiety gave way to boredom as the sun made its daily trek across the sky. The sun had been before them when they left early that morning, lighting their path ahead, but now it sunk behind them, shimmers of orange glinting off the waves as twilight approached.

Dusk and dawn, that's when predators came out to hunt.

If they were going to catch anything, it would be now, but they didn't even glimpse another shark on the field cameras, much less a mermaid. Either Killian's navigational calculations had been wrong, or they couldn't outsmart the ocean-born species with a lure.

Walsh's humming continued, just a bit louder than before. He normally stuck to classic rock tunes, but the sound took on a slight melodic quality. As the older fisherman flew through the motions of net repair, fingers twisting and tying, knotting and unknotting, he swayed rhythmically on his crate seat, tapping out a beat with his boot. *Thump, thump, thump.*

Otherwise, it was quiet on deck. No voices, just the sound of waves sloshing against the hull, the occasional sea bird squawking overhead, flying lazy circles around the boat. Even the constant rumbling of *Dawn Chaser*'s engines faded into the background, just ambient noise on an offshore fishing vessel.

"...When the night comes," Walsh sang with a rasping breath.

"When the night comes," he repeated, his voice softer, more melodic this time. Almost sweet and crooning.

Wait.

The engine cut, and Killian and the others lurched forward from the sudden change in momentum.

Dawn Chaser drifted forward, and without power the bow turned, slowing until she was beam to the oncoming waves, striking their exposed side over and over, rocking them violently. Killian lifted his handheld radio to his lips. "Branson?"

A loud, screeching scrape against the hull dulled the answering static, followed by the jolt and snap of the crane cables as they pulled taut.

"Branson!"

Metal groaned. And the boat began moving ever so slowly...backward.

She's pulling the boat.

"Pull up the net!" Lila shouted. "Pull it up! We have her!"

Killian glanced over to the field cameras. There was no mistaking the siren's electric blue bioluminescence writhing on screen. "Branson, engage the crane!" he called, but there was no answer.

Fuck. He'd find out what happened to his friend later. They were out of time.

Dashing to the crane, he switched the machinery on, the soft grind and whir of gears a soothing contrast to his panic. The cables jerked as the creature in the net thrashed, fighting the ascent, but they held.

The others crowded near, straining to get a look over the stern. "Get back!" he shouted above the machinery, taking Jackie and Lila by the arm, the two closest to the edge, and pulled them away. While they wouldn't get sucked under by a motionless propeller if they went overboard, there was a feral, flesh-eating mermaid down there.

The cables clanked, dripping seawater as they lifted the net, the backward motion of the boat slowing. It stopped entirely when their catch breached the surface below.

The engines and his best friend remained silent.

"Jackie, go check on Branson. Everyone else, stand clear..."

With a fierce hiss, Lorelei darted forward, and grabbed the front of his shirt, wrenching him toward her. As he stumbled into her arms, a confused curse on his lips, he heard something tear, and felt a sharp pain across his back.

Steadying himself, he followed Lorelei's angry gaze to see a pair of cold, electric blue eyes leering back, and a grinning mermaid reveal her mouthful of razor-sharp teeth. Arm outstretched, she held up one wicked claw, a drop of blood beading at the tip. His blood.

Without breaking eye contact, she brought that claw to her lips and licked it clean.

There was a flash of movement to his right—Walsh punched a button on the crane's control panel, and the net yanked roughly upward, away from everyone on deck. The mermaid screeched.

"Killian, I can't get Will to budge. His eyes are all glazed over, like he's in some kinda trance...Holy shit!"

He could only imagine the sheer shock on Jackie's face.

The mermaid swung above deck, shrieking and thrashing violently in a blur of black, electric blue, and silver like an angry cat. With another push of a button on the control panel, she hit the deck with a hard thud and slumped over, weighed down by the netting. She quieted as her gills began to seal shut, ribs expanding and contracting with laborious effort, wheezing and gasping each breath from unused lungs.

"She's swapped over breathing mechanisms." Lila edged closer, glowing with scientific fascination.

The mermaid's head snapped up, and locking her eyes on Lila, she began to hum.

Pulling out a diver's knife, Lila continued forward. "We have to free her," she said, wearing a dazed look.

"No, stop!" Killian caught her wrist and wrapped an arm around her middle to hold her back. The mermaid continued to hum but shifted her gaze to Killian. Lila struggled against him, but he maintained his hold.

Walt dashed over to pry the knife from Lila's hands. "Baby, what are you doing?" he cried.

Stepping in front of the mermaid and glaring down at her, Lorelei commanded, "Knock it off."

The creature hissed, eyes flashing with anger. But she stopped humming to instead examine Lorelei. Sniffing, she glanced from her to Killian and back. "Two-Legger lover," the mermaid spat at Lorelei.

She ignored the insult and crouched down to eye-level. Something sparkled around the siren's neck. "You speak?"

"Of course, I do." The mermaid jutted out her chin defiantly. "Just because we eat Two-Leggers, doesn't mean we can't or won't learn their language. It's so much easier to lure them with sweet promises."

Peering closer, Lorelei recognized the sparkling object—Mackenzie Coldwater's necklace. Fury rose, heating her skin and making it prickle. Pointing to it, she growled, "You murdered my friend."

Recognition flickered across the siren's face. Eyes darting to Lorelei's arm, she flexed her hand. "Ah, yes. I remember you now, Shorewalker.

But you have it all wrong. Two-Leggers are a decadent food, and sometimes good to mate with, but they're not our friends. How can you be friends with food?"

How can you mate with your food? Lorelei wanted to shout it but held her tongue. For now. "Two-Leggers—people—they're not food," she bit out. Retrieving one of the cans of meat that they stored in the deck box, she opened it, and heard the mermaid inhale deeply. "This is food." She tossed her the slippery slab.

It landed with a splat on the netting that bound the mermaid, but it didn't hinder her from snatching and greedily gobbling it up. "More."

Lorelei fed her two whole cans worth, and as the cravings abated, the mermaid ate less desperately. "This isn't Two-Legger flesh?" Blue-Eyes asked, holding up her last bite.

"No. That's pig—it's a land animal."

"Pig," the mermaid repeated, examining the can closely. She flicked the aluminum with a sharp claw. "We find these in sunken ships sometimes. Usually they hold foul Two-Legger food, but never anything as good as this pig."

"People store a lot of their food like that so they can keep it for a long time without spoiling. They don't eat things while they are alive," Lorelei explained, crouching back down.

The mermaid nodded in disgusted fascination. "They eat dead things."

Lorelei marveled at how both true and extremely gross that sounded. Setting down the can, Blue-Eyes took off Mackenzie's necklace, dangling it between them. "I'll gladly exchange this for enough pig to feed my people."

"I think that can be arranged," Lorelei said diplomatically, though it wasn't anywhere close to a fair trade considering the fact that Blue-Eyes had probably eaten Mackenzie. She held out her hand to take it.

The mermaid dropped the necklace into her palm, frowning. "I'm sorry for your friend." The apology was a little stiff, but not disingenuous as far as Lorelei could tell. Blue-Eyes seemed to understand her anger and hurt well enough, just not the crime itself.

Unsure of what to make of that, Lorelei wordlessly pocketed the necklace. "If you think people are food and not friends, then why do you, um, 'mate' with them?"

"Our men are born very sick," she explained, pointing to her head to indicate the type of illness. "It wasn't always that way, but now they're far t too dangerous to couple with." Lorelei grimaced, and the mermaid continued, "But it's always more enjoyable when we mate with Two-Leggers, who aren't as likely to inflict pain with their blunted claws and teeth. They're like us enough for it to work, and babies are easier to carry when they're wanted." Blue-Eyes looked briefly at Killian and said, "We once befriended people, and perhaps we still would, if only they didn't taste so good now. Can't be friends with a creature that drives us mad with hunger. And other wants."

In a morbid, twisted way, Lorelei began to understand how food and mate weren't mutually exclusive to her kin, having experienced the unsettling phenomena for herself. "Eating this helps me maintain control of those urges," she told the other siren, pointing at the empty can, "so they don't rule me."

Blue-Eyes leaned forward, expression thoughtful. "So, it does." The promise of control seemed to interest her.

Although Lorelei was afraid to know the answer, she asked the question that had been burning in her mind since she found out about her oceanic origins. "How does someone like you or I become a Shorewalker?"

The mermaid gave her a look that oddly resembled sympathy. "Most of us have Two-Legger blood in our veins after generations of our foremothers mating with them. There are less and less left of our kind who do not. And because of that, we can shift and walk the shores if we choose to, but we never do beyond an occasional prowl for mates. A Shorewalker is made when one of our men hurts one of your women, and she escapes, giving birth on shore. It doesn't happen often. Our men usually try to kill their mates."

Oh my God. All blood rushed from her face. Too unsteady to remain crouching, she sat down on deck. *My mother was...I'm a...*

"It's not dissimilar to dolphins, believe it or not," Lila interjected grimly. "They are some of the biggest assholes in the sea."

"But it looks like we've discovered the reigning champions," Jackie quickly followed, revulsion dripping from every word.

Why was the deck spinning?

The mermaid shot Lila and Jackie dirty looks. To Lorelei, she said, cutting through the dizziness with her stern tone, "Next time you meet one of our men, you kill him, Shorewalker child. That's what we do to survive."

Lorelei nodded numbly, remembering the night Blue-Eyes and her four companions killed the male stalking her. She vaguely registered promising to heed this advice, her mouth moving automatically. That reckless abandon should've scared her into silence, but she kept on talking, trying to drown out the roiling thoughts in her head. "We'll give you all the canned pig you want, but you have to promise us that you and your people won't eat humans ever again. And we'll also have to take you back to shore with us."

The mermaid narrowed her eyes. "I don't have to do anything. And I certainly won't become a Shorewalker like you. Who're you to demand such a steep price of me?"

Bristling, Jackie stepped in. "Listen here, sea hag. You're not going to have much of a choice. You and your kind ate a ship full of ours."

"Your kind makes us and every creature living in our ocean sick," the mermaid fired back. "You've killed far more than we ever could. What's one ship compared to that?"

Putting a hand on Jackie's shoulder before things escalated further, Lila said, "We're trying to stop doing that, but maybe we can help each other. You stop eating us, and we stop making you sick, or at least try to as best we can."

The mermaid folded her arms across her chest and fixed the scientist with a hard look. "As best you can? You don't make a very convincing argument, Two-Legger."

"The world—the shore—is filled with lots of people." Lila tugged on one of her curls, stretching it straight, a nervous tick Lorelei hadn't noticed before. "Convincing every single one to stop polluting is, um, probably not going to happen."

"The ocean is filled with us. Also not so easy to convince, even with this canned pig to quell our cravings." She motioned to an empty can.

"All either of us can do is our best," Walt interceded, holding out his hands diplomatically. "There's going to be mistakes on either side, folks who don't care to change, but that's no reason to fight each other over it and let it ruin our goodwill."

The mermaid respectfully inclined her head to him. "What would happen to me if you brought me to shore?"

Caught off guard by the question, they all looked at each other, hoping someone would have a good answer. None of seemed to know how to explain to a sentient creature that they planned to study them in captivity—indefinitely.

"We want to study you," Lorelei answered, too tired to sugarcoat the truth. But even if she'd thought of gentler phrasing, it felt too much like lying and manipulation.

The mermaid crushed a can of potted meat with her hand and pointed one clawed finger. "No," she seethed. "That's not how you broker peace. You're too much like the Two-Leggers who raised you, Shorewalker child—just taking and taking and taking without offering anything meaningful in exchange."

This was going to hell in a hand basket rather quickly. "I'm sorry, that's not my intention," Lorelei began, scrubbing her cheeks. *God, this was stressful.* Frankness wasn't working, and she didn't exactly learn how to handle interspecies diplomacy in Public Speaking 101. "I don't want to be a taker. Please tell us what a fair exchange would be, and we can go from there?"

"First of all, you'll return me to the sea with more of this canned pig if there's to be any hope of my people abstaining from human flesh. If I go with you, and leave my pod behind, who will enforce whatever deal we strike here today?"

That was a fair point.

"Okay," she agreed. "What else do you want?"

"Human healing is renown even to us. For all that you poison the sea and sicken seafolk, you've an uncanny ability to pinpoint illnesses and heal yourselves. I want you to heal us. It's not just our men who are sick

—you, me, the rest of our kin, we're all beholden to cravings for human flesh. The canned pig is a soothing salve, but it's not real, lasting change."

Lila perked at the mention of healing and crouched down to speak with the siren on eye-level. "You mean like find a cure?"

"Yes, Two-Legger."

Scratching her head, Lila was silent for a moment, lost in thought. "That depends on what's causing the sickness," she answered cautiously, but there was a hopeful spark of scientific excitement kindling in her eyes. "Could be a mental illness, which can be treated, but not cured. But maybe it's related to pollution—like toxic chemicals in the water. Or maybe it's caused by a disease like rabies or cetacean morbillivirus. But I'd have to run tests and collect blood and skin samples from other mermaids before I could attempt to puzzle it out."

The siren narrowed her eyes. "You need one of us to study to find a cure? Fine. I'll send you one of our own, but just one. No more. I'll not subject any more to the Shorewalker fate than needed. And you must promise me you won't cause any more suffering in the process than is necessary. After watching you squirm at my peoples' ills, I can tell you have a conscience—don't betray it."

"We won't," Lorelei promised without giving it a second thought, but Lila wrinkled her nose. Something wasn't sitting right with her.

"I understand your concerns," she said, "but I'll need additional samples if I'm going to successfully figure out what's causing the sickness and how to cure it. The good news is, I can come out here and collect them—just small amounts of skin and blood. Nothing too painful. Just a little pinch. How's that for a compromise?"

The siren ran a claw across her lips, considering the idea. "You'd truly come to us to do this? That would be agreeable."

Lila rose to her feet and turned to the rest of the group. "I think I can do it. I'm not an epidemiologist, but I have solid connections in the field."

Hope fluttered in Lorelei's chest, the first she'd felt after the grim revelation about her parentage. A cure would be life changing. She wouldn't have to fear losing control and hurting the people she loved.

They could stop what happened to *The Osprey* from ever happening again. Humans would be safe, and the mermaids would be free from this maddening, all-consuming hunger.

A cure might even save their species.

Walt stepped forward and took his daughter by the shoulders. "My smart girl. I'm so proud of you. If there's any scientist on this planet brilliant enough to figure this out, it's you. But this could take a long time. And it's possible you may not find the answers you want. Answers a whole community in the sea below us are counting on, if you promise this. All I'm saying is make sure you make a promise you can keep. Set expectations."

Fierce love and determination shone in Lila's eyes. She hugged her dad tight.

The siren spoke up. Her tone was somber. "I understand you'll find answers if there are answers to be found. But if there aren't any, we'll have to accept that, but you must still supply us with canned pig if you want to prevent more of your kind from dying."

It wasn't a threat. Just the reality of the situation.

After conferring with the group, Lorelei agreed to the deal. She wanted to be happier about it, and this potential cure, but the thought of taking one of her own into captivity dampened that glimmer of hope and made her stomach churn. While she could fill the role as Lila's primary test subject herself, she didn't have the courage to face the whole world with her secret.

"What's your name?" Lorelei asked the siren.

She tilted her head. "Undine."

"That's a German name." Like hers.

"Is it?" Undine shrugged. "Names whispered in the ears of humans sometimes make their way to shore."

Placing her hands on her hips, Jackie cleared her throat. "Well, *Undine*. Are you going to keep your word and find us your replacement?"

Without warning, Undine let out a shrill, piercing whistle. Everyone on the boat except Lorelei keeled over and covered their ears. Glaring at Jackie, Undine said, "I lead our pod. They listen when I call impatient, demanding, Two-Legger."

A moment later, there was a splash in the water nearby. Jackie reached for her large thermos, as if ready to bash in anything that climbed over the side and got too close.

"See?" Undine grinned, revealing her pointed teeth.

Jackie shuddered.

"Give me another can of pig," Undine commanded with her hand outstretched.

Lorelei wordlessly gave her another, which the mermaid opened and chucked over the side. They heard another splash, followed by the unpleasant sound of loud chewing.

Once appeased, a dark-haired mermaid climbed over the side of the boat holding the now empty can. A juvenile, she appeared docile but eyed them all warily with gleaming golden eyes.

Like two other mermaids Lorelei had seen before, this newcomer's fins fanned out in several orange shades with slashes of the same silvery color as her scales. Perhaps they were relatives.

The juvenile mermaid knelt beside Undine.

They conversed in another language—a combination of hand signs and flashing bioluminescence. Whatever was said, the conversation ended with the younger mermaid bowing her head in agreement. To Lorelei's surprise, her tail split down the middle as she shifted to a crouching position in semi-human form. Save for the scales along the sides of her legs and feet, Nireed's lower half appeared completely human. But then again, Undine had said that most of their kind had human blood in their veins. They *could* shift but chose not to.

"This is Nireed. She will go with you to shore. Now, do you have more of this food you promised?" Undine took the can from Nireed and tossed it to Jackie.

The reporter fumbled but managed to catch it. She looked to Killian in question.

"The crates are below deck," he answered.

"Come on," Walt waved to Jackie. "We'll go get them."

"Undine, how long ago did the sickness set in?" Lorelei asked.

"Two generations ago when our men turned against us, and our grandmothers and mothers sought comfort with Two-Leggers. The madness set in not long after."

"Could mating have caused the madness?"

Undine shook her head. "No. Our kind and theirs began mating long, long ago. Not as often, but often enough to know this madness is new."

When Walt and Jackie returned with two crates, Undine motioned to Nireed and where Mackenzie's necklace had hung around her neck. "With this, our debt is paid, for now. If you keep your promises, there will be peace."

"How will we get the food to you?"

Undine smirked. "Two-Leggers are good at dumping things in the ocean. Do that. We'll find it and give back the cans." She chirped an instruction to Nireed, and the second mermaid heaved the crates brought up from below decks overboard.

"How often?" Killian asked.

Undine looked pointedly at him and winked. "Every time, fisherman." She tore through the netting with startling speed, and in a flash of scales and fins, dove over the side of the boat.

The escape was so sure and effortless, it begged the question: had they ever truly ensnared her? Maybe Undine *let* herself be captured. But why? As Lorelei stared out over the water, where Undine had disappeared beneath the waves, cold sea air cut through her fleece jacket, making her shiver.

A soft whimper drew her attention back on deck.

Nireed who'd obediently stayed behind while her mistress swam away, was balled up in a crouch, making herself as small as possible, shaking either from cold or fear or both.

They tried speaking with her, but unlike Undine, she didn't seem to know any English.

Pangs of sympathy and guilt stabbed at Lorelei's heart. The mermaid was young and quite literally out of her depth, a fish out of water, her future uncertain. Their mission had been technically successful, but it didn't feel like a victory.

With a weary sigh, Lorelei handed Nireed another can of faux human meat, and that seemed to cheer her up a bit.

Motivated by food.

"Shocker Undine didn't leave behind a mermaid who could actually speak to us," Jackie muttered, shooting an icy glare at the ocean.

Lila shrugged. "It's not like I get to talk to the marine life I study, anyway. I'm a marine biologist, not an anthropologist."

"Were you hoping to get a quote?" Walt teased, draping a blanket around Nireed.

While the mermaid flinched when the material touched her skin, she accepted it as she had the food and huddled by the deck box to eat, never taking her eyes off them.

"It would have been nice," Jackie huffed.

"Maybe it's for the best," Lila began. "As we discussed before, we don't want anyone to know what really happened to *The Osprey's* crew. The families shouldn't be put through that. And we know what the response will be if it gets out. Merfolk will be hunted to extinction."

Jackie glanced at Lorelei. "And if that happened? Extinction, I mean," she trailed, prompting Lila to continue. "It sounded like they're headed there already."

Lila elaborated. "We don't know yet how these creatures impact the ecosystem. Wiping out a whole species can have disastrous effects for us all."

These creatures?

Though her voice was shaky, Lorelei finally voiced the thoughts she'd kept to herself. "They aren't animals. No more than I am. Yes, they act on their instincts—albeit people-eating ones at times. And yes, their social standards aren't the same, but all that's different between them and me is I was raised by humans. And when my biological origins caught up with me, I had you guys to turn to for help. As much as I hate what they did to my crewmates, they're not completely to blame. This hunger, this sickness Undine spoke of, it controls them. They're just doing what they must to survive."

Killian wrapped his arm around her shoulder and squeezed.

Lila looked stricken. "Lorelei, I didn't mean—"

"I know. But think we need to take this even more seriously than we have been." They had a mermaid hiding behind the deck box, shrinking herself down as much as possible and watching them warily as if *they* were the threat. "Nireed's our responsibility now."

"You're not wrong, Lorelei," Jackie said, tucking her hands under her arms. When she looked at Nireed, her expression softened in a way it never had for Undine. "And I'm sure Lila will take good care of her. But the reality is your kind has proven to be dangerous to humans, and they seem self-aware enough to know that they're eating *people*, not just other animals. So, while I understand where you're coming from, my sympathies only go so far. It's also in the public's interest that we study Nireed, especially now that a ton of folks are going to be looking for the others. People-eating aside, their ability to compel people is quite alarming."

The reporter's words eased some of her conscience. Not every reason they had for doing this was self-interested.

"Speaking of compulsion, did you see how Undine reacted when she first came onboard?" Lila asked the group. They nodded. "The first thing she did was compel Will to shut off the engine. I'm willing to bet they don't approach modern boats at all, because the propellers and noise from the engines freak them out. Lorelei, your hearing has adjusted for life on land, but in the ocean, theirs must be a lot more sensitive."

Jackie pulled a small notepad from her back pocket and began jotting down notes. "Dr. Branson, she compelled you. What did it feel like being under her control?"

"Uh, freaky?" Lila arched her brows.

Tapping her pen against her lips, Jackie looked at Killian. "She tried doing the same thing to you—I think to get you to let go of Dr. Branson. But it didn't work. Were you just able to resist it better?"

He scratched the scruff along his jawline, brow furrowing. "Are you sure she did? I didn't feel anything."

Jackie nodded, biting the tip of her pen. "She was staring at you with her beady little sea hag eyes." Turning to Lorelei, she added, "Look, I heard you what you said earlier, but I don't trust Undine. After that horror movie of an entrance, I think she's up to something."

"I mean, she's their leader. My best guess is she was scoping us out.

But ultimately the deal we made with her is beneficial to the both of us. She's just looking out for her people." Looking up at Killian, Lorelei added, "You can't be completely immune if I can—" but before she could finish that thought she remembered they were in mixed company and blushed.

"Interesting." Lila tapped her lips thoughtfully. "You know, I think it has to do with your relationship," she surmised, waving between the two of them. "Killian, it's like you're already attuned to Lorelei's song. You can't be called by another siren, because it's as if Lorelei has already staked her claim on you."

His hold around her slipped down to her waist. "That's kinda hot," he murmured privately into her ear. This man. She grinned and bumped him with her hip.

Pocketing her pen and notebook, Jackie coughed to get Lorelei's attention. "You couldn't understand what Undine and Nireed were saying, could you?"

Lorelei shook her head. "How could I? I was raised human. Language is learned, not inherently known."

Crossing her arms, Jackie looked between Nireed and the rest of the group. "Do you think she might try something with us? While I appreciate that Undine's kept her word so far, and seemed reasonable when making the deal, I can't help but think she might have ulterior motives, and that Nireed's part of her plans. Or equally possible—there are no ulterior motives—but what if Nireed chafes under Undine's orders and decides to go rogue?"

Lorelei shook her head. "I'm not getting that vibe from her. But I could be wrong. We should probably put her in the tank tonight. And I'll stand watch since her singing doesn't affect me."

"Doesn't affect me either, apparently. I'll split the watch with you." Killian brushed back a tendril of hair loosened by the sea wind. His tone brooked no argument.

CHAPTER

FORTY-SIX

NIREED SCREECHED AND CUPPED HER HANDS OVER HER EARS when the engines restarted, sensitive to the sound, but Lorelei coaxed a pair of noise-cancelling headphones onto her head. The mermaid settled, distress ebbing away the moment everything fell into blissful silence. She curled up in a coil of rope and fell fast asleep.

The headphones couldn't go into the tank with her later that night, so Lorelei tasked Killian with finding a pair of foam earplugs.

Observing Nireed's relaxed, vulnerable expression, Lorelei felt unexpectedly protective of her. It stemmed from the guilt she felt at holding the fellow mermaid captive and subjecting her to the world's curiosity. This was the price of her own anonymity.

Hand sliding into her coat pocket, Lorelei's fingers brushed Mackenzie's necklace in cold reminder and her anger flashed. Despite the kinship Lorelei was beginning to feel toward Nireed and the others, another part of her still thought this was just payment for the destroyed lives of *The Osprey's* crew.

While nothing could ever adequately repay that debt, at the same time, Lorelei also thought reducing Nireed's life to a glass tank, an ongoing series of tests, and the relentless gaze of onlookers was too steep a price. The moral and ethical quandary made her head spin.

She didn't know what she should feel.

And yet, later that night, when helping Nireed into her seawater-filled tank, she vowed to make sure the siren's life onshore was as comfortable as possible and to release her if it ever became unbearable.

Coming to stand beside her, Lila watched as Nireed settled inside. Relief washed over the mermaid's face and her drying, flaking skin healed. Even this short time away from water had emotionally and physically taxed her.

"Penny for your thoughts."

Lorelei voiced the vow she made to herself, and Lila agreed to follow suit, making it a pact between them. No matter what, the day Nireed couldn't handle the study anymore, they'd set her free.

"Working with marine life with this level of sentience is completely unprecedented," Lila said vulnerably, arms wrapped around herself.

Even knowing the good that would come from studying the species, the marine biologist also couldn't help but question whether doing that was right. Nireed's dubious consent, and Lorelei's reality check, sobered her initial excitement. For the first time since taking organic chemistry in undergrad, Lila felt completely out of her depth, and the whole world, particularly the scientific one, would be watching and scrutinizing her work.

"Maybe you could talk to the director about getting an anthropologist onboard or a linguist," Lorelei suggested, giving her a little nudge. "And plan an intersectional study."

Lila brightened. "That's a good idea."

THAT EVENING, AFTER SITUATING AND SECURING NIREED IN her saltwater tank, the group met in the pilothouse for a discussion. "Undine said that the ocean was filled with her kind, but how many of them could actually be out there?" Lila wondered out loud. "They sound like a pretty self-destructive species. The males rape and kill the females. The surviving females kill the males."

Jackie grimaced. "Well, the females apparently rape human men for babies. But how often can that happen? It wouldn't be very discrete."

The reminder made Lorelei nauseous.

For much of her life, she'd contemplated her history, her parentage, but never had she regretted digging into the past more than now. Murderous sea creatures? Fine. She was finally coming to terms with that. But rapists? A child born of...

"It wouldn't be discrete," Killian reasoned, taking her hand under the table, a lifeline in the storm overtaking her mind. "But I don't think most would admit to it, and less so by a mythical sea creature."

Branson agreed, but added, "The stories also talk about seduction. Maybe some of it is consensual?"

Jackie snorted. "Up until they become the wrong kind of snack."

Branson shot Lorelei a sympathetic look. "Sorry, I tried."

Pushing the roiling thoughts in her head deep, deep down, she shrugged. "It is what it is," she said, sounding much calmer than she was. "But if Lila and her research team find out what is making us sick, and can develop a real cure, or treatment, that won't be a problem anymore. And it might save the species."

Jackie pulled out her notebook and flipped back a couple pages. "That's right. She said we taste good and drive them crazy with hunger, but that they used to be friends with us."

"Before we get back to shore, we need to get our story straight," Killian said. "Some of the things we know can't be shared without jeopardizing Lorelei's anonymity. For instance, we can't talk about Shorewalkers. Or we have to seriously fudge the details, because a lot of what we know is because of Lorelei."

Frowning, Lila ticked off all such knowledge on her fingers. "Why we picked this location when the sightings were close to shore. Why we fed Undine and Nireed canned pork. How we know they like to eat and/or mate with people—oh boy. There's a lot to fudge."

Killian folded his arms across his chest and rubbed his chin as he thought. "Lila, I can say we were having weird issues with our netting being shredded at some of our fishing sights. So, after you didn't find anything near shore, you can say you decided to check it out with us. As for the canned pork, recreate the same test you did with Lorelei for show. The rest—let the folklore fill in those blanks."

Wanting to get it exactly right, Jackie scribbled vigorously in her notepad.

"Mm. That's the story I'll tell my boss, since he authorized the search," Lila began. "But the board has no idea I went out and did this. We have to cook up a second story—the public story."

Jackie groaned and scratched out the entire page she'd just written. "You gotta be kidding me," she muttered to herself.

Lila suggested that they say Nireed was bycatch fishermen caught while assisting her with research on new trawling gear to hit the market, and its impacts on seafloor habitat. The board had already approved a similar project plan before she was asked to develop the museum.

"That works!" Jackie said hurriedly, as if doing so would prevent any additional story changes.

"Now that we got what we came for, is it a good time to mention that reporter guy's story went viral early this morning?" Lila said sheepishly, eliciting a series of surprised exclamations.

"Babe. You didn't think to tell us then?" Branson pinched his brow, sounding rather tired.

"I thought it would add unnecessary stress!"

Knowing first-hand the fragility of ship morale, Lorelei sided with Lila. "The possibility was already hanging over our heads. Not knowing didn't make us any less efficient. At least Jackie knows now that she's going to have to pull an all-nighter writing her counter article."

The reporter made a face, knowing this was true.

Feeling bad for the woman, Lorelei said, "I'll go fill up that humongous thermos of yours."

And truth be told, she desperately needed something to do with her hands.

CHAPTER
FORTY-SEVEN

WHEN THE REST OF THEIR GROUP HAD GONE TO BED, Killian put *Dawn Chaser* on autopilot and set Lorelei up on a cot in the pilothouse. He would take the first watch.

"How are you doing?" Although he already suspected the answer, he wanted to give her the space to talk about it.

Paling, she pulled the blankets to her chin with trembling hands. "Sick to my stomach." Her voice barely tipped above a whisper. "I haven't been able to stop thinking about what Undine said, about what happened to my mother." She squeezed her eyes shut, as if the words hurt too much to speak. Still, she forced them out. "I've always wondered why my biological mother gave me up, more out of curiosity than anything else. Greta was everything I needed and more, so I never had room to miss the one who birthed me. But out of all the possible reasons I considered, I never thought this would be the one. My human birth mother is out there somewhere dealing with this trauma alone, and I wish I could hug her. I know that wouldn't 'fix' anything, but if she's alone..."

Lorelei didn't finish the sentence.

His heart ached to see her in such pain.

Crouching beside her, he smoothed back her dark auburn hair, frizzy and disheveled from a day out on deck. "Do you want to try to find her?"

Face falling further, she picked some fuzz off the blanket. "I would love to meet her, but what if that was triggering? Hurting her is the last thing I'd want to do."

Grasping for words and coming up short, he combed his fingers through her hair instead.

"I know that none of what happened is my fault, but it still sucks."

"Maybe Undine was wrong. Or lying."

Disagreement etched hard lines in her expression, a protest about to follow, but she stopped herself, suddenly. "Yeah, maybe. I guess I'll never know."

"Even if it's true, don't take that weight on yourself," he continued. For as much as he didn't trust Undine, what mattered most was whether Lorelei believed it to be true. And if she did, he needed to be sensitive to it. "It changes nothing, helps no one."

She nodded but did not respond any further than that.

How Lorelei had gotten so far inland remained a mystery. Unless... her biological mother fled the coast, running as far away as possible from the ocean. That made a lot of sense, but why run to Upper Peninsula, Michigan? Did she know Lorelei's adoptive mom?

Whatever the case may be, he was at a loss for how to comfort her and take away the pain she felt. What he would give to be able to do that. "Get some rest, Lorelei," he said finally. "It's going to be a long night."

He tucked the blanket around her and leaned forward to kiss her forehead.

Although they agreed to share the watch, he had no intention of waking her up. After the day she'd had, filled with its heavy revelations, Lorelei could use all the sleep she could get. He'd stand the watch himself.

Bringing the cot up here—he'd just wanted to keep her close.

CHAPTER
FORTY-EIGHT

RUBBING A FINGER ALONG THE WORN, SMUDGED EDGE OF the newspaper column, Lorelei reread Jackie's article. She'd bought the paper at the local grocery and returned to it often, even weeks after its original print date.

"You ever gonna stop reading that thing?" Lila teased, barely looking up as she clacked away on her laptop. They sat across from each other at Killian's kitchen table, enjoying a rare work from home day.

"Just can't believe that it's real." Lorelei shook out the paper just as she'd seen her mother do countless times. Greta had never been without the morning paper at the breakfast table. "The world knows about mermaids now. And are mostly freaking out in a good way."

Despite Jackie's deep distrust of Undine, and wariness of her intentions, it was a fair and honest piece. Her reporting delicately treaded the line between fact and a healthy advisement for caution, cleverly guising all her warnings in allusions to folklore. Only time would tell if the deal they made with the mermaid would come back to bite them.

Lila interrupted the thought, snarking, "What, not a fan of the upcoming Mermnado movie?"--

Tornado-riding mermaids. Lorelei shrugged. "I'd see it."

"You would?"

"Who doesn't love comically terrible CGI and face-nomming? Maybe it'll be so bad it's good."

"Nah," Lila drawled, eyeing her skeptically. "But ply me with enough wine beforehand, and maybe I'll go with you, anyway. Gonna talk through the whole movie though."

"That's the only way to do it," Lorelei grinned, but a potential hang-up made it falter. "Do you think the theater will be crowded with tourists?"

Normally the cold months were quiet and gave the locals reprieve from bustling summer activity, but Haven Cove, Maine had become a media feeding frenzy and tourism hotspot.

"Ugh. Probably. Let's wait to stream it then."

"How are the award applications coming?" Lorelei asked. "And the contracts?"

Lila qualified for a number of Woods Hole Oceanographic Institute awards and was in talks with NOAA and National Geographic for research partnerships.

The marine biologist groaned, slumping to the tabletop, lightly banging her head against the surface, poufy cloud of curls swaying each time. "Girl, I just want to look at fish. I'm not good at writing about myself. And legalese bores me to tears."

"Want some help? Words don't scare me." And she grew up with a County Judge for a mother.

Lightning fast, Lila shot up and spun around the laptop, pushing it across the table. "Take it. It's yours." She bounced out of her seat and began rooting around the cupboards, quickly finding Lorelei's chocolate stash. From one dessert hound to the other, Lorelei respected her efficiency, and folding the newspaper and setting it aside, Lorelei slid Lila's laptop in front of her.

Several hours of wordsmithing and translating contract language later, and they opened a bottle of well-deserved wine.

"Did the board approve your promotion?" Lila asked, supplying them both with generous pours.

"Yup." Excitement and pride swelled within Lorelei's chest, a goofy grin overtaking her face. "Just need to sign a few things and then I'm officially Museum Director."

Lila shimmed with delight and clinked their glasses together.

It was a dream come true. The museum project, under her direction, would include a sizable mermaid exhibit, as well as a public memorial for *The Osprey* crew. The world could never know what truly happened, but it could honor and remember them. That sobered her a bit and reminded her of the tabloid-eques piece that had swept them down this path.

It was clear to her now that Ed Knudsen's article had been a grieving man's cry for help.

While Lila leafed through the takeout menus cluttering their junk drawer, Lorelei opened her email, and after finding his contact information at the paper, began to type. She was no stranger to grief, and no one should ever have to endure it alone.

CHAPTER
FORTY-NINE

ONLY ONE LOOSE END REMAINED.

Cut off all ties with Carrie. Make it abundantly clear that she was not to come anywhere near them or Killian's seaside home ever again. The decision to confront his ex was necessary, but it made Killian quiet, pensive.

When Lorelei asked why, wondering if maybe he had doubts, he'd said he'd never thought it would come to this. That the woman Carrie was and the woman she became was so completely different, a clear-cut line had to be drawn in the sand.

Boundaries weren't a problem with her fifteen years ago, but now she trampled over them like inconvenient weeds. Getting her way, and being right, had become more important than respect.

After getting the address from Will, Killian drove to Carrie's house, and Lorelei tagged along for emotional support. They parked out front in his pick-up truck and walked up the front porch steps hand in hand, snow crunching underfoot. They paused at the ruby red door, sharing a long look.

She squeezed his hand tight, lending him strength.

Time to get this over with.

With a deep breath, he knocked on Carrie's door, jostling the out-ofseason autumnal wreath hanging there, brown wicker adorned by fall leaves, pinecones, and acorns.

Carrie must have been in a room nearby because she came to the door quickly, dressed in pressed slacks and a cashmere sweater. Surprise brightened her face upon seeing Killian at her front door, but that quickly vanished when she turned her gaze to Lorelei.

The woman visibly flinched.

In as calm a voice as he could muster, Killian began laying down his terms. He'd never shown a temper with Lorelei, except that one time when she'd gotten hurt, but his patience for Carrie was already on thin ice. One interruption and this had the potential to escalate quickly.

Rubbing soothing circles across his knuckles with her thumb, Lorelei wordlessly reminded him she was there, that he wasn't alone. He returned the gesture with a light squeeze. She'd come along to be a calming force, and it seemed to be working. His temper remained caged.

Asking a people-eating mermaid to mediate ex-girlfriend problems? There was a joke in there somewhere.

To Carrie's credit, she listened, even though the rising color in her alabaster cheeks made it apparent that the moment Killian stopped talking, she'd fly into a fit of rage.

This wasn't going to end well.

The moment his mouth closed for more than three seconds Carrie unleashed. "Killian, you can't be serious! A restraining order? I haven't been on your property since I took that stupid video!"

Which wasn't all that long ago.

It was a Herculean effort to not roll her eyes. While warranted, goading Carrie was the last thing either of them needed. It would only draw out this encounter longer than it needed to be.

"Yeah, well, you don't exactly inspire confidence that the last time is the last time. This is your final warning before we go through with it." Killian crossed his arms. "You've already had more than enough chances."

"Ugh. You're unbelievable!" Carrie smacked her hand against the door frame.

Hackles raised, and eying that hand for one wrong move, Lorelei repressed the urge to step in front of Killian. Some sort of territorial, protective instinct was compelling her to get between him and his ex.

That woman had an unsettling habit of hitting things when she got mad.

"Is it really so hard to respect my boundaries?"

"Don't flatter yourself! I'll admit I needed closure at first. But then one of those fish people attacked me. Was I supposed to just shut up about it and pretend it never happened?" She paused and stared Lorelei dead in the eye, issuing a challenge. The predator that hid within did not like that. "No one else was going to give a shit," she added darkly.

Temper flaring, Lorelei's gums and nail beds ached as her sharp edges threatened to come out. So much for being a calming force. She tried to affect a calm tone. "What happened to you was terrible. But you're wrong about no one giving a shit. We give a shit. We just handled it differently than how you wanted."

Carrie rolled her eyes. "Don't feed me that bullshit. You didn't do anything."

"Think for just a minute. What were animal services going to do? What were the police going to do? What was bitching on the fucking internet going to do? We went to Lila and handled it ourselves. If you don't believe me, watch the live feed of the mermaid tank." Her control over her temper slipped, and she spat out the last words, "She didn't end up there because we did nothing."

The bullheaded woman just shook her head, arms folded across her chest. "She's not the one who bit me. I don't have a score to settle with her. I'm after the sea bitch with red hair."

Her blood ran cold, and Killian, who stood beside her shoulder to shoulder, tensed.

She knows.

Carrie continued irritably, "Now, if you'll excuse me, I've got shit to do." She promptly slammed the door in their faces.

Or maybe not…

If Carrie truly knew she was the "sea bitch with red hair," she would have said so in no uncertain terms, right? She wasn't the sort of person to pull punches. Throwing a person's flaws and wrongdoings in their face was a favorite Carrie pastime, second only to snooping.

As much as that woman's rudeness and accusations of incompetence made Lorelei want to rip out her hair, she'd take that over the alternative any day. Carrie could never find out she was a mermaid. That information was a weapon, and Carrie would use it without hesitation to gut her like a fish.

"That's over with," Killian exhaled deeply and wrapped an arm around her shoulders.

Still shaken, Lorelei leaned into his touch, drawing on his solid frame for warmth and comfort. "Let's go home."

CHAPTER

FIFTY

Leaning against the door frame to Lorelei's office, Killian held a bouquet of flowers, watching his love hard at work. He'd been away at sea for nearly a week, and down at the docks for the past five hours, but now his homecoming was complete.

Discarded heels on the floor beneath her desk, she sat cross-legged in her chair, lower lip bit in concentration. She furiously typed away at her computer, quietly humming a familiar upbeat tune.

> *That's what we do with a drunken sailor*
> *That's what we do with a drunken sailor*
> *That's what we do with a drunken sailor*
> *Early in the morning*

Drawn in by the darting motions of her fingertips, he noticed that she'd painted her nails a rich dark brown. Warm. Inviting. Not the pretty pinks or sultry reds she'd worn before.

A stupid wide grin bridged his face.

He wasn't trying to be sneaky, but she was so immersed in her work that she didn't look up when he approached her desk. To think that he could sneak up on his vicious siren girlfriend, a predator by nature with a predator's instincts. He coughed quietly to get her attention, trying not to startle her, but she jumped anyway, looking up at him with a wide-eyed expression.

But once she fully registered him, a bright smile erupted.

Bounding out of her chair, Lorelei closed the distance between them and threw her arms around his neck. A kiss followed. "I wasn't expecting to see you until dinner time."

"Wanted to surprise you."

"Are those for me?" She gestured to the flowers in his hand.

"Of course," he grinned, offering them to her.

"They're lovely. Thank you." She put them in the ceramic vase that had taken permanent residence on her desk for this exact purpose. His routine of bringing flowers began with Lorelei's promotion to Museum Director but seeing how much she loved getting them led to another bouquet, then another. He was just too enthralled by her smiles to stop.

"Can I steal you away for a little bit?"

"Sure," she replied, brushing back a strand of hair that had come loose from her fishtail braid. "I could use a break. What do you have in mind?"

"I was thinking a short walk on the shore path."

"Give me one minute." Lorelei hurried back to her desk to save her work and log out of her computer. Then she fished out a pair of wool socks from her work bag and located her snow boots by the door. Once she donned those, her winter coat, gloves, and hat, she looped her arm around his and let him lead the way.

They strolled leisurely along the shore path, snow crunching beneath their boots. The frigid temps and deep snows of January had finally brought peace and quiet to Haven Cove from the relentless mermaid craze.

Killian frequently glanced down at Lorelei, her cheeks rosy from the cold.

"What?" She laughed, catching him in the act.

Kicking a clump of snow with his boot, he shoved down his growing nervousness, and asked, "How do you feel about engagements after a short period of dating?"

A teasing smirk played on her lips as she raised one arched brow. "Why, are you thinking of proposing?"

"It's been on my mind." He shrugged, trying to keep it casual, but felt anything but. "Don't worry, I'm not going to do it right now."

The smirk faded. For a moment, she appeared lost in thought, but whatever it was, made her lips quirk upwards as if recalling a fond memory. "What if I want you to?"

"Well." He turned. "As it happens, I did bring the ring." He reached inside his jacket and pulled out a brown wooden box.

Her gloved hands flew to her mouth. "Oh, you weren't kidding," she said softly, eyes twinkling with joy.

Stepping closer, he touched his forehead to hers, their clouded breath coalescing together as one. "Will you marry me, Lorelei?"

"Yes." The way she beamed up at him made his heart soar.

With a wide smile to match, he removed her glove and slipped the ring onto her finger. When it was firmly in place, she gave him a fierce hug that was almost too tight. That bone-crushing mermaid strength of hers…

He wouldn't have it any other way.

"Do you like it?" he chuckled.

"Oh gosh," she laughed, releasing him.

Finally examining the ring encircling her finger, her eyes widened in wonder. Taking off her other glove, she traced the pearl, accent diamonds, and gold band with her finger. Their lives, their love, were intrinsically tied to the sea. He picked this ring to honor that.

"It's perfect," she breathed, voice hardly a whisper. "I love it."

Wrapping an arm around her waist, he pulled her close, anchoring her to his side. The love of his life. His future wife. God, he couldn't stop smiling. "Shall I walk you back to your office?"

She looked up at him as if he'd grown two heads. "I can't concentrate on work now."

Of course not. That's not what he intended. "Do your blinds close?"

he asked, tracing her lower lip with his thumb, his grin growing mischievous.

But Lorelei's turned positively wicked. Her green sea glass eyes flashed, glowing for a single moment, as she threaded her fingers through his. "Follow me, Captain."

He followed.

CHAPTER
FIFTY-ONE

One Month Earlier

Watching from behind drawn curtains, Carrie waited for Killian and his new girlfriend to drive away. The doors and windows were locked but would that be enough? Carrie needed to see *her* leave.

She'd been blind. So, so blind.

Once they were out of sight, Carrie sunk to her living room floor and screamed into clenched fists. The near constant throbbing of her leg and that memory of swirling red hair in icy water haunted her every waking thought and terrorized her sleep. Not a single moment spared her from feeling powerless and afraid. She hated the pitying looks people gave her on the street as she limped by on her crutches. It reminded her all too well of things she'd rather forget.

But most of all, Carrie hated Killian Quinn and Lorelei Roth for being right.

She'd been slowly going mad since the day she left Haven Cove for New York City. And it had been getting much, much worse since her return.

She hadn't seen it before, the resemblance, but anger had a way of revealing the truth about someone, about the ugliness hidden within. And now she couldn't unsee it.

It made no logical sense, she knew, but Carrie swore Lorelei looked just like the mermaid who'd tried to kill her.

Thank you for reading! Did you enjoy? Please add your review because nothing helps an author more and encourages readers to take a chance on a book than a review.

And don't miss more in the Haven Cove series with book two, SONG OF LORELEI, available now! Turn the page for a sneak peek!

Also be sure to sign up for the City Owl Press newsletter to receive notice of all book releases!

SNEAK PEEK OF SONG OF LORELEI

KILLIAN

Science quantified the mystical, boiled it down to logic, data, and biological processes. But there was a kind of magic to new discoveries, and the discovery that murderous sirens lurked in ocean's deep captivated the world and brought the New England fishing industry where they'd been found to its knees.

Myth had become universal truth, and modern fishermen wanted no part of it.

The sirens should have scared away *Dawn Chaser*'s crew, but stubbornness outweighed fear, and they did not flee the Gulf of Maine like most of their offshore competition.

Idle chatter and laughter rang out across the decks as the crew prepared the nets, and Captain Killian Quinn listened to them from the pilothouse, their muffled voices drifting to where he stood at the helm. He couldn't make out the words, but their cheer was unmistakable, and the corners of his mouth lifted.

This could have been just another day at sea.

Strong morale was good for crew retention, and these days, that's what kept him in business. But more than that, his crew was like a family to him, more so than his own flesh and blood, and he liked hearing them in high spirits.

A sharp ping from the boat's navigation system jolted Killian from his thoughts. Glancing down at the charts, the sectioned off area he programmed into the computer flashed up at him, and the small smile he wore died.

He slammed the throttle forward.

Dawn Chaser's engines rumbled loudly as it crossed into siren territory. The louder the better to repel any uninvited visitors.

Killian waved over the helmsman. "Take over for me and maintain speed." Crossing the pilothouse to look out the back window, he lifted his personal radio to his mouth. "Noise cancellation headsets on now."

A hush fell over the crew, prey animals alerted to lurking danger.

Every man reached for the black headsets hooked to their utility belts, and fitted them over their ears, their movements almost in complete unison with one another. Given the threat they faced, deadly siren song, it was an ironic display of puppetry, and Killian the puppeteer. But instead of supernatural manipulation, they were compelled by trust.

He hoped that trust was not misplaced.

The crew yanked off the tarps covering crates of canned meat, their tribute to the seafolk. They shuffled about the task in silence, casting wary glances over the side for movement in the waves below—the telltale flash of bright, colorful scales just beneath the dark surface.

How oblivious he and his crew had once been to the vicious sirens of the deep—as dangerous as they were beautiful with their wicked claws, razor-sharp teeth, and dark hunger for human flesh. Though the sailors of old must have gotten drunk on grog during their long, cold months at sea, the superstitious tales they told about seafolk were true.

Killian clenched his jaw. He wasn't one for grog, but he could use a shot of whiskey right about now.

It had almost been a year since news broke across the world about the sirens' existence. Many fishermen and sailors reconsidered their professions, but not even a school of bloodthirsty merfolk stopped Killian's crew from coming to the pier before sunrise each day. A seafaring life was all they'd ever known. They didn't want or know how to do anything else. For them, that was reason enough to stay on.

Not that there were a lot of job alternatives in rural, coastal Maine. The logging industry wasn't what it used to be, and while increased tourism was a boon for commercial real estate development, construction jobs were hard to come by with the influx of ex-fishermen looking for new careers. But with their competition thinning out, the pay Killian could now offer was quite compelling.

While money couldn't buy bravery, it certainly helped.

The noise cancellation headsets Killian gave to his crew had a built-in radio communication system that allowed them to talk with one another without succumbing to the sirens' seductive crooning. They were designed by an acoustics physicist hired by Dr. Lila Branson, the marine biologist credited with discovering the siren species, and Killian's good friend. She had one in captivity and brought in a physicist to study the frequency of her call. With three loved ones in the fishing industry—a husband, a father, and a close friend—Lila had spared no expense pushing the project along.

After donning his own headset, more for show than safety, Killian jogged down the pilot house steps and joined his crew. He didn't need to wear it, but he couldn't explain to them how he was immune to most siren song.

He wore the ear-coverings slightly off-kilter, allowing in outside sound. He would adjust them soon, but he needed to hear those roaring engines just a bit longer for his own peace of mind. If they ran strong, the hearing-sensitive sirens would not come anywhere near his boat.

One by one, his crew members nodded to him as he passed. Even as the sun pierced through the clouds overhead, hot and bright, their sun-tanned faces paled. They squinted at him through the light, waiting. This part of their offshore runs never got any easier. The anticipation. The fear that *this time* something might go wrong. But they always toughed it out for the bountiful promise of a good haul. When they fished just beyond siren territory, skirting its edges, they never went home empty-handed.

Killian took stock of his crew.

Despite the summer's heat, they shivered in their boots. No, not shivered. *Quaked.* Only Walter "Walt" Walsh, a former fishing captain, and Will Branson, Killian's lead deckhand and best friend, stood steady. Walt held a wide stance, dark brown thumbs casually hooked through his front belt loops, and Will crossed his arms, heavily freckled, "tan" for his ruddy white skin, both men a picture of cool and collected, but their lips were pinched tight. They understood better than anyone else on the crew exactly what they faced out here on the open water.

Killian unclipped a knife from his pocket and unfolded the blade. He crouched before the crates of canned pork and slashed open the tethers holding them in place, hoping the quick motion hid his trembling hands. With a barked command from Branson, the crew sprung to life, hefting crates away from the stack. Killian's own fear wasn't forgotten but working with his hands helped. Idleness only allowed fear to dig its ugly claws in deeper.

All around him his crew wedged crowbars beneath the lids, the wood creaking as it splintered and was pried apart. Waves splashed against the hull, and the boat's engine continued to roar. There was also a weird ringing in his ears, but likely had to do with the headset sitting half on, half off.

And yet, despite all the noise, his crew's silence was the loudest of all.

He adjusted his headset, fitting it snugly over his ears. The engines, the waves, the ringing, everything disappeared, save for the low staticky hum of an open radio channel. The crew tore off the rest of the lids and prepped the crates for dumping overboard.

While everyone threw themselves into work, the youngest crew member, Ian, stared blankly ahead at the water, frozen to the spot. The sandy-haired kid didn't even blink when another crew member bumped into him. Or squint at the sun, for that matter, even though he'd taken off his sunglasses, the skin directly around his eyes shone a lily white where the rest of his face was deeply tanned.

The glare off the water should've been blinding. Kid was probably damaging his eyes staring like that.

Killian clasped the young man's shoulder and found it damp to the touch. "You okay?" His voice crackled across the comms.

Ian blinked twice and looked up at him. The hairs at the back of the young man's neck rose above prickled gooseflesh, and although his eyes were glassy and unfocused, he nodded. The movement was slight, barely a dip of the chin.

Killian squeezed his shoulder. "It'll be all right." The kid didn't usually get this worked up, but some days the fear of what lurked below just gripped tighter. "Why don't you give Walt a hand with that crate? Helps to stay busy."

"Okay," Ian mumbled.

Killian left him to grab a broom. With his crew handling all the heavy lifting, the least he could do was sweep up wood shards and tether cuttings. Just because he was captain didn't mean he was above the work.

As he went to open the deck box, a round, black object, with its center cut out like a donut, caught his eye against the steel deck. He crouched down and picked it up, squishing it between his fingers. Wrinkled foam. Like the cushioning in their headsets, which not only provided comfort, it also created the sound-blocking seal.

One side was slightly tacky, like glue, and there were puncture marks all throughout like someone's dog had used it for a chew toy.

"Ian! Where d'you think you're going, son?" Walt called out, his voice loud and clear over the radio. Killian glanced over to where the young man had last stood but the spot was empty. "Ian?" Walt repeated, his voice dropping low in volume. The seasoned fisherman took a hesitant step forward, his brow furrowed, a strong gust of wind whipping back his mane of tight, curly white hair.

The kid didn't respond.

Killian rocked back on his heels for momentum and leapt to his feet. He followed Walt's gaze to the pilot house steps, where Ian steadily climbed up. There was no hard rule saying he couldn't be there, but there wasn't a reason for him or other members of the crew to be. Their place, their work was on deck.

Although Ian was no model for good posture, his shoulders were slumped more than usual, the movement of his lanky limbs slowed as if filled with wet sand. When the kid paused on the steps to tilt his head and shake, Killian half expected seawater to trickle out.

And that's when he saw it.

Shit.

Ian's noise cancellation headset sat off kilter on top of his head... because he was missing the ear-padding on one side.

He dashed after the kid.

How had he not seen it before? He should have been paying better attention. While the tech was effective, it wasn't foolproof. Unless the earpieces sat snuggly over top the ears, creating a seal that blocked out sound, the headsets lost all their protective qualities.

Ian continued to the door. "It's so loud," he whined, reaching for the handle.

The memory of a mermaid named Undine thrashing on deck, clawed hands covering her ears from the sound of the boat's engines, spurred Killian up the stairs. When they caught Undine in their nets, she hummed until Branson shut off the engine, and she almost successfully compelled Lila to set her free.

"McAdams! Don't let him shut the engines off!" Killian shouted to his helmsman.

"Wha—oh, shit. Ian, what the hell are you doing?"

The comms crackled with the sounds of a scuffle.

As Killian bounded up the steps, two at a time, he felt the vibrations from another set of feet pounding up the stairs behind him.

"Right behind you, Cap," Branson's voice assured.

A loud *thunk*, followed by a sharp cry over the radio, chilled Killian's blood. He lurched forward, bracing himself against the pilot house door. Not because they sped up, but because the boat had abruptly stopped, its engine cut.

"Open those crates and then get yourselves below deck," he ordered the others, wrenching the door open.

Inside, McAdams lay unconscious on the floor.

Armed with a paper weight, Ian stood guard over the navigation console, trembling. Killian stopped short and raised his hands. Ian may not have been a sturdy kid, but he was scrappy.

"Whoa, easy there, Ian. You can put that down. I'm not going to hurt you."

"Captain, we gotta keep these engines off," Ian pleaded. "They're too loud."

"Okay, no problem. I just need you to look at me, listen to the sound of my voice, and set the weight down. Can you do that for me, Ian?"

The kid's eyes remained glassy, but he lowered his arm.

Killian licked his lips nervously. He needed to get to the console asap, but he didn't want to hurt the kid to get to it, if he didn't have to. "That's it. Good. Now can you take a step toward me?" He gestured the kid forward.

Ian planted his feet and shook his head.

Somewhere behind Killian, Branson grumbled under his breath and brushed past him. Ian swung the paperweight at the lead deckhand's head as he approached, but Branson blocked his wrist and socked the kid right in the face. The paperweight clattered to the floor, and Ian followed, knocked out cold. Stepping over him, Branson reached for the controls, blood trickling from his busted knuckles.

"Did he—?" Branson swore, slamming his palm on top of the console. "He broke the key in the ignition."

Cries of panic erupted over the comms. "Cap! They're swimming for the boat!"

"Get below now," Killian barked, dashing outside. He silently cursed the siren's supernatural swim speeds.

In just a matter of seconds, they were scaling the side of his boat.

"Hurry, man! Hurry!" a crew member yelled.

The whole lot of them were bottlenecked at the stairs. Walt took up the back of the line with a crowbar in his hands, his face a mask of fierce resignation. He would defend the crew until his last breath, if need be, but the old man wouldn't stand a chance. None of them would.

Pulling a gun from his hip holster, which he'd bought for emergencies exactly like this, Killian fired a warning shot into the air.

The sirens hunkered down and shrieked. If it weren't for the headset he wore, his own ears would be ringing right now.

Please let that be enough to scare them away.

The sirens shook their heads, flinging water from strands of sea-soaked hair. When the shaking stopped, seven pairs of eyes locked on the last of his crew, funneling through the door.

They kept climbing.

Oh, hell no.

Killian fired another shot and trained his gun on the nearest one—a dark-haired creature with amber eyes and silvery scales streaked with orange.

Pressing her ear to her shoulder, she glared at him and hissed. But her gaze didn't stray to the rest of the crew. Message received...he hoped. While he wouldn't hesitate to shoot, doing so probably wouldn't bode well for future fishing expeditions. And what would Lorelei think? All her peacemaking efforts swallowed whole.

He swiped his brow with the back of his arm to keep the sweat from burning his eyes.

One by one, seven sirens slinked over the side, one scaled leg after the other. Their claws clicked against the metal as they walked on all fours across the deck toward the abandoned crates. They tore into the canned pork, ripping apart the aluminum tins and cramming the meat into their mouths, canning juices running down their chins.

Bile rose at the back of Killian's throat. He looked away before he spewed his lunch all over the deck.

At least it wasn't his crew they feasted on.

A door slammed shut beneath Killian, the vibration from the door's swing coursing through his boots. Every siren on board jumped, hackles raised. He prayed they didn't rush the door and try to batter their way in, but they returned to their meal with little more than a few dirty looks cast in his direction.

"We're all in," Walt radioed. "Get yourself back into the pilot house and bar the door."

Killian exhaled. "We're good. They're just chowing down on deck. I'm gonna stick around and make sure they leave."

The radio fell silent, long enough that Killian didn't think he would respond, but the old fisherman replied in a soft voice, "Be careful, son."

He would wait until they had their fill before attempting to shoo them away. Best not get between them and one of their favorite meals. He wasn't about to present himself as dessert.

The sirens wore arm and neck pieces fashioned from metal taken from past offerings of canned meat, unaware how ridiculous wearing the canned pork brand appeared to their two-legged prey. If he wasn't so freaked out about having people-eating sirens crawling around on his boat, he would have laughed.

When they were all safely back on shore, he would have to tell Lorelei, and maybe then he could laugh with his feet planted on solid ground, and the only siren in sight more likely to kiss him than eat him.

The sirens just kept eating and eating, their bellies bulging from their gorging.

What about the rest of the pod? Shouldn't they be leaving enough for them? And where was Undine? He didn't think the leader of the sirens would approve of this. As he understood it, their regular potted meat tribute was meant to be shared, and it was supposed to keep the sirens away from his boat, not hosting a family dinner on deck.

Leave. Just take it all and go.

Why draw it out? It didn't make any sense. Sirens disliked being above water.

Maybe this was a rogue group, or maybe Undine sanctioned this breach of their agreement to demonstrate her power, to show the humans who really held all the cards out in the open ocean.

A dull ache formed behind Killian's eyes.

He waited until the seven sirens onboard slowed their eating. They sat back, lounging on deck, and patted their rounded bellies, making themselves at home. His temper flared. Switching off his mouthpiece, so he didn't blow out the eardrums of his crew, he yelled, "All right, you've had enough. Get the fuck off my boat!"

They looked up in unison. He made a shooing motion to emphasize his point.

The amber-eyed one cocked her head to the side and smirked.

The nerve...he shot the crate next to the siren, sending splintered wood flying. They all jumped back, covering their ears and snarling.

"GET. OFF. MY. BOAT," he repeated, pointing out at the water. If this provoked an attack, he had another magazine in his pocket. He didn't want to have to use it, but he would.

Beneath his boots, the whole boat vibrated, the engines roaring to life. Branson must have found a way to pry the broken key out and used the spare. The sirens shrieked and hurtled themselves over the side. He watched their brightly colored bodies streak away before they dove down into the deep.

Why did the engines send them away and not the gunshots? Was it one loud noise too many? Or was it the continuous drone that bothered them? He sat heavily on the steps, *Dawn Chaser* chugging along at full speed. He didn't get it, but whatever it was, he was grateful they were gone.

He switched his mouthpiece back on. "They're gone. You can come out now."

One by one his crew filed out onto the deck. He didn't have to say anything. They just began hurling the remaining crates of canned pork over the side and cleaned up wood shards, empty cans, and splattered meat. In all their years together at sea, *Dawn Chaser*'s fishing crew had never seen anything that would make any of them even think the word "siren" or "mermaid." But his dealings with Undine last year opened a door he could not close. And despite his best efforts to keep the siren's hunger for human flesh in check, it only seemed to embolden them further.

Killian swiped a hand over his face. He failed his crew today and could lose them. Not that he'd blame them. Vicious mermaid attacks weren't what they signed up for.

The sirens must have planned this. That they happened to be singing while Ian was wearing a faulty headset couldn't be a coincidence. It made him suspect that they might always sing when his boat entered their waters, lying in wait for the moment he and his crew showed weakness, hoping for exactly what happened here today.

But then why hadn't he heard their song when his own headset was askew? There was that weird ringing, but it hadn't felt compulsory. Maybe it had something to do with the fact that he was attuned to only one siren's song—the love of his life, his wife-to-be.

Lorelei.

He'd pulled her from these very waters almost a year ago, when the ship she was on sank, its entire crew devoured by her murderous kin. But as a Midwest transplant, who at the time had never been to sea, Lorelei hadn't known what she was. The maritime tragedy awakened that dormant part of her, and with her transformation, came cravings for human flesh.

If it weren't for Lila's help, Lorelei might've been lost to him, irrevocably called to the deep, and unable to resist the carnivorous drive that turned loved ones into prey. She could have been one of the sirens scaling the side of his boat today.

Arms draped across his knees, he stared out over the water, wondering if they were still nearby, lurking, following, waiting for another mistake. This wasn't the first time he'd had an unfriendly siren on his boat, but every day for almost a year, he'd hoped and prayed it would be the last.

A series of events led Killian, Lorelei, and a small knit group of their closest friends and family to live capture a mermaid—Undine—the siren's leader. And they made a deal. Potted meat in exchange for safe passage. A "cure" in exchange for a siren to study.

Because the siren hunger for human flesh wasn't innate. It was viral.

Every time, fisherman.

Undine's last words haunted him. She'd said it with a wink that was a disturbing mix of flirtation and warning. No skipped meals. No tribute could mean retaliation. He'd been diligent, but maybe she *was* behind this, but whatever the case might be, he would be a fool if he thought this incident was just a fluke, and the last of their troubles with the sirens.

The prey animal that he was felt it down to the marrow with chilling certainty.

Dawn Chaser was marked. And so was he.

Don't stop now. Keep reading with your copy of SONG OF LORELEI available now

And sign up for the latest news, giveaways, and more from at www.dmniccoli.com

Don't miss SONG OF LORELEI, book two of the Haven Cove series, available now, and find more from Desirée M. Niccoli at www.dmniccoli.com

Her song is a lure he cannot resist.

Even after brokering a deal with the vicious merfolk who stalk his offshore fishing lanes, Captain Killian Quinn has had one too many onboard his boat for comfort. His livelihood, and life, as well as that of his crew's, depends on his ability to maintain peace. One wrong move and the *Dawn Chaser* could become a floating charcuterie board, and he'd never see again the one mermaid he wouldn't mind take a little nibble out of him.

A sinister craving for human flesh leaves Lorelei Roth with no other choice. She must aid the study of one of her own to find a more permanent solution to protect the ones she loves. As enthralled by all her sharp edges and seductive siren song as her fiancé may be, the threat of becoming the wrong kind of snack is never far enough away.

While they're close to a breakthrough treatment, doubt gnaws at Lorelei as she watches a fellow mermaid languish in a tank, enduring endless rounds of tests and denied the healing touch of the sea. Is one mermaid's declining health and happiness too steep a price for freedom? And if so, what sacrifices is Lorelei willing to make to set it right?

All reviews are **welcome** and **appreciated**. Please consider leaving one on your favorite social media and book buying sites.

For books in the world of romance and speculative fiction that embody Innovation, Creativity, and Affordability, check out City Owl Press at www.cityowlpress.com.

ACKNOWLEDGMENTS

Called to the Deep was born on a ladder trail in Maine. So, I first want to thank my brainstorming buddy Devin, because without her, and our hours long conversation about murderous mermaid behavior and biology while hiking in Acadia National Park, this book wouldn't have been nearly as interesting. And I want to thank her not just for that initial brainstorming session, but for subsequent ones, and for connecting me to Dr. Sean Todd at the College of the Atlantic in Bar Harbor. Dr. Todd graciously humored me with a very fun, speculative conversation about mermaid physiology and habitat, as well seafloor topography and cetacean morbillivirus. I took a lot of artistic liberties, but that conversation was invaluable for this book and its upcoming sequel.

Next, I want to thank Tee Tate, my editor at City Owl Press, for helping me through the homestretch of edits. It's easy to rush things when the end is in sight, but Tee coached and cheered me across the finish line. She understood and nurtured the horror elements I love in this story just as much as the romance and coaxed from me the spooky polish *Called to the Deep* needed.

My agent Kaitlyn Johnson of Belcastro Literary Agency has been the best champion of this bonkers romance featuring people-eating mermaids. The moment I saw she had creepy mermaids on her manuscript wish list, I knew we had to work together. Not only do I value her insight and guidance, I admire her proactiveness within the book community, and I can always count on her for brainstorming sessions, morale boosts, and silly SPAM jokes.

My writing pals Katie Erin, Ingrid Pierce, and Morgan T. Jackson came in clutch with their positivity passes during post-deal editing, as well as Katie Rose and Dani Frank for flooding my DMs with good vibes and fun times. I, like a lot of writers, struggle with imposter syndrome, so their words of encouragement, love, and emotional support reminded me to believe in myself, too.

My squad of beta readers: Alexandra, Kyle, Victoria, Stacia-Fe, Lizzie, Laura, and Ally—their insightful feedback picked me up when I was down and got me fighting for my manuscript in the querying trenches when my energy and morale were zapped. We have this book in our hands because of them. I'm thankful for every minute they slogged through those rough early drafts with me, and all its cringey parts, and still found something kind to say.

A special shout out to my beta boo Alexandra for being my second pair of eyes for everything—Tweets, emails to readers, even the front and back matter of this book—and for being there to listen and talk every time things felt like too much. And to Victoria for letting me read *Called to the Deep* out loud to her, so it wouldn't feel so lonely.

All my friends and family have been incredible throughout this book's publishing journey, and I'd be remiss if I didn't thank them for accepting, if not embracing, a creepy, flesh-craving mermaid romance. But I want to give a special shout out to my mom, who told me the more the merrier with regards to the sexy bits. Now I have no shame about my family reading them! I also want to give a special shout out to my brother Tre, who has been hyping me from day one and so sweetly sharing posts about all my bookish victories. And my dad, for bravely listening to all my podcast guest appearances, and the FUN discussions I have with my peers.

My husband Kyle has been my rock, my everything. He's seen me through every hill and valley of this emotional rollercoaster ride, read over my earliest drafts, helped me brainstorm individual scenes and characters, and provided invaluable knowledge about search and rescue operations, Gulf of Maine fisheries and treating hypothermia. But wait! There's more. He couldn't just stop at being my biggest champion and greatest love, he also had to go and be my in-house editor and character artist, too.

Puma Thurman, Editor-in-Chief, kept my notebooks and keyboard warm. Neglecting them was an oversight on my part, and I'm deeply sorry I didn't keep the keyboard smashes—creative differences and all that. Pawdry Hepburn was the most dedicated outside writing buddy and protectress. She ate every single bug she could get her paws on, no doubt saving me from many vicious attacks. Thankfully, she hasn't caught a spicy sky raisin.

To the book community, and the monster lovers, thank you so, so much for all your boosting and support! Promoting can feel weird and lonely, but you make it feel far less so. And to those who've stuck with me the longest, spreading the word about *Called to the Deep* years in advance of its release, thank you so, so much for your patience and for cheering on my lovely vicious mermaid and her sea captain beau.

xoxo,
Desirée

ABOUT THE AUTHOR

By night, Desirée M. Niccoli writes adult romance featuring vicious monsters, villains, and the supernatural, often served with a side of eco-horror and paired with (mostly) emotionally intelligent characters and heart. By day, she is a public relations professional living the nomadic military life with her husband and two cats Pawdry Hepburn and Puma Thurman. Although born and raised in Pittsburgh, Desirée has since lived in coastal Maine (where her spooky heart truly lies) and Maryland.

Want to be the first to get a look at covers, sneak peeks, and more? Sign up for her newsletter and find more at www.dmniccoli.com.

 facebook.com/dmniccoli
twitter.com/dmniccoli
instagram.com/author_dmniccoli

ABOUT THE PUBLISHER

City Owl Press is a cutting edge indie publishing company, bringing the world of romance and speculative fiction to discerning readers.

Escape Your World. Get Lost in Ours!

www.cityowlpress.com

 facebook.com/YourCityOwlPress
 twitter.com/cityowlpress
 instagram.com/cityowlbooks
 pinterest.com/cityowlpress

Made in the USA
Middletown, DE
18 July 2023

34838820R00205